A TREASURY
OF VICTORIAN
DETECTIVE
STORIES

A TREASURY OF VICTORIAN DETECTIVE STORIES

Edited by Everett F. Bleiler

CHARLES SCRIBNER'S SONS / NEW YORK

A Note on the Text of This Volume

The stories in this collection have been taken from many different sources, which do not always agree with one another on matters of style. Original punctuation and other stylistic points have been followed exactly. Although obvious typographical errors have been corrected, variant spellings in place and personal names have been allowed to stand.

Copyright © 1979 Everett Bleiler

Library of Congress Cataloging in Publication Data

Main entry under title:
A Treasury of Victorian detective stories.

    1. Detective and mystery stories, English.
2. English fiction—19th century.   I. Bleiler,
Everett Franklin. 1920–
PZ1.T7148   [PR1309.D4]   823′.0872   78-26908
ISBN 0-684-16055-2 (CLOTH)
ISBN 0-684-17640-8 (PAPER)

1 3 5 7 9 11 13 15 17 19   F/P   20 18 16 14 12 10 8 6 4 2

PRINTED IN THE UNITED STATES OF AMERICA

CONTENTS

A TREASURY
OF VICTORIAN
DETECTIVE
STORIES

Introduction

Queen Victoria acceded to the throne on June 20, 1837, and died on January 22, 1901. Within that same period occurred the birth and development of the detective story. It was written in short stories and in novels; it appeared in periodicals, newspapers, and books; and it took many different forms. In a certain sense everything in the development of the detective story since 1901 has simply been an expansion or refinement of ideas and techniques that originated in Queen Victoria's day.

Take the various branches of the detective and mystery story as they are recognized today. The scientific detective story? It is usually believed to have begun with R. Austin Freeman in Edwardian England, when his Dr. Thorndyke operated a private crime laboratory and used the resources of zoology, human biology, chemistry and other sciences to trap criminals. Yet back in the 1860s "Waters," one of the unidentifiable pseudonyms of the era, was examining blood stains under a microscope to determine if the corpuscles were human, and Andrew Forrester, Jr.'s, female detective, Mrs. G____, caused her lab man to identify dust and animal hairs under the lens.

Hard-boiled detectives? The detective story is supposed to have left the vicarage and the house party with Dashiell Hammett and Raymond Chandler and other *Black Mask* authors in America in the 1920s and 1930s. But the British street literature of the 1850s and 1860s knew that a spade was a spade and did not hesitate to say so. For example, Tom Fox, detective, could investigate a sordid murder in a brothel while the prostitutes commented about their lives.

Procedurals? The Americans in the 1940s are supposed to have been the first to show the interest inherent in detailed police procedures used to solve a realistic crime, as opposed to watching the flashy deductions of a gifted amateur. Yet most of the earlier crime stories of the 1850s and 1860s in Great Britain were intensely concerned with matters of police procedure.

Female detectives who do not think it is an "unsuitable job for a woman"? Two female detectives had their adventures recorded back in the 1860s, and in the 1890s Loveday Brooke was regarded highly.

Ingenuities? Sealed rooms? Impossible crimes? Poe started them back in the 1840s, and the American John B. Williams, M.D., and the Englishman Andrew Forrester, Jr., in the 1860s, each devised sealed rooms and difficult crimes of some ingenuity. Fantastic crimes? L. T. Meade specialized in crimes that involved weird scientific apparatus or curiosities of science back in the 1890s.

The list could be continued. Let it be enough to say that the ideas were present in the Victorian period, and if they were not belabored with hundreds of repetitions, as they are today, they are all the more interesting for their novelty.

Unfortunately, the Victorians, while surprising experimenters in detective and mystery fiction, tossed aside many good ideas after trying them once or twice, and these ideas were not remembered when the twentieth century began. The twentieth century had to work out its own variations on the basic themes of death and justice.

How did the Victorians start it all?

History began with Edgar Allan Poe back in the early 1840s, when his great amateur detective, the Chevalier Dupin, solved three mysteries that had baffled the police of Paris. Paris, in one case at least, was New York, for Dupin, in "The Mystery of Marie Rogêt," tried to solve the murder of Mary Rogers of Manhattan, a historical crime that took place in New Jersey, right across the Hudson.

Before Poe was the prehistory of the detective story. Prehistory was richer than we used to think, but most of it was material that dropped aside and withered away after the work of Poe and his followers became known.

The important literature before Poe can be summarized quickly. In 1794 appeared the novel *Things As They Are*, by William Godwin (1756–1836), the social theorist and father of the author of *Frankenstein*. It narrated the adventures of Caleb Williams, a prying young man who suspected his benefactor of murder and did not rest until he had uncovered evidence. In backwoods America, in 1801, Edgar Huntley, in the novel *Edgar Huntley* by Charles Brockden Brown (1770–1810), wandered through the wilderness trying to discover who had murdered his friend. In 1827, back in England, *Richmond*, a novel of unknown authorship, carried a Bow Street Runner through five cases. In New York, in 1828, William Leggett, a minor American author, showed how a crime could be solved by means of ballistics. And there were many other detective stories before Poe, although most of them were trivial.

But with Poe a new era began, for he assembled the loose strands that had been lying about and interwove them with new material into a detective story form that still survives. With Poe begins the chain of amateur detectives who are cleverer than the official police; the fairly moronic Watsons who are lost in admiration of the detective; the process of ratiocination, or reconstructing complex events by observing and interpreting minor clues; mysterious crimes in sealed chambers; and much more.

Literary innovators and creators of forms are often not recognized in their day, and often generations must pass before their work is absorbed. But this was not the case with Poe. Within the two decades following the appearance of Dupin, Poe's work was read and imitated to some extent in America and England. In France, however, he found his ablest, most important direct follower, Émile Gaboriau.

Gaboriau (1832–1873), who had saturated himself in Poe's works and declared Poe to be his master, created the first mature, full-fledged detective novel. This was *L'Affaire Lerouge* (*The Widow Lerouge*), which appeared in 1865, in periodical parts. The story of a somewhat unsavory widow who was mysteriously murdered in her cottage, it leads the detective, Père Tabaret, into a nest of misdirections until he and the reader finally discover who the murderer was. All the complexities then neatly fall into place.

A little later than Gaboriau was the English novelist Wilkie Collins (1824–1889), whose *Moonstone* (1868) was the first important detective novel written in English. Collins and Gaboriau between them firmed out the detective novel, with characteristics that have lasted until today. Their chief contribution, probably, was their clear recognition that in a detective novel everything should focus on crime and detection, and not on secondary plots. The unitary novel they wrote, however, passed out of view for several decades; indeed, not until A. Conan Doyle's *Hound of the Baskervilles* (1902) did another truly first-rate pure detective novel appear in England. Doyle's earlier stories, *A Study in Scarlet* and *The Sign of Four*, were really detective short stories with adventure novels appended.

The detective short story in Great Britain, however, seems to have been independent of Poe for a time. This was the so-called casebook story, which was the narrative of an individual police case, related by the professional detective concerned in it. Fairly realistic in crime, sometimes sentimental, sometimes sensational and melodramatic, such stories were quite different from the cerebral, well-plotted stories of Poe.

The first casebook story was "Recollections of a Police-Officer," purportedly by one Inspector Waters of the London Police. Obviously an outgrowth of great public interest in the new London police system, it was followed by similar stories, which were gathered together in book form, first in New York in 1852, then in England in 1856.

The name "Waters" now shifted from the detective to the author and under the name "Waters" soon appeared several similar collections of stories centered around other investigators. The odd thing about the author "Waters," however, is that we do not know his identity.

"Waters's" casebook stories were soon copied by other authors, and in the late 1850s and 1860s came the first outburst of detective stories in England. Collections of stories were occupied with the doings of police detectives, private detectives, amateur detectives, sheriffs, customs officers, female detectives, lawyers, and doctors acting as detectives. Among the more important authors in this minor industry were "Waters," Andrew Forrester, Jr., Charles Martel, William S. Hayward, Charles Hillyard, Robert Curtis, John B. Williams, James McGovan, and William Henderson.

Many odd things are to be found in these casebooks, if one can locate copies, for they are impossibly rare. There are instances of realism and naturalism, and there are also melodramatic situations that might have been taken from a bad stage. There is psychological detection based on the manipulation of emotion, and there are scientific detectives. There are stories that are simple narratives, and there are stories that have begun to move toward structured fiction. Unfortunately, most of these potentials were not realized beyond a few individual stories, and between 1870 and the appearance of Doyle's short stories in the early 1890s British detective fiction did not advance, either in the novel or in the short story.

This is not to say that Victorian literature ran short of crime, mystery, and some detection after 1870. The three-volume domestic novels provided plenty of such material for readers. While they centered on social relations, crime and informal detection often took place in the background. Sometimes the reader was taken along the path of a crime and shown the gradual unraveling of a mystery; sometimes a heroine was placed into deadly peril, from which she had to extricate herself.

A surprisingly large number of Victorian novels held such themes. Such novels cannot, as a rule, be considered pure detective stories, since the detectional side was often secondary in importance within the novel. But such novels were often sensational, and they did form the third great body of crime and mystery fiction during the Victorian period.

Sensational novels came into prominence in the early 1860s with two important works. These were *Lady Audley's Secret* (1861–1862) by Mary Braddon and *East Lynne* (1861) by Mrs. Henry Wood. *Lady Audley's Secret* is the story of a bigamous wife who tries to conceal traces of her former marriage by attempting to murder her first husband. *East Lynne* contains two plots: the story of an adulterous wife who returns to her household in disguise to become the governess of her own child and, secondly, a murder mystery with a fairly sophisticated concealment. A third important mystery novel of the day was J. S. LeFanu's *Uncle Silas* (1864), which related with ghoulish relish and wonderful atmosphere the attempts of a young heiress to escape being murdered for her money.

One author, as the reader probably knows, was primarily responsible for the reemergence of pure detective stories in the late 1880s and early 1890s. This was Arthur Conan Doyle. The first Sherlock Holmes story, *A Study in Scarlet*, appeared in 1887; it was followed in 1890 by *The Sign of Four*. Neither novel attracted much attention. But when *The Adventures of Sherlock Holmes* began to appear serially in *The Strand Magazine* in 1891, Doyle suddenly found himself one of the most popular authors in Great Britain, and also one of the most imitated. These *Strand* stories were responsible for the second great explosion of detective literature in England.

Doyle and Holmes dominated detective fiction well up into the twentieth century, but other authors are still remembered today. There was Arthur Morrison (1863–1945), the chronicler of London slum life, who wrote about Martin Hewitt, a suave detective not too dissimilar to Holmes; L. T. Meade, who collaborated with either Clifford Halifax or Robert Eustace, to produce chains of stories based on oddities of science or thought; Fergus Hume (1859–1929), author of *The Mystery of a Hansom Cab*, surely one of the least worthy best sellers of the day; Guy Boothby, B. Fletcher Robinson, Huan Mee, and many others.

During the 1890s many different types of detective story were written. There were stories about private detectives of great skill, and about police detectives equally competent. There were society detectives, female detectives, medical detectives, and occult detectives; there were puzzle stories, crime stories involving masterminds, and other types of fiction, much of which is still worth reading.

The stories in this present volume have been selected to show the great variety of detective material that was available in Queen Victoria's day. They are the best that Queen Victoria could have read, had she read detective stories.

E. F. Bleiler

CHARLES DICKENS

(1812–1870) was greatly inter-ested in judicial and police reform, and several of his stories reflect this interest: Oliver Twist (1837–1839), Barnaby Rudge (1841), and, of course, Bleak House (1852–1853), with Inspector Bucket. Only one of his novels, however, could be termed a full-fledged detective story. This was The Mystery of Edwin Drood (1870), his last, unfinished novel, which generations of scholars and cranks have tried to finish.

During Dickens's lifetime the British police systems were revolutionized. In London the old Bow Street Runners and the police-court magistrats associated with them were abolished, and their place taken by the new Metropolitan police of New Scotland Yard, the so-called Peelers or Bobbies. Dickens gave quite a bit of favorable publicity to the new police, as can be seen in "Three 'Detective' Anecdotes."

"Three 'Detective' Anecdotes"

I.—THE PAIR OF GLOVES

"It's a singler story, Sir," said Inspector Wield, of the Detective Police, who, in company with Sergeants Dornton and Mith, paid us another twilight visit, one July evening; "and I've been thinking you might like to know it.

"It's concerning the murder of the young woman, Eliza Grimwood, some years ago, over in the Waterloo Road. She was commonly called The Countess, because of her handsome appearance and her proud way of carrying of herself; and when I saw the poor Countess (I had known her well to speak to), lying dead, with her

throat cut, on the floor of her bed-room, you'll believe me that a variety of reflections calculated to make a man rather low in his spirits,
came into my head.

"That's neither here nor there. I went to the house the morning
after the murder, and examined the body, and made a general observation of the bedroom where it was. Turning down the pillow of the
bed with my hand I found, underneath it, a pair of gloves. A pair of
gentleman's dress gloves, very dirty; and inside the lining, the letters
Tr, and a cross.

"Well, sir, I took them gloves away, and I showed 'em to the
magistrate, over at Union Hall, before whom the case was. He says,
'Wield,' he says, 'there's no doubt this is a discovery that may lead to
something very important; and what you have got to do, Wield, is,
to find out the owner of these gloves.'

"I was of the same opinion, of course, and I went at it immediately. I looked at the gloves pretty narrowly, and it was my opinion
that they had been cleaned. There was a smell of sulphur and rosin
about 'em, you know, which cleaned gloves usually have, more or
less. I took 'em over to a friend of mine at Kennington, who was in
that line, and I put it to him, 'What do you say now? Have these
gloves been cleaned?' 'These gloves have been cleaned,' says he.
'Have you any idea who cleaned them?' says I. 'Not at all,' says he;
'I've a very distinct idea who *didn't* clean 'em, and that's myself. But
I'll tell you what, Wield, there ain't above eight or nine reg'lar glove
cleaners in London,'—there were not, at that time, it seems—'and I
think I can give you their addresses, and you may find out, by that
means, who did clean 'em.' Accordingly he gave me the directions,
and I went here, and I went there, and I looked up this man, and I
looked up that man; but, though they all agreed that the gloves had
been cleaned, I couldn't find the man, woman, or child, that had
cleaned that aforesaid pair of gloves.

"What with this person not being at home, and that person
being expected home in the afternoon, and so forth, the inquiry took
me three days. On the evening of the third day, coming over Waterloo Bridge from the Surrey side of the river, quite beat and very
much vexed and disappointed, I thought I'd have a shilling's worth
of entertainment at the Lyceum Theatre to freshen myself up. So I
went into the Pit, at half-price, and I sat myself down next to a very
quiet, modest sort of young man. Seeing I was a stranger (which I
thought it just as well to appear to be) he told me the names of the
actors on the stage, and we got into conversation. When the play was
over, we came out together, and I said, 'We've been very compan-
ionable and agreeable, and perhaps you wouldn't object to a drain?'
'Well you're very good,' says he; 'I *shouldn't* object to a drain.' Accordingly, we went to a public house, near the Theatre, sat ourselves

down in a quiet room up-stairs on the first floor, and called for a pint of half-and-half apiece, and a pipe.

"Well, Sir, we put our pipes aboard, and we drank our half-and-half, and sat a-talking very sociably, when the young man says, 'You must excuse me stopping very long,' he says, 'because I'm forced to go home in good time. I must be at work all night.' 'At work all night?' says I. 'You ain't a Baker?' 'No,' he says, laughing, 'I ain't a baker.' 'I thought not,' says I, 'you haven't the looks of a baker.' 'No,' says he, 'I'm a glove-cleaner.'

"I never was more astonished in my life, than when I heard them words come out of his lips. 'You're a glove-cleaner, are you?' says I. 'Yes,' he says, 'I am.' 'Then, perhaps,' says I, taking the gloves out of my pocket, 'you can tell me who cleaned this pair of gloves? It's a rum story,' I says. 'I was dining over at Lambeth, the other day, at a free-and-easy—quite promiscuous—with a public company—when some gentleman, he left these gloves behind him: Another gentleman and me, you see, we laid a wager of a sovereign, that I wouldn't find out who they belong to. I've spent as much as seven shillings already in trying to discover: but if you could help me, I'd stand another seven and welcome. You see there's Tr and a cross, in side.' 'I see,' he says. 'Bless you, I know these gloves very well! I've seen dozens of pairs belonging to the same party.' 'No?' says I. 'Yes,' says he. 'Then you know who cleaned 'em?" says I. 'Rather so,' says he. 'My father cleaned 'em.'

" 'Where does your father live?' says I. 'Just round the corner,' says the young man, 'near Exeter Street, here. He'll tell you who they belong to directly.' 'Would you come round with me near?' says I. 'Certainly,' says he, 'but you needn't tell my father that you found me at the play, you know, because he mightn't like it.' 'All right!' We went round to the place, and there we found an old man in a white apron, with two or three daughters, all rubbing and cleaning away at lots of gloves, in a front parlour. 'Oh, Father!' says the young man, 'here's a person been and made a bet about the owner-ship of a pair of gloves, and I've told him you can settle it.' 'Good evening, Sir,' says I to the old gentleman. 'Here's the gloves your son speaks of. Letters Tr, you see, and a cross.' 'Oh yes,' he says, 'I know these gloves very well; I've cleaned dozens of pairs of 'em. They belong to Mr. Trinkle, the great upholsterer in Cheapside.' 'Did you get 'em from Mr. Trinkle, direct,' says I, 'if you'll excuse my asking the question?' 'No,' says he; 'Mr. Trinkle always sends 'em to Mr. Phibbs's, the haberdasher's, opposite his shop, and the haberdasher sends 'em to me.' 'Perhaps you wouldn't object to a drain?' says I. 'Not in the least!' says he. So I took the old gentleman out, and had a little more talk with him and his son, over a glass, and we parted excellent friends.

"This was late on Saturday night. First thing on the Monday morning, I went to the haberdasher's shop, opposite Mr. Trinkle's, the great upholsterer's in Cheapside. 'Mr. Phibbs in the way?' 'My name is Phibbs.' 'Oh! I believe you sent this pair of gloves to be cleaned?' 'Yes, I did, for young Mr. Trinkle over the way. There he is, in the shop!' 'Oh! that's him in the shop, is it? Him in the green coat?' 'The same individual.' 'Well Mr. Phibbs, this is an unpleasant affair; but the fact is, I am Inspector Wield of the Detective Police, and I found these gloves under the pillow of the young woman that was murdered the other day, over in the Waterloo Road?' 'Good Heaven!' says he. 'He's a most repectable young man, and if his father was to hear of it, it would be the ruin of him!' 'I'm very sorry for it,' says I, 'but I must take him into custody.' 'Good Heaven!' says Mr. Phibbs again; 'can nothing be done?' 'Nothing.' says I. 'Will you allow me to call him over here,' says he, 'that his father may not see it done?' 'I don't object to that,' says I; 'but unfortunately, Mr. Phibbs, I can't allow of any communication between you. If any was attempted, I should have to interfere directly. Perhaps you'll beckon him over here?' Mr. Phibbs went to the door and beckoned, and the young fellow came across the street directly; a smart, brisk young fellow.

"Good morning, Sir,' says I. 'Good morning, Sir,' says he. 'Would you allow me to inquire, Sir,' says I, 'if you ever had any acquaintance with a party of the name of Grimwood?' 'Grimwood! Grimwood!' says he, 'No!' 'You know the Waterloo Road?' 'Oh! of course I know the Waterloo Road!' 'Happen to have heard of a young woman being murdered there?' 'Yes, I read it in the paper, and very sorry I was, to read it.' 'Here's a pair of gloves belonging to you, that I found under her pillow the morning afterwards!'

"He was in a dreadful state, Sir; a dreadful state! 'Mr. Wield,' he says, 'upon my solemn oath I never was there. I never so much as saw her, to my knowledge, in my life!' 'I am very sorry,' says I. 'To tell you the truth; I don't think you *are* the murderer, but I must take you to Union Hall in a cab. However, I think it's a case of that sort, that at present, at all events, the magistrate will hear it in private.'

"A private examination took place, and then it came out that this young man was acquainted with a cousin of the unfortunate Eliza Grimwood, and that, calling to see this cousin a day or two before the murder, he left these gloves upon the table. Who should come in, shortly afterwards, but Eliza Grimwood! 'Whose gloves are these?' she says, taking 'em up. 'Those are Mr. Trinkle's gloves,' says her cousin. 'Oh!' says she, 'They are very dirty, and of no use to him, I am sure. I shall take 'em away for my girl to clean the stoves with.' And she put 'em in her pocket. The girl had used 'em to clean the stoves, and, I have no doubt, had left 'em lying on the bed-room mantel-piece, or on the drawers, or somewhere; and her mistress, looking round to see that the room was tidy, had caught 'em up and put 'em under the pillow where I found 'em.

"That's the story, Sir."

II.—THE ARTFUL TOUCH

"One of the most *beautiful* things that ever was done, perhaps," said Inspector Wield, emphasising the adjective, as preparing us to expect dexterity or ingenuity rather than strong interest, "was a move of Sergeant Witchem's. It was a lovely idea!

"Witchem and me were down at Epsom one Derby Day, waiting at the station for the Swell Mob. As I mentioned, when we were talking about these things before, we are ready at the station when there's races, or an Agricultural Show, or a Chancellor sworn in for an university, or Jenny Lind, or any thing of that sort; and as the Swell Mob come down, we send 'em back again by the next train. But some of the Swell Mob, on the occasion of this Derby that I refer to, so far kiddied us as to hire a horse and shay; start away from London by Whitechapel, and miles round; come into Epsom from the opposite direction; and go to work, right and left, on the course, while we were waiting for 'em at the Rail. That, however, ain't the point of what I'm going to tell you.

"While Witchem and me were waiting at the station, there comes up one Mr. Tatt; a gentleman formerly in the public line, quite an amateur Detective in his way, and very much respected. 'Halloa, Charley Wield,' he says. 'What are you doing here? On the look out for some of your old friends?' 'Yes, the old move, Mr. Tatt.' 'Come along,' he says, 'you and Witchem, and have a glass of sherry.' 'We can't stir from the place,' says I, 'till the next train comes in; but after that, we will with pleasure.' Mr. Tatt waits, and the train comes in, and then Witchem and me go off with him to the Hotel. Mr. Tatt he's got up quite regardless of expense, for the occasion; and in his shirt-front there's a beautiful diamond prop, cost him fifteen or twenty pound—a very handsome pin indeed. We drink our sherry at the bar, and have our three or four glasses, when Witchem cries suddenly, 'Look out, Mr. Wield! stand fast!' and a dash is made into the place by the swell mob—four of 'em—that have come down as I tell you, and in a moment Mr. Tatt's prop is gone! Witchem, he cuts 'em off at the door, I lay about me as hard as I can, Mr. Tatt shows fight like a good 'un, and there we are, all down together, heads and heels, knocking about on the floor of the bar—perhaps you never see such a scene of confusion! However, we stick to our men (Mr. Tatt being as good as any officer), and we take 'em all, and carry 'em off to the station. The station's full of people, who have been took on the course; and it's a precious piece of work to get 'em secured. However, we do it at last, and we search 'em; but nothing's found upon 'em, and they're locked up; and a pretty state of heat we are in by that time, I assure you!

"I was very blank over it myself, to think that the prop had been passed away; and I said to Witchem, when we had set 'em to rights, and were cooling ourselves along with Mr. Tatt, 'We don't take much by *this* move, anyway, for nothing's found upon 'em, and it's only the braggadocia* after all.' 'What do you mean, Mr. Wield,' says Witchem. 'Here's the diamond pin!' and in the palm of his hand there it was, safe and sound! 'Why, in the name of wonder,' says me and Mr. Tatt, in astonishment, 'how did you come by that?' 'I'll tell you how I come by it,' says he. 'I saw which of 'em took it; and when we were all down on the floor together, knocking about, I just gave him a little touch on the back of his hand, as I knew his pal would; and he thought it WAS his pal; and gave it me!' It was beautiful, beau-ti-ful!

"Even that was hardly the best of the case, for that chap was tried at the Quarter Sessions at Guildford. You know what Quarter Sessions are, sir. Well, if you'll believe me, while them slow justices were looking over the Acts of Parliament to see what they could do to him, I'm blowed if he didn't cut out of the dock before their faces! He cut out of the dock, sir, then and there; swam across a river; and got up into a tree to dry himself. In the tree he was took—an old woman having seen him climb up—and Witchem's artful touch transported him!"

III.—THE SOFA

"What young men will do, sometimes, to ruin themselves and break their friends' hearts," said Sergeant Dornton, "it's surprising! I had a case at Saint Blank's Hospital which was of this sort. A bad case, indeed, with a bad end!

"The Secretary, and the House-Surgeon, and the Treasurer, of Saint Blank's Hospital, came to Scotland Yard to give information of numerous robberies having been committed on the students. The students could leave nothing in the pockets of their great-coats while the great-coats were hanging at the hospital, but it was almost certain to be stolen. Property of various descriptions was constantly being lost; and the gentlemen were naturally uneasy about it, and anxious, for the credit of the institution, that the thief or thieves

---

*Three months' imprisonment as reputed thieves.

should be discovered. The case was entrusted to me, and I went to the hospital.

" 'Now, gentlemen,' said I, after we had talked it over; 'I understand this property is usually lost from one room.'

"Yes, they said. It was.

" 'I should wish, if you please,' said I, 'to see the room.'

"It was a good-sized bare room down-stairs, with a few tables and forms in it, and a row of pegs, all round, for hats and coats.

" 'Next, gentlemen,' said I, 'do you suspect anybody?'

"Yes, they said. They did suspect somebody. They were sorry to say, they suspected one of the porters.

" 'I should like,' said I, 'to have that man pointed out to me, and to have a little time to look after him.'

"He was pointed out, and I looked after him, and then I went back to the hospital, and said, 'Now, gentlemen, it's not the porter. He's, unfortunately for himself, a little too fond of drink, but he's nothing worse. My suspicion is, that these robberies are committed by one of the students; and if you'll put me a sofa into that room where the pegs are—as there's no closet—I think I shall be able to detect the thief. I wish the sofa, if you please, to be covered with chintz, or something of that sort, so that I may lie on my chest, underneath it, without being seen.'

"The sofa was provided, and next day at eleven o'clock, before any of the students came, I went there, with those gentlemen, to get underneath it. It turned out to be one of those old-fashioned sofas with a great cross-beam at the bottom, that would have broken my back in no time if I could ever have got below it. We had quite a job to break all this away in the time; however, I fell to work, and they fell to work, and we broke it out, and made a clear place for me. I got under the sofa, lay down on my chest, took out my knife, and made a convenient hole in the chintz to look through. It was then settled between me and the gentlemen that when the students were all up in the wards, one of the gentlemen should come in, and hang up a great-coat on one of the pegs. And that great-coat should have, in one of the pockets, a pocket-book containing marked money.

"After I had been there some time, the students began to drop into the room, by ones, and twos, and threes, and to talk about all sorts of things, little thinking there was any body under the sofa—and then to go up-stairs. At last there came in one who remained until he was alone in the room by himself. A tallish, good-looking young man of one or two and twenty, with a light whisker. He went to a particular hat-peg, took off a good hat that was hanging there, tried it on, hung his own hat in its place, and hung that hat on another peg, nearly opposite to me. I then felt quite certain that he was the thief, and would come back by-and-bye.

"When they were all up-stairs, the gentleman came in with the great-coat. I showed him where to hang it, so that I might have a good view of it; and he went away; and I lay under the sofa on my chest, for a couple of hours or so, waiting.

"At last, the same young man came down. He walked across the room, whistling—stopped and listened—took another walk and whistled—stopped again, and listened—then began to go regularly round the pegs, feeling in the pockets of all the coats. When he came to THE great-coat, and felt the pocket-book, he was so eager and so hurried that he broke the strap in tearing it open. As he began to put the money in his pocket, I crawled out from under the sofa, and his eyes met mine.

"My face, as you may perceive, is brown now, but it was pale at that time, my health not being good; and looked as long as a horse's. Besides which, there was a great draught of air from the door, underneath the sofa, and I had tied a handkerchief round my head; so what I looked like, altogether, I don't know. He turned blue—literally blue—when he saw me crawling out, and I couldn't feel surprised at it.

" 'I am an officer of the Detective Police,' said I, 'and have been lying here, since you first came in this morning. I regret, for the sake of yourself and your friends, that you should have done what you have; but this case is complete. You have the pocket-book in your hand and the money upon you; and I must take you into custody!'

"It was impossible to make out any case in his behalf, and on his trial he pleaded guilty. How or when he got the means I don't know; but while he was awaiting his sentence, he poisoned himself in Newgate."

We inquired of this officer, on the conclusion of the foregoing anecdote, whether the time appeared long, or short, when he lay in that constrained position under the sofa?

"Why, you see, sir," he replied, "if he hadn't come in, the first time, and I had not been quite sure he was the thief, and would return, the time would have seemed long. But, as it was, I being dead certain of my man, the time seemed pretty short."

ANDREW FORRESTER, JR.

is one of the great might-have-beens in the history of the detective story. Although his earliest work was in imitation of "Waters," he soon enlarged the scope of the British detective story with new themes, creating plotted stories as opposed to narrated reminiscences. Forrester was also the first, apparently, to recognize the importance of Poe's work. Unfortunately, his stories received no attention, although they were a generation ahead of their day.

Forrester's three books are Secret Service, or Recollections of a City Detective *(1863),* The Revelations of a Private Detective *(1863), and* The Female Detective *(1864). The last title is the first collection of stories about a female detective, preceding William S. Hayward's* Revelations of a Lady Detective *by about six months. Two other books published under Forrester's name are partial reissues of earlier volumes.*

About Forrester himself nothing can be said. In all probability his name was a pseudonym, but judging by internal indications Forrester was an intelligent, well-educated, well-read man, possibly with legal training. We might speculate that he stopped writing fiction when he was established in another profession.

"Arrested on Suspicion"

I may as well say, at once, that this statement never could have been made had I not been, as I remain, an admirer of Edgar Allan Poe; and if ever I have time, I hope to show that his acts were the result, not so much of a bad, as a diseased mind. For one thing, I believe his eyes were affected with an inequality of sight, which, in itself, was enough to overbalance a very exciteable brain.

But Poe has nothing to do with my statement, except as its

15

prompter. My name is John Pendrath (Cornish man, as I dare say you see in a moment), my age is twenty-eight, and I live with my sister Annie. We are all that are left of our family, which you must see by the name was equally good and old. I need not say what I am; because, though I feel no shame for my work, I do not care about it, and hope, some day, when the Lord Chancellor wakes up, to be able to go back to Cornwall.

However, it seems I am writing about myself, and that is not my intention; which, indeed, is to show how much individual good such a writer as even the condemned Edgar Poe can do, and even on this side of the Atlantic.

As I and my sister cannot afford a house of our own, we live in apartments—two bedrooms and a sitting-room, generally second floor; Annie having the room behind our parlour, and I camping in a garret. I do not say we are very happy, because of our chancery affair; but we are generally cheerful—always so, except when we hear about costs, which is all we do hear of our famous suit.

When we had been in Aylesbury Terrace, Bayswater, about six weeks—on the second floor—I was coming home as usual, when, in the ordinary way, I found Annie at the usual meeting-place.

"Annie," said I, "what's the matter? Have you heard any good news?"

"No, Jack; but when I don't come to meet you, and I run down to open the door, you look twice before you give me my Cornwall kiss."

"Why, Annie," said I, "what do you mean?" for I hate a mystery without a statement. This arises, I suppose, through my liking for mathematics.

"Jack, dear," said she, "I have a double."

"No, Annie," I replied, "that can't be, or I shall go courting."

"Upon my word, Jack," said sister Annie, "I felt inclined to ask myself whether I had gone out and come home with a stout lady, aged forty, in black silk, when I saw them come to the door: and now I've left them behind, under our rooms, I ask myself—in fun, you know—whether I have come out to meet you."

Of course then, I understood. Annie had made a statement.

"Oh," said I, "a mother, with her daughter, apparently, has taken the first floor of No. 10, Aylesbury Terrace, and the supposed daughter is certainly something like you."

"That is the history itself, John," said sister Annie, "if you take out *apparently*; for I heard the younger call the elder, 'ma, dear;' and I am sure they have taken the first floor, because the door was open as I came down, and I could not help seeing that they were eating slices of bread and marmalade."

"Oh!" replied I; for I could say nothing else.

And when I saw the young person come up the house steps next morning (Sunday), it seemed to me that she resembled Annie in some degree; but my sister—like most women I think, had exaggerated the likeness. She would have passed for Annie with a stranger, but not with me.

Annie was also wrong in saying they had taken the first floor. The mother (apparent), alone lived in our house, and the daughter, said to be married, lived elsewhere.

Well, I hope my sister Annie has no more curiosity than most women; but, as I am away all day, and she is lonely, I can't blame her for looking out of the window, though I have, perhaps, sometimes told her it was a pity she could not find something better to do. So, she could not help noticing four daily facts:—

1. That the younger woman came every morning.

2. That the mother and daughter (apparent) went out together.

3. That they seldom left the house two days running in the same clothes, and frequently exchanged their cloaks and shawls on the same day.

4. That the occupant of the first floor always came home alone.

I put these premises before myself—though, perhaps, it would be, as a rule, below a man to interfere in such matters as these—and I came to this conclusion:—That the husband of the daughter had quarrelled with the mother; that, therefore, the mother and daughter went about together, while the husband was away at his business; and that they were rather vulgar, well-off women, who liked to go about and show their finery.

I had no need to tell Annie to avoid Mrs. Mountjoy and her daughter, Mrs. Lemmins. She felt neither was a companion for her. I mention this because Mrs. Mountjoy made advances to Annie, which, however, ended on her side; for in spite of the assurances of Mrs. Mountjoy's respectability by our landlady, Mrs. Blazhamey, Annie and I kept our own opinions.

I suppose Mrs. Mountjoy had been in the house about a month, when I noticed a little blue-stoned ring on Annie's left hand. Of course I said nothing about it, since she did not, though I saw it was new. I am not one of those men who pry into women's actions. You know we do not like them to pry into ours.

Well, the thunderclap came as suddenly as I am about stating its particulars to you. I was at work, when a cab drove up to the door, and out came Mrs. Blazhamey. I shoved her into the waiting-room for the public, and then listened for her to speak. The poor woman seemed quite overwhelmed for some moments, and though I did not move or utter a word, I dare say I was white enough.

"Oh, sir," at last, she said, "Miss Annie's took up for shop-liftin'!"

If you ask me how I felt, I cannot tell you. But I am sure of this—that within ten seconds I was thinking wholly of my sister. I know Mrs. Blazhamey believes me to this day a brute; but I hope I am not cynical when I say, that most of the people who give way to a deal of emotion generally seem to have a quantity of big I's mixed up with their grief. I dare say, though, I am a cold sort of man.

What was to be done? See Annie, if possible. It was then ten minutes to four, the hour at which we closed. I obtained an easy permit to leave, and jumped into Mrs. Blazhamey's cab. I did not speak, after learning whither we had to go, till we met a hansom cab, into which I and the poor woman with me exchanged.

Of course, I am not going to give the particulars of the meeting. I have only to state facts, so I will only say that Annie, after a little while, was almost as cool as myself. She had been arrested at three, and now it was half-past four. That she would not be taken before the magistrate till half-past eleven the next morning was the first news I gained. Then I asked the inspector on duty, and the policeman who had brought Annie to that place, for the particulars of the case.

They were these: The prisoner, Annie—do not suppose I am going to conceal any fact, so I say prisoner—had been shoplifting the district for some time, in company with a companion about forty years of age. The prisoner had been identified by a jeweller who had been robbed; and one of the rings stolen from his shop was found on her left hand—it being sworn to by a private mark.

I may tell you that this statement was given to me with mock gravity by the inspector, on my calm representation that it was a case of mistaken identity. I need not add that I know my sister ran no chance of condemnation; but scandal has always got some weight, and therefore I had two ends to meet—her immediate liberation, and the arrest of the true depredators.

I need not state that both Annie and I saw how the ground lay—she had been arrested for Mrs. Lemmins (so called); and in a moment I comprehended the daily change of dress, and the return of the woman Mountjoy alone in order to avoid the greater chance of detection after a robbery by remaining with her companion.

Annie comprehended my warning glance as our eyes met, when the inspector, in the charging-office, stated the case; and I have no doubt he thought we knew the suspicion was strong. But I think I staggered him when I said—"Do thieves usually wear the jewellery they steal?"

"Good bye, Annie," I said; and I could not trust myself to kiss her—nor did she offer to touch my cheek.

Now, what was to be done? Here were the facts. Annie could not be released till the next day, and I had about eighteen hours in

which to work for her, and procure the arrest of the women going by
the names respectively of Mountjoy and Lemmins. Had they taken
the alarm? If so, how long? If not, what extent of time would they
require in which to learn how matters stood—when might they infer
my sister and I would suspect them? So far, there had passed but
two hours and a-half since the arrest. Had they heard of it in that
time?

"Can I have a detective in my employ, if you please?" I said to
the inspector.

"Two," the official said; who, in spite of the calmness of apparent fact against Annie Pendrath, was, I saw, interested by my action.

"One," I said; and a soft-looking, quiet, almost womanly man,
with fair hair and weak, soft blue eyes, a man about thirty-five, was
placed at my disposal.

We three—myself, the constable (named Birkley), and Mrs.
Blazhamey—left that station in a cab called, and then I said—

"Mrs. Blazhamey, the real thieves are your precious drawing-
room lodger and her friend."

"What, Mrs. Mountjoy!" screamed our landlady; "why, she's a
lady."

"So she may be, but she's a thief."

"Then out o' my house she goes the moment I gets home."

Of course, this was just the kind of answer I expected. I had
balanced it this way: if I do not tell Blazhamey, she will carry the
whole history up to Mountjoy the moment we reach home; while if I
inform her, she will put the woman on the alert.

"Mrs. Blazhamey," said I, "will you make five pounds? Yes, I
see you will. Go to your daughter's at Kensington-park—don't come
home till half-past ten, and I'll pay the note down to-morrow at
twelve."

Of course, she made a thousand objections; but she was packed
off, at last, in another cab, and I and the policeman drove to Ayles-
bury-terrace.

"Policeman," said I, "if this woman is still in the house, she
must only leave it in your company. I'll take the responsibility of
charging her; but I don't want you to take her (if she's there) till I
give you the word. I want to catch her friend."

"Lor', sir! do yer think her frind'll turn up, and do yer think
she's there? Lor' bless yer, sir! they takes an 'int in a hurry. They've
hooked!"

"If she is still there," I said, "will you watch opposite till I've
put a canary cage in the second-floor front right-hand window, looking *into*, and not from the street?"

The blue-eyed detective, the most innocent-looking man I ever saw, opened his azure eyes; and the end of it was, that he agreed to my proposal, which was but natural.

"It may be hours you'll have to wait," I said.

"Days," replied the man, with the best laconicism I ever witnessed.

We left the cab before reaching the house, and then separated to opposite sides of the street. It struck seven as I went up the garden path.

There she was, at the window, reading a yellow-covered book.

She could not have taken the alarm, I thought, or she would not be reading. I had up the servant directly. Did she know why her mistress had left the house in the afternoon?

"No," the girl replied. "She was very much flustered, and only said, 'It can't be—it can't be.' "

She (witness) did not know the beginning of the affair, because she had been out on an errand, and when she came back, missus had her every-day bonnet on. She went out with a policeman. I may here add, that Annie had sent the policeman to our lodgings to Mrs. Blazhamey; having forethought enough not to send to me at the establishment. I than asked the girl whether Mrs. Mountjoy was in at the time.

"No," the girl said; "she com'd in at five."

Had any letter arrived for her?

"No—not even a note, mister," the girl replied.

Now, I could have had Mountjoy arrested at once, but I had learnt that the criminal classes are, as a rule of business, very faithful to each other, and therefore I felt that the apprehension of Mountjoy might prevent that of Lemmins. If the latter heard of Annie's arrest first, I felt sure that Mountjoy would be in some way informed of the matter; while if our fellow-lodger was the first to acquire the knowledge, the accomplice would be in some way warned. The priority of information would chiefly depend upon this condition—to the residence of which woman was my sister nearest when she was arrested?

I went to the window, after dismissing the servant, and there was that blue-eyed man, who no one could take for a police-officer, eating nuts, and with a couple of newspapers under his right arm. I saw Mrs. Mountjoy was safe, but it was her accomplice I wanted to encompass.

Nothing occurred up to ten minutes to eight, except Mrs. Mountjoy calling for some warm water; but at that time a woman limped up the garden, and carrying a basket of clothes, which, it seemed to me, was just home from the laundress. She did not come in, but she left the basket, and quietly went her way.

Almost immediately after she had closed the gate, the detective opened it, and before he reached the door I had my hand on the lock.

"Quick!" he said, pushing past me; "that's a 'complice—the letter's in the wash."

The girl was coming out of the drawing-room, having taken in the basket, as I ran down to the door; and as the policeman pushed past me and up the stairs without the waste of a moment, I am quite sure the basket had not been carried into the room more than a quarter of a minute, when the officer followed it.

Half a glance satisfied the man. The linen on the top of the basket had been roughly turned over. There was no letter in Mrs. Mountjoy's hand, but I saw it was trembling. She was seated in the chair near the window, exactly as I had seen her when I came home, but the book she had been reading was on the table.

The officer looked from me to the basket, flinging an expression into his blue eyes I never should have thought could characterize them; and then turning to the woman, he said—

"Come—the game's up."

"I don't understand you," said the woman.

"I does," added the officer; and continued to me—"will you go and fetch a cab, sir? I dare say the lady'ud rather not walk."

Upon the removal and charging of the woman I need not dilate, as those circumstances have nothing to do with my statement.

What I wanted was the letter, which I felt sure, without the help of the policeman, had been brought amongst the linen.

She had not had time to read it, and, therefore, it would not be destroyed, unless she had recognized the policeman's step at the bottom of the staircase, and had managed to annihilate it while he and I were ascending the staircase. The officer appeared to have been aware of the value of the letter equally with myself; for when I returned to the house, he had manacled her hands, as he told me afterwards, to prevent her from touching the letter if she had it about her.

Under the policeman's directions, I kept my eyes on the ground from the drawing-room to the cab—(I seem to be writing the word "cab" very frequently; but the fact stands, that I was in one cab or another by far the better part of the score of hours between Annie's arrest and the end of my statement)—and I was quite sure the letter was not dropped during the passage. Again, when we reached the station-house, the vehicle was closely examined, and even the ground over which we passed to the charging-office.

Then the woman was closely searched. I was told that even her hair was examined minutely, and the basque of her stays taken out. But all to no purpose—the letter was not found. That some kind of communication had been made, or rather attempted, I was certain, for the policeman had recognized the apparent laundress as a hanger-on, and general thieves' go-between.

The conclusion both I and the officer came to before we left the station was, that the letter, or note, was in the drawing-room, and still in the basket.

It was clear she could not have found and read the warning, however short, in the few moments that elapsed while I ran down stairs and up again with the constable. It would take some seconds to reach the chair in which she was seated, and further time in which to hide the communication.

The constable said, "p'raps she swallered it," as a kind of preparation for the worst. But I was not inclined to accept this theory, notwithstanding he urged that it might have been a mere scrap of paper; because it seemed impossible that it could have been found, masticated, and swallowed in the time.

When the officer and I returned to the house, it wanted a quarter to nine. You see, time was progressing.

And now began the search for the letter. And here it was that I think my experience beat that of the police constable; for, after we had ransacked the basket, and were quite sure the letter was not within it, *he* began the ordinary routine search, while I sat down and began to *think*. The constable supposed I was broken down, and so he said—

"Chirrup, sir."

Whereupon I answered him—

"Go on, officer; I'm searching, too."

I suppose he was inclined to laugh, for he turned away to the stove. It was summer time (August), and so there was no fire in the grate. The officer, being at the stove, began examining it.

"Any ashes on the ground?" I asked.

"Why, you don't suppose she burnt it? It's hid," the man replied.

"Any soot on the hobs or hearth?"

"No," he replied.

"Then the top moveable flap of the stove has not been moved. Could a letter—take this card—be thrust between the damper and its frame?"

"No," said the man; "there's a hedge to it."

"Then, what are you staying about the stove for?" I asked.

The man turned, looked at me, his foolish-looking jaw dropped low, and then he said—

"You knows a thing or two, mister—you do."

Of course I do not wish to hide from the reader that I was trying to copy Edgar Poe's style of reasoning in this matter; for confessedly I am making this statement to show how a writer of fiction can aid the officers of the law.

"I shall do the regular round," said the officer, beginning to the right of the fire-place.

Now, as I sat, I was exerting all my reason to deduce the probabilities of the place of concealment from the facts known. I remembered that in the case of a search for a letter by the French police, recounted by Poe, that while the officers were hunting for the missive, even in the very legs and backs of the chairs, that it was stuck in a card rack, openly, with a dozen others; and though this knowledge was the basis upon which I built up my argument, yet, of itself, it was valueless, for I felt it would require a mind far beyond the common-place—a condition which did not distinguish Mountjoy—to imagine and rapidly complete a mode of concealment which should be successful by its very candour.

I felt that this woman had concealed the communication—if, indeed, it were not destroyed, a supposition I refused to entertain—in such a manner as a child would conceive, with the superaddition of some dexterity, the result of the shifting and elusive nature of her life.

I was still pondering, when the officer came to the bookcase, which was locked.

"Yere'll be a job, to hunt all through them books," said the blue-eyed, amiable officer, in a confidential tone.

Now, had the bookcase been opened? I got up, and looked at the projecting ledge of the escritoire portion, below the bookcase. The dust had been blowing that day, and the upper part of one of the windows was still open. A glance showed me the case had not been unclosed, for the particles of dust lay equally over the ledge; and I noticed that the opening, or key-door was furnished with an inner green silk curtain, which was shut in, and protruded below the bottom of the panel. Had it been opened, this curtain must have broken the regularity of the dust, which was *not* disturbed. So, again, the fine, white, pulverous particles lay on the upper part of the two knobs of the escritoire slide—a fact which proved to me that the escritoire had not been opened, as in that case both handles must have been touched.

My argument was so clear, that the officer did not even hesitate to admit I was right.

"And what about the cupboard under the askertor?" he asked.

"Search it," I said, "though I doubt if it's there. She was a stout woman, and would avoid stooping."

"Ha!" answered the officer approvingly; but he examined the cupboard, and found little else than china in it.

Still I sat, for I felt I could thus more easily concentrate my thoughts than by standing. And do not suppose that all this time I did not think of Annie. The fact is, I knew I could best serve her by acting exactly as though I was doing an ordinary duty, rather than one of love. Indeed, if people would but think of themselves a little less than they do, they would often-times get through more work than most men manage.

"Officer," I said, after a pause, in which he had looked over the chairs, under the table-cloth, and in all parts of the ebony inkstand—even fishing in the ink with a pen, and catching nothing worth the taking. "Officer, will you examine the joins of the wall-paper from the ground, to about six feet high?"

"Very well, mister; but will you help me move the heavy things?"

"Only note the joins you can see," I said, adding, with the first smile I had indulged in since the morning, "I don't think she had them out and back again in the time it took us to come upstairs—see if the joins fit and are flat."

This was a long piece of work for the officer, and dusk was coming on as he made half-way round the apartment.

"Look at the cracks in the mantelpiece, where the flat and the top of each pillar come together? Nothing! Well, and now the edge of the carpet all round the room, where the edge can easily be raised."

I dare say you will wonder that I did not help actively to search. I was hunting with my brains. Was it possible, I thought, that always anticipating a visit from the police, she had some easy place of concealment for pieces of jewellery and small articles of value, and into which she had conveyed the letter?—of the existence of which there could be no doubt, for we found that the tumbled linen belonged, some of it to children, and some of it to grown-up men, while a pair of stockings were unfolded, "and," said the constable, "somehow, a stockin' allers is the pest-bag among 'em."

Could such a place of immediate concealment be a slit in the carpet? This might be the case, and I suggested the idea to the officer.

"Then hadn't we better have the carpet up!" he asked.

"It will cause a great waste of time," answered I, "and we will not do so till we have done searching elsewhere."

But I found this idea so clung to my mind, that it impeded the progress of my thought. So, deciding that I must settle this point before I proceeded to another, I sat devising a means of ascertaining if there were a slit in the carpet without hauling it up. Soon I found one. If I took up one end of the carpet, and flapped the air under it, the dust you will always find under a lodging-house carpet would rise, and fly in a little cloud through any cutting.

The officer saw the force of this argument, and it was put into operation.

But nothing came of it; and I think it was at this point that my official friend began to break down, saying—

"Derpend upon it, she swallered it."

Then he began to hunt again—this time behind the pictures, but I soon called his attention from them by saying—

"The moderator-lamp."

"Ha! I didn't think o' the lamp," said the officer.

But we found nothing in the lamp beyond disappointment.

Time, however, had not been lost; for the field of observation was nearly gone over. The letter, or scrap of paper, was not below the wall-hangings, for not one of the seams was loose, or wet with paste or gum. It was not up the chimney, not even concealed in the paper ornament in the stove, nor about the bookcase, lamp, chairs, or table; nor, in all probability, was it under the carpet.

"The tea-caddy," I said, after a pause.

The caddy was easily opened, for Birkley had brought the woman's keys with him; but it was searched to no purpose. And when the night had well closed in, and Mrs. Blazhamey had come home (before her time, though), and hindered us, we were no nearer a satisfactory result than we had been at the commencement of the search. By this time, the carpet had been taken up, the pictures down and out of their frames, every loose book about nearly pulled to pieces with examination, and even the bell-pulls unripped. The sacking of the chairs, the bottom of the fender, the cornice of the bookcase—a hundred spots, nine-tenths of which must have been totally inaccessible to the woman in the time at her disposal, had been examined, and with equal want of success.

"Derpend upon it, sir, she swallered it," said the officer; and I think it was this persistency on his part which intensified my obstinacy in believing that the warning was in the room. I wanted to be by myself, to think without interruption, to follow the action of the woman,; and with this end in view, I said to the officer—

"Go to the station, and see if they have heard anything."

"Holl right!" said he; "but, derpend upon it, she swallered of it *down*."

The officer gone, and Mrs. Blazhamey almost forced out of the room, which by this time looked like a wreck, I sat down in the midst of the furniture, and asked what next was to be done. And then, with that repetitory process which, I am told, is common during intense thought, I began conceiving once more the idea of what the woman must have been about when she first supposed a police-officer in the house.

How many seconds had she been in doubt before the officer and I entered the room? I had accepted Birkley's theory that she had recognised the policeman's tramp when he was at the bottom of the stairs; but was I justified in accepting that theory? How if she had no suspicion till the door handle was turning? If such were the case, the scrap of paper would be within a foot of the right side of the chair in which we found her seated. You see, being left to myself, I was adding to the repetition of my thought.

Suppose I went through *her* actions from the opening of the linen basket to the entry of myself and the officer?

You may declare this action childish, but you are wrong.

I went to the basket, supposed that I opened a stocking, and then went to the chair, thinking to myself that she, a stout woman, and naturally agitated by the arrival of the warning, would take a seat; and what more natural, since she was going to read by the coming twilight, than to go to the window?

I took the chair, exactly as we had found her, my right side to the window, and then supposed myself startled by the opening of the door. This fright would be followed by the involuntary attempt to hide the letter *by the right hand*. I flung my hand behind me, and it lodged in the folds of the cord-knotted curtain.

The discovery was far easier than putting on a worn glove—which is sometimes a rather difficult operation. My fingers positively rested on the paper, a mere scrap, torn from a wide-margined newspaper, and which had been easily thrust into the folds where the damask was gathered.

We had been at fault by crediting the woman with too much cleverness. We had supposed that she had anticipated and prepared for our coming when we were at the bottom of the stairs; and acting upon that belief, we had been wandering all round the room when our investigation should have been confined to a square yard.

Nor was I blameless on another score. I had presupposed the woman to be not intellectual enough to avoid a distinct concealment; whereas, the rapidity of our coming had caused her to do by accident that which a clever and prepared criminal would do by premeditation—placing the letter where nobody would think it worth while to look, as being under one's very eyes.

Will you believe the statement that now I had found the scrap of paper I saw that it was *visible* as it lay in the folds of the curtain, which had positively been unhooked by the constable that he might examine the shutter-cases with facility?

But do not suppose my labours were over. Not that I refer to the perusal of the *cipher* as a labour; I defy an ignorant cipher to puzzle me. Exactly as you would never dream of looking for a hidden letter in a blotting-case, so a merely confused Roman-letter cipher (if the word in such an instance as this is applicable) is infinitely more difficult to analyse than a system of actual, arbitrary signs. I had always been able to read an arbitrary cipher after a study of twenty minutes. I was only twelve, when I found a little packet in my cousin's room containing a lock of hair and some words in arbitrary cipher, which I analysed in half a minute; for seeing two words flourished all about, I supposed they formed the lady's name, found that the fourth and sixth letters of the first, and the second and fifth of the second, were similar, so successfully guessed, in far less time than it takes to write about, that the MS. and lock referred to our neighbour Phoebe Reade.

Cunning, ignorant people, I am told, always use an arbitrary cipher, almost as easy to read as A B C. I may tell you that Mrs. Mountjoy's letter gave me little trouble. I found it at nearly a quarter-past nine, and at half-past it was written out for the benefit of the police. It was in a simple character.

And as I can have no secret in this matter, if you are willing to learn the process, which has few regular rules, here it is to study. You may acquire it in five minutes.

X⅂H. I+ +IL. ⅃ ZU⊥. H⅂U/.
　　1　　　　2　　　　　3　　　　4

X⊢U\. X⊐X⅂. HXX⊢. X⊢. ZU
　5　　　　6　　　7　　　8　　9

⊐⊐U⊢UH. /⅂I. HI. X⅂H /⊥
　　9　　　　10　　11　　12　　13

U. X\I⊥⊓. X⅂H / ⅃ U\XI. XV
13　　14　　　　15　　　　16　　　17

I\. ⊐X/⅃∧. X⅂H. ++⌐⊥\. HI. H
17　　　18　　　19　　　20　　　21　22

⅂⅃⌐X IX⊐X⅂H. I. ⊐X∧U⊥+
　22　　　　23　　　　24　　　25

∧U⅂I ⊐U.
26　　　27

Now, I dare say all this appears very mysterious to the general reader. There never was a more candid arbitrary alphabet put together. In the first place, the straight-line character of the writing told me it was simple. Alphabets curve as they rise in the thought which they embody. It will be seen that here there is no curved line.

Now, when you are fairly sure you have a simple cipher, and written in the English language, you hold the key to it with this one piece of knowledge—that the most frequently used letter in our language is e. Very well, then, find that character which is most frequently repeated, and you may be pretty certain it is e. In this case, you will find the leading figure is X. It is repeated sixteen times.

Now, we have a more than merely supposed e. The next question is the frequency, if any, with which a series of characters is repeated. You will find that the first word marked by a stop is repeated four times in twenty-seven words, or better than one in seven. This, then, must be a common expression. Take the next newspaper, and you will find the word "the" the most frequently repeated. But here comes an important contradiction. The first word agreeing with "the" has certainly three letters, but then it begins, instead of ending, with X. Now, you will find that the character representing e begins many words in this sentence, and ends none; whereas, the rule in English is, that e rather ends than commences words.

Take this fact into connection with the known truth that the thieves talk "back," or reversed English, and the contradiction is cleared away—each word is begun to be written at the end. We have then three letters, t.h.e. Now, if you go on to the sixth word, you will find we have the characters representing t.h.e, and that they spell (in the right direction) he-e. Now, the only ordinary word with this combination is "here." Therefore, we have now four letters, t h e r. If we now hunt out a word in which all these characters occur, we shall find it at 23, which runs there-. The sixth character must be an s, because it's the only natural terminal to the word there's—short for "there is."

We have now five letters, t h e r s.

We will now take word 24, following "there's." It can't be I—"There's I" is an impossible phrase. But there is only one other ordinary English word of one letter besides "i"—it is "a." "There's a" is a natural mode of expression. We have now six letters, t h e r s a.

Now, you must settle the short words before you can touch the long. We have got "the" and "a," and the words in which t, h, and e are commonly combined with one another. Let us now pass to other short words. Take 21. One of the letters of this word we already know to be "a;" what is the second? The two commonest words with which a is combined, and at the same time not preceded by the only letter word "i," thus as "I am," which is not the case here—are "as," and "at." Now, this letter is already a direction, in the shape of a warning. Every known circumstance in the case proves this, and therefore the word "at" is more likely to be used than "as," which is a word, when used grammatically, very seldom seen in common letter-writing. We will suppose 21 to represent "at," and then we shall find the same word at 11, which confirms the belief that these characters represent "at." And this conclusion supports the supposition referring to the "s" and "t" character. To continue. The word 22, which follows 21, we now find to stand e - - ht; and this partial elucidation reciprocally acts with word 21, to form the likely phrase in such a letter—"at eight."

Then we now have, as discovered letters—t h e r s a i g—eight letters. There are now enough upon which to build up the first skeleton of the revised letter, and thus it stands, the unknown letters being represented by small hyphens, and the words wholly wanting by the figures with which they have been already allied:—

> The ga - - s (3) - - -t - - -e here -eet -e t - - -rr- - a- - at the (13)
>   1   2   3   4   5   6   7   8   9   10 11 12 13
> - -a-e the se- - - - - -a-e - - -er the - -i- - at eight theres a - - - -er
>   14   15   16   17   18   19   20 21 22   23 24   25
> sh - - (27).
> 26 27

Now, 7 and 8 reciprocally suggest "meet me," and so we add "m" to our list of letters—now nine; and the t - m - rr - - after "meet me" confirms that reading, and which makes this word "to-morrow." This gives the letters "o" and "w," making in all eleven letters. Taking 5, "I find "o" and "m" are the second and third characters; therefore, I infer the first is "c." Now we have twelve letters. I also find that the second letter of word 4 is "o," which gives "- o - t," which, taken in connection with the letter being a warning, and the two following words, "come here," I take to be "don't." This rendering yields me two more letters, "d" and "n," which make in all fourteen.

The elucidation now stands:—

> The ga - -s - -own. Don't come here. Meet me to-morrow, and
>   1   2   3   4   5   6   7   8   9   10
> at the o-d - -ace, the second ca-e -nder the cl - - - at eight there's
> 11 12 13   14   15   16   17   18   19   20 21 22   23
> a - -ower show on.
> 24 25   26 27

Now, putting aside the first sentence, the first words we have to clear up are 13 and 14. Let us suppose it is "something place," and we are right, for the "l" drops into the centre of word 13, and we have "old place." This yields letter "p" and "l," and now we can add a letter to word 3, which from "--own" becomes "-lown."

We now arrive at word 17, where there is one letter wanting, and this we must for the present pass, and come to (18)-nder. This must be "under," and so we add "u" to the list; but it is useless, for it occurs only this once in the entire paragraph.

We now reach word 20, to which we can only add "l," which makes it cli--. And it will be remarked that the two most important words in the letter are still defective. However, the word 20 is soon elucidated, by going on to 25, to which we can now add the letter "l"—thus we get -lower, which, taken with words 26 and 27, gives "flower show on." We therefore find that word 20 is "cliff." The double "f" in word 2, makes it "gaff." We have now only *two* characters to decipher; the composition standing thus:

"The gaffs -lown. Don't come here. Meet me tomorrow at the old place, the second ca-e under the cliff at eight. There's a flower show on."

Now it is clear the missing letters are two, neither of which is used more than once. Then we have only to find the missing letters, and see which will fit in, to solve the problem. These letters are b, j, k, v, x, y, z.

The only letter which will agree with -lown is b, by which we get the sentence "The gaffs blown"—pure thieves' English, perhaps even something like good Anglo-Saxon. It means, the meeting-place is discovered and overthrown. "Gaff" is doubtless the talking-place, from *gabian*, to talk; while, probably, the word "blown" is based upon the idea of giving a blow—to blow, when the past participle in Saxon English would be blown—"beaten down."

Coming to the word ca-e, we find that v only will fit, and so we get "the second cave under the cliff at eight to-morrow" as the gist of the missive slipped among the folds of the curtain.

One word before I proceed with my story. Give me little credit for reading that cipher. I did it in less than twenty minutes; though it strikes me I may as well give the alphabet of this cipher, and also the appearance of the missive when reduced to ordinary letters. Here, first, is the alphabet—very simple and elementary:

The back reading stood thus:—eht sffag nwolb tnod emoc ereh
teem em worromot dna ta eht dlo ecalp eht dnoces evac rednu eht
ffilc ta thgie sereht a rewolf wohs no.

You would hardly suppose this was merely reversed English—
would you?

As I have said, the reading of the letter was nothing, but its
application was another matter—another business to continue the
thread of the clue in the nip of my mind till it was wound off the reel
by the re-introduction, under the auspices of the police, of Mrs.
Mountjoy to young Mrs. Lemmins.

What were the coming facts before me?

These—that Lemmins expected (since the go-between false
laundress had got clear from the house)—Mountjoy to meet her at
eight, in the second cave under the cliff, and that a flower show
would take place.

Now, it was summer time, and, therefore, I might take the
words "flower show" as literally meant; for, in connection with the
correspondents, it meant theft at the *fête* in question. Now, where
was this *fête* to be held? I was at a loss to tell whether it was next day
or the following. If next day, the meeting for eight referred to the
morning. If the following, it might mean eight in the evening.

But first for the spot. It must be populous, because the flower
show was talked of in London, and because thieves thought it worth
while to canvass the place. Secondly, it must be at the sea-side,
because only at the sea or water-side is the cliff called by that
name—at all events by Londoners.

Then I got at these suppositions, or rather facts. That a flower
show was to take place either the next day or the following at a sea-
side place distinguished not only for cliffs, but with caverns, or
caves, in them, and that Lemmins would be in the second either at
eight in the morning of the following day, or at that hour in the evening.

Was the place far away? It seemed to me not, because the context of the letter so plainly inferred that the recipient could easily
reach the spot, since the exact hour was named. Now, if I could only
find out, by an advertisement, where a flower show was to take place
within a couple of days, the locality being a cliffy, sea-side locality,
in all probability full of visitors—for I had heard of thieves going to
the sea-side with honest men—why, the chances were that I should
trap the woman.

Where was the place, and how could I find it out?

It was clear it could not be on the *east coast*, because it is flat
from the mouth of the river to Hull, or nearly so; neither, if very
near home, could it be below Brighton, for thence the shore is level,

or if not level, more or less unprovided with *cliffs* over a wide range of country.

Then the place in question, in all probability, stood either in Kent or Sussex. By this means I got my facts into a very narrow line, for I had but to examine the papers of both counties to ascertain whether or not a flower show was advertised. But here a new difficulty arose. It was now a quarter to ten, and all places of business, all reading-rooms were closed. Perhaps, however, the *fête* was advertised in the "Times," my second-day's copy of which was in our sitting-room. Ten minutes' search resulted in disappointment; but my eyes had caught an advertisement, all letters to be addressed to some initials, care of Messrs. Mitchell and Co., town and country news-agents, Red Lion Court, Fleet Street. The question I asked myself was, whether I should call at this office, in the faint chance of finding it still open, or go on at once to the London Bridge terminus, and take the night-mail to one of the several sea-side places, one of which I believed was the appointed place of meeting. My decision in favour of trying the office rested on the ground that, with a fast cab, to call on my road to the station, it would not delay me more than a quarter of an hour.

The cab (I find I must continually refer to cabs) took me into Fleet Street in considerably under the half-hour, and, to contract this portion of my narrative, for the simple reason that it is commonplace, I found a woman cleaning out the office. She was much flurried, and, I think, somewhat confused, in consequence of being so late at her work. With that extraordinary and simple belief of the very ignorant in the sacred nature of papers, she would not let me lay a finger upon one of the files of papers hung about the office; but with that other belief in the absolute power of money, I applied the great "progressive how much" argument with her, and which, supported by the assurance that print was not writing, led to my triumph upon another step of my journey; for at about the sixth hook I found a pile of (I think) *Kentish Observers*, or *Gazettes*, and soon I discovered (the information being in a prominent position) that a flower show was to be displayed on the very next day at the Tivoli Gardens, the context intimating that certain omnibuses would run at regular intervals from Ramsgate and Margate.

The inference stood that "the second cave under the cliff" was either at Ramsgate or Margate, and as I was driven on to the station, I turned over in my mind the various ways in which I could arrive at a just conclusion before I started, or while going down the line.

Absurd as was the question—"Are there any caves in the cliff at Ramsgate or at Margate?"—I put it to several railway porters; but they knew nothing about either place. And I have found generally that railway porters know nothing of their respective lines. In this strait, and after questioning the young woman in the refreshment department, and the policeman on duty, who, I think, felt somewhat inclined to arrest me on general grounds, I bethought me of buying a guide-book to the coast; but the railway book stall was blank with shutters, and the only acquisition I could make was the London and South Eastern Railway time-table; and this publication I was turning over, not so much disconsolately as with vexation, when an outline map fell open before me.

It was but natural that I should look at the relative positions of Ramsgate and Margate; and the investigation of the map formed another link in my chain of—may I say?—circumstantial evidence. The map showed me that the coast about Margate was more exposed to the action of the sea than the other marine town. Knowing that the indentation of the shore by sea water is, in a measure, effected by the formation of channels, or caves, the inference stood, that Margate was more likely to be the goal of my journey than the other town.

To Margate I went, making inquiries, however, when changing trains at Ramsgate, in order to ascertain if there were caves in the cliff of this latter place.

The reader who knows Margate is aware I was right.

But we did not catch our felon till ten a.m., for the tide was up, and the caves, which in the eyes of the children are such enormous caverns of darkness, were unapproachable. And, indeed, when the tide had receded sufficiently to allow of the approach of myself and the policeman I employed, I feared for my success, as I could discover no woman walking towards the "second cave," with her back towards me, and in whom I could trace a resemblance to the person called Lemmins. But the officer was right when he surmised that perhaps she had started from the "other end," referring to the break in the cliff at the point where the Preventive Service Station is built.

She was so surprised at the arrest, that she had not a word to say; for, as I implied from the copy of a telegraphic message we found on her, she had been informed that all was going well.

And as the magistrate of the district police court in which my sister had to appear was more than ordinarily late that morning, we reached the court before Annie was brought forward, and so when her eyes drifted round the court, they met mine. But we had already seen each other at the police cell door, and she knew that the actual thieves were in custody. Seen together, my sister and the younger prisoner were very distinguishable; but had the jeweller's man, upon oath, declared that Annie was Mrs. Mountjoy's companion, I do not think he should have been blamed.

I have now reached the end of my intended narrative. My purpose was to show that action in misfortune is better than grief. I have not referred to any pain, degradation, or consequence, which resulted either to my sister or myself, in consequence of her terrible arrest for shoplifting. I have merely stated, as logically as I could, a series of facts, inferences, and results, with the aim of pointing out that very frequently there is a deal of plain sailing where some people suppose no navigation can be effected.

"WATERS"

"WATERS" is an embarrassment. Although he is the originator of the British detective short story, nothing is known about him. His name is said to have been William Russell, but he is not to be confused with either William Russell the correspondent of the London Times or with William Clark Russell, the author of sea stories. Waters's dates are unknown, but he probably died before 1900.

Waters has the distinction of establishing the detective short story in Great Britain. His tale "Recollections of a Police-Officer" by "Detective Police-officer Waters" appeared in Chambers's Edinburgh Review *in 1849; it was soon followed by other adventures, which were gathered into book form in America in 1852 and in Great Britain in 1856. Waters wrote other books of pseudofactual cases:* Recollections of a Detective Police-Officer, Second Series *(1859);* The Experiences of a French Detective Officer *(1861);* Experiences of a Real Detective *(1862), and others.*

"Murder under the Microscope"

In a straggling, sandy district known as Stape Hill, not far from Poole, Dorsetshire, there dwelt in 1844, a man not more than forty years of age, if so much, but so bowed, withered by care and disappointment that he looked to be sixty at the very least. His name was Joseph Gibson, and he had once carried on business as an oil and colourman, in High-street, Islington. He failed in 1843, but managed, by effecting a compromise with his chief creditors, to save about four hundred pounds from the wreck. He had been some years separated from his wife, an attractive woman, by whom he had one pretty, delicate girl at the time of the failure. His own life was wrapped up in that of Catherine; and medical authority warned him

that only country air, and that for some years to come, could permanently establish her health. Whilst earnestly pondering how their future lives could be shaped so as to secure that primary object, his eye
hit upon an advertisement in the *Times*, announcing to agriculturists
and others that a farm of one hundred acres, partly arable, partly
pasture, with convenient dwelling-house, out-buildings, &c, situate
at Stape Hill, market town of Poole, was to be let on lease, at the
low rental of fifty pounds per annum. The stock, implements, &c,
were to be taken at a valuation, which would certainly not exceed
three hundred pounds, including the growing crops, the season
being late in the year; possession to be given on Michaelmas-day,
then ten days distant only. Satisfactory reasons for the throwing up
of so desirable a homestead by the last tenant would be given, and so
on after the manner of such schemes for gulling the unwary. A
transparent trap like that could not have imposed upon the least intelligent of practical farmers. He would have known that you might
as well have attempted to cultivate seashore sand as arable and pasture land near a populous English market town, inclusive of a convenient dwelling-house and requisite out-buildings, which the proprietor was willing to let at ten shillings annual rent per acre. But to
town folk there is a fascination in the prospect of occupying land
which blinds them to the most self-evident facts. Application in person only was to be made to Mr. Arthur Blagden, of Finsbury-
square. This gentleman was a solicitor retired from business, and a
native of Dorsetshire, in which county he possessed large property,
especially in Poole and its vicinity. He was a man of somewhat eccentric habits, and very close, almost penurious, in his expenditure.
The Dorsetshire rents he always collected twice a year in person.

The Staple Hill Farm appeared to be precisely suited to Gibson;
it being, the advertisement stated, one of the healthiest places in the
United Kingdom, and apparently requiring no more capital than he
possessed for adequate cultivation. As to not being himself a practical agriculturist, that deficiency the diligent study of such books as
"Farming for the million," &c., would quickly supply. Joseph Gibson having so resolved, betook himself to Finsbury-square without
delay, saw Mr. Blagden, who, when informed that the applicant really possessed four hundred pounds in cash, readily accepted him as
a tenant for Stape Hill Farm, a coloured drawing of which he placed
before Gibson, who was so delighted with the picture of rural felic-
ity which it presented that he carried it away to show his child. A
lease for fourteen years was to be immediately prepared at the tenant's cost, and on the 28th of September Mr. Blagden would go
down with him to Dorsetshire to give possession of the estate and
stock.

The preceding tenant, Mr. Blagden candidly informed Gibson,

had not prospered at the farm—was, in fact, at that moment a prisoner for debt; but he was an idle, dissolute fellow; encumbered, too, with a large, idle family, and a slatternly wife, who would never do well anywhere. Mr. Blagden had gladly taken the farm and stock off his hands—pleased to be shut of Edward Ridges, even at a considerable sacrifice.

Possession was given—Joseph Gibson installed in his rural domain—monarch of all he surveyed; spavined horses; lean and for the most part, barren cows, a score of decent pigs; and growing crops, such as they were; inclusive. Three labourers (one of them of the name of Somers) on the farm; and Jane Somers (an elderly maid-of-all-work and dairy-woman) were retained. Somers and his wife slept on the premises.

A very short time sufficed to dissipate the fond illusions which the swindled oil and colourman had indulged in. Staple Hill Farm would have consigned any man to a debtor's prison who could not afford to lose at least one hundred pounds per annum upon it. It was a sad awakening from a pleasant dream. His eyes were suddenly opened to the bare-faced fraud practised upon him by Mr. Blagden on the very next market-day, in Poole, after that gentleman, having collected his rents, left for London. The poor victim, who zealously falling in at once with market habits, dropped in at the Roebuck—an inn patronised by the bulk of the farmers, to not one of whom he was personally known—had the pleasure of listening to a very enlightening conversation, carried on in undertone by two or three of the guests. One asked who it was that that cunning devil, Blagden, had let Staple Hill Farm to? To which the reply was: —"A Cockney tailor, or something of the sort, who had got a few hundreds, which the avaricious old leech would soon suck him dry of. He had taken handsome hansel already, by making out that the stock on the place was worth three hundred pounds, and had got the rhino, so at least Jem Somers said—the covetous old hawk's factotum, sly as his master, and a sweet nut for the devil to crack some day or other." "Three hundred pounds!" says another; "the unconscionable, thieving skinflint. Why it was all valleyed to Blagden by poor Ridge's creditors for a hundred and forty pounds! and money enough too. Ah, well! the London tailor must soon take to his goose again; though he be goose enough himself, for that matter. Well, if folks will meddle with things they don't understand, they must pay their account with being done uncommon brown, especially if they come in old Blagden's way."

This was something like the substance of the conversation, as related to me about a twelvemonth after it occurred, by Nicholas Price, one of the interlocutors; my business in Poole being to ascertain if any ill-blood had existed by Gibson and Blagden, how engen-

dered, and how hot—inflamed. "Something turned the talk," Price
said, "to other matters, and about two hours passed—the silent
stranger, as he and others noticed, drinking hot brandy-and-water as
if it were so much water—when, all in a minute, up the said stranger
speaks, says he's the Cockney tailor they had been talking about, and
wants to know if it was positive true that Blagden was such a swin-
dling blackguard as they made out. 'If so,' said the excited stranger,
'I am a ruined man! My name is Joseph Gibson. It is I who have
taken the Stape Hill Farm; and if what you have said is true, may
God do so to me and more also but I will have the villain's heart's-
blood before many months have passed!' " Genuine fury, earnest
passion always impresses, rebukes men for a time to silence, and no
one spoke in answer. Price and his companions were not desirous
that their confidential chat with each other should be made a town-
talk of. Everybody disliked Blagden, but few would have chosen to
make him their personal enemy. "What I want to know is," continued Gibson, who did not appear to be exactly drunk, though he
had really tossed down his throat during those two hours nine shilling glasses of brandy-and-water—his speech, his legs being steady,
firm (the devil of drink, as frequently happens, was mastered by the
far mightier demon of revengeful rage)—"what I want to know, and
will know, is, whether or not the stock and growing crops at Stape
Hill Farm were valued to Blagden at one hundred and forty
pounds?" This fierce query was replied to by Mr. Philips, a master-
harness-maker at Poole, who had before spoken upon the subject.
"That is Gospel-truth," said he. "I am one of Ridge's creditors,
under the assignment which he made for the benefit of all (though
some haven't accepted it), and my name is to the receipt for the one
hundred and forty pounds paid by Blagden, just three weeks agone,
for the stock and crops upon them acres of hungry sand which he
calls Stape Hill Farms. A precious farm! It was plenty of money too.
Let me advise the gentleman from London," continued Mr. Phillips,
in the very words he used, as well as his memory served him, "that
if he have given three hundred pounds, as some say he have, for
what will not bring in more than a hundred odd, to throw up the
place at once, and let first loss be last loss. As for taking Blagden's
heart's-blood, that is very wild, foolish talk."

    At hearing that, Gibson dropped back into his chair without
speaking a word, motioned a person near a bell to ring it, signed to
the answering waiter for another glass of brandy-and-water, and sat
drinking till he fell, helplessly drunk, upon the floor, and was carried
to bed. It was late the next day when he left the Roebuck, and he
was never again seen in the house.

    Gibson had never been addicted to drink; and in ordinary circumstances, till of late years, when misfortunes gathering thickly about him cankered his temper as it bowed his form, as it blanched his hair—had been a man of generally placid demeanour, though capable, when roused, or rushing into the most violent extremes. This I ascertained from his former neighbours in Islington. It must not be forgotten either, that he had set his life—more than his own, his child's life—upon the desperate cast of success in the farming experiment. To play falsely with such a man, in such a mood of mind, was playing with fire.

Somers and his wife managed to pacify him for a time by confident assertions that the land was very fair land, and the stock, properly tended, would realize a profit upon the three hundred pounds. What he had heard at the Roebuck was mere malicious gossip; nothing more. Thus heartened, Gibson persevered; working, at such labour as he was fit for, like a slave. He had one prime source of consolation, which could be no deception—Catherine's health improved wonderfully at Stape Hill; and could he but manage to make both ends meet, he should be well content with his bargain.

That he soon found to be impossible. Wages, manure, horse-keep, his own domestic expenses—trifling as was the last item—quickly ate up his ridiculously insufficient capital. Stock, half-fattened, was sold at ruinous prices; and two months before Michaelmas, 1845, he, after looking carefully and boldly into the state of his affairs, was fain to recognise the terrible fact, that he must give up the farm; and, with scarcely a sovereign in his pocket, return to dingy, stifling London, with his now blooming daughter; to seek there means of eking out miserable life, and die there. Catherine soon as he, perhaps sooner. The slightest hint of leaving Stape Hill paled the newly-blown roses on her cheeks, one of the reasons why being that she, on most fine evenings met "William down at the stile," the said William being the blithe-looking, well-respected son of a building carpenter and timber-merchant, whose place of business was less than a mile distant from Staple Hill Farm.

This success induced Gibson to again go minutely over his accounts, and the result this time was, that if Mr. Blagden could be persuaded to let the rent—the whole twelve months' rent—stand over to the following year, he might rub on, and eventually by growing only root crops, pull through. But if the retired attorney would insist upon being paid the fifty pounds, the amateur agriculturist did not see how it would be possible to get through the year whilst the crops were growing; hardly then. Still, it might be barely possible to do so.

On the 30th of September, 1845, Blagden, (arrived from London on the previous day) called at Staple Hill for the year's rent. He

came in a one-horse gig, which, as he was in the habit of doing, he
had hired at the Roebuck, Poole. It was growing dusk when he
reached the place; he stayed about two hours, and it was quite dark,
except for a faint starlight, when he left in high dudgeon.

There had been a stormy scene between him and Joseph Gibson, at which were present Catherine Gibson and James Somers,
who had cleverly or cunningly, managed to keep well both with the
tenant and the proprietor.

Blagden flatly refused to wait one day longer for his rent. The
terrified tenant's beseeching remonstrances; the daughter's tears;
even the pretty positive opinion of Somers that were the time asked
for granted, Mr. Gibson might come round—had no effect upon the
retired lawyer. To end the matter, he took his pocket-book, which
being stuffed with Bank of England notes, he ostentatiously spread
open, selected a ready-drawn, stamped receipt for fifty pounds from
a number of others, placed it upon the table, drew forth his watch,
and said he would just wait half an hour for the money; if it were not
then forthcoming, he should leave, and on the morrow an execution
for the amount and costs would be put in. Furious, maddened with
rage and disappointment, Gibson leapt at his landlord, and inflicted
a severe.blow upon his face, at the same time howling forth threats
of direst vengeance.

The misguided man was forcibly separated from Blagden by his
daughter and James Somers. The landlord (Catherine afterward told
me) remained quite cool; and but for the quiver of his ashen lips, the
calm, deadly ferocity which gleamed in his grey eyes, any one might
have believed that the assault was a trifling matter, of no importance
whatever.

There was a slight lull after the storm and Catherine, taking advantage of it, said: —"I will go and ask Mr. Finch to advance my father forty pounds upon the piece of carrots he has bought. They will
be digged next week. We have quite ten pounds in the house, and
shall then be able to pay the rent in full."

"You have just twenty minutes, Miss Gibson," said the imperturbable lawyer.—"Just twenty minutes—not one more or less. The
cowardly assault committed upon me," he added, with a flash of
hell-fire at his tenants, "a court of law shall pronounce upon! Somers, see the horse is put into the trap."

Somers said that should be done, and left the room to do it.
Miss Gibson left at the same time. She was gone but a quarter of an
hour. Mr. Finch was out, and Mrs. Finch said he never paid money
till he was in possession of the goods purchased. Mr. Blagden took
no apparent notice of what Catherine Gibson said, waited till the
half-hour was exactly expired, took up his watch, wrapped his long
fur-collar about him, and left.

Soon after it was light the next morning, two sailors on their way to join a vessel in the harbour of Poole came upon the dead body of Mr. Blagden, lying across the narrow but high road. A little distance off was the horse and gig; the animal, one of its forelegs broken, was suffering great torture; and both shafts of the gig were broken. Immediate alarm was given, and before long a number of people came up, by whom it was at first supposed that Mr. Blagden had met his death by accident. The horse, a high-spirited animal, had perhaps bolted, and the gig coming in contact with one of the trees, which dotted each side of the road, had been turned over with great violence, and Mr. Blagden, hurled upon the hard road, had probably been killed instantaneously. A very cursory examination sufficed to show the fallacy of that surmise. There was a deep wound in the back of the dead man's neck—apparently delivered by a sharp axe, which had cut through the stand-up collar of the cloak he wore. No question but that he had been struck from behind. Robbery had been added to murder; the deceased gentleman's pocket-book, purse, and gold watch were gone. There was another wound in the crown scalp, sufficient in itself to cause death, and which must have been inflicted when the head was bare, as there was not the slightest cut visible in the texture of the hat, which was found some yards off. The murdered man's clenched hands were filled with the gravel of the road, grasped no doubt in his agony, and suggestive that he must have been either forced upon the ground or kneeling when the mortal blow was dealt. But how had the gig been stopped—the horse flung down, and reduced to so pitiable state? A question that not very readily answered. Two or three days subsequently a clothesline, almost new, one end of which had been recently cut, was found by a woman, buried under the hedge of a cottage, situate between the spot where the murder was committed and Stape Hill Farm. One of the woman's hens, in scratching under the hedge, had brought it to the surface. The circumstance was spoken of, but no importance was attached to it. The murdered man had not been strangled. The buried cord could not therefore have been the instrument or one of the instruments, of death! Still, it was odd that the full half of a long, new clothes-line should have been carefully buried near the scene of the awful crime!

No sooner was the murder, and the circumstances connected with it, known at Poole, than every finger pointed to Joseph Gibson, the tenant of the Stape Hill Farm, as the murderer. His savage threat at the Roebuck was remembered; and it was known to several persons that his sole chance, admitted to be so by himself, was that Blagden should let the year's rent then due stand over till the following Michaelmas! One person, of the name of Frost, who had done some smith's-work for Gibson, having told him he was trusting to a broken-reed in relying upon lawyer Blagden's generosity, received for reply, that "Blagden would be very unwise to provoke him too far!" This expression was held to indicate a settled determination in Gibson's mind to kill his landlord, should the required favour be refused. A skilled detective would have drawn an inference just the reverse of that. No man, unless he be delirious with drink or rage, hints of his intention, under certain contingencies, to commit murder!

Joseph Gibson, unprovided with professional aid, was taken before the coroner's inquest, and the cumulative evidence brought against him was certainly staggering. The scene at Stape Hill, already given,—the assault by Gibson upon the attorney, and his ferocious menaces,—Blagden's threat to distrain early in the next day,—the vain attempt by Catherine Gibson to borrow money of Mr. Finch to make up the rent—were capped by the discovery, in Gibson's bureau in his bed-room, Stape Hill, by the Poole police, of the genuine stamped receipt for the money, which Blagden had placed tauntingly upon the table, and taken away with him. Unceremonious verdict of wilful murder against Joseph Gibson, who was forthwith committed on the coroner's warrant to Dorchester jail!

This narrative I heard from the daughter, with exception of the conversation at the Roebuck, of which she herself had heard but a vague, indistinct report from her father.

It has been stated that Mr. Joseph Gibson was and had been long separated from his wife, a person of remarkable personal attractions. Neither her maiden name nor that which she has since the separation passed under need be printed in these pages. It is sufficient to say that she was an orphan girl and a milliner's assistant when Gibson foolishly fell in love with and married her. As often happens in such cases, the disappointment was mutual. Gibson at the time had quite a splendid shop, was in the first flush of a year's promising business, kept two servants; which items summed up meant, of course, nothing to do, a well-furnished table, silk and satin dresses, cabs to theatres, &c. In short, the life of a ladyship, *minus* only the title. And the bridegroom, no doubt, expected to be imparadised in the smiles and endearments of the entrancing milliner's assistant to the full end and term of his natural life. Well, the business did not answer so well as might have been reasonably expected—one servant was first lopped off, omnibus must serve for a cab, with the rest of such disagreeable declines in life. The husband (time and familiarity are such disenchanters) discovered that his wife was not quite the angel he had supposed, and—and the young lady was frail. A separation took place, and the guilty wife had since continued to live in splendid sin. Twenty years ago only a rich man could obtain a divorce—the matrimonial chain yielded only to a golden file—and Mr. and Mrs. Gibson were still of course, in legal parlance, man and wife. The woman, however, was not all bad; few are—neither man nor woman, none that I have known; and having read the report, copied into the London papers from the *Poole Herald*, of the proceedings at the inquest on Blagden's death, she forwarded to her daughter Catherine, a draft, in a feigned name, for one hundred pounds; and at the same time, so influenced—not directly, of course—influential persons, that I was commanded to proceed to Poole and Stape Hill, and minutely investigate the case. A letter from "the friend" who had forwarded the one hundred pound draft, addressed to Miss Gibson, preceded me; and I was welcomed with tears of trembling hope. I think that Catherine guessed that "the friend" was her fallen mother; but she hinted nothing of the kind, and indeed it was not till all was over that I myself had any notion— a matter after all of supreme indifference—as to who pulled the strings by which I was set in motion.

It was a very, very ugly affair. Before going into the business with Miss Gibson, I, in accordance with invariable tactics, made myself thoroughly acquainted with the case against us—in this instance the case for the Crown. A sight of your adversary's cards is a good step towards winning the game. The sight, however, of the formidable cards held by the Crown in "Regina *v.* Gibson" did not at all reassure me.

The Poole police had not only deposed that the prisoner, when surprised in his bed on the morning of the murder, so late as eleven o'clock—he that usually rose by six at latest—exclaimed when he saw the officers, who had not spoken a syllable respecting the murder of Blagden, not even mentioned that gentleman's name, opening his bureau, he cried out, "Ah! it's all over with me. I shall be hanged, I suppose, for that devil Blagden. Take me away at once." After that betraying avowal, he assumed the mask of sudden silence—not speaking another word except when, as they were going along the road with him, in a chaise cart, towards Poole, one of them, when passing or nearing the spot where the crime had been committed, said, "I can't but think Blagden fought hard for his life, whoever murdered him."

"Whoever murdered Blagden!" exclaimed Gibson with a fearful start, "what are you talking of? Robbed him perhaps?" "Murdered and robbed him," said the officer; "but, mind, no one asks you to let out about it." At hearing which, the prisoner gave a loud cry, and fainted or pretened to faint away.

Since then he had not said a word upon the subject; the attorney who appeared for him when he was examined before the magistrates having "reserved his client's defence." Since then there had been found at Stape Hill, in an outhouse, a sharp billhook, the blade and handle of which were stained with blood. It was such an instrument as might, the surgeon who had examined the body deposed, have inflicted the wound which deprived the deceased Blagden of life; and thrust away amongst old rags and other lumber, in a place which Miss Gibson admitted her father could only have access to, was an old apron, just such a one as the prisoner sometimes wore, covered with blood-stains. These evidences—dumb, yet endowed with miraculous voice—had been carefully sealed up, and remained in possession of the local police. Catherine Gibson endeavoured to account for the blood upon the finely-sharpened bill-hook, by saying that her father had a few days before the death of Mr. Blagden chopped off the head of a gander, which bled very much. Gibson did not however, she admitted, wear the bloody apron upon that occasion. None of the money belonging to Mr. Blagden, neither notes nor coin—he had a small canvass bag full, or nearly so, of sovereigns—had been found, nor had the gold watch. It had all, no doubt, been cunningly concealed; but he (the officer with whom I was conversing) had little doubt that with patience and perseverence they should discover the hiding-hole.

"Does it not strike you as somewhat remarkable," said I, "that Gibson did not also cunningly conceal the stamped receipt, the most damning piece of evidence against him? It *might* be legally impossible to prove that the notes and gold, even the watch, belonged to Mr. Blagden; *might* be I say—though that, as regards the watch, is a violent supposition. But the receipt, about which there can be no mistake—the man must have lost his head not to have concealed or destroyed that."

"He, no doubt, intended to produce it in bar of the claim for rent which would be made by the deceased's representatives!"

"Although Somers could prove that he had not paid the rent, and Mrs. Finch that she had refused to Catherine Gibson the means of doing so? Queer to my mind that. Still the easily discoverable possession of the receipt is, however looked at, unaccountable. It can only be explained by the axiom that whom God determines to destroy he first deprives of reason. Did I understand you to say that the prisoner had been fully committed for trial by the magistrates as well as by the coroner?"

"Yes; fully committed in reality, not formally. The magistrates, having no doubt whatever of the prisoner's guilt, declared their intention of fully committing him for wilful murder; but he will be again brought before them the day after to-morrow, for the completion of the depositions. At present he remains in Poole Jail."

"The day after to-morrow! Oh, by-the-bye, is the clothes-line, or half of a clothes-line, scratched out by a hen from under a hedge, handy?"

"Yes, it is here. I will show it you. But I really do not see what possible connection that can have with the murder."

"I do not say it has; still I should like to see it."

It was shown me.

"Humph! A new line—one of the best make. A new line spoiled to no purpose. This piece is not above six yards long; sharply severed, too; and there is a slip-noose at one end!"

"True enough; but what use could have been made of it in effecting the murder?"

"Well, a very efficient use; but we will speak of that hereafter. Keep it safe if you please. The hedge where it was scratched up was not road gravel, I suppose; and there are many particles of road-gravel, sticking to this line, or I am mistaken. Have you leisure to go with me to the scene of the murder?"

"Yes," replied the officer, "I will go with much pleasure."

The notion which had struck me about the clothes-line was derived from a former police experience near Hereford. How the horse had been thrown down with such violence as to break one of its legs—a singularly sure-footed animal too—had puzzled the natives. Now, it had come out in the Hereford business—which ended in nothing, the person robbed having refused to prosecute—that the robbers had, in that case, thrown the gentleman's horse (he also drove a gig) down by a very simple expedient. A line was dropped in the dark across the road, attached by a running noose at one end to the stump of a tree, at about two feet from the ground, which suddenly tightened as the horse came swiftly up, would bring down the surest-footed beast in the world, with terrible violence. The same trick might have been played upon this occasion. I was pretty sure it had been; and the other portion of the clothes-line might suffice to hang whoever could be proved to have had it in his possession on the night of the murder.

The place where the horse must have fallen was just the spot where such a device might be resorted to with success. The road was narrow, level; the horse would be going at its swiftest pace; and there was an oak-sapling on one side, round which the running noose could be slipped, and fixed at any height. One man, having the other end in his hand, and *seizing the exact moment* for raising it, could throw any swift horse down. Yes; but to do so was scarcely to be expected of a Cockney oil and colourman—one too prematurely feeble, aged. No, no; if that trick had been played, it was by some one whose eyes could see in the dark as well as by daylight; one possessed of nerve, quickness, decision, which would bring down a partridge before it had fluttered its wings thrice.

"Clever poachers about here?" I carelessly remarked, speaking to my brother-officer.

"I should think so. Rum fellows to meet with of a dark night too!"

"Mr. Gibson, the prisoner, can hardly be one of that sort, I should think?"

"God bless you! no. I should hardly think he knows a snipe from a partridge, except when they are cooked; nor how to so much as load a gun."

"Have you any first-rate moonlight fellows about here?"

"Yes; but the cleverest, by a long chalk, is gone out of that line—Jem Somers, as live at Stape Hill. He used to be an out-and-outer. He's not exactly such a bad sort," continued the officer, "as everybody, or almost everybody (Mr. Blagden liked him very much) says he is. He's very sorry, seems almost heart-broken about this horrible affair—Mr. Gibson and his daughter having been, he says, so very kind to him. He thinks, if he can't get a tolerable situation, which he can hardly expect now Mr. Blagden is dead, of going to America."

"America! Well, he'll have plenty of sport there. I suppose such a tender-hearted gentleman would be most grieved for the fate of his oldest friend Mr. Blagden."

"No, really, no. He is most distressed about Gibson and his daughter. Tears come into his eyes every time he speaks about them. Why," continued the greenly-guileless officer, "Why to get out of him, before the coroner and magistrates, about what passed at Stape Hill between Gibson and Blagden, when there was such a row because Gibson could not pay his rent was like pulling the very teeth out of his head."

"But it came out, as the teeth would, at last. He's a 'cute chap, too, I am pretty sure, as well as soft-hearted?"

" 'Cute, I should think so! Catch a weasel asleep, and you may chance to drop upon Jim Somers when he's got one eye shut."

"He lives, you say, in the same house with the Gibsons?"

"Yes; but not exactly. They have a place to themselves that joins on like to the farmhouse, but yet separated from it."

"I understand. They have their castle. Every Englishman—the humblest—likes that, if the castle is a wooden one, the roof thatched with furze. Their own poultry, pig, and washing-yard also, I suppose?"

"Yes; quite distinct from the farmhouse. Jim's wife showed me over it the other day."

I was pleased at that; for it had occurred to me that I should like to *see Jim Somers' last new clothes-line or what remained of it.*

I had a long conference with Catherine Gibson; but it was far from a heartening one. When she had done, I said:

"There is one circumstance I should be glad to hear from your own lips, if you choose to honour me with your confidence. I mean, of course, if you can throw any light upon the seeming mystery. It is this: how came the receipt for the rent due (fifty pounds) in your father's possession!"

The young woman's face flushed—the flush, I was sure, of shame. She cast down her eyes, and remained silent.

"If I am to be of any service, I must know *all*," said I, gently, but firmly.

"I understand that," said Catherine Gibson, not uplifting her eyes. "I will tell you. Mr. Blagden, in his hurry and passion, did not observe that it had dropped on the floor; and left, supposing, no doubt, that he had replaced it in his pocket-book. After he was some time gone, my father saw the piece of paper, picked it up, and—and—"

"Appropriated it, you mean to say; or had some indistinct notion—a very foolish notion—that it might be a bar to the execution to be put in on the morrow. And when the police called on the morrow, the still wilder notion arose in his mind, that an intention, if he had really intended such a crime, of *stealing* the receipt, was equivalent, under the circumstances, of having really done so. Absurd! but I can readily understand such a feeling. Your father, perhaps, drank more than usual that night, after Mr. Blagden's departure?"

"Oh! more, much more. My father is a very abstemious man."

"So I have been told. The receipt stumbling block, as far as I am concerned, is removed. The man Somers and his wife are, I am told, very kind and serviceable to you in this sad crisis?"

"Very kind and attentive; more so than ever they were."

"I should much like to see Somers. Perhaps I could glean something from him or his wife which, though deemed unimportant by you and them, might in my eyes be of significance. Is he within?"

"His wife is not, but he is—in the next building which adjoins this. Shall I say who you are?"

"Not that I am a detective-officer, if you please. It would not, perhaps, so much matter that Somers should know my vocation; but if I am to serve your father, I must work, like a mole, in the dark. Say simply, and which is the truth, that I am a friend from London, anxious to assist your father in his, I trust, passing trouble."

"I will do so. He will be here in three minutes."

"Not of the least use, James Somers, to fence with me with that smoothly-loose tongue of yours; to look modestly, sorrowfully upon the floor with those catlike eyes. *I know you, and that you are the murderer of Mr. Blagden!*

"A moment after Miss Gibson passed out at the front, I left by the back door, making a trivial excuse to the servant, and saying I

would return in a moment. You came out of your house with Miss
Gibson, and I took the liberty of walking in. Had I been seen by either of you, it would have been easy to say that I went to tell you I
would prefer seeing you and Mrs. Somers (she not being then in the
way) on the morrow. Neither of you did see me. But I saw in a large
table drawer, which I took the liberty of inspecting, the longest half
of a clothes-line, sharply cut, of the newness, colour, and, I think,
rather peculiar twist of that found under the hedge. It's not likely
you'll miss it before it has answered the present purpose I shall put it
to; and if you do, the last thought that will enter the cunning—but,
as I can see plainly enough through the flat-crowned, animally
shaped skull—uneasy, palpitating brain of yours, that it is now in
the coat-pocket of a London detective officer. Though of itself hardly
strong enough to make a halter for that bull-neck of yours, it will
perhaps enable me to find something that will. Oh! you have nothing
more to say, except to repeat how "mortal sorry" you be for the
young missus, and for Mr. Gibson too! I have no doubt, Somers,
you are a feeling man, and especially just now you must feel very
strongly. I am sure you do. I have nothing more to ask. Miss Gibson
is positive that her father is innocent, and we must trust to Providence to make the truth manifest. To-morrow I may, or may not,
call to see your wife. Good-day, Miss Gibson. I have promised to
dine with an acquaintance in Poole, and must be gone."

The end of clothes-line which I had brought away from Somers'
place precisely matched with that in possession of the Poole police;
colour, size, twist were identical, and both pieces made up in length
that of an ordinary clothes-line. If the county magistrate—to whom
the officer I had previously spoken with, whose name I forget, volunteered to introduce me—had any brains in his head, he would, in
a case involving such issues, grant a warrant to search Somers' premises. The magistrate fortunately had brains in his head. I mentioned
the Hereford affair, showed him the sundered clothes-cord, and
declared my willingness to make oath that I had sufficient grounds
for suspecting James Somers of having murdered and robbed Mr.
Arthur Blagden, to justify the issuing of a search-warrant. I had
brought written testimony as to my detective acumen, signed "Rich-
ard Mayne;" and it is probable that that as much, if not more than
the evidence of the clothes-line, decided him to grant the warrant,
which was placed at once in the hands of the police officer, whose
name I have forgotten, and off we both set without delay for Stape
Hill.

Somers and his wife were greatly scared by our visit, the man
especially so, upon finding that Miss Gibson's friend was a London
detective.

Our search was ineffectual, so far as that no property of the murdered man could be found; neither notes, gold, or watch; but a very sharply-ground hand-axe, put away in a corner-cupboard, attracted my attention. "This is your husband's axe?" "O yes; our axe!" I examined it minutely. First with the naked eye, then with a strong magnifier, which I was seldom or never without. The axe had been washed, not so very long ago; and, though nothing was visible to the naked eye, my magnifier discovered upon the blade, not only spots of red rust, which might not be stains of blood, but a number of what looked to be minute fibres of fur sticking to the stains. On removing the wooden handle, we saw distinct marks of blood, which I concluded had been washed, as it were, into the socket. The man saw those marks, and turning cadaverously white, exclaimed that he had killed a snared rabbit with it not long before.

"A rabbit?"

"Yes, a snared rabbit."

"You have killed nothing else with it?"

"Oh no!"

"You had better take this axe with you, at all events," said I to the local officer. "It may be of no consequence; still you had better take possession of the instrument."

Once when I attended a lecture by a celebrated man, he had stated that every animal had in its blood globules differing in size from those of any other kind. This knowledge had been arrived at by very slow steps. There was no doubt, however, of its scientific accuracy, or that with the aid of a powerful microscope a professional man of skill and experience could decide, without chance of committing a mistake, from the slightest stain whether the blood, if blood, had flowed in the veins of a human being or other animal. It was the same with minute fibres of fur, hair, &c. This he had said was a most valuable discovery, and he instanced the fact that in France an innocent man might have been convicted of murder owing to a knife having been found in his possession stained with what had every appearance of blood, which stain examined by a skilled gentleman through the microscope was proved to be lime juice.

The lecture had made a great impression on me at that time, and it occurred to me that here was a case in which such a discovery, such a power, would prove invaluable? The fur cloak collar of the murdered man, it will be remembered, had been cut through; the skull had also been split by the assassin. Were those minute fibres of fur sticking on the blade of the axe, fibres of rabbit fur, or of that, whatever it might be, of which the cloak collar was made? and were there any, the slightest shreds of human hair mingled with those particles of fur? Then as to the blood upon Gibson's billhook, and upon the old rag of an apron; was that human blood?

In the scientific replies to these questions lay the issues of life and death as regarded the prisoner Gibson; and as, although not knowing *who* "the friend" was that sent Miss Gibson the one hundred pound draft, I knew how to communicate with him or her, I determined to do so without delay, and I started in a gig for Dorchester ten minutes after I had so determined, there not being a moment to spare—reached London by train, and with the potent agency of "A Friend's" purse, engaged the services of the most eminent professor of that especial branch of anatomical science in the metropolis, with whom I returned to Poole.

The court was crowded on the day when it had been expected that Joseph Gibson would be finally committed for trial—a rumor having got afloat, that owing to the Detective that had been sent down from London, strange discoveries had been made. Poor Gibson looked more like a ghost than a man. He believed himself to be the doomed victim of a relentless fate—that nothing, no accident could—that God would not reveal the truth.

The billhook, the apron, the axe were placed upon the table, and Professor Ansted (by whom they had been carefully examined) gave his evidence: it was clear, decisive. The blood upon the billhook was *not* human blood; of that he said there could be no possible doubt. The stains upon the apron were red paint, containing peroxide of iron. (Gibson, when oil and colourman, no doubt had to grind his own paints, and when so occupied used the apron.) The stains upon the axe, found in the house of Somers, were human blood (there were human hairs sticking on them); and the particles of fur were not rabbit but squirrel fur the fur of which the murdered man's cloak collar was made!

Seldom has evidence—almost supernatural it seemed to the astounded audience—produced a deeper impression than did Professor Ansted's. The finger of God appeared to be visible in it! "William," who had proved himself a true lover throughout, burst into tears, as he pressed forward and shook the prisoner, and his daughter, standing close to her father, warmly by the hands.

The magistrates, who appeared to be somewhat mystified, bewildered, retired to consult with each other. Returning into court, the chairman announced, that relying upon the evidence of so distinguished a gentleman as Professor Ansted, a warrant for the apprehension of James Somers would be immediately issued; but that for the present it was not thought prudent to discharge the prisoner Joseph Gibson. The case would be adjourned for three days.

The magistrates were saved any further trouble in the matter by the murderer himself. An acquaintance in court, specially employed for that purpose, had ridden off to Stape Hill directly the decision of the magistrates was declared; who, of course, apprised Somers that a warrant was out against him for wilful murder, and that the officers would be there almost immediately to arrest him. The despairing felon heard the news with a savage growl, and a moment or so afterwards desired to be left alone.

The door of the room, in which his wife (weeping, sobbing, wringing her hands the while) said we should find him, was fastened on the inside. We burst it open; and a shocking spectacle presented itself. Somers was lying dead on the floor, in a pool of blood, self-murdered; he had cut his throat with a razor. On a small table we found a scrap of writing in his hand:—"It was I, not Gibson, that killed Blagden. I had owed him a bitter grudge a long time, though he didn't think it. D--n him, he ruined me body and soul when he sold me up eight years ago. What I wish particularly to say is, that my wife is as innocent as a babe in the business. She don't even know where the money and watch is, or that I have such things. They are hidden away in a box under the flagstones of one of my pig-styes—the right hand one going out. That is all I have to say. I thought of going to America; and now I'm going to ——, if there is such a place, which I don't believe. The Peeler was right about the clothes-line; that was just how it was done. ——J. S."

The money, watch, &c., we found as indicated. All doubt respecting the terrible business being at an end, Joseph Gibson was forthwith discharged from prison. His case excited much sympathy. The executors of Arthur Blagden allowed him to throw up his farm, forgiving him the arrears of rent; and he, with the help, I believe anonymously conveyed through the daughter of "A Friend," took a smaller and culturable one not very far off from Stape Hill; and has since, I have been told, prospered tolerably. His daughter, I saw by the local paper which some of them sent me now and then, married "William."

ANONYMOUS *The authorship of "The Woman with the Yellow Hair" is unknown. It first appeared in* The Dublin University Magazine *for November 1861. It was then reprinted in* The Woman with the Yellow Hair and other Modern Mysteries *(1862), which was possibly the first anthology of detective and mystery stories.*

The date November 1861 is significant, for if "The Woman with the Yellow Hair" had been published after 1862, it would have seemed derivative from Lady Audley's Secret *by Mary Braddon.* Lady Audley's Secret, *however, began serialization in* Robin Goodfellow *in July 1861, but the periodical failed after only a few chapters of the story had been published, and it was not until March 1862 that* Lady Audley's Secret *was started afresh in* The Sixpenny Magazine.

"The Woman with the Yellow Hair.—A Tale"

Chapter I.—THE HOUSE

Not one of the pattern tenements which your story-teller can contract for in his first chapter, and have built for himself according to the traditional models, with plenty of gables mullioned, embayed windows, an inner skin of very black oak, and an outer one of damp, green ivy, furnished for his money. No regimental yews of "cawing" rooks (these are the professional epithets); no "quaint" gardens, still hedges, trimmed and shaved; no sundials; no ghost's walk where my Lady Mary in white is reputed to promenade under chilly circumstances. There were none of these traditional accidents which would almost seem *de rigueur;* yet it had claims to a certain stern romance of its own. Gables and oak panels have not a strict monopoly of the business of solemn adventure.

No. This Redgrange was a square block of a mansion, very

heavy, even to overloading of the ground beneath it; very plain, and with cheeks of a subdued rubicund tint. That colour had once been flaming red, but had crusted into a mellow and sober tone. There were two rows of tall ungainly windows, slim and narrow; and the great hill-side of the roof was dotted plentifully with whole villages of little cots, where, indeed, the accommodation was indifferent, admitting of no more than a man's head and shoulders, stretched forward to look at the view. There were whole brigades of these garret windows.

It was a very gaunt place, indeed. It lay in a sort of blasted heath, which had sternly rejected all efforts at conciliation in the way of plantation, and would display its back in a bare, unfurnished, and almost mangy state through all time. Planting would not do, save immediately about the house itself, where some tall funereal trees herded dismally together, and clung timorously to its skirts, which, at a distance, gave the effect of its being wrapped in the folds of a dark pall. It was, in short, a house with nothing very remarkable about it; a disagreeable and uncomfortable thing to look at; but, no doubt, good and substantial quarters within. A warm place in the savage winters, for the walls were in parts ten and twelve feet thick. Note well, too, that the nearest post town was ten miles away.

At night—take it to be a gloomy moonlight night—standing a few paces from the hall-door, those two flanking clouds of Erebus, those black patches of trees which adhered in a cowardly manner to the great house's sides, seemed to draw us slowly into their dark bosoms, with purpose of swallowing and never rendering us again. There was the blighted waste of a lawn behind us, stretching away, bounded afar off by some base and draggled hedge-rows, bringing with it a sense of loneliness and awe, quite insupportable. Creeping round to the back, where lay what was called the gardens, there was an indescribable wilderness of rank luxuriance, of trees, bushes, shrubs, choking each other, and gasping for want of breathing-room; and of walks swallowed up in flower-beds, and flower-beds merged into walks. The plague of neglect has fastened on the place, it was eaten up with the leprosy of decay. It must have been long since neat-handed gardeners had trimmed, and raked, and clipped, and performed their other dainty functions under my lady's own eye. Down at the end was a rude jagged gap, a shapeless hole, which had once been a neat archway in the green hedge, shaved smooth as a wall. This was the threshold to a bowling-green, and beyond the bowling-green, now no more than a pure meadow of rottenness, where, indeed, it would be difficult to bowl now, and where bowler, if he tripped, would be lost to view in lank grass, high as corn— beyond the green, which by courtesy and out of respect to fallen greatness, may still bear its old name, was a very sad pond, once politely known as ornamental water, now degraded almost into a slimy ditch, round whose edge were some melancholy al fresco ruins, some plaster, temples, and arcades, on which time is preying with a gentle decay, whose plaster skins are flayed away, and whose laths protrude nakedly. This was the glorification for some fete or gala; and the conception clearly was, that the noble company should wander down of an evening through the lath and plaster arcade, then white and snowy as paint could make it, and, leaning on the balustrade, look across the water at the moon's reflection, or the theatrical gondola, built by a scenic artist, which, no doubt, did its part in the show. That heap of collapsed boards, crunched first, then rotted out of all shape, was, no doubt, the original stage-boat.

That was a short and dismal description of all that and those, the capital messuage, with all the rights and easements thereunto appertaining; a solemn, surly, and somewhat awful mansion, which needed only that it should have a good look out into an adjacent grave-yard, say just under the windows, to be a respectable ghostly house of the old established pattern.

Now, the mystery of all this corruption and neglect was simply this: that some two and twenty years ago, the father of the Faithfull family had been found one darkish winter's evening, when they sent to call him for dinner, hanging stark stone dead from one of the great bed-posts in a state-room. There was a wood fire flickering up and down fitfully, and by that light there was a swinging shadow on the shining floor. Thereupon the Faithfull family broke up scared, and fled the place in a sort of horror-stricken rout.

Chapter II.—THE TENANTS

Twenty-two years is a long span. It will efface even that black splash of a figure swinging from that grim gallows of a state-bed. There comes a season of drought for widow's tears; and for the young—for those specially who were no more than just launched upon life— these ogres of infancy lose their horrors with years; so that at this date, Mrs. Faithfull has been long drawn from private contemplation of her terrible ogre by outside duties; and now become a stern commanding matron, of awful presence, and yet affable manner, who has been, in the smoke of battle, a skilful captainess in those ball and drawing room skirmishes, has at last fought the good fight over her daughters' bodies, and brought back a prize for her bow and spear.

A word now for these two daughters—the eldest, Janet Faithfull, the youngest, Mary Faithfull. The eldest fairhaired, smooth-faced, with a sort of weary blue eye, that she was always dropping towards the ground; a dreamy reflective manner, and yet a ready tongue, which streamed with odd conceits and remotely fetched fancies, so that she was sure to draw people to cleave to *her* specially, even out of a mere surprise and wonder. Very pretty, though more of a latent prettiness, was this eldest daughter of the Faithfulls; one, too, whom quiet, unworldly mammas would shrink from instinctively, and caution their best-loved male child against. That quiet, unworldly mamma, she could cuff, flout, turn inside out, and riddle through and through with arrows—morally speaking, of course. For that younger daughter, she was no more than an ordinary girl, one that we all know well enough in this or that particular family; one of a file of daughters, neither plain nor pretty, neither odious nor delectable, neither dull nor brilliant, but a good average thing. She was her sister's sister, that was all. She was one of the Miss Faithfulls— "that other one, you know—not the sharp clever one"—(so she was spoken of), and her name was Mary. She was the foil and the helot of that elder sister.

Now that elder sister was about being married to one Henry St. John Smith, Esq., of Burd Castle, a very desirable man—a possible baronet, and income of say eight to ten thousand a year. A great "catch," said the vulgar genteel. A poor mean-souled cur, that had thrown himself away, said disappointed trappers, grinding their teeth. Where were his eyes for their own little dears? Anathema upon his dull senses. So, lose no more time, and let us bait for fresh quarry. Henry St. John Smith, Esq., has passed the usual probation—the probation by balls. In that medium had the two atoms gravitated towards each other. At the proper period came the result; and it was proposed to Miss Jane Faithfull to become Mrs. St. John Smith, and possible baronet's wife—not Mrs. Smythe, for he had not yet been prevailed on so to vulgarize his name. And drawing all our cords together the result of the whole is this, that the heavy grim house has been furbished up, the damp partially driven out, the walks weeded, and tremendous wholesale clearings made in the wild bush region behind. With the garden razor has the bowling-green been shaved, with the garden scissors has the hedge been snipped and chopped into smoothness, and the green dead man's hole, where the stage boat paddled, skimmed neatly with a gigantic spoon. Some plastering and patching healed the sores in that poor Lazarus of a sham temple, and it blazed out brightly in holiday clothes of shining white paint. And to grow to a point at once, it being a traditional custom with the Faithfull family that all who took the matrimonial plunge should do so under that roof, the family absent so long had now journeyed back again to the old roost, and that stony-hearted grim monster of a building had been coaxed, and trimmed, and brightened, in something like a surly toleration.

And there was news come by mail that the brothers, bridegroom and his best man, were at this time posting down by speedy stages, and would arrive by a particular night, fixed and looked for. The millinery stores and other nuptial impedimenta had been laid in. The rite would take place in about a week—grim, cold, dry-bones of a rite, in proper keeping with the house.

Chapter III.—THE GUESTS ON THE ROAD

As Jane Faithfull had a subsidiary sister, so had St. John Smith a sort of worshipping brother, a deifying Williomo—a sober, reflective, and somewhat heavy youth, that took time to honour the receipt of an idea. He had to do with the sea as Lieutenant Smith, and was simple and almost guileless as men of that profession usually are. He had come home on the news, and did not relish it, though he had not yet seen Jane Faithfull. He was even earnest with his brother to break off the business, urging that Jane was no wife for him. These traits of character, which his brother told with rapture, turned him more and more against her; but when he found that he could not prevail, he, like a wise and heavy seaman as he was, gave over battling with a head wind, and was now actually beside his brother in a postchaise whipping down to that lonely house.

They had been journeying all day, from very close to dawn, all along wild roads, where the way had to be asked, and were now towards five o'clock, when it was growing to be dark, jangling and creaking up to a miserable sort of post-house, very bleak-looking and rusted, with a kind of escaped convict and hunted down look. A rusted woman came out and said that this was Braynesend, while one of the brothers said that was all right, and bade her look sharp and have the horses put to. Then said the younger brother, who had been any thing but a cheerful mate all the road—

"I wish—I wish we could go back."

"Why?" said the other, shortly.

"Because it will lead to no good. Ever since morning I find myself getting more and more depressed. This is a miserable overture for a marriage."

The elder brother, who had felt the influence of this grim landscape too, was inclined to be moody, and made him no answer.

"It is not too late," said the younger, eagerly. He had not touched on this delicate subject the whole day. "It might be averted—put off. The whole thing has been done in such a hurry, any thing will be a reasonable excuse. You know," he went on, gathering courage from the other's silence, thinking, indeed, he was making an impression. "You know I have been against the business from the beginning. You know she is not the person for you. I have heard——

"Confusion!" said the elder brother, dashing down the window savagely. "You must stop this. Am I to sit here and listen to this talk—what do you mean, I say? Who gave you a right to preach to me? Here, put those horses to—quick!—get on, get on. Will you never buckle that trace!" And he shut up the window with as violent a bang as he had let it down. "Now," said he, with something like a threatening manner to his brother, "don't speak to me again on this matter. I won't take it from you. My mind's made up."

His brother turned very red at this hostile language, and had as angry a rejoinder on the tip of his tongue; but he checked himself, and lay back in his corner of the chaise without a word. After this burst it was not likely there would be much conversation. So it grew darker, and they plunged into a yet wilder prairie, the old provincial chaise jangling and clattering most unmusically. This was not, as the younger brother remarked, a cheering overture to an epithalamium. They should have had smiling meadows, and pastoral Lubins and Phyllises, and flowers, and trellis-work, instead of this stiff, stark, iron-bound country. It was a dismal progress both for bridegroom and for best man.

Chapter IV.—YELLOW HAIR

Now, here are lights as from gaol windows: and with a prodigious clatter, a whole prison-yard full of convicts' chains jingling about them, they drive up triumphantly to the door of the heavy mansion.

But inside no gaol surely. Warmth, light, domestic comfort, cheerful hues, graceful women's figures, and not the hard savage outlines reasonably to be expected in such a district. So we leave our dismal forebodings in a small bundle among the straw on the floor of the postchaise, and enter shaking hands and receiving welcome, with an overflowing delight.

So it was with that bridegroom at least. The brother was still moody, as from a sense of injury. Janet Faithfull, in the character of a beautiful weird woman, for to-night, sat near to her husband *in posse*, stroking that yellow hair of hers. The brother kept looking at her with looks of constraint and almost open aversion. They went in and ate at a snowy round table, groaning with excellent things, while the family sat round and admired. They were two hungry men, for the grim country had whetted their appetites; and the bridegroom, as he grew warm, and what may be called comfortable, laughed and told their day's adventures, being corroborated now and again in a curt, grudging fashion, by the younger brother. All this while the yellow-haired woman leant upon her hands, her elbows rested upon the table, and watched the performance in a dreamy fashion—of course, wrapped up in that lover of hers—of course, devouring with her eyes those adored motions and gestures, as he devoured her.

These things—this little ceremonial of devotion—may be accepted as understood—a supererogation even to mention. But the younger brother took his food seriously, and dealt forth with heavy news to the matron, seasoned with a sort of ponderous dough of his conversation, all the while scowling distrustfully at the yellow-haired lady.

Then they finished, and the bridegroom, still in boisterous spirits, and joyous over his prize, stole her off into an adjoining room (which it seems is the privilege in this species of novitiate), and told her, by way of entertainment, all his faint-heartedness and dismals, during the day. Then we hear her voice for the first time. (She had been listening in that passive, almost insensible way of her own, which with her became almost a charm).

"That strange brother of yours gave you sensible advice."

"What, to go back, give all up; do you tell me this, enchantress?"

"Yes," she said, almost coldly, "you and I cannot look into futurity; who knows how we shall suit each other? We are not divines; there may be at this moment, in you, undeveloped, a ripe savage, a royal brute, wife beating, wife reviling, dissipating, drunken. In me a sleeping demon, I am thinking," and she began as usual, stroking her yellow hair; "what safeguard have we against these things? You may be yet cursing me, and I tearing my hair."

The possible husband looked at her gloomily.

"I can see one thing for certain," he said; "you are a very curious enchantress. Where do you get these wild notions?"

"Out of history, the newspapers, common talk. Now," she said, leaning her hand upon her chin, "tell me, how long have you known me, what do you know of me after all? You have, of course, like all rapturous lovers, lived ages since you have seen me; but now, considering it quietly and rationally, do you not know *very* little of me?"

This strange line of conversation mystified the bridegroom wonderfully, and tamed down those splendid spirits of his. But he looked at her steadily for a moment.

"I would wager all I have most precious in the world, that you will never turn out different to that opinion which I now have of you. I know you, present and future."

Her answer was a laugh, loud, and a little harsh. Then she put back her hair and rose, laid her arm on his, and casting away that philosophic manner of hers, became loving. They passed out of the room together.

Exeunt slowly. All have dropped away fitfully, one by one to rest; and so closes that day. Night was now to set in.

Chapter V.—THE FIRST NIGHT

Henry St. John Smith, Esquire, as being of the worthier blood, and the more honoured man, was privileged with a grand state bedroom all to himself. His brother, as being of humbler quality, was packed away up a great stone back-stair, to a row of bachelors' lodgings, all along a stone corridor, where, indeed, he might have his pick and choice. There were no other bachelors, so he had the whole range to himself; and to say the truth, did not very much relish this segregation. He had an instinct that he was not very far from the roof. Luckily he was not very profound in the family legends, or he would have learnt that here, on this very stone corridor, that lamentable hanging business took place, down at the very end, in the last room of all, now fast locked. He had not this to think of. He was rather thinking of how he had found no opportunity of speaking the soft word which turneth away wrath to his brother, before retiring. Nay, the good-night he had received was a fixed scowl, and a whisper from the yellow-haired lady on his arm, who swept by him scornfully.

"He has told her every thing," he said to himself, as he laid the light upon the table. "Naturally enough she will dislike me. She has an instinct already that I am her enemy. A strange creature, interesting—something over her that draws and repels." He thought, as he lay down, that he had been foolish to turn a woman who would be so related to him, into his foe. Possibly there was no mischief in her. Possible perfections that—well, all that was to be seen. And he slept the sleep that seamen sleep.

With all the renovations, no one had thought of moving the ancient clock bell, cracked through and through, which jangled out the hours irregularly, in an old perch of its own, with a wheeze, and a gurgle, and a rattle. A veteran bell, long in the family, somewhat asthmatic in its brazen throat. Now, it came to pass, that the wind rose a little this night, and a small slate detached, came clattering down the slope of the roof, and thence toppling over, escaped with a sonorous crash upon the window sill of the seaman, who awoke.

Lifting himself in bed and wondering—for it was as though some one had tapped loudly at his window—he first heard the asthmatic bell jangle out some disorderly chiming, and then strike two! He heard the rooks disturbed in their slumbers, entering indignant protest. He heard the wind shouldering its way through the tall ghostly trees, with moaning excuses. And there was a bluish moonlight outside. He found that his tongue was cleaving to the roof of his palate, and that he was altogether very parched and feverish.

For a plain seaman he would have relished handsomely the

water-jug already in the room, but a memory of soothing drinks, cooling malts, refreshing wines, laid purposely outside the drawing-room door, wooed him irresistibly—invited him down. A draught under such conditions comes not too often—so with a marvellous promptitude he was up and dressed in a minute—at least, in that partial al fresco dress which he judged sufficient for the occasion. No light: but he knew the road, having habitually an eye for all manner of bearings—then opened the door cautiously, and slipped down the stone-stairs. Feeling his way, he actually had his hand on the door of that chamber where the hanging business—so unpleasant for the family—had taken place. There was light enough—moonlight—from the windows, as he descended; a window at every landing. Thence he got into the long corridor—thence on to the great landing, where was the welcome grape. He took a grateful pull—all in the shadow— and much comforted, feeling like a well-watered flower bed, turned back on his road again.

Hush! a break of light overhead, flashing through the banisters, as if a door had opened and closed again, for the light had vanished as quickly. It was undesirable to be surprised in this rude wood-man's garb, so we had best get home to Bachelor's Lodgings as speedily as possible. But hark!—tread—then interval, and tread again. Rather—for the boards are very aged and wheezy—creak, with a pause of suspension—and then creak again—the seaman, in his rude garb, aghast. Some one coming down stealthily—and in the dark. He must get away, and made a step back within the half-opened drawing-room, but accompanied with a loud crack under his foot. He had best not move farther, for *his* boards were tell-tale too. Creaking now draws nearer—grows less cautious and more frequent—seaman, not daring to breathe, looking out in the direction, where all is darkness. Creaking now changed into a tread—a soft, light tread on a carpet drawing nearer. Ah! yes, closer and closer, until the watcher's heart thumped and thumped again.

The drawing-room was at the top of the great flight of stairs from the hall, and there was a great tall window, which rose up from the bottom of the first flight, and directly faced that drawing-room door. Outside this tall window was a cold, bluish veil of moonlight, which made all the paths down the grand flight very clear and distinct. The light step very close now. Hush!—not a breath, and something brushes by very softly and mysteriously. There, now it is full on the grand flight, descending, floating—a woman's figure, in a sort of gray shawl. Now it has reached the bottom, and stops looking out through the tall window, leaning her arms on the sill. Then turns her head slowly, full in the blue moonlight, by which it is to be seen that her hair is yellow. Then she vanished away down the lower flight.

Pausing an instant, and much relieved, the seaman bethinks him of returning to his room, but will first descend softly to that tall window and see what prospect it commands outside. It looks out towards the back of the house, over the tangled gardens, bowling-green, and even so far as the plaster ruins and dilapidated stories beyond. They were now bathed in the blue lake of moonlight, and really bore themselves, with a decently decayed air, like sham Tinterns and Melroses. The ragged laths and plaster were softened down at that distance, and the younger brother, leaning his arms upon the sill of the tall window, gazed at it thoughtfully, and though not of a versifying nature, could not but think it very poetical. It wanted but a little life—a figure or two.

Now he started again, though almost reckoning on that apparition. There, directly below him, emerging from the porch, gliding over the tangled luxuriance of the garden, stole along the figure of the yellow hair, and the gray shawl, now set on plaidwise. Doubtful at first, *was* it yellow hair, until about the middle of the garden, where was the old sun-dial, the figure stopped, and moving round slowly, bringing face and hair into the light with a flash. Yellow hair, indeed! It positively turned it into molten gold. The face was fixed on the window, and for a moment he thought himself discovered, but she turned again and moved on slowly.

This seaman loved life rather than sleep, and relished adventure prodigiously. He was not surprised. His was a simple salt-water heart; but he could make nothing of this midnight wandering. "A strange creature," he said, "a witch. She looked very like a witch when she turned up her face that time." We have, all of us, a particular curiosity, a thirst for spying, which may be called mean or not, according to the mood.

So he slipped down stairs softly, found a door with the bolt drawn, and was out in the blue moonlight in a moment.

Chapter VI.—SPIRITS

He did not take the centre by the old sun-dial, as she had done, but skulked along cautiously in the shadow under the old hedges. He stepped very softly, indeed, then coasted round the whole circumference of the bowling-green, until he got to the little narrow arch cut in the hedge. Here his passage was exposed, but he slipped down upon his hands and knees, and crept through like a dog, then crawled into the shadow again, and looked round for her.

He was just at the edge of the old piece of ornamental water; there green scum curdled thickly at his feet. She was not there, but for all the broad moonlight, so full was the place of dark shadows by thick trees and tangled shrubberies, she might have been within a yard of him. So he stopped and looked round him very cautiously, but he could see nothing. His eye fell on the green curdling pond, and it flashed upon him, what if this had been her aim—a speedy deliverance from an odious alliance. It was a morbid, far-fetched idea, and yet, coupling it with this unaccountable disappearance, this devouring of her, as it were, by the earth, it became barely possible.

Hark!

He crept on still farther round the rotten arcade, peeping through its open arches every now and then, until he reached the centre, where it broke out at the back into a glorious burst of pavilion, and looking round the corner, still carefully, he saw at the far end the yellow-haired figure leaning over one of the old plaster balustrades, and talking softly.

Talking to one whom he could not see. He was barely half-a-dozen yards from where she stood—and could hear the tongue in which she spoke, which was not English. He listened carefully: it was Italian. He had been at Leghorn in his shipping rounds, and knew the ring of that sweet tongue well enough; knew, too, most its commoner coinage that circulates in commoner talk. He would have given any price to have drawn nearer, and seen the other party to the dialogue, but this was too dangerous, so he waited and listened, and heard her quiet tones, so clear in the loneliness of that night and place, sounding all the endearments and musical caresses of that affectionate language. It was "Mio Caro," and "Carissimo," breaking out every now and again. He was indignant—boiling over with a seaman's honest indignation; and he was glad, very glad, that those forebodings of his had received such triumphant corroboration.

He waits many minutes, the sympathizing dialogue still going on—hungering, thirsting, for a glimpse of the troubadour. At last, a head, with glossy, curling, black hair, and a trimmed black beard and moustache, was lifted up over the balustrade, as though the owner had been standing on a stone, and the younger brother saw his face very clearly, indeed.

After that he was satisfied. "The land-lubber! I shall know him again," he said, as he crept away. But that standing on the stone and consequent lifting of the bearded head was but the preamble to farewell, which was sealed by another short ceremony, which the seaman did not see. So before he had skulked away many yards along the arcades he heard the step close after him; he managed, however, to get safely into the bowling-green, and skirted round lightly, as before, sheltered in the shadows of its circumference. She took her way straight across it, musingly, with her eyes upon the ground, carrying in her hands, too, a little black hood, which she did not seem to care to put on. Just as she had finished her transit he had finished his half circuit, and they both met face to face, at the little evergreen arch of entrance.

She gave no scream, only a little start.

"So," she said, "you are the appointed detective. You have been watching me."

"Have seen and heard all," he answered; "you have betrayed my unfortunate brother, but he shall know it all in the morning—no, within the next hour."

She looked at him a moment, mournfully, tying and untying the strings of her hood.

"I knew it must come to this at last. I have had a presentiment of it for long. I was a fool to expect a dream to last for ever."

The younger brother almost laughed as he listened to her; he was astounded at her coolness.

"You are a strange creature," he said, at length; "are you pretending this indifference?"

"A strange creature," she said, almost fiercely—"that is your judgment—because I dare not think or choose for myself—because I am dragged a fashionable slave to the market, set up and sold—because I then take a stolen liberty for myself, you get scornful in judgment on me, and tell me I am a strange creature."

Then she threw a hood from her with a sudden, and drew herself up. He could see her eyes flash in the moonlight. Her yellow hair was loosing on her neck. He thought she was a bold dangerous woman, but still a fine creature.

"You—neither you nor he know my true story—all that I have borne, that I am bearing—the miserable childhood, the grinding oppressions. But, sir, you have done your detective's duty well—your gallant, chivalrous duty of hunting a woman—you will be rewarded for it, no doubt."

The other was ashamed.

"I can assure you," he said, in a softer voice, "it was an accident—altogether an accident. On my honour, I had no intention of watching you."

She looked at him steadily.

"I believe you," she said, "from my heart—I do. There is honesty in your face. Yes, I do believe you."

The yellow hair, but carelessly put up at first, had now at last got free, and came tumbling in a perfect gush to the ground. The younger brother was dazzled, and forgot the beginning of a reproving speech he had ready.

"She is a queen," he thought, "but a wicked queen."

"I trust *you*," she went on; and as she spoke she began pacing up and down a short way each time. "But, of course, you would not believe my story—what I could tell about this business; and I could tell you much about it."

"I am not the savage you make me out," said the seaman indignantly. "Any reasonable explanation that would set you right with me shall be willingly accepted."

"I would scorn to give it," she said. "Never!—not to you."

He coloured, and said anxiously—

"You told me you believed me."

"True," she said; "but I shall speak it all to him. There will be, of course, the vulgar *exposé*, the hackneyed break-off, the vile fetching and carrying of the news. You and he will go away free. I shall return to gaol."

A very mysterious creature, thought he, and yet attractive. To be pitied a little.

"I know how all this came about. You had a dislike to me from the beginning—before you saw me—a cruel prejudice which has coloured all your opinions and actions. I saw it in your face when you entered the house—a deep-seated, rooted aversion. You laid yourself out to destroy me."

"No, no," said he, very eagerly, "nothing of the kind. I do, indeed, own to not liking this marriage much. Why, I cannot say. But as to any unreasonable prejudice, I can assure you you do me injustice."

"No matter," she said. "You must, of course, do what is your duty at any sacrifice to me. That is of small account. So let us go in. Tell your brother all, without delay or disguise. It is, as you say, your duty. It will be a relief to me—Good-night."

"But," said the other, still lingering, "you could surely explain. Don't go without a word at least. Give me some explanation, no matter what."

"No," she answered, "I have none. None that would satisfy you. It would be useless too. It will be all over in the morning."

"But why," said he, impatiently, "should you set me down as this cruel vindictive enemy, that will hear nothing, and is bent on destroying you. Do you suppose I wish to hunt you down. Do consider this matter carefully. We will speak of it in the morning."

She looked at him for a moment doubtfully.

"I do not think you are my enemy after all. Perhaps I misjudged you. Forgive me if I have. As you say, there is no need of rousing the whole family from their sleep, and having a splendid *exposé*. It will keep until morning, when I shall denounce myself!—Good night once more."

If ever there was a mermaid sitting on the rocks and singing poor fascinated sailors on to shipwreck, it was this woman with the yellow hair. A dangerous deadly mermaid, whose skill and artfulness knew no depth. She flitted away before him, and was gone in a golden flash.

"There is some mystery under all this," said the foolish mariner, whose boat was getting in among the shoals. "It is plain that she dare not speak; and yet I could swear she is innocent."

Then lay down with a smirking satisfaction and a pleased moral elevation, and very soon was sleeping fast.

Chapter VII.—BATTLE

They all met at breakfast in that buoyant humour which in country houses usually effervesces at that meal, more particularly when nuptial rites are drawing on. Down came the scattered members of the family, and fell gaily into their ranks. Down came the elder brother quite boisterous, and by-and-by the younger, rather troubled and nervous, and later on still, the woman with the yellow hair.

His heart began to thump as he heard her step—as she entered he grew violently red. But she was as a mermaid only can be. The boisterous flew at her, and swallowed her up. The other skulked up to her in a confused, disordered way, and blushing painfully. She was without a ruffle, and looked at him with astonishment, and calmly hoped his room had been comfortable. The foolish seaman stammered "yes," and found his brother's eyes fixed sternly on him.

After breakfast said she to her lover—

"Come out, and let me show you our gardens and plaisaunces. You shall admire the strangest conceits, perfect marvels of the topiary art, our ponds of gold and silver fish, and fairy-like arcades. Come," she said, "let us visit Arcadia—a little dilapidated, it is true."

The seaman was confounded at this sang froid. He would have rather chosen to have avoided the place. But, no doubt, she had chosen this opportunity to tell her secret. What perversity—what folly. So when the elder brother bounded away to his room, and they were alone, he drew near and said—

"You are not going to betray the secret—*our* secret?"

There was an assumption of partnership—a joint communion, that it was plain jarred upon her. At least so he gathered from the long, haughty, almost contemptuous look she fixed upon him.

"Why not," she said. "I shall have no Damocles' sword hanging over my head; neither will I let any one hold me in their power even for a single day. Do not think it." She then drew herself up after the manner of haughty queens in plays and novels. The poor driveling seaman was lost in admiration and penitence. "Do you think I have no courage for such a sacrifice? I should glory in braving the world. You do not know how little I care for the opinions of the outside world. I spurn the voice of the vile mob. Let them talk as they will. I have my own heart—my brave heart, to support me, and of those stout friends who will be content to believe and yet not see."

Superb, splendid, dazzling creature, thinks the poor driveller.

"You do not then put me among your Saint Thomases," he said, a little bitterly.

She laughed savagely.

"What am I talking about. Friends! God knows I have but few of them. But I can trust him—perhaps you. He is very happy this morning—is going to be very happy all day long. Why not leave him for this short span in his dream. He will know the worst too soon, poor soul, and will awake to bitterness. Shall we do this?"

"With all my heart," said the other. "Whatever you will. My sole most devout wish is to please you."

She was looking at him steadily, and with the poor dupe translated into a smile of soft encouragement, when the brother entered and carried her away. The seaman striding through air, and conscious of a new and strange excitement, betook himself to the fields, where he wandered about for hours, gloating over his secret. He there drivelled to himself, and blushed to find himself thinking with satisfaction over the dissolution of his brother's nuptial contract. From afar off, looking towards the old house, he could see the horses being brought round, and the pair going out for a ride. Then he himself set forth upon a long day's walk, far upon the fells, struggling for many hours with the steep places and rocky passes, coming home towards evening tolerably fatigued. As the fresh, healthy mountain air played upon him, and his limbs became braced with honest exercise, a more wholesome train of thought came back upon him. After all, that old sea training, and the brave innocence of spray and ocean, was *not* to be swept away in one unguarded moment. He blushed literally, as has been said, to find himself in so shabby, so unhandsome, perhaps so wicked a character. Presently he was descending the hills with a firm step, as it might be a quarter-deck, and with a new fixed resolution to assert himself, casting away from him, for very shame sake, every hint and thought of that absurd—as it now seemed—hallucination. He found himself a little out of the road, and brought round without his own will by the back of the old house—very far to the back, at the rear of the old garden, and he could see the jagged, tattered edges of the plaster arcades peering over the hedges. It would be a shorter way home, so he jumped the ditch and landed successfully.

Voices, and voices that he knew. He peeped through one of the shattered arches, and saw across the green pond the pair walking round and round the bowling-green. They were talking very earnestly and lovingly. He saw them, and with a sour expression you may be sure. He crept softly round the arcade, meaning to surprise them, or perhaps to play Mr. Detective, having done so once before with success, for a few seconds: only for a few seconds, then reveal himself.

"And you dislike poor Ned," said the lover, laughing.

"A poor, weak fool, yet dangerous, very dangerous, as are fools sometimes." She said this very spitefully, and the dupe turned pale.

"He is not your favourite brother—is he, St. John, dear?" she said, in a wonderfully coaxing manner. "No, I thought not—was sure not. I myself should not trust him too much. Do you know, dearest St. John, it has struck me that he does not relish your approaching marriage *too* much."

The brother's brow darkened.

"Yes, he had an unworthy sort of feeling about the business which I could not have believed him capable of. What penetration you have, darling."

Brother number two scowled again and ground his teeth behind the hedge.

"Though, indeed," she added, "it is shabby of me to abuse him. I can see, that though his enemy from pure report of me, I have since merited his approbation. He approves of me generally, I believe."

"Ha! indeed," said the elder brother. "I began to suspect him this morning. And has he dared," he added, raising his voice.

"No, no," she said, patting his arm; "the poor sea-calf may worship when he likes, but it shall be from a long way off. Now, you must promise me not to be angry with the poor sea-calf."

"You are an angel," said the lover. And they passed out of the bowling-green towards the house. Some one followed them gnashing his teeth with fury. He met her in half an hour on the stairs. (He had been watching for her.) There was rage and mortification in his face.

"Sea-calf!" he snapped out.

Not the least discomposed she answered him—

"Again, Mr. Detective! It is a habit."

She passed on. But she was troubled.

"I will never make love in a bowling-green again."

They all met at dinner, and the second brother barely spoke a word. He was chewing the cud of his revenge. To-morrow morning brother should know all. The shrewd mermaid read all this in his face.

Chapter VIII.—THE LAST NIGHT

With every morsel of his joint, and fowl, and *ragouts*, he swallowed
down his vengeance; he fed it fat all the time. Disclosure should
come the first thing in the morning. It was too much, that savage
personal ridicule. He would have no mercy. Those weak simple na-
tures feel all things on the raw; and in return, smite hip and thigh.
He was clumsily jocose all the evening, and made as though he were
in boisterous spirits. The elder brother measured him now and again
scornfully. She played the downcast penitent mermaid, the broken
bruised reed, with imploring eyes and piteous entreaty, whenever
the other was looking in an ordinary commonplace direction, which
was indeed but seldom. It was as who should say, you are powerful,
and strong, and my master; but be merciful. But the seaman looked
truculent and ferocious, and would not soften.

In the drawing-room that night, just before they began some
obstreperous small plays; just, too, as he was listlessly turning over a
quarto book of prints, he felt a little twisted scrap of paper drop
down upon the plate of Venice, after Turner; and at the same moment heard a rustle of dress floating away in the distance. He opened
it cautiously, and with skill, for he was now grown to be a complete
and scientific conspirator; and read, pretending all the while, to be
absorbed with his plate of Venice, after Turner, words to this effect:

"You have misconceived me. You have heard but half. You
know not all that is behind, or the difficult, the cruel game I have to
play. Your brother loves me to madness, and is a tiger *for jealousy*. I
must soothe him at times. He suspects that I do not love *him* to madness. If you would come to-night about the same hour, and to the
same place, I *could* explain much, and make all clear.

                                                    JANET"

The dupe read and read again. He thrilled with exultation. He
was a conqueror, a slayer. This mermaid had felt his power, was his
slave. But the sea-calf! He that was ugly. How stupid of course—
a blind, to hoodwink that elder one, with his absurd and troublesome dotage. Were there not legends among them aboard the frig-
ates, that but give seamen a chance, and they bore all before them.
He was triumphant, exultant, and when her face next looked towards him, he threw her a beaming glance translated into "yes."

They broke up about midnight: and about an hour after, when
the old cracked bell, high up in its little shed, was wheezing out one
o'clock; the younger brother opened his door softly, and stole
down—not in the light careless way he had descended before, but
this time guiltily, in a cowering undignified fashion. He was afraid

that some might be abroad. He trembled at every shadow. He found the bolt free, and passed out into the garden. There was blue moonlight out to-night.

Yet even here again this poor weak seaman was not too much to blame. The resolutions of his late mountain walk were not utterly trampled down—it was more surprise, curiosity, and a sailor's feeling of adventure that was at work. Any peripatetic, unordained preacher who would have improved the occasion and admonished an erring might only spend his labour as so much superfluity. Who shall nicely balance by the pennyweight the adjustment of resolution and conflicting motive, and gauge the pressure of this and that force or temptation? Not certainly those who are *outside*, still more, not a mere story-teller. So then, he stole down, this seaman brother—not with every resolution shattered, but obscured rather, and in suspension.

All, therefore, was very dark. There were no shadows to scare him, but the whole was a pure waste of impenetrable darkness. He nearly ran foul of the lonely sun-dial in the centre. There came a strange terror over him at this harmless shock. He felt degraded, and half wished to turn back, for this seemed to him a base unworthy intrigue, of which he was ashamed. A midnight plotter against his brother; this did not sound too respectable.

Here was the bowling-green—he had felt his way so far—and here now he was at the edge of the green pool. He could make out indistinctly enough the crazy architecture on the other side.

He heard a low soft voice call to him—call to him by his Christian name—his heart leaped within him. Yonder was the mermaid on the rocks, and this poor weak, trusting mariner must reach her, though he dash his skiff to pieces. He ran round by the way he knew, the half circle to the right. Voice again, rather to the left calls out softly, "not that way, not that way, come by this side."

O fatal singing of the syren; better be deaf, blind, a hundred times. The ship is already among the breakers, and yet he was not wicked wilfully, but rather weak; and so in a tempest and perfect whirl of transport he runs round by that fatal left side.

On that fatal side had been cut, in the fine old flourishing days, a sort of feeding-trough, which led to the river, and supplied the green pond. What, with slime, and weeds, and water-plants, it was overgrown completely, and bore the likeness of dry land. It was very deep, and worse than all, there was a tangled net of thick vegetable strings at the bottom, about as effectual as snares or gins to rabbits; so that a heedless and eager Christian, hurrying on at dead of night, would be precipitated, as through a trap, into the green compost, and be held fast by the limbs, in the toils of the cruel monsters at the bottom.

There should have been fencing surely, or warning of some kind, for it is indeed a terrible thing to be thus choked with a cold green slough.

Chapter IX.—L'ENVOI

After an interval the great marriage—great, at least, for that lonely part of the country—took place. No impediment heeded its progress; even the unaccountable absence of the younger brother, who, it was currently supposed, through the eccentricity of his profession, had fled in the night and gone to sea again. He was always odd, and would turn up one of these days. It was a very sumptuous ceremony, and everybody was rejoiced. Lovely looked the bride; lovelier looked the shining golden hair, absolutely lustrous in the sun that was pouring in through the church windows: it was the hair of a water mermaid. And the organ rolled out a hymn euphonious, as their hands were joined; and there was a blessing implored on their heads; and it passed over that yellow hair, and no doubt fructified. Let us sing allelujah with the choir!

She, who drives about in that deep, dark blue brougham, one of the most "stylish" in the capital, is Mrs. St. John Smith. She leaves her cards. She is very beautiful and placid, and with a line—her yellow hair is famous; and she has really nothing to trouble her.

TOM FOX *was the pseudonym of John Bennett (dates unknown), a small London publisher and minor writer of popular fiction. His books, unlike those of the Victorian lady novelists, were not aimed at middle-class readers but were curb literature, sometimes a little on the raffish side, as can be seen from the suggestive titles of certain of his books:* Revelations of a Sly Parrot *(1862),* My Wife's Earnings, A Tale of the Married Women's Property Act *(1873), and* Simon Peter and Pio Nono at the Gates of Heaven *(1880).*

Tom Fox; or, The Revelations of a Detective (1860) has an earthy quality and naturalism that are refreshing after the counting houses and drawing rooms of most of the contemporary crime literature. On the pictorial title page of Tom Fox *is the following verse:*

He played his part so well, I took him for my friend;
But when I had confided all my guilt to him,
Alas! for me, I found him—a "DETECTIVE."

"The Revelations of a Detective"

Society has at length been seriously called to that plague-spot of great cities, the "Social Evil." Evil, indeed! And none but a Detective knows its magnitude. His avocation as a crime-hunter brings him in contact with this sin of sins, when it is obscured from the public eye, and takes shelter in its own polluted refuges. Regardless of being stigmatised by mankind, sentimental or "beery," I, Tom Fox, Detective, being of sound mind, do affirm the "Social Evil" to be the greatest of evils. I have seen it wrapped up, and I have seen it

in its nakedness—I have seen it drunk, and I have seen it sober—I
have seen it rich, and I have seen it poor; but I have never seen it
without the reflection that it is the curse of the age.

I was very glad indeed to be present at the recent "tea and toast
meeting," convened by ministers (who are not always engaged in
such practical Christianity) for the regeneration of these "Fallen
Angels." The press may heap ridicule on the attempt, if it pleases—
(and it pleases to do many unaccountable things, and not the least remarkable of its anomalies is the encouragement it gives to quackery
and humbug, in its advertising columns)—but I say that it was a step
in advance when these poor victims of *man*-kind were brought
together and appealed to in the old tones of love, which have never
rung on their ears since the downward step was taken.

Depravity assumes many forms, many disguises; but none so
pitiful to the eye of virtue,—so abhorred by the public mind,—so
corrupting in its influence,—so antagonistic to a country's welfare,—
so blighting to the influence of youth, as the woman who has lost her
shame; as she who, from whatever cause, lewdly stalks forth by
night and day, gaily decked off in borrowed dresses, feathers, paste-
jewellery, paint-plastered cheeks, flicking her perfumed handkerchief
in the face of some susceptible passer-by, and with other unseemly
overtures, lures him to a neighbouring house of ill-fame. Perhaps
some youth who becomes so enamoured with the tricks of the harlot,
that he robs his friends or his employers to support her; perchance
her wiles and smiles entrap some weak husband from his fidelity to
her home, and once having forfeited his honour, he too becomes the
harlot's victim.

I will now give the reader a revelation from my note-book of
two sisters—Jane and Mary Chester—whose fearful annals on the
pavé will show more of the horrors of the Social Evil, and the causes
that led them to its membership, than any reflections upon it. I shall
blend my facts into the form of a story, which, I think, will give
them an additional interest.

"Is this the house where the old gentleman was murdered?"

"Yes, and his body lies in that room, where the yellow blind is
pulled down."

"Serves him right, for going to such a horrid house!" remarked a
respectable old lady, who made one of a crowd that had been attracted, from morbid curiosity, before the door of a small house of
ill-repute, in an out-of-the-way street, at the west end of London, to
gather all the information concerning the murder of a wealthy old
farmer, which had just been discovered. The aged lady spoke so
loudly, so excitedly, that the crowd encircled her, and poured a tor-
rent of questions on her, thinking that she knew more of the matter
than they.

"Who's done it?" asked a young clerk, who was wending his way to his City office.

"My eyes! a murder!" exclaimed a butcher's boy, whose tray proved a great nuisance to the crowd he made his way among.

"Has he been robbed as well as murdered?" inquired a woman with a child in her arms.

"Is it a bad house?" demanded a stalwart man, with a long whip in his hand, and who had pulled up his waggon of coals outside the crowd. When he had satisfied himself of all "perticklers" he and his mate adjourned to a neighbouring "public," to talk the matter over a pint of "arf an arf."

"I know no more than you do about it," said the old lady, at the earliest opportunity she could get to reply.

The crowd increased—every one that passed paused before a decent looking house, but a house known in the neighbourhood as one of accommodation for the gay yet unhappy members that contribute so largely to the "Social Evil" of the Metropolis.

The attention of the crowd was diverted by the entrance into the narrow thoroughfare of the street-newsman, who got a living by selling "Last Dying Speeches" under the gallows, and when nothing extraordinary enough occurred in real life, he would readily invent something to excite the imagination and tastes of the credulous and ignorant. He limped slowly along the street, with an illustrated pamphlet in each hand, and several copies stuck under each arm, crying with a loud, sing-song voice, "Only one a'penny! a full, true and particular account of a dreadful murder and robbery of a wealthy farmer by two gay women!" &c. And such indeed was the sad, unexaggerated truth, and the man succeeded in selling a great number to the excited crowd by which he was surrounded.

It was deep in the autumn of the year, and the keen cold wind which moaned through the branches of an elm that was planted in the grounds of a public-house at the corner of the street, scattered its yellow leaves over the heads and at the feet of the mob who congregated round the house in which Murder reigned.

All eyes were now cast in the direction of myself, two policemen, and a woman, who hastily came down the street towards the ill-fated house, but the crowd was so compact and close, that it was with difficulty we could penetrate it. The woman was middle-aged, and there was considerable disturbance betokened in her dissolute-looking countenance; the rouge that had been thickly laid on the previous night, had been partially washed away by her tears. She looked like a woman of fashion that had dressed in extreme haste, and while everything she wore was of the gayest character, there was a dirty, faded, and stale appearance about her. While her bonnet was of a rich velvet, her hair was uncombed, and looked as if she had just risen from her pillow; her rich large-patterned shawl, too, was in strange contrast with dirty unlaced boots; nor was there much harmony with glittering rings, and fingers that were shaded with dirt, and a face agitated more with alarm than sorrow. She was the landlady of the house.

"Stand back! stand back!" cried I to the crowd, pushing aside two gaping, wonder-struck countrymen, equipped with agricultural implements, who pressed on our heels as we waited at the door of the house, while the woman let us in with her latch-key.

"Stand back!" I again shouted, now obliged to use my staff on the heads of some of the mob who made endeavours to follow us into the house. The doctor's brougham now came rattling along, and dispersed the crowd before it. I, the landlady, and doctor soon found our way to the chamber of horrors, and the window-blind was drawn up for the admission of light for the careful examination of the murdered.

A dismal sight presented itself! I will save my readers the pain of description further than by stating that an elderly gentleman, with short silvery hair, lay on the carpet, cold in death, and bathed in blood that flowed from a gaping wound in his skinny throat. That he had struggled for his life there were evidences to corroborate; his veiny hand clutched the carpet as if he still held his murderer, and the toilet water-bottle and soap were on the floor. He lay in his shirt, while his handsome suit of clothes, with the pockets turned inside out, were scattered about, some on a chair, some on the floor.

It is painful enough to behold the passions of the young leading them to houses of ill fame; but when we find men there whose feet are tottering to their graves, our disgust and indignation know no bounds. Can there be a more pitiful sight than to see a man, whose very brows are grey with age, dallying with a lewd woman? What more sorrowful—more contemptible—than to find the hoary-headed walking in the path of shame and criminality?

"He is dead," said the doctor, as he knelt down to examine the nature of the wound.

"Oh! it will be the ruin of me," blubbered the gay landlady. "I wouldn't have had such a thing happen in *my* house, for the world."

"Who slept with him?" I inquired.

"Two girls brought him here at about twelve last night, and engaged the room; and they all seemed happy enough; and the poor gentleman sent the servant for a bottle of wine, and some walnuts— and there is the shells and the empty bottle. I never saw a person so merry for his years—he took a girl on each knee, and sang, "How happy could I be with either."

"Was he sober?" asked I.

"Well, I should say, not quite, but still there was nothing particular to notice."

"Did you observe whether he had a watch or any jewellery?"

"Oh, yes. I saw a gold watch and chain, and a valuable mourning-ring; and when he gave the girl the money for the wine, I saw his purse was full of money."

"Did you drink with him?"

"I did. Oh, I won't deny anything at a time like this."

"When did you discover the murder?"

"Not half-an-hour ago."

"It is now nine o'clock," I said to one of the officers. "Who slept in the house last night?"

"Well, besides me and the servant, who slept in the back parlour, and the poor gentleman and the two girls, who slept in this room, there was two men, who was waiting for two women, took the first floor front; a man and a woman slept in the second-floor front: and another couple in the second-floor back."

"Do you know any of the parties?" I inquired.

"Oh dear no; I should have a large acquaintance if I knew everybody who came here. One of the men who took the first-floor front, I noticed had a cast in his eye."

"What time did the girls leave who slept with the murdered man?"

"That I don't know; but my servant says she heard them leave about six in the morning."

I conferred aside with the surgeon, and then, after obtaining from the landlady and servant a further account of the "ladies" who they supposed had slept with the farmer, their dress, their height, their ages, their features, and their complexions, one of my men quitted the house, but soon returned with a parish shell, in which the ghastly body was placed, and, followed by the crowd, was conveyed to the public-house at the corner of the street for immediate inquest. Of course, the showy landlady and her servant were summoned to attend the coroner, and were subjected to a searching investigation. Nothing, however, was elicted that could criminate either of them with the murderous deed, and they were left free to pursue their detested course of life.

When the fat and tawdrily-dressed landlady returned to her "virtuous" home, she and her slip-shod, all-of-a-heap servant, or drudge, sought the room that had so lately been the scene of inhumanity. When she again cast her large grey eyes on the blood-stained floor, she clasped her hands together, and exclaimed to her attendant—

"To think, Hannah, that this mess should have been made in

my best room! I hope to ____ the infernal husseys may be found and hung for it! Why, look here—there's blood on the best counterpane! there's blood on the carpet! there's blood on the chair-cushion! Oh, my! oh, my! oh, my! there's blood everywhere! Get some gin, Hannah; I feel so sick. Do you hear, fool! get a pint of gin, and don't stand staring there like a jackass in a field."

"Don't be passionate, mum—*I* didn't make the mess," said Hannah.

"Who says you did? You'll have to clean it up, though."

"So I 'sposes," she sullenly observed. "I wish the old sinner had been in ____ afore he'd com'd here!"

"And so do I, Hannah, and the girls with him."

"Ah, missus, it'll take a sight of soda to wash *that* away," pointing to the bloody spot where the corpse had lain.

"Get the gin, Hannah, for I'm sick to think on it!" exclaimed the landlady, taking from her gold-bound porte-monnaie a crown-piece. "Ha! this is the very coin the gentleman, whose blood lies at your feet, Hannah, put into my hand as a present for the room. Take it, and spend every farthing of it"—dashing it with disgust on the floor. "Buy brandy, Hannah—gin won't be strong enough for a time like this. If they asks you anything at the public, best be mum;—know nothing;—it's a ticklish time, Hannah, and the least said the soonest mended. Be quick, for I've not yet had a drop to drink all the morning—and I'm blest if I'm not afraid to stop in the room by myself."

The red-armed, blotchy-faced, big-bosomed, thick-lipped, sleepy-eyed drudge, with a bottle under her dirty apron, and her two heavy gold drops in her long red ears, went her errand, and soon returned with the "O-be-joyful"—their slang term for ardent spirits.

"That's very welcome!" said the landlady, after tossing off a glass of the spirit. "Now help yourself, Hannah. Lord! what would poor creeturs that is in trouble do without a drop of drink? I'm woman enough for anything now—that is, I shall be after a glass or two more. Here's to the speedy discovery of the murderers, Hannah!" tossing off a second glass.

"And may I be at the hanging of 'em," responded Hannah, tossing off *her* second glass.

"Hanging's too good for 'em," said the landlady, filling her third glass. " 'Pon my soul, Hannah, I can hardly believe that the two young creeturs that the old fool came home with could have done such a thing."

"Don't *I* though," responded Hannah. "I seed enough of their conduct to show me they were not chickens about town."

"Was the gentleman in liquor, do you think?" inquired the landlady, showing symptoms that the brandy was doing its work on the brain.

"He was much on, missus—I seed that direkly I opened the door, for he chucked me under the chin, and stroked my nose."

"It's all a mystery to me, Hannah—a deep mystery. I can't yet see the occasion for the murder."

"You *must* be in a fog, then. Didn't they rob him?"

"To be sure they did—in that observation you are perfeckly correct. But I maintain there was no occasion to murder the old soul—they might have had his swag without that same doing. Depend upon it there is a mystery in this affair. Take another glass, Hannah, and I'll have another glass; a drop of spirit calms me. It's been an awful fright to me, Hannah, and the end of it will be that I am a ruined woman. You know what a good trade I was doing—beds full from morning to night—beds from attic to kitchen—all let at good prices. And although I say it, mine was as respectable a conducted house as any house of its kind in London. And the girls knew that same; and, for the matter of that, so did the gents who come with them. The accommodation was good—everything clean—and you always kept a civil tongue in your head. But nobody will ever come again, and I shall be ruined."

Here the wicked old woman broke into loud laments, and fits of sobbing.

"It will all blow over, missus," said Hannah, coaxingly. "I'll soon get the house to rights, and the girls will bring their gents as reg'lar as ever."

"It's a marked house, Hannah, and you're an old fool for saying that the circumstances will blow over. Look at it—look at the counterpane—look at the carpet—look at the chair cushions! 'Pon my soul, if I stay here much longer I shall go mad. D____d if I don't feel I had rather the wretches had killed me than have brought this disgrace upon a 'respectable' house."

"Don't take on so, missus; we'll soon get up the 'spectability of the house ag'in. Lord! a glass or two of gin to the young ladies as use for to cum here will do that."

"You gallows fool!" exclaimed the landlady, looking unutterable things at her consoler, while her large breasts perceptibly moved up and down as they peeped over her low dress.

"What for, missus?" inquired Hannah, in the deepest surprise.

" 'Taint the young ladies as we have to consider, it's the gents as comes with 'em! Think they'd trust themselves in a house where a murder had been committed?"

"Gents is not so particular as you think for, missus. They'd foller a woman anywhere."

"There's truth in that," said the landlady, filling her fourth glass with neat brandy.

A large, sleek, black cat here walked in, and would have lapped the dead man's blood, but the women hallooed it back, and the scowling animal slowly retreated to the region below.

"I'm just thinking, Hannah, what a row there'll be about this in the papers!"

"Likely 'nough, mum: an p'raps the very men, if we did but know, who writes 'em and prints 'em have been here themselves for accommodation. We know who *has* been here—don't we, mum?"

"Hush, hush, Hannah—I know what you mean. Honour among thieves—he paid us well not to mention it."

"Oh, that's all right missus," said Hannah; "but I never shall forget the bowl out as long as I live. I 'spose the parish clerk thought we never went to church, and of course we could'nt know him. Ha! ha! he was mistaken. I thought he would have died when I called him by name!' "

"All the world over—people cry loudest agin what they likes most. But no mistake, Hannah, you always heerd me say so in my sober senses, ours is a wretched trade for women, and I'm sure if it wasn't for a drop of spirits now and then to keep my heart up, I should often have destroyed myself. What should we poor wretches be, Hannah, without the comfort of the bottle?"

"It's too late to be virtuous, so we'd better not talk about it. What can't be cured must be endured. We mustn't blame ourselves, neither, missus."

"Who, then?"

"Men! who hunt us for their pleasure, and then despise us. The villain that sedooced me, tried twenty things before he succeeded; he knew I was a poor orphant girl, and he pretended to be my friend: then the old game, promised to marry me—then led me astray; then I might go to the devil for what my *friend* cared. And to the devil I shall go; and as true as God's in heaven, the villain that sedooced me, and then left me to be hunted down by the world, will be there to see me. That's a comfort, anyhow."

However vulgarly expressed, there is so much truth involved in Hannah's words, that I cannot resist pausing to remark upon them. *The sin of prostitution lies at man's door.* Man is woman's snarer; he lays traps for her with infinite cunning; catches the frail innocent, feasts on her, then loathes her, and "whistles her off, and lets her down the wind to prey at fortune."

The concert-room, dancing saloon, the town and country fairs, tea-gardens, and gin-palaces, are the nets of man's invention, dexterously laid to entrap poor woman. The "Social Evil" is man's evil; by him it was brought into existence, by him it is nurtured, by him it grows—and, to reiterate Hannah's words, as "sure as God's in heaven, man will be answerable for it."

The two women, the landlady and her drudge, sat maudling over the brandy until both were half intoxicated, when the former proposed that they should have some tea, and wind up the auspicious day in the gallery of an adjacent theatre.

While the wretched scene was being enacted by the two women at the now notorious brothel, I and others of the police were taking vigilant steps for the capture of the murderers. Every wall, and every hoarding of London, were speedily plastered with large placards, offering a heavy reward to any who discovered them, and a free pardon to all except the actual murderer; simultaneous measures were also actively taken to discover who the murdered gentleman was.

At the end of the second day, a dissolute-looking young man, of shabby appearance, appeared at the workhouse, and claimed the body of the murdered as his grandfather, and to whom he was heir.

It transpired that the deceased was Squire Hepburn, a wealthy farmer from Kent. In life the old gentleman heaped upon *himself* all the luxuries the world could afford, while to others he was peculiarly penurious. He ate by himself—he drank by himself—he lived on his estate by himself. He formed no friendships—he cultivated no affections. One passion, for an old man, he possessed in abundance—a passion that had rioted in his blood from youth to age—animal desire for women. Many a young cottager on his estate he had ruined, and left to her fate. Oh! rare poetic justice—he lived only to deceive and debase woman, and by woman his blood was shed. He had married a tender-hearted lady, but his abominable habits of life soon snapped the bond asunder, and the tomb received her. She left a son to his care, but from his birth he was handed over to stranger hands, and brought up at a low sum per week. The cruel father virtually disowned him, and left him to grow to manhood with the smallest possible assistance. He reached man's estate and married, but a raging epidemic of the period swept him and his wife to the grave. He left behind him a boy seven years old—William Hepburn, the grandson and heir of griping old Squire Hepburn—the young man who now stood at the workhouse door identifying the body of the grandfather he had murdered!

Young Hepburn knew his grandfather well, for since the death of his father he had appealed in vain to him for assistance. The youth, William Hepburn, left so early to his own resources in London, it need cause no surprise that he should associate with cunning lads and wicked lads—with thieves and prostitutes—people who were "a-fly to everything," and sturdy advocates of community of property. There were one or two of this confraternity of a more des-

perate character than the rest, and knowing young Hepburn's relationship to the rich old squire in Kent, continually advised his death,
arguing, as the "old buffer" must go soon, "he might as well go first
as last." Ned Stammers—a bull-dog faced man, who generally spoke
with folded arms—suggested a "nocturnal visit and a crack on the
head, and the job's done—and who's to know?" While Sam
Johnson—honoured name—"that he should be eased of his life on
the highway."

"Don't shrug your shoulders, Bill," said Sam, to young Hepburn, as they sat over their pipes and their beer; "for if what you
tells me is correct, the sooner such an old ____ as your grandfather is
gone to kingdom-come, the better for society. I should like to do the
job very much, if I was paid for it, mind ye, and it was a reg'lar understood thing among us all."

Little did the old squire dream, as he wandered beneath the rising sun to see that all his labourers were at their early duties on his
wealthy estate, that a council of death was hatching his destruction,
and his own grandson at the head of the council! Yet so it was.

I will now give a pen and ink sketch of Sam Johnson. He had a
ghastly cast in one eye, a pale long face, and very red thin lips; tall
and consumptive in appearance, and consumptive in character, for
he seemed never to tire of eating and drinking—but he never fat-
tened on his food.

Sam Johnson, though a burglar and murderer, was a pleasant
fellow, and especially so with a quartern of gin before him, and a
pipe in his mouth. But when luck was against him, and he could not
get his "comfort," he was morose and ill-tempered; and when there
was a "job on"—as now, when he was inciting his wavering companion to murder old Hepburn—he was grave, earnest, logical, and
would easily persuade any one disposed to sin, that it was "all right."
He was indeed a "character," and such he was designated by his
"pals."

"I would murder him," said Sam, "because he is a miser—and,
in course, a useless member in society. I would murder him (D___n
it, there's a fly in the gin!) because he starves you—and the Bible
says, Life for life. I would murder him (Give us a bit of baccy, Bill,)
because you would then get all his chink, and it would be scattered
for the good of yourself and others."

"There's no getting over that," said a somewhat voluptuous
young woman, who leant her folded arms across the table, while
Sam poured out his oratory and his logic. This was Jane Chester,
and Sam Johnson was her "man," or "bully," and Jane Chester was
his "woman," and she gave him all the produce of her prostitution,
and never dared to differ from him, or her painted face would be
decorated with an eye of blackberry hue; for when Sam addressed

himself to Jane's tender organ of sight, it was always in a *striking* manner. Jane saw she had pleased Sam, and she resumed the trotter she had been engaged upon with additional gusto and relish, and toned her stomach with a glass of gin.

"I don't see it, Jenny," said Mary Chester, who, in a happy state of "beer," leant her head and bonnet upon William Hepburn's shoulder—for the same relationship existed between these two, as between Jane and Sam.

No pen could sketch greater profligacy than that which reigned so triumphantly here. The four human beings—(if I must so dignify them)—could fall no lower. Amongst themselves, the mask was torn off—their wretchedness was naked. To see these two abandoned women (sisters too!) who at one time must have been shocked at an evil word or gross allusion—whom their Maker had created beautiful, and who still retained marks of their beauty—to see them thus fallen to depths almost too low to rescue them,—should stir society from its lethargy, until it had fathomed the cause of this monstrous "Social Evil," and swept it from England's shores. But the chief cause *is* known—poverty and the cruelly low prices that young girls and women receive for their unremitting labour,—these are the accursed causes of prostitution, which now by night and day fill the village, the town, and the city.

Mary Chester advised William Hepburn not to be concerned in the murder of his grandfather. She "didn't see it."

Young Hepburn, also, "didn't see it"; but he wouldn't mind the murder if he was sure not to be "lagged" for it.

"Leave that to me," said Sam Johnson. "First, let us all be in it."

"No," interrupted Mary Chester: "I'm none so jolly happy,—yet I'm none so tired of life to be hung out of it."

"You're a fool, Mary!" exclaimed Jenny. "See how jolly it would be for all of us, if the old man was out of the way, and your Bill had his property. *You'd* cut it fine enough, I know."

"May be Bill then would cut *me*," replied Mary.

"That be ____!" exclaimed her gallant protector.

"I like you for that," said Mary, patting young Hepburn's puffy cheeks, and playfully pulling his whiskers.

"Let's all be in it," reiterated Sam Johnson, "and close the affair over half a pint of gin."

"Best leave me out," said Mary Chester. "Lord! in one of my sleep-walking and sleep-talking fits I should blab the whole thing, and hang you all!"

Let us observe that Mary Chester was subject to fits of somnambulism, and frequently rose from her bed in her night-dress, and wandered down the old staircase, to the horror of any who had been sleeping with her; nor could she be aroused to consciousness or wakefulness until her naked foot came in contact with the stone pavement, or some other particularly cold substance. Our picture ably represents her in one of these unfortunate and dangerous trances; another might have shown her sister Jane at a gay house of accommodation, in the purlieus of the Haymarket, dallying with a "swell" she had passed the night with, and who has just made her a present, and is taking an "affectionate" leave of her. This illustrated phase of the "Social Evil" would convey at a glance more than a pen could portray in a volume. Of course, the presents the poor wretches receive from their evil supporters are handed over to their fancymen for "gin and baccy."

> "Oh! that the gods would put in every hand a whip.
> To lash such rascals, naked, through the street!"

It is a singular fact, but nevertheless true, that the majority of these poor fallen women form strong attachments to the men they live with, and bear from them the greatest cruelties, and think nothing too degraded to furnish them with the means to live in idleness and dissipation. These "fellows" may be seen on the heels of their tricked-out paramours, while they trace the *pavés* of our great thoroughfares, and as the women catch their victims, they (the men-monsters) hang about the very door of the brothel to clutch the money paid them for their sin.

William Hepburn had not much to say upon the subject of his grandfather. Oh! that he could enjoy or reach the old man's wealth without the old man's slaughter!

"You would never find me turning out of your bed then, Mary, to let some one else lie with you! I've heard, Sam, that he is the richest man in Kent."

"And you the poorest man in London," sneered Sam. "Was I you, Bill, it wouldn't be long afore *I* was the richest man in Kent— 'specially when nothing but an old miserly life prevented it."

"It's a fine chance, Bill," followed on Jane Chester, flinging the bones of their trotter into the fireless grate.

"Let us hear, Sam," said Hepburn, "how the job should be done."

"Don't hear nothing about it," said the somnambulist, "for you shall have nothing to do with it."

"Don't let a woman rule you, Bill," said Johnson.

Mary darted a swift keen glance at the last speaker, and would have flung the glass that stood before her at his head, had not Hepburn prevented her.

"You ugly wretch, what do you mean?" she exclaimed. "I hate

Jenny for living with and maintaining such a leary-eyed hound as you."

"That's my business," interposed Jane. "He'll do well enough for me."

"Haven't you an engagement to keep?" said Bill to Mary, wanting to get her out of the way; for, silent as he had hitherto been, he could not shut his eyes to the immense advantage it would be to him were his grandfather dead. He was his heir, and he had often and often secretly longed to taste the pleasures of wealth.

"I see," said Mary, "I'm not wanted. I'll be even with all of you yet,"—and made a speedy angry exit from the room. But she *had* an afternoon engagement with a "gent," and she went straight to the harlot's dresser to borrow her night plumes; for in the dirty plight in which she left her room a dog would have shrunk from her.

When she had left for her velvet and feathers, the three, who were pretty well of one mind on the subject of the murder, spoke freer and bolder.

"But what of Mary?" suggested Sam Johnson.

"Leave her to me," said Bill. "When she's drunk I can do anything with her. Only let us see the way clear, and I'll go in for the job. He's been a stingy villain to me and my father. Had he done his duty——"

"But he hasn't," interrupted Sam, "and I'm d——d if I wouldn't be one with him."

"You like Mary, and Mary likes you, Bill," said Jane; "and you both do things spicy—you know you do. Sam's often heard me say that you was born to be a 'gent.' And I know devilish well what Mary likes—every thing tip-top. Nobby togs, plenty of lush, cutting it slap at the Argyle and Cremonne, cards, theatres, and the races."

"Aye, aye, old gal, and you like these luxuries as much as Mary."

"Don't I, though! I just do, Sam, and I will chance my neck for them. I'm tired of the streets, I can tell you. Bah! it's a sickening life for a woman to be pulled about by every fellow she meets."

"Whew, whew, whew!" whistled Sam, "You are getting as virtuous as Mary."

"I'm in—if you can plan it neatly," said Hepburn.

"Your hand, old boy! Yours, Johnny! I know I can depend on you, gal,"—shaking Jane's hand heartily.

The dreadful compact was made.

"Mind, if we succeed, it's share and share alike, Bill?"

Hepburn hesitated.

"Oh, yes; share and share alike," repeated Sam—and Jane Chester backed her "man."

"Agreed; now for your plans, Sam."

"First of all, Mary *must* be made a party, or she will have the pull on us."

"Well?" said Bill, paying the most earnest attention to Sam's murderous stratagem, while Jane Chester paid equal attention.

"Mind ye, it's none so easy a matter to murder a man now-a-days," said Sam; "it wants a little cutting and contriving, as the woman said when she wanted to make a new gown out of an old un."

"But you've got a plan?" said Hepburn.

"Lord! don't be in a hurry," he replied. "Mind, you're all in it—Mary and all."

"Score it down in writing, if you like," said young Hepburn.

"That would puzzle me to do, more than the murder; writing's a thing I never was a fist at. No occasion neither, Bill, for that—we shall have plenty of pull upon each other if things are not righteous and above board with either of us."

Furthermore to the same effect was spoken before Sam unravelled his plan of action, which was simply this:—That Jane and Mary Chester should wait outside the tavern, which old Hepburn used when he came to London, and which was known to his grandson, and when he was inflamed with drink, that they should entice him to accompany them to the house where he was subsequently murdered; and that when he slept, the women should give them warning, and they were to enter and do the deed.

"But what if we fail to get him to the house?" suggested Jane.

"There's no fear there; for when he's in liquor he takes with the first woman that offers—so the villagers say on his estate," said Hepburn.

The three friends having settled to steep their hands in an old man's blood on the morrow night, and after another glass round, dispersed themselves to their different "callings." Jane Chester stepped at once to her dresser's, and soon appeared in black velvet tunic and flowing red skirt, then fluttered about the entrance to Her Majesty's Theatre, as gay and happy as a gorgeous butterfly. The gin had made her merry, and when she was merry she always sang and pirouetted on the pavement. Sometimes—well, often if the reader likes—she took the glass too much, then she would do a little boxing, and a great deal of swearing. Mary Chester was bad enough, but Jane was worse. The only vestige left of their sex, innocence, and humanity, was, that the sisterly feeling had not perished with their other virtues. They felt themselves sisters—they clung to each other as sisters; and though they might now and then have a "tiff" between themselves, they would allow no one to insult or injure the other.

It was a cold, comfortless night, and Sam Johnson, while dancing attendance on his "woman," buttoned his over-coat to the throat,
lit his short pipe, and thrust his dirty hands into his pockets. Sometimes he and Jane might be seen for an instant exchanging a word or
two; at others he might be discovered in the centre of a group of
other "unfortunates."

Oh, happy chance for Sam—business turns by! The blandish-
ments of Jane—her tuneful "With a fal lal lal! With a fal lal lal!" has
won the admiration of Mr. Green, secretary to one of our charitable
institutions, who was "rayther" the worse for his after-dinner glass.
Jane "twigged" the happy state of Mr. Green, and made much of
him, and still singing "with a fal lal lal!" they adjourned to an adjoining oyster-opener, for a few "natives"—then to the Argyle Rooms
for a dance and sherry-cobbler. They danced to very weariness, and
they drink to very drunkenness, and so happy they get, so jocose, so
obscene, so facetious, so insulting, that they are politely ejected from
the room.

Thus Jane Chester, and in a very similar manner Mary, passed
the night before the murder. Young Hepburn's influence and his gin
succeeded with Mary, and she made one of the deadly party.

Well, the murder was done, and "they were all in it." But it sat
not easy on Mary's mind, and her sleep was oppressed with a sense
of the horrid deed. William Hepburn had the old man's body removed into Kent, and with himself as chief mourner—

"To mimic sorrow when the heart's not sad"—

it was interred in the village church.

The funeral over, it was arranged that the grandson and heir
should take possession—and he would have done so, but for a trifling obstacle,—there was a **LAST WILL AND TESTAMENT** in
the way. Young Hepburn left his companions at a small public-
house on the estate, one morning after the funeral, and set out over
the heather with a heart big with joy to assume mastery of the estate.
Oh! what castles he built up in his imaginations as he hastily trod
among the heather! He would gamble, race, drink, dress—he would
_____ But his hand is on the knocker of the door, and the knocker
knocked as never knocker knocked before. So loud—so imperative
was the summons, that a respectable attorney, who happened to be
there in the interest of the rightful heir or heiress, replied to it, leading by the hand Bessie Gordon, a maiden of sixteen—an illegitimate
daughter of Squire Hepburn, and to whom only a month before he
had left the whole of his large property.

"Who is at home here?" inquired William Hepburn.

"This young lady, sir," replied the attorney. "Pray, what is
your pleasure, sir?"

Hepburn was confounded, and stammered—"My pleasure is to take possession of the estate."

"By what right, sir?"

"By right of inheritance, to be sure. I am the squire's heir."

"Well, you might have been a month ago, it is true, for then there was no will in existence; but since the execution of this parchment deed, attested by indisputable testimony, this young lady became the squire's heir, and is now mistress here."

"That be d——d!" exclaimed the disappointed scoundrel. "That won't do for me."

"That's to be regretted—but it will do uncommonly well for Miss Gordon."

By the time the disappointed heir had returned to his friends in murder, they were half intoxicated. When they learnt the news—when young Hepburn with hellish oaths, said there was not a d——d farthing for any of them—it quite sobered them. The spirit-flush deserted the cheeks of Jane and Mary Chester, and an ashy paleness overspread them.

Sam Johnson, for a while, was mute with wonder—then he drew the pipe from his mouth, dashed it to the ground, and swore that Hepburn was playing them false.

"A d——d fine idea!—to murder a man—"

"Hush! hush!" said Jane, "we don't know where we are."

"I think it's me that should holler about it," said Hepburn; "I've lost most."

We forbear picturing any further the scene that ensued. Indeed, we could not, without filling our page with slang and oaths.

The four made the best of their way to London; by the time they reached there, they were all mad with drink, passion, and disappointment.

This night was to be the last of Mary Chester. After she and Hepburn had slept some time at their London lodgings, the poor woman arose sleeping from her bed, and talked of the old man's murder. Young Hepburn awoke, and followed her to the door and to the top of the high flight of stairs. While she stood in this position, he, seized with a sudden impulse of brutality, pushed the sleeping wretch from the top to the bottom. She awoke no more, but gave a heavy groan, ejaculated "Farewell, Bill!" and died. Hepburn then, to disguise the deed, placed a stool by her head, as an evidence that she must have fallen over it from the landing. This, combined with her known affliction of walking in her sleep, favoured Hepburn's innocence.

But justice does not always sleep. Not many days after the parish burial of Mary Chester, Hepburn and Johnson concocted a burglary in a dwelling-house in the outskirts of London. I detected them, and lodged them in prison. At their trial it was proved that great brutality had been shown towards a servant of the house who had heroically defended his master's property. They were sentenced to transportation for life, and at this present time they are working in the convicts' gang in a foreign land.

Jane Chester was now left alone, and with the aid of dram-drinking she managed, poor wretch! to pursue her "calling," until time robbed her of all her outward charms. Then, utterly slighted by the world, beggared and sick, she gave herself up to misery and despair. In an insane moment she sought the "Bridge of Sighs," and daringly took the life God gave her.

A few nights before this, in an insane moment, she suddenly sprang from her wretched couch, and, to the alarm of those who stood by, she persisted she saw the ghost of her mother beckoning her away.

CHARLES MARTEL

CHARLES MARTEL, if the slightly doubtful entry in the British Museum Catalogue is correct, was the pseudonym of Thomas Delf (1810–1865), a London bookseller and scholar who had prepared translations and original works on art technique. His best-known book was Principles of Colouring in Ornamental Art *(1866), which had reached its eighteenth printing by the 1890s. Delf also compiled a standard reference work,* Appleton's Library Manual *(1847), which listed and classified some twelve thousand books.*

In 1860 two books of short stories appeared under the pseudonym Charles Martel. These were The Diary of an Ex-Detective *and* The Detective's Note-book. *While the individual stories vary greatly in quality, several are concerned with aspects of scientific detection, and Martel seems to have consulted the official detectives of the City of London. Several of Martel's plots anticipate better-known later literature; he was the first to show a private detective recovering a lost naval treaty.*

"Hanged by the Neck: A Confession"

I.

I am about to lift the veil of mystery which for ten years has shrouded the murder of Maria G——; and, though I lay bare my own weakness, or folly, or what you will, I do not shrink from the unveiling. No hand but mine can perform the task. There was, indeed, a man who might have done this better than I; but he wrapped himself in silence and went his way.

I like a man who can hold his tongue.

On the corner of Dudley and Broad Streets stands a dingy-brown house, which, judging from its obsolete style of architecture, must have been built a century ago. It has a very cocked-hat air about it—an antique, unhappy look. It is now tenanted by an incalculable number of Irish families; but at the time of which I write it was a second-rate lodging-house of the more respectable sort, and rather largely patronised by poor but honest literary men, tragic actors, and pretty ballet-girls.

My apartments in Dudley Street were opposite this building, to which my attention was directed, soon after taking possession of the rooms, by the discovery of the following facts:—First, that a very charming *blonde* lodged on the second floor front of "over the way," and sang like a canary-bird every morning; second that her name was Maria G____; third, that she had two lovers—short allowance for a *danseuse*. If ever poetry and pathos took human shape it was christened Maria G____. She was one of Beauty's best thoughts. I cannot tell if her eyes were black or hazel; but her hair was bronze-brown, silken, and wavy, and her mouth the perfection of tenderness. Her form was rich in those perfect curves which delighted the old Greek masters. I write this with no impure thought. But when she lay in her little room, stark, and lifeless, and horrible, the glory faded from her face, then I stooped down and kissed her, but not till then. How ghastly she looked! Eyes with no light in them, lips with no breath on them—white, cold, dead!

Maria G____ was a finer study to me than her lovers. One of them was commonplace enough—well dressed, well made, handsome, shallow. Nature manufactures such men by the gross. He was a lieutenant, in the navy I think, and ought to have been on the sea, or in it, instead of working ruin ashore. The other was a man of different mould. His character, like his person, had rough lines to it. Only for the drooping of his eyelids, and a certain coarseness about the mouth, he would have been handsome, in spite of those dark, deep-sunken eyes. His frame would have set an anatomist wild—tall, deep-chested, knitted with muscles of steel. "Some day," said I, as I saw him stalk by the house one evening, "he will throw the little lieutenant out of that second-floor window." It would have been a wise arrangement.

From the time I left off short jackets women have perplexed me. I have discovered what woman is not; but I have never found out what she is. I cannot tell to this day which of those two men Maria G____ loved, or if she loved either. The flirtation, however, was scandal enough for the entire neighbourhood; but little did the gossips dream of the tragedy which was being acted under their noses.

This affair had continued for several months, when it was reported that Maria and Julius Kenneth were affianced. The lieutenant was less frequently seen in Broad Street; and Julius waited upon Maria's foot-steps with a humility and tenderness strangely out of keeping with his rough nature. Mrs. Grundy was somewhat appeased. Yet, though Maria went to the Sunday concerts with Julius Kenneth, she still wore the lieutenant's roses in her bosom!

If I could only meet with an unenigmatical woman!

II.

I was awakened one morning by several quick, nervous raps on my room door. The noise startled me from a most appalling dream.

"Oh, sir!" cried a voice on the landing, "there's been a dreadful murder done across the street! They've murdered Maria G____!"

"I will get up." That was all I said. I looked at my watch. It was nine o'clock. I had overslept myself; but then I I sat up late the night before.

I dressed myself hastily, and, without waiting for breakfast, pushed my way through the crowd that had collected in front of the house, and passed upstairs unquestioned to the scene of the tragedy. When I entered the room there were six people present—a tall, slim gentleman, with a professional air, evidently a physician; two policemen; Adelaide Woods, an actress; Mrs. Marston, the landlady; and Julius Kenneth. In the centre of the chamber, on the bed, lay the body of Maria G____. The face of the corpse haunted me for years afterwards with its bloodless lips, the dark streaks under the eyes, and the long silken hair streaming over the pillow. I stopped over her for a moment, and turned down the counterpane, which was drawn up closely to her chin.

> "There was that across her throat
> Which you had hardly cared to see!"

At the head of the bed sat Julius Kenneth, bending over the icy hand which he held in his own. He seemed to be kissing it. The gentleman in black was conversing in undertones with Mrs. Marston, who wrung her hands every other moment and glanced towards the body. The two policemen were examining the doors, closets, and windows of the premises. There was no fire in the grate, but the room was suffocatingly close. I opened a window and leaned against the casement to catch the fresh air. The physician approached me. I muttered something to him.

"Yes," he began, "the affair looks very mysterious, as you remark. Never so little evidence of anything. Thought at first 'twas a case of suicide: door locked, key on the inside, room in perfect order; but then we find no instrument with which the subject could have inflicted that wound on the neck. Party must have escaped by the window. But how? The windows are at least thirty feet from the ground. It would be impossible for a person to jump that distance without fracturing a limb, even if he could clear the iron railing below. Unpleasant things to jump on, those spikes. . . . Must have been done with a sharp knife. The party meant to make sure work of it. The carotid cleanly severed. Death in about a hundred seconds."

The medical man went on in this hideous style for ten minutes, during which time Kenneth did not raise his lips from Maria's hand. I spoke to him; but he only shook his head in reply. I understood his grief; and on returning to my room I wrote him a note, the purport of which will be shown hereafter.

The *Evening Herald* of that day contained the following article:— "MURDER IN BROAD STREET.—This morning, at eight o'clock, Maria G____, the well-known *danseuse*, was found murdered in her bed, at her late residence on the corner of Broad and Endell Streets. There was but one wound on the body—a fearful gash on the neck, just below the left ear. The deceased was dressed in a ballet costume, and was evidently murdered immediately after her return from the theatre, by some person or persons concealed in the room. On a chair near the bed lay several fresh bouquets, and a long cloak which the deceased was in the habit of wearing over her dancing dress on coming home from the theatre at night. The perfect order of the apartment, and the fact that the door was locked on the inside, have induced many to believe that the poor girl killed herself. But we cannot think so. That the door was fastened on the inner side proves nothing, excepting that the murderer was hidden in the chamber. That the room gave no evidence of a struggle is also an insignificant fact. Two men, or even one strong man, grappling suddenly with the deceased, who was a very slight woman, would have prevented any great struggle. No weapon whatever was discovered on the premises. We give below all the material testimony elicited by the coroner's inquest. It explains nothing.

"*Harriet Marston* deposes: I keep a lodging-house at 131, Broad Street. The deceased has lodged with me for the past two years. Has always borne a good character. I do not think she had many visitors; certainly no male visitors, except a Lieutenant King and Mr. Kenneth, to whom she was engaged. I do not know when Lieutenant King was last at the house; not within three days I am confident. Deceased told me that he had gone away for ever. I did not see her last night when she returned from the theatre. The street door is never locked; each of the lodgers has a latch-key. The last time I saw the deceased was just before she went to the theatre, when she requested me to call her at eight o'clock, as she had promised to walk out with 'Jules,' meaning Mr. Kenneth. I knocked at the door eight or ten times, and received no answer. I then grew frightened, and called one of the lodgers, Adelaide Woods, who helped me to force the lock. The key fell out on the inside as we pressed against the door. Maria G____ was lying on the bed with her throat cut. The quilt and the strip of carpet beside the bed were covered with blood. She was not undressed. The room presented the same appearance it does now.

"*Adelaide Woods* deposes: I am an actress. I occupy a room next to that of the deceased. It was about eleven o'clock when she came home; she stopped ten or fifteen minutes in my chamber. The call-boy of the Olympic usually accompanied her home from the theatre. I let her in. Deceased had misplaced her night-key. I did not hear any noise in the night. The partition between our rooms is quite thick; but I do not sleep heavily, and should have heard any unusual noise. Two weeks ago deceased told me that she was to be married to Mr. Kenneth in June. She and Mr. Kenneth were in the habit of taking walks before breakfast. The last time I saw them together was yesterday morning. I assisted Mrs. Marston in breaking open the door. [Describes position of the body, &c., &c.]

"Here the call-boy was summoned, and testified to accompanying the deceased home on the night of the murder. He came as far as the steps with her. The door was opened by a woman. Could not swear it was Miss Woods, though he knows her by sight. The night was very dark, and there was no lamp burning in the entry.

Julius Kenneth deposes: I am a machinist. I reside at No. __, F__ Street. I have been acquainted with the deceased for eighteen months. We were engaged to be married. [Here the witness's voice failed him.] The last time I saw her was yesterday morning, on which occasion we walked out together. I did not leave my room last evening. I was confined to the house by a cold all day. A Lieutenant King used to visit the deceased frequently. It created considerable talk in the neighbourhood. I did not like it, and requested her to break off the acquaintance. Deceased told me yesterday morning that Lieutenant King had been ordered to some foreign station, and would trouble me no more. Deceased had engaged to walk with me this morning at eight o'clock. When I reached Broad Street I first learned that she had been murdered. [Here the witness, overcome by his emotions, was permitted to retire.]

"*Dr. Underhill* deposes: [this witness was very voluble and learned, and had to be checked several times by the coroner. We give his testimony in brief.] I was called in to view the body of the deceased. A deep wound on the throat, two inches below the left ear, severing the left common carotid and the internal jugular vein, had been inflicted by some sharp instrument. Such a wound would produce death almost immediately. The body bore no other marks of violence. The deceased must have been dead several hours, the *rigor mortis* having already supervened. On a second examination with Dr. Rose the deceased was found to be *enceinte*.

"*Dr. Rose* corroborated the above testimony.

"The policeman and several other people were examined, but the statements threw no light on the case. The situation of Julius Kenneth, the lover of the unfortunate girl, excites the deepest commiseration. The deceased was nineteen years of age. Who the criminal is, and what could have led to the perpetration of the cruel act, are mysteries which, at present, threaten to baffle the sagacity of the police."

I could but smile on reading all this solemn nonsense. After breakfast the next morning I made my toilet with extreme care, and presented myself at the police office. Two gentlemen, who were sitting with the magistrate at a table, started to their feet as I announced myself. I bowed to the magistrate very calmly and said,—

"*I am the person who murdered Maria G____!*"

Of course I was instantly arrested. The *Globe* of that evening favoured me with the following complimentary notice:—

"THE BROAD-STREET HOMICIDE: FURTHER DEVELOPMENTS: MORE MYSTERY.—The person who murdered the ballet-girl in Clark Street on the night of the 3rd instant surrendered himself to the magistrate this morning. He gave his name as Paul Larkins, and resides opposite the scene of the tragedy. He is of medium height, and well made; has dark, restless eyes, and chestnut hair; his face is unnaturally pale, and by no means improved by the Mephistophelean smile which constantly plays upon his lips. Notwithstanding his gentlemanly address, there is that about him which stamps him villain. His voluntary surrender is not the least mysterious feature of this mysterious *affaire*; for, had he preserved silence, he would have escaped detection beyond a doubt. He planned and executed the murder with such skill that there is little or no evidence against him, save his own confession, which is inexplicable enough. He acknowledges the crime, but stubbornly refuses to enter into details. He expresses a desire to be hanged immediately! How he entered the room, and by what means he left it after committing the heinous deed, and why he brutally murdered a woman with whom, as it is proved, he had had no previous acquaintance, are enigmas which still perplex the public mind, and will not let curiosity sleep. These facts, however, will probably be brought to light during the trial. In the mean time the greatest excitement reigns throughout the city."

At four o'clock that afternoon the door of my cell turned on its hinges, and Julius Kenneth stood face to face with me. I ought to have cowered in the presence of that injured man, but I did not. I was cool, Satanic; he feverish and terrible.

"You got my note?" I said.

"Yes; and I have come here as you requested."

"You know, of course, that I have refused to reveal the circumstances connected with the murder? I wished to make the confession to you alone."

He turned his eyes on mine for a moment, and said, "Well?"

"But even to you I will assign no reason for having committed this crime. It was necessary that Maria G____ should die. I decided that she should die in her chamber, and to that end I purloined her night-key."

Julius Kenneth fixed his eyes on me.

"On Wednesday night, after Maria G——— had gone to the theatre, I entered the street door by means of the key, and stole unobserved into her chamber, and secreted myself under the bed, or in that small clothes press near the window—I forget which. Some time between eleven and twelve o'clock she returned; and as she lighted the candle I caught her by the waist, pressed a handkerchief saturated with chloroform over her mouth, and threw her on the bed. When she had ceased to struggle, and I could use my hand, I made a deep incision in her throat. Then I smoothed the bed-clothes, and threw my gloves and the handkerchief into the grate. I am afraid there was not fire enough to burn them!"

Kenneth walked up and down the cell in great agitation; then he suddenly stopped and sat down on the bed.

"Are you listening? I then extinguished the light and proceeded to make my escape from the room, which I did in so simple a manner that the police, through their very desire to discover wonderful things, will never find it out, unless indeed *you* betray me. The night, you will remember, was remarkably foggy; it was so thick, indeed, that it was impossible to see a person at four yards' distance. I raised the window-sash cautiously, and let myself out, holding on by the sill until my feet touched the left-hand shutter of the window beneath, which swung back against the house, and was made stationary by the catch. By standing on this—my arms are almost as long as yours—I was able to reach the iron water-spout of the adjacent building, and by that I descended to the pavement."

Kenneth glared at me like some ferocious animal.

"On gaining the street," I continued, "I found that I had thoughtlessly brought the knife with me—a long, slim-bladed knife. I should have left it in the room. It would have given the whole thing the appearance of suicide. I threw the knife———"

"Into the river!" exclaimed Kenneth, involuntarily.

And then I smiled.

"How did you know it was I?" he shrieked.

"It was as plain as day," I returned coolly. "Hush, they will hear you in the corridor. I knew it the moment I saw you sitting by the bed. First, because you shrank instinctively from the corpse, though you seemed to caress it. Your grief throughout was clumsily done, sir; it was too melodramatic. Secondly, when I looked into the grate I saw a handkerchief partly consumed, and then I instantly remembered the faint, peculiar smell which I had observed in the room before the windows were opened. Thirdly, when I went to the window I noticed that the paint was scraped off the iron brackets which held the spout to the adjoining house. The spout had been painted three days previously; the paint on the brackets was thicker than anywhere else, and had not dried. On looking at your feet, which I did when I spoke to you, I remarked that the leather on the inner side of both your boots was slightly chafed."

"If you intend to betray me——" and Kenneth thrust his hand in his bosom. He had a pistol there.

"That I am *here* proves nothing of the kind. If you will listen patiently you shall learn why *I* acknowledge the crime, why *I* would bear the penalty. I believe there are vast, intense sensations, from which we are shut out by the fear of a certain kind of death. This pleasure, this ecstasy, this something which I have striven for all my life, is known only to the privileged few—innocent men, who, through some oversight of the law, are *hanged by the neck*. Some men are born to be hanged, some have hanging thrust upon them, and some (as I hope to do) achieve hanging. For years and years I have watched for such a chance as this. Worlds could not tempt me to divulge your guilt any more than worlds could have tempted me to commit your crime. A man's mind and heart should be at ease to enjoy, to the utmost, this delicious death. Now you may go."

And I turned my back on him. Kenneth came to my side and placed his heavy hand on my shoulder—that red right hand which all the tears of the angels could not wash white. It made me shudder.

"I shall go far from here," he said, hurriedly. "I cannot, I *will not*, die now. They dishonoured me. Maria was to have been my wife: so she would have hidden her shame! She is dead. When I meet *him* then I shall have done with life. I shall not die till then. And you—they will not harm you—you are a maniac!"

The cell door closed on Julius Kenneth.

I bite the blood into my lips with vexation when I think what a miserable failure I made of it. Three stupid friends who had played cards with me at my room on the night of the murder proved an *alibi*. I was literally turned out of prison, for I insisted on being executed. Then it was maddening to have all the papers call me "a monomaniac." I a monomaniac! I like that! What was Pythagoras, and Newton, and Fulton, and Brunel?

But I kept my peace; and impenetrable mystery shrouded the murder of Maria G____.

III.

Three years ago, in broad daylight, a man was shot dead in the park. A hundred eyes saw the deed. I went to the man's funeral. They buried him with military honours. So much for Lieutenant King!

The first grey light of dawn straggled through the narrow window of the cell, and drove the shadows into the farther corner, where Julius Kenneth lay sleeping. A summer morning was breaking on the city.

In cool green woods millions of birds stirred in their nests, waiting for the miracle of morning; the night-trains dashed through quiet country towns; innumerable shop-boys took down innumerable shutters; the milkmen shrieked; the clocks struck; doors opened and closed; the glamour of sleep was broken, and all the vast machinery of life was put in motion.

But to the man in jail it was as if these things were not.

As he lay there, slumbering in the increasing light, the carpenters in the prison-yard were raising a wooden platform, with two hideous black uprights supporting a horizontal beam, in the centre of which was a small iron pulley. The quick sound of the hammers broke in on his dreams, if he had any. He turned restlessly once or twice, and pushed the hot pillow from him. Then he opened his eyes and saw the splendid blue sky through the window.

He listened to the hammers. He knew what the sound meant. It was his last day on earth. *Vive la bagatelle!* He would have more sleep; so he closed his eyes again.

At six o'clock the jailer brought him his breakfast, and he devoured it like an animal. An hour afterwards two attendants dressed him in a melancholy suit of black, and arranged his tangled hair. At seven the chaplain of the prison entered the cell.

"Would his poor friend," he said, approaching the wretch, "turn, in this last sad hour, to Him whose mercy, like the heavens, spanned all things? Would he listen for a while to the teachings of One whose life and death were two pure prayers for mankind? Would he have, at this awful moment, such consolation as he, a humble worker in God's vineyard, could give him?"

"No; but he would have some brandy."

The unscientific beast! I could pity him—not that he was to be hanged, but because he was not in the state of mind to enjoy the ecstatic sensations which I am convinced result from strangulation. The chaplain remained with the man, and the man yawned.

The ponderous bell of St. Paul's modestly struck eight as the High Sheriff paused at the foot of the scaffold, while the prisoner, followed by the indefatigable chaplain, complacently mounted the rough deal steps which lead to—can anybody tell me where? To the top of the scaffold. Quite right!

I shall not forget that insensible, stony face, as I saw it for a moment before the black cap screened it from the crowd. Why did they hide his face? I should like to have studied the convulsive workings of those features.

In the stillness of that June night they took the body away in a deal coffin, and buried it somewhere. I don't know where. I have not the slightest idea where they bury that sort of man.

ANONYMOUS

"Tale of a Detective" appeared in a collection of short stories entitled A Race for Life and Other Tales, *published by the Religious Tract Society in the early 1870s. Its authorship is unknown.*

The stories in A Race for Life and Other Tales *were written to edify young adults, and religion and morality were worked into the stories in various ways. Sometimes the piety of the characters was extolled; at other times morality emerged from the action itself. In "Tale of a Detective," however, the moralism is applied in one solid lump at the end of the story; everything that precedes it, except for the mildly allegorical names, might have appeared in a secular collection of sensational fiction. Perhaps the author had finished a detective story and found that he or she could sell it if a few moralistic passages were added at the end of the story. Perhaps the editors felt that the luridness of an ordinary detective story might carry an unsuspecting young reader into the moral.*

"Tale of a Detective"

It was in the summer of 1845 that I was sent for, the following case explained to me, and the unravelling of it placed in my hands.

I had better, in the first place, premise that the names both of places and individuals are, purposely, fictitious: it were needless to wound afresh hearts which have already been well nigh broken by shame and sorrow.

"Mr. Clutch," said my superior officer, "I have sent for you because I have greater confidence in your acuteness and ability than in that of any other officer in the force."

I bowed low to the compliment, though I am wrong to call it by that name; for the kind and warm-hearted man who was then one of our chief officers never paid empty compliments, but really meant what he said. I cannot let this opportunity slip of recording my deep obligations to Mr. Frankman for the unvarying kindness with which he treated me whilst I was under his command, and of thanking him most gratefully and cordially for the confidence he placed in me, and for the friendship with which he honoured me.

Mr. Frankman resumed.

"The case, as far as I understand it, is this: Mr. and Mrs. Winter, people of large fortune, living at a place in _____shire called Northcourt, have had their house broken into, and have lost an immense amount of plate. I have not sent for you before because, considering this affair merely in the light of a simple burglary, I hoped to be able to work it out without your assistance, knowing besides that your time was always fully occupied in trying to untie knots which had puzzled every one else. However, this Northcourt burglary has assumed that character now; our people have been ferreting and 'worriting' about it for the last fortnight, and all to no purpose: and so now it legitimately belongs to you, if you will undertake it."

"Most readily, sir," I replied; "but I am afraid the scent must be rather cold."

"Yes, I am afraid so; but I don't like to give it up: the scent is not only cold, but gone altogether it appears: however, you are the man to recover it, if it is to be recovered. You will do your best, I know."

Again thanking Mr. Frankman for his high opinion of my detective powers, and promising to do my best to deserve his approbation, I requested him to furnish me with all the particulars of this burglary, as far as he knew them.

Mr. Frankman referred to his reports, and gave me the following account of the robbery, which appeared to have been committed by very practical hands.

On the morning of the 15th of June, the under housemaid at Northcourt, upon going into the dining room to open the shutters, discovered that someone had already performed that duty for her, though not exactly in the usual way. In fact, she found not only the shutters of one of the windows open, but a pane of glass missing. Plate glass though it was, it had been most scientifically removed; and as the pane was a large one, plenty of room for the admission of a man had been thus obtained. Upon this discovery, Sarah hastened up to the housekeeper's room, and after knocking till she was tired and receiving no answer, she opened the door and peeped timidly in. This was the girl's own statement. She called, "Mrs. Softly! Mrs. Softly!" but still no answer: the room was quite dark, except where the sun streamed through the chinks in the shutters, so that she could see nothing; but she thought she heard strange noises from the bed. Now, Mrs. Softly the housekeeper was married to Mr. Softly the butler, and Sarah's sense of propriety forbade her to enter their room uninvited; but the strange noise continuing from the bed, and she getting no answer to her repeated calls, she could stand it no longer, but rushing to the windows she threw open the shutters, and the brilliant June sunbeams fell upon a scene which "frightened her almost out of her wits."

Mr. and Mrs. Softly lay side by side in bed, making uncouth sounds, and looking fearfully red in the face. In short, they were gagged, and bound hand and foot. Sarah speedily released them; and as soon as the butler could speak, he blubbered out (for the poor man actually cried in his vexation), "The plate-chest—the—villains, the key!—oh the villains!"

The house was of course soon thoroughly aroused, and Mr. Winter made acquainted with what had happened.

The butler's account was as follows. He was suddenly awakened out of a sound sleep by a sense of suffocation: upon opening his eyes he saw a man in a black silk mask leaning over him, and busily employed in, as he believed, strangling him; but he was only adjusting the gag, which he quickly effected; he then strapped his hands tightly to his sides, tied his legs together, and fastened them securely to the bed-post, which effectually prevented him from attempting to get up. He was surprised, he said, not to hear a word from his wife during all this time, and was afraid at first that the man might have murdered her; but he was soon relieved on that score by the appearance of another masked figure on the other side of the bed, who had performed towards Mrs. Softly the same office that had been so effectually performed on him.

As soon as the two men had so fastened the butler and his wife as to insure their silence, they began to search the room; Mr. Softly's eyes followed them in the greatest alarm, for he began to guess their errand, he said; and his fears were very shortly verified. One of the men took a bunch of keys out of Mr. Softly's breeches pocket; he looked at the butler as he did so, and laughed, as much as to say, "I see by your face that I'm on the right tack." He soon found the object of his search—the key of the plate-chest: another look at the butler, and another low laugh, showed his knowledge of the value of the prize he had gained.

The men immediately left the room, merely shutting the door after them; and Mr. Softly, half strangled and powerless, was left to the full enjoyment of a knowledge of the intended robbery, without being able to do anything either by word or deed to prevent it. He described his sensations to have been at that time quite overpowering. "To think," he said, "that all that beautiful plate was being took away by them villains, before my very face almost!" And then the loss to his poor dear master! he couldn't bear to think of that. In short, he was in a dreadful state of mind, by all accounts, and blamed himself for sleeping with his door unlocked. Had it been

locked, the villains would probably have awoke him in breaking it
open, and the burglary might have been prevented; nay, it should
have been prevented, unless they had taken his life; for Mr. Softly
would not have yielded up the key of his plate-chest except with his
life. The burglars had made a clean sweep of it. Plate to the value of
2000£ and upwards had been carried off, and amongst the rest were
several valuable old relics, which had been in the family a long time,
and were highly prized by Mr. Winter.

Suspicion fell upon a man of the name of John Post. He had
been formerly, and not very long since, under-footman at Northcourt, but had not given satisfaction to Mr. Softly, who complained
of his carelessness and idle habits, and he was consequently dismissed. This man had been taken up upon suspicion, had been examined, and discharged. His apprehension was owing in a great
measure, if not entirely, to the hints and inuendoes of Mr. Softly;
but when Post was under examination, it was mainly the evidence of
Mr. Softly which exculpated him; and it was remarked upon, as a
proof of the butler's conscientiousness, that although he was evidently no friend to Post, still he would not allow his dislike to influence him.

Since the discharge of John Post, no one had been apprehended
even on suspicion; no clue to the depredators could be discovered;
the affair was wrapped apparently in an impenetrable mystery.

The history of the Softlys was this. He had originally been footman in Mr. Winter's family, then under-butler, and eventually had
been raised to the dignity of butler, in which capacity he had acted
for the last fifteen years: altogether he had been about five-and-
twenty years in Mr. Winter's service. As soon as he was appointed
butler, he made known his wish to marry Mrs. Winter's maid, to
whom, he said, he had been attached for several years. The housekeeper was about to leave; and Softly, in obtaining his master's permission to marry, obtained also the situation of housekeeper for his
wife. Mr. and Mrs. Winter were kind-hearted, easy-going people,
who possessed the not uncommon dislike to trouble which character-
izes many rich folk; and, moreover, they liked both Softly and Ann
Cook, both of whom they had every reason to consider trustworthy
and honest. Ann Cook, thought not so long in the family as Softly,
had been lady's maid more than five years, and had therefore been
over fifteen years at Northcourt at the time of the burglary.

Having received all the information on the subject that Mr.
Frankman was able to afford me, I took my leave. I must confess
that I never felt less sanguine as to the result of any search in which I
had been employed than I did in this. It is true that I already suspected two people; but how was I to get at them? There is, I am
sure, an inward expositor or revealer of secrets, as well as an inward

monitor in man: I have over and over again entertained a perfect and entire belief in the guilt or innocence of particular people—a belief founded on no grounds that I could at all explain, substantiated by no outward proof; and yet it has been as strongly impressed upon my mind as though I were well assured of the fact by positive evidence; and what is more extraordinary still, my suspicions, impressions, belief, or whatever the feeling may be called, almost always turned out to be true. Now, in this instance I had, almost from the very first mention of the man's name, felt an irresistible conviction that Softly the butler was implicated in the burglary at Northcourt. No matter how improbable it seemed, I thought so all the same; I couldn't help it. It could not be that I was prejudiced against the man, since I had never heard his name before in my life. In vain did I say to myself, "This Softly has been upwards of twenty-five years in Mr. Winter's family; he is an old, respected, and valued servant." In vain I said this; the ready answer was in my heart, "Ah, he had a hand in the robbery for all that."

I tried to reason and argue myself out of this suspicion at first, but at length I gave into it. But how was I to act? As I said before, how was I to get at the people I suspected? It was quite clear that their master did not suspect them, though I did; and I knew from experience that it was ticklish work interfering between master and servant—as bad as between man and wife, pretty nearly. However much a man may abuse his own servants, he never likes anyone else to abuse them. I once had a lesson with regard to interfering about a gentleman's drunken coachman that I did not readily forget.

And now I was about to tax another gentleman's servant with a worse crime a good deal than drunkenness—with robbery—a robbery, too, committed under the most aggravating circumstances of guilt, involving a breach of trust of the most flagrant description. And moreover, in this instance, the man's master, so far from ever having himself spoken ill of his servant, had the highest opinion of his trustfulness and integrity, and invariably spoke of him in the highest terms. Besides all this, I had not a tittle of evidence to disprove his right to his master's confidence—nothing but my bare suspicions—the morbid effect of a naturally suspicious nature, I suppose. It was thus I argued as I walked home after my interview with Mr. Frankman. Reason and common sense seemed both against my conclusions, but they were not shaken a bit. I continued obstinately to accuse the Softlys in my mind, though I "pooh-poohed" the idea with my lips.

"Well," thought I, "at all events I must do something." It was still early in the day, about eleven o'clock; I should just be in time for the 11.30 train; so I hailed a cab, jumped in, and told the man to go to the ____ station as fast as he could.

Northcourt was about fifty miles from London, and the station at which I was to get down (which we will call Gravelly) was barely a mile from the house. Arriving at Gravelly, I immediately started on foot for Mr. Winter's residence: it was a sultry afternoon, and I walked slowly, endeavouring to form some plan of proceeding, but I could hit upon nothing. I could inspect the premises and ask questions; but all this had been done already, and to no purpose. So on I walked, pondering and racking my brain for an idea; and in that state of uncertainty I arrived at Northcourt. "I will trust to accident," I said to myself, as I rang the bell. I wanted, if possible, to see Mr. Winter before the butler had seen me, though I scarcely knew why; for certainly I had no intention of commencing my compaign by denouncing Softly to his master. The door was opened by a footman in a smart livery.

"Is Mr. Winter at home?" I asked.

"He is in the stable yard, sir, but he will be in presently," replied the man.

"Mr. Softly, he is in I suppose?" I don't know why I said that because I hoped he was not, I believe.

"Oh yes, he is in;" and then he added, as though my inquiring for Softly had put it into his head, which, no doubt, it had, "You are come about the butler's place, sir, I suppose." Here was the chance, here was "the accident;" and I was not slow in taking advantage of it.

"Oh, here is master," said the footman.

I turned round, and saw a tall, thin, elderly man coming towards me.

I touched my hat, and the footman said something to him, explaining my object, I suppose. He told me to follow him into his study, and began to catechise me as to my last place, my character, recommendations, etc., when I stopped him, telling him that I had not come, as the footman supposed, to look for the situation of butler, but that I was an officer in the detective force, sent down from London to endeavour, if possible, to discover the authors of the late robbery at his house. I further told him that the moment the footman had asked me the question about the butler's place, it had occurred to me that it might be useful to assume that character; and if, therefore, Mr. Winter thought good, I would take up my residence at Northcourt for a short time, in the capacity of butler; but I insisted on one thing, namely, entire secrecy as to my true character. I assured him that if a breath of suspicion was raised as to that, my plan would be defeated. After some little demur on his part, he agreed, though he said he did not expect any good result from my sojourn in his house. I saw very clearly that he did not relish the implied suspicion of some one in the house, to which my plan very plainly pointed. Indeed, he asked me point-blank if I suspected any of the servants; I replied that I had no actual grounds of suspicion against any one; but that, all other means having failed, I should like to put this scheme of mine into practice as a last resource, though I candidly acknowledged that I was not myself very sanguine of success.

A man, however rich he may be, does not give up 2000£ worth of plate without a struggle, especially when great part of it is old family plate, that could not be replaced. Mr. Winter therefore agreed to my plan; I was to be taken upon trial; Softly was to leave in a fortnight; and as this was my first situation as butler, having hitherto acted only in the humbler capacity of serving-man, I was to come at once, that I might learn some of the duties of my new profession under the careful guidance of Mr. Softly.

Before leaving, I was introduced both to the butler and the housekeeper. They received me very kindly, Softly especially so: he said he was glad his master had engaged me; he had no doubt I should do very well; it was a very easy place; and, for his part, he should be delighted to put me up to any little peculiarity of his master's; more than that he was certain I should not require: I knew my business well enough, he was sure. Why he was it would be difficult to say; but, however, he was very civil, and moreover exactly the sort of person I expected to find him. He was about fifty years old, short, stout, of a florid complexion, with thin, light, sandy sort of hair, rather bald, and with a pair of restless grey eyes, which were never quiet for a moment. To say that he never looked me in the face would not be strictly true: he very frequently did, when I was not looking at him; but he never met my eye if he could help it; the instant I observed him, he *snatched* his eyes from my face, as it were, to come back again when the coast was clear.

Mrs. Softly was a little woman, somewhat prim and starched in her manner; she had fewer characteristics than her husband, and was probably, I settled, entirely under his control.

I was to return to London that evening for my clothes, and to come back to Northcourt, to enter upon the duties of my new situation, on the morrow.

It had been agreed between Mr. Winter and me that I should take the name of Hunt, with whom he had been in correspondence, and had just decided not to take; but this determination Softly did not know, whilst he *did* know of the correspondence. The object of this arrangement was that no suspicion might be raised in his mind on account of my very sudden engagement. I expressed to Mr. Winter my surprise at hearing that Softly was leaving him: so old and valued a servant, I said, would be a great loss to him I feared. He said he would indeed, but that he could not think of standing in the way of his advancement in life: he (Softly) had taken a violent fancy into his head that he could make his fortune in Australia, and consequently to Australia he was going; he did not think Mrs. Softly much fancied the plan, but she had been talked over, he supposed, by her husband; and he hoped they would succeed, for they were a worthy couple, and had served him and Mrs. Winter faithfully for many years.

"How long," I asked, "has this Australian scheme been on foot, Mr. Winter?"

"Oh, for some months—it must be six months, and more than that, since Softly first spoke to me about it. Poor fellow," he added, "he was nearly giving it up when that robbery occurred; he offered to do so if I wished it; he said he would stay here, and serve me for nothing, till the loss of the plate was made good, if he lived as long; indeed, he said more than that—he actually offered to give me 1000£ which he had saved, he and his wife, during their service, towards repaying the loss of the plate, for which he always blamed himself, though quite needlessly I think. Of course I did not listen to either of his proposals; but they tell well for the man's feelings—poor Softly!"

I made no comment, and shortly after my interview with Softly and his wife I took my leave, declining Mr. Winter's kind offer of sending me to the station in his dog-cart.

I wanted to be quite alone for an hour or two; so, after I had walked about half the distance to the station, I turned off the road into a wood, and, selecting a shady spot under a fine old beech, I lay down at full length, to cool myself and to think over my future proceedings. In this comfortable situation, after the heat and dust of the road, I not unnaturally fell asleep: I must have slept for some time, for when I awoke the sun was getting low, and the trees were casting long shadows over the opposite slope. I was just looking at my watch, to see if I was in time for the 7.30 up train from Gravelly, when I heard footsteps approaching; presently the sound of a man's voice came distinctly on my ear; I started, for I knew the voice instantly: it was Softly's; some one answered him: there were two there, but I did not recognise the second voice. A path ran through the wood, near to the old beech under which I was lying, and along this path the two men were walking. I could not see them, the bushes were too thick; but as they came nearer I could hear what they said plain enough: they were strolling leisurely along.

"What sort of fellow does he look like?" said the stranger.

"Oh, nothing particular—a good sort of a young man enough, I dare say," replied Softly.

"And the squire has engaged him, has he?"

"Yes, as good as engaged him: he is to come to-morrow on trial;

he is to be placed under my instructions; I am to teach him his duty."

"Ha! ha!" laughed the stranger, "no one better able; but is he a sharp fellow, likely to suspect anything, or to pry about, and meddle with matters in which he has no concern?"

"Not he; he will never set the Thames on fire; he seems a good-humoured, easy-going young man, as I said before; but there's not much in him—I saw that at once."

"Ah, well, all right, then—don't want—lurking—my house——"

And that was all I could hear; they had passed by too far for me to catch another syllable, though I listened with all my ears, for I was very anxious to hear what more they had to say.

I dared not attempt to follow them, as I should certainly have been heard in forcing my way through the bushes. I was therefore obliged to content myself with what I had got, and that, though apparently very little, I considered a good deal, for it confirmed my suspicions of the butler. It was quite evident that he had something to conceal, and it did not require a conjuror to discover what that something was.

But the fellow's impudence! I have not much in me, haven't I?—a soft easy-going sort of chap, eh?—capital!—and I chuckled to myself as I walked towards the station.

Thinks I to myself, thinks I, "I'll make you dance to another tune, Master Softly, before we part, or I'm much mistaken:—not much in me, eh?"

The fact is, I was rather nettled, I suspect, at old Softly's mean opinion of me, though I didn't own it.

I was in plenty of time for the 7.30 P.M. train to London, where I arrived in due time.

The next day I packed up my things and started back for Gravelly; there I found a dog-cart waiting to convey me and my portmanteau to Northcourt. I got there just as the servants were going to dinner. I accordingly joined them, and after dinner adjourned to the housekeeper's room to discuss divers good things, only allowed to upper servants. I will not break faith, and betray those whose salt I have eaten; but I strongly suspect that masters and mistresses have very little idea of the exceedingly small difference which often exists between the eating and drinking of the housekeeper's room and the dining room.

I found the Softlys as agreeable and condescending as people in their high position could be towards a tyro like myself; they imagined this to be my first introduction, as an inmate, to "the room," and consequently expected me to be rather overawed by the grandeur of the furniture, and the superior elegance of their own manners and behaviour over what they supposed my natural sphere, the servants' hall. It was very amusing. I frequently sought occasion to talk with Softly about the late robbery, although never allowing him to suppose that I was more interested in the affair than as a piece of gossip. If he seemed inclined to enter into it, which at first he was not, I listened attentively; if, on the contrary, he tried to shirk the subject, I always allowed him to do so, nay, helped him—so fearful was I of raising his suspicions.

Softly had one great fault: he was too fond of the bottle. I never saw him drunk; I don't believe any one ever did; but I saw him muddled very frequently during the fortnight I was at Northcourt. I could not for some time make out how it was he got muddled, for he drank very little at dinner, and very little in "the room," and he was scarcely ever in the pantry by himself: when he had done his work, he always came into the housekeeper's room, and sat there; he liked the company of the ladies, he used gallantly to say.

At length I discovered that Softly, in his afternoon walks, invariably looked in at "The Winter Arms," a public-house in the village, kept by a man of the name of Soak. This Soak held but an indifferent character in the neighbourhood; he had formerly been under-gamekeeper to Mr. Winter, but had been dismissed upon suspicion of selling the game—a suspicion which, I was told, amounted in point of fact to certainty. He was a married man, and had a large family; and Mr. Winter, who was the kindest hearted and most credulous man I ever saw, pitying his destitute condition, and relying on his promises of amendment, allowed him to take "The Winter Arms," lending him a sum of money to begin with.

About a week after my arrival at Northcourt I was sent into the village with a message from Mrs. Winter; when, just as I was passing "The Winter Arms," out bolted Softly in my very face, and immediately behind him stood a dark, tall, ill-looking man, with whom he had evidently just parted.

Softly turned very red at first, but quickly recovering himself said to the man in the doorway, "You'll be sure to send those things up as soon as they arrive."

"Yes, yes, Mr. Softly, you shall have 'em directly they come, depend upon that." I started—I had heard that voice before—but when? I could not call to mind that I had ever seen the man, but his voice I was perfectly certain I had heard.

Softly explained to me that he had been speaking to Soak about a barrel of beer, or porter, or something that ought to have been left at his house by somebody—the carrier, or the railway man; but the fact was I didn't hear, or at least take in, a word he said; there was a confused murmuring in my ear all the time he was talking, but what it was I had no idea. I was thinking the whole time where it was I had heard that man's voice—it was so strange that I could not recognise his face!

At length it struck me all of a sudden. "I have it!" I cried in my excitement. "You have it! what is it you have?" said Softly, in the greatest astonishment. I saw my imprudence, and for an instant I was quite abroad; I didn't know what to do. Luckily for me Softly was not so great a conjuror as he fancied himself. By an adroit turn of the conversation his attention was diverted to another topic.

Softly was not naturally a sharp fellow, but the consciousness of danger had engendered suspicion.

We parted at the stable-yard gate; he said he must go in, as he had something to attend to, but there was no occasion for me to come in unless I chose.

Part II.

"Oh! oh!" said I, as soon as my friend Softly had disappeared; "so it was you, Mr. Soak, was it, whose voice I heard in the wood with the butler? Come, come! the plot begins to thicken." I strolled into the village again, and passed the Winter Arms. Mr. Soak was sitting on a bench with his back against the wall of his house, a pipe in his mouth, and a jug of ale on the table before him. I entered into conversation with him, but he was not very sociably inclined; he gave me rather short answers, and so I did not think it expedient to touch upon the robbery. "I'll bide my time," thinks I; "it won't do to hurry matters." I had, almost immediately after my arrival at Northcourt, struck up an acquaintance with Sarah the under housemaid. She had, it will be remembered, been the first to discover the burglary, and had also found the Softlys bound hand and foot in their bed.

Sarah was a stout, rosy-cheeked girl, of about eighteen years, cheerful and chatty in general, but occasionally visited with musing fits, which seemed to me unnatural for one of her age and spirits. We soon became great friends. I talked to her frequently about the late robbery, and very soon satisfied myself that she knew more than she chose to tell; for she was too young to be able to keep a secret from one so accustomed to worm them out as myself. I cross-questioned her a good deal, though with apparent indifference, as to the state in which she found Softly and his wife—whether they were red in the face, or black in the face, whether they complained of being in pain; which was tied the tightest; and, as I expected, she grew confused and red, and contradicted herself several times: it was quite evident that she had never been cross-examined on the subject before. Why the authorities had taken it for granted that her statements were all true, and why they never suspected the possibility of deception on her part, it would be hard to say. It seemed clear to me that she had been repeating a lesson, which some of my questions had confused, and had caused her to trip and stumble somewhat. For instance, I asked her whether she found the Softlys' door locked or unlocked. She said "unlocked."

"It is very odd it should have been so," I remarked. "One would have thought that the burglars, such finished workmen as they appeared to have been, would have known their business better than to leave the door unlocked; a turn of the key would have been very little trouble, and would have prevented either Softly or his wife from getting out of the room, even if they had got their hands and legs free: time was, of course, a great object with the robbers."

"Oh yes, to be sure!" said poor Sarah; "how ever could I make such a mistake? The door *was* locked sir, of course. I remember turning the key now, and wondering why it was locked." I looked at her as she said this: her face was scarlet. I quite pitied the poor girl as she remarked that "she had made a mistake"—"*in her lesson*," she might have added.

I then talked to her of the wickedness of the deed, and how every one implicated in it would be punished when they were caught, which, sooner or later, they would surely be; "even those," I said, "who know of the robbery and conceal it will be as severely dealt with as the actual perpetrators, unless they have the honesty and good sense to come forward and make a clean breast of it": in that case, I doubted not, that any one who had no hand in the actual robbery would be forgiven. Sarah listened to all this attentively, and she fidgeted about, and seemed frightened and uneasy in her mind; but she never made any answer. Once or twice I thought she really was going to confess all. She told me she had something to say to me, something about which she wanted to ask my advice; but she never got any further. After trying to make me promise not to breathe it to any one—which promise of course I managed to evade—she would burst out crying, and say she could not tell me! and then it was in vain attempting to get anything out of her. I felt satisfied that she was an accomplice in the robbery, though to what extent I could not guess. I had no doubt she had been bribed, probably with a new dress, to assist in some minor way, and I was really anxious to get her to confess, for I liked and pitied the girl. I was sure she was not naturally dishonest; and I had no doubt that even in this business she had been imposed on, and had not been told the extent and magnitude of the crime in which she had been implicated, and from which I felt certain she would gladly release herself if she dared.

Of course, upon such strong suspicion I was authorized to arrest her, and I had little doubt but that, in her terror, she would have disclosed all; but then she certainly did not know where the plate had been taken to, and I wanted to get *that*, as well as the burglars.

The moment she was arrested, the plate would have gone into the melting-pot, and that was exactly what I wished to avoid. At present I felt pretty sure that it was still plate, and safely packed somewhere or other, ready for a start to Australia. So I kept the arresting of Sarah as a last resource, determined to act upon that if all other means failed. The time was now drawing nigh when the Softlys would leave Northcourt. I had become on very friendly terms with Softly, and had accompanied him more than once to the Winter Arms, and drank a glass of brandy and water with him. Brandy I discovered to be the particular liquor favoured by Mr. Softly. It was strange that his man could rob his master of 2000£ worth of plate, and yet not drink his brandy; he might have done so, I am convinced, with perfect impunity, for the keys of the cellar, as well as of the plate-chest too, were in his keeping: but no, he never did; a glass or two of sherry or port now and then, just the end or the beginning of the bottles, was the extent of his depredations, as far as I ever saw. I used to frequent the Winter Arms chiefly for the purpose of getting on friendly terms with Mr. Soak, but I never succeeded; that worthy regarded me with eyes of suspicion up to the last moment of my stay at Northcourt; he was a very cunning fellow, and a difficult customer to manage. If ever I ventured an observation about the burglary in his presence, his eyes were upon me in an instant; he watched me as a cat would watch a mouse, ready to spring on me if I had said a word to justify his suspicions. I was therefore obliged to be very cautious; not that I was afraid of the man, but I was afraid of his finding out my true character.

Softly had been very busy packing several large trunks and chests ready for his start to the other side of the globe, and he had asked me to help him, which of course I did. It amused me very much to see the display of honesty he made; he over-did it, of course: those sort of people always do; and instead of allaying, he confirmed my previous suspicions or rather conviction of his roguery.

He had not only ostentatiously paraded before my eyes every single thing he put into his boxes, but he even went the length of unpacking one large chest, under the pretence that it was badly packed; and more than that, when they were all finished and corded, and we sat down and wiped our brows, for it had been hard work, he said, "There! you're witness that I've nothing in any of these boxes that don't belong to me, Hunt! One doesn't like to leave a house so soon after a robbery has been committed with a suspicion on one's character, you know; though master would as soon suspect, I don't know who, as me!—his own wife almost."

"Oh you precious rascal! to abuse such trust and confidence," I thought.

My bed-room was at the end of a long passage, and immediately facing my door were the stairs leading up to the maids' rooms. On the first landing, in a small room, slept Sarah: why an under house-maid should have a room to herself, when the upper housemaid shared hers with the upper laundry-maid, was in itself a suspicious circumstance, at least so it appeared to me. I asked Sarah the reason one day, and she was again suffused with blushes, and stammered out something about "Mary—house—and the laundry-maid being cousins, and so they wished to share their room." Next to Sarah's room was a housemaid's closet, where pails, brushes, mops, brooms, and all sorts of things were kept; it was a very narrow, dark, deep closet, and had evidently been taken off Sarah's room, from which it was divided merely by a lath and plaster partition: so thin at the end of the closet, that I had little difficulty in making a hole with my knife, sufficiently large to enable me to see into the room when nec-essary. I had examined it one day when Sarah was engaged else-where, and had observed that in one corner the paper was torn and ragged: it was accordingly exactly behind that spot that I made my incision, one piece of torn paper more or less not being likely to be discovered.

For many nights I passed hours in that closet, but neither heard nor saw anything to repay me for my trouble; but still I persevered, for I felt sure that some one would pay Sarah a visit before long. I had overheard Mrs. Softly whispering to Sarah; I had come sud-denly upon them once or twice when they were evidently holding very secret and confidential communication, and felt pretty certain that these interrupted conversations would have to be finished at some future time, and no time so likely as the dead of night. I was satisfied that my exhortations to Sarah about the wickedness of the robbery had not been thrown away; neither had my assertions regarding the punishment which would sooner or later overtake the burglars and all connected with them. She several times referred to that, and also to the probability of forgiveness which any one, not the actual perpetrator of the robbery, might obtain: by this I could see that she repented of her part, whatever it was, in the transaction; and no doubt this repentance had been noticed by the Softlys, who would naturally be both averse to, and alarmed at it, and would do all they could to bring back her mind to their way of thinking on the subject. That this was the cause of their frequent conferences I was pretty sure, from several words which I had caught at different times addressed to Sarah, both by Softly and his wife.

I may as well say here, that although I watched Softly and Soak as closely as possible, and used my utmost endeavours to circumvent them, to entrap one or the other into some sort of an admission by way of a thread to catch hold of, however tangled a skein it might be, to guide me in my search, I never could overhear but one word likely to be of the slightest service to me: that word was "Hardy."

I had been feigning sleep, as I frequently did when in company with those two worthies; my arms were on the table, and my head on my arms. Softly and Soak had been whispering together for about ten minutes, and I was straining every nerve to hear what they were saying, but in vain; when Softly said rather louder than usual, "What name did you say?"—"Hardy," replied Soak. "But hold your tongue, can't you!"

He did hold his tongue, or at all events he modulated it below my power of hearing, and I thought very little of my grand discovery: it wasn't likely that Hardy would help me to get back Mr. Winter's plate. Much I thought; but, according to the habits of a detective, I took a note of the name the moment I was alone.

And now the Softlys had only two more nights to spend at Northcourt. I was in my usual place at midnight, although I began to think myself a great blockhead for passing so many hours to no purpose in that dark, uncomfortable closet: still, there I was, and after remaining an hour, I began seriously to think of going to bed, and of giving up these nightly vigils; but upon second thoughts I determined to stay where I was. "Only two more nights of it, the two most likely nights, too! I won't give it up," I said to myself; and scarcely had I said so, when I thought I heard a board creak on the stairs. Breathlessly I listened, my flagging energies all alive in a moment; in a few seconds there was another creak—then another—but no sound of a footstep; the person coming had no shoes on, I was sure of that. Presently I heard a hand upon the door of the closet in which I was; the handle turned—the door was opened—it was pitch dark, and I could see nothing.

"Sarah! Sarah!" whispered a voice I well knew. Footsteps now advanced into the closet; nearer and nearer they drew to me; when suddenly down clattered a mop, or a broom, on the top of a tin hip-bath, which I knew of old, and always gave a wide berth to when I entered my hiding-place.

"Dear me! oh! whatever is that?" cried terrified Mrs. Softly.

I heard Sarah's door open, and immediately after her voice was at the door of the closet. "Mrs. Softly, you have gone wrong," she said; "this way; give me your hand—you've got into the closet."

And then I heard footsteps retreating, and presently a light was struck in Sarah's room, and I looked through my chink, and there were Sarah and Mrs. Softly sitting on the bed, not five feet from my look-out. It would unnecessarily lengthen this (I fear) already too long story, were I to relate all I saw and heard through the hole in the wall; I will, therefore, briefly state that Mrs. Softly counted out five-and-twenty sovereigns on the bed. "There," she said; "now,

Sarah, you and Tom Dark can marry as soon as you please. And as for the plate, why what great matter is it to master, a few bits of silver more or less, rich as he is? He'll soon get more in its stead; but you, if you was such a fool as to let this opportunity slip by, might wait long enough before you could get five-and-twenty sovereigns together; and as for Tom Dark, he'd get tired of waiting, and no blame to him either."

With such talk the artful woman combated all Sarah's scruples, laughing at them, at her, and at the robbery itself, which she treated as a capital stroke of cunning and ingenuity—making all their fortunes and hurting no one. Her strongest weapon, however, was Tom Dark; she worked him well and effectually: it was evident that Sarah was much attached to him, and that, but for him, she would neither have entered into the conspiracy at first, nor have kept to it then; but her love, aided by cunning Mrs. Softly's sophistry, carried the day. She took the twenty-five pounds, which sum was ten pounds more than had been originally promised her (it was easy to understand why the bribe was increased), and promised secrecy as to the robbery, now and for ever. I could plainly see that her better feelings rebelled against what she was doing; but her love for Tom Dark was too strong for her honesty—and she fell.

With regard to the plate itself, the only clue to its existence I got hold of, was a promise on Mrs. Softly's part that two or three old family relics, which Sarah pleaded for, knowing how much Mr. Winter valued them, should be returned. Of course I knew they would not be; but I believed in their existence, feeling sure that, had they gone through the fire, Mrs. Softly would at once have said so, as that would have relieved her from the necessity of a useless falsehood. After more than an hour's conversation, the housekeeper crept silently away, and I stole off to my room.

Nothing further occurred at Northcourt. The morning of the Softlys' departure arrived. I accompanied them to London, having, I told Softly, some business there. He seemed at first averse to the arrangement, I thought, though he said nothing; but he very soon got over any feeling of the sort, and indeed, several times on our way up, said how glad he was that I was with them: it broke the parting (the hypocrite!), having some one with them whom they knew, and hoped that I would come on board "The Caroline," and see them off: they were to sail that afternoon at five o'clock.

I promised to be there in time—a promise I was not very likely to break. We parted at the station. The Softlys had a good deal to do—things to buy, and people to part from: they should not be on board before four o'clock, they said. It was then half-past eleven.

The moment they left me I took a cab, and drove to Scotland

Yard. I saw my chief for five minutes, told him that I hoped before night to be able to report good news, and applied for an assistant.

My chief asked no questions, only smiled, and said, "Certainly; take any one you please." I accordingly chose a steady, un-policeman looking young man of the name of Tough, and started for Blackwall, where "The Caroline" was lying.

The moment we arrived on board I asked for the captain. Unfortunately he was on shore, and not expected back till near the time of sailing, but the first mate was at my service. I had rather have spoken with the captain, but there was no alternative. I told the mate who I was, and what was my mission (having first bound him to secrecy). I then asked for a list of his freight, with the names of those at Melbourne to whom boxes were directed or consigned. After some little delay I obtained this list, but the name I looked for was not there.

I then spoke to the steward: "Had any boxes belonging to the passengers arrived on board yet?"

"Oh yes, a good many."

"Have any arrived for Mr. or Mrs. Softly?"

"No, none."

"They have a cabin to themselves, of course?"

"Oh yes, certainly, one of the best."

I would go and see it.

I went below, and the very first thing my eyes lighted on, as the steward showed me into the cabin, was a large chest. I walked up to it, and looked at the direction:—

"Mr. Hardy,

Melbourne."

"Favoured by}
Mr. Softly."}

A smile of triumph rose to my lips. Here it was at last. I had run my game to earth, sure enough.

"I thought you told me that nothing had come on board for Mr. Softly?" I said to the steward.

"I had forgotten this box, sir; it came on board late last night, after I was gone to bed. I was told of it this morning, but forgot all about it."

I saw that the man was speaking the truth. I tried to lift the chest, but couldn't move it with my utmost strength.

Quite satisfied, I left the cabin, and went upon deck.

Of course I did not leave the ship again. About four o'clock the captain came on board. I immediately told him my name and business, and the discovery I had made. He promptly offered me every assistance in his power towards capturing the Softlys. "All I want you to do," I replied, "is simply this: the moment the Softlys come

on board, before they have time to go below, say out loud: 'A chest
has come on board directed to "Mr. Hardy, Melbourne," favoured
by some one—does it belong to any one here?' Say that, captain, if
you please, and leave the rest to me."

He promised he would do so. We had scarcely done speaking
when the Softlys appeared, with a boat full of luggage.

Mrs. Softly came up the side first, her husband following close.
The instant his foot touched the deck, the captain spoke—"Does any
one here own a chest, directed to 'Mr. Hardy, Melbourne?' "

"Yes, I do; where is it?" said Softly, quickly.

"In your cabin, sir," replied the captain.

"Oh, it's all right, it belongs to me—that is to say, it is in my
care." So saying, he went below, his wife staying on deck to see
their luggage safe out of the boat. I beckoned to Tough, and followed Softly. I opened the door of his cabin, and walked in: he was
standing before the chest, looking at it with a very well satisfied
smile on his countenance, which he was destined soon to lose. He
started on seeing me; but, recovering himself in a moment: "Ah,
Hunt!" he said, "come to have a look at our cabin? Not a very grand
affair; not so big as the pantry at Northcourt; but it will serve our
turn, I dare say. Why, what now?"

I placed my hand on his shoulder. "Mr. Softly, you are my
prisoner: that chest contains Mr. Winter's plate."

He turned deadly pale, but spoke not a word. At that moment
Tough entered, and, at a sign from me, slipped the handcuffs on. At
the touch of the cold iron, Softly started and shrunk back; but resistance was useless, and he felt it to be so. Utterly dejected and
cowed, he sank upon the chest, and, covering his face with his
hands, he sobbed aloud. He was a poor, pitiful, cowardly rogue.

Little more remains to be told. Softly and his wife were placed
in safe custody, and I returned to Northcourt that night, taking
Tough with me. Immediately upon my arrival I arrested Soak, and,
very much against my will, poor Sarah.

Mr. Winter was thunderstruck when I told him that I had discovered the burglars, and who they were. The ingratitude of Softly
and his wife affected him far more than the loss of the plate had
done.

Sarah was allowed to turn queen's evidence against the rest,
though without any promise of pardon. Her statement of the burglary was as follows. The plate was all taken, she believed, to the
"Winter Arms" in the first place; where it went to afterwards she
never knew. When it was all removed, Softly and Soak took out the
pane of glass in the dining-room; Soak then tied and gagged the
Softlys, she (Sarah) assisting him. When this was done, it was time
for her to begin her day's work; accordingly, she went down stairs,

saw the pane of glass out of the dining-room window, and gave the alarm, as previously agreed on. The rest is known.

On searching the "Winter Arms," several pieces of the missing plate were discovered.

The evidence against all the prisoners was conclusive. The two Softlys and Soak were transported for life. Sarah was pardoned, as much in consideration of her artless and simple character, which had been so shamefully imposed upon by her wicked and unscrupulous fellow-servants, as on account of the important evidence she had given.

Nearly ten years after the events above recorded, I received a letter, dated Toronto, Upper Canada, and signed "Sarah Dark." It was, I may say, a beautiful letter. The writer began by thanking me for my kindness to her when at Northcourt, and for my endeavours to persuade her to do what was right. She said that she had been on the point of confessing all to me a hundred times, but that her love for Tom Dark had prevented her; she would, had she confessed, have been obliged to give up the twenty-five pounds bribe, and then she could not have married him.

"But," she went on to say, "I have learnt that one must not do evil that good may come of it—for good never will come of it." And then she said that, although pardoned by the judge, she could never pardon herself, and that her shame was so great that she could not remain in her own country, and she had told Tom Dark so; whereupon he, who still loved her in spite of her wickedness, had proposed marrying at once and emigrating. Her family and friends all looked coldly on her: she had no chance of getting another situation: in short, she consented, and a month after the trial they were on the sea, bound for America.

For two or three years they had a hard struggle to live; but after that it pleased God, in his great mercy, to make them acquainted with the Rev. J. M——: of him, she declared, she could never speak or think without tears of love and gratitude filling her eyes.

He had found them almost destitute and despairing; for Tom was sick, and had been unable to earn a penny for several months past. "Mr. J. M—— visited us daily," she wrote, "after he first found us out. He relieved our temporal wants; but oh! Mr. Clutch, he did better, far better than that; he read the Bible to us, and explained it as I never had heard it explained before; and I was so miserable on account of my past sins, that one day I fell down on my knees as he was reading about the Prodigal Son, and I said, whilst my tears blinded and almost choked me, "Oh, Mr. M——, I have sinned so dreadful!' and then I told him everything. Yes, Mr. Clutch, everything, I kept back nothing; and, would you believe it, he cried too: he did indeed, and he said, 'Joy shall be in heaven over one sinner that repenteth, more than over ninety and nine just persons, which need no repentance.' I could not understand that blessed passage, then, Mr. Clutch, as well as I can now; but I have, through the kindness and patience of dear Mr. M——, been brought to a sense of my own sinful nature, and I now read the Bible daily, and love it; and Tom and I have now got over all our troubles, and he has plenty of work. I thought you would like to hear of our well doing, and so I took the liberty to write to you.

"I return thanks on my bended knees every night for His great and undeserved mercies to me; and I do not forget you in my prayers, Mr. Clutch, for it was you who first put my sin plainly before me, and made me wish to get rid of it."

It was, as I have said, a beautiful letter. I am not ashamed to own that it brought the tears into my eyes.

MARY BRADDON

(1835–1915) (Mrs. John Maxwell) was the most popular lady novelist of the nineteenth century. Her famous work, Lady Audley's Secret *(1861–1862), went through scores of editions in Great Britain and America and was performed countless times in many stage versions. It is the story, as is well known, of a beautiful lady who tumbled a superfluous husband into a well. In addition to being a best seller, it has been highly regarded by the critics. As Thackeray said of it, "If I could plot as well as Miss Braddon, I would be the greatest novelist in the English language."*

Miss Braddon wrote more than seventy novels and many short stories; her exact bibliography is not clear because of anonymous and pseudonymous work. She was also editor of Belgravia Magazine *and the mainstay of her husband's publishing house. Most of her early fiction contains crime, mystery, and detection, but it must be admitted that her work is not uniform in quality.*

"Levison's Victim"

"Have you seen Horace Wynward?"

"No. You don't mean to say that he is here?"

"He is indeed. I saw him last night; and I think I never saw a man so much changed in so short a time."

"For the worse?"

"Infinitely for the worse. I should scarcely have recognised him but for that peculiar look in his eyes, which I dare say you remember."

"Yes; deep-set gray eyes, with an earnest penetrating look that seems to read one's most hidden thoughts. I'm very sorry to hear of this change in him. We were at Oxford together, you know; and his place is near my father's in Buckinghamshire. We have been fast friends for a long time; but I lost sight of him about two years ago, before I went on my Spanish rambles, and I've heard nothing of him since. Do you think he has been leading a dissipated life—going the pace a little too violently?"

"I don't know what he has been doing; but I fancy he must have been travelling during the last year or two, for I've never come across him in London."

"Did you speak to him last night?"

"No; I wanted very much to get hold of him for a few minutes' chat, but couldn't manage it. It was in one of the gambling-rooms I saw him, on the opposite side of the table. The room was crowded. He was standing looking on at the game over the heads of the players. You know how tall he is, and what a conspicuous figure anywhere. I saw him one minute, and in the next he had disappeared. I left the rooms in search of him, but he was not to be seen anywhere."

"I shall try and hunt him up to-morrow. He must be stopping at one of the hotels. There can't be much difficulty in finding him."

The speakers were two young Englishmen; the scene a lamp-lit grove of trees outside the Kursaal of a German spa. The elder, George Theobald, was a barrister of the Inner Temple; the younger, Francis Lorrimore, was the son and heir of a Buckinghamshire squire, and a gentlemen at large.

"What was the change that struck you so painfully, George?" Lorrimore asked between the puffs of his cigar; "you couldn't have seen much of Wynward in that look across the gaming-table."

"I saw quite enough. His face has a worn, haggard expression, he looks like a man who never sleeps; and there's a fierceness about the eyes—a contraction of the brows, a kind of restless searching look—as if he were on the watch for someone or something. In short, the poor fellow seemed to me altogether queer—the sort of man one would expect to hear of as being shut up in a madhouse, or committing suicide, or something bad of that kind."

"I shall certainly hunt him out, George."

"It would be only a kindness to do so, old fellow, as you and he have been intimate. Stay!" exclaimed Mr. Theobald, pointing suddenly to a figure in the distance. "Do you see that tall man under the trees yonder? I've a notion it's the very man we're talking of."

They rose from the bench on which they had been sitting smoking their cigars for the last half-hour, and walked in the direction of the tall figure pacing slowly under the pine trees. There was no mistaking that muscular frame—six-feet-two, if an inch—and the peculiar carriage of the head. Frank Lorrimore touched his friend lightly on the shoulder, and he turned round suddenly and faced the two young men, staring at them blankly, without a sign of recognition.

Yes, it was indeed a haggard face, with a latent fierceness in the deep-set gray eyes overshadowed by strongly marked black brows, but a face which, seen at its best, must needs have been very handsome.

"Wynward," said Frank, "don't you know me?"

Lorrimore held out both his hands. Wynward took one of them slowly, looking at him like a man suddenly awakened from sleep.

"Yes," he said, "I know you well enough now, Frank, but you startled me just this moment. I was thinking. How well you're looking old fellow! What, you here too, Theobald?"

"Yes, I saw you in the rooms last night," answered Theobald as they shook hands; "but you were gone before I could get a chance of speaking to you. Where are you staying?"

"At the Hotel des Etrangers. I shall be off to-morrow."

"Don't run away in such a hurry, Horace," said Frank; "it looks as if you wanted to cut us."

"I'm not very good company just now; you'd scarcely care to see much of me."

"You are not looking very well, Horace, certainly. Have you been ill?"

"No, I am never ill; I am made of iron, you know."

"But there's something wrong, I'm afraid."

"There is something wrong, but nothing that sympathy or friendship can mend."

"Don't say that, my dear fellow. Come to breakfast with me to-morrow, and tell me your troubles."

"It's a common story enough; I shall only bore you."

"I think you ought to know me better than that."

"Well, I'll come if you like," Horace Wynward answered in a softer tone; "I'm not very much given to confide in friendship, but you were once a kind of younger brother of mine, Frank. Yes, I'll come. How long have you been here?"

"I only came yesterday. I am at the Couronne d'Or, where I discovered my friend Theobald, happily for me, at the *table d'hôte*. I am going back to Buckinghamshire next week. Have you been at Crofton lately?"

"No; Crofton has been shut up for the last two years. The old housekeeper is there, of course, and there are men to keep the gardens in order. I shouldn't like the idea of my mother's flower-garden being neglected; but I doubt if I shall ever live at Crofton."

"Not when you marry, Horace?"

"Marry? Yes, when that event occurs I may change my mind," he answered, with a scornful laugh.

"Ah, Horace, I see there is a woman at the bottom of your trouble!"

Wynward took no notice of this remark, and began to talk of indifferent subjects.

The three young men walked for some time under the pines, smoking and talking in a fragmentary manner. Horace Wynward had an absent-minded way, which was not calculated to promote a lively style of conversation; but the others indulged his humour, and did not demand much from him. It was late when they shook hands and separated.

"At ten o'clock to-morrow, Horace?" said Frank.

"I shall be with you at ten. Good night."

Mr. Lorrimore ordered an excellent breakfast, and a little before ten o'clock awaited his friend in a pretty sitting-room overlooking the gardens of the hotel. He had been dreaming of Horace all night, and was thinking of him as he walked up and down the room waiting his arrival. As the little clock on the mantelpiece struck the hour, Mr. Wynward was announced. His clothes were dusty, and he had a tired look even at that early hour. Frank welcomed him heartily.

"You look as if you had been walking, Horace," he said, as they sat down to breakfast.

"I have been on the hills since five o'clock this morning."

"So early?"

"Yes, I am a bad sleeper. It is better to walk than to lie tossing about hour after hour, thinking the same thoughts, with maddening repetition."

"My dear boy, you will make yourself ill with this kind of life."

"Don't I tell you that I am never ill? I never had a day's illness in my life. I suppose when I die I shall go down at a shot—apoplexy or heart disease. Men of my build generally do."

"I hope you may have a long life."

"Yes, a long life of emptiness."

"Why shouldn't it be a useful, happy life, Horace?"

"Because it was shipwrecked two years ago. I set sail for a given port, Frank, with a fair wind in my favour; and my ship went down in sight of land, on a summer's day, without a moment's warning. I can't rig another boat, and make for another harbour, as some men can. All my world's wealth was adventured in this one argosy. That sounds tall talk, doesn't it? but you see there is such a thing as passion in the world, and I've so much faith in your sympathy that I'm not ashamed to tell you what a fool I have been, and still am. You were such a romantic fellow five years ago, Frank, and I used to laugh at your sentimental notions."

"Yes, I was obliged to stand a good deal of ridicule from you."

"Let those laugh who win. It was in my last long vacation that I went to read at a quiet little village on the Sussex coast, with a re-tired tutor, an eccentric old fellow, but a miracle of learning. He had three daughters, the eldest of them, to my mind, the loveliest girl that ever the sun shone upon. I'm not going to make a long story of it. I think it was a case of love at sight. I know that before I had been a week in the humdrum sea-coast village, I was over head and ears in love with Laura Daventry; and at the end of a month I was happy in the belief that my love was returned. She was the dearest, brightest of girls, with a sunshiny disposition that won her friends in every direction; and a man must have had a dull soul who could have withstood the charm of her society. I was free to make my own choice, rich enough to marry a penniless girl; and before I went back to Oxford I made her an offer. It was accepted, and I returned to the University the happiest of men."

He drank a cup of coffee, and rose from the table to walk up and down the room.

"Frank, you would imagine that nothing could arise to interfere with our happiness after this. In worldly circumstances I was what would be considered an excellent match for Miss Daventry, and I had every reason to believe that she loved me. She was very young, not quite eighteen; and I was the first man who had ever proposed to her. I left her, with the most entire confidence in her good faith; and to this hour I believe in her."

There was a pause, and then he went on again.

"We corresponded, of course. Laura's letters were charming; and I had no greater delight than in receiving and replying to them. I had promised her to work hard for my degree, and for her sake I kept my promise, and won it. My first thought was to carry her the news of my success; and directly the examinations were over I ran down to Sussex. I found the cottage empty. Mr. Daventry was in London; the two younger girls had gone to Devonshire, to an aunt who kept a school there. About Miss Daventry the neighbours could give me no positive information. She had left a few days before her father, but no one knew where she had gone. When I pressed them more closely they told me that it was rumoured in the village that she had gone away to be married. A gentleman from the Spanish colonies, a Mr. Levison, had been staying at the cottage for some weeks, and had disappeared about the same time as Miss Laura."

"And you believed that she had eloped with him?"

"To this day I am ignorant as to the manner of her leaving. Her last letters were only a week old. She had told me of this Mr. Levison's residence in their household. He was a wealthy merchant, a distant relation of her father's, and was staying in Sussex for his health. This was all she had said of him. Of their approaching departure she had not given me the slightest hint. No one in the village could tell me Mr. Daventry's London address. The cottage, a furnished one, had been given up to the landlord, and every debt paid.

I went to the post office, but the people there had received no direction as to the forwarding of letters, nor had any come as yet for Mr. Daventry."

"The girls in Devonshire—you applied to them, I suppose?"

"I did; but they could tell me nothing. I wrote to Emily, the elder girl, begging her to send me her sister's address. She answered my letter immediately. Laura had left home with her father's full knowledge and consent, she said, but had not told her sisters where she was going. She had seemed very unhappy. The whole affair had been sudden, and her father had also appeared much distressed in mind. This was all I could ascertain. I put an advertisement in the *Times*, addressed to Mr. Daventry, begging him to let me know his whereabouts; but nothing came of it. I employed a man to hunt London for him, and hunted myself, but without avail. I wasted months in this futile search, now on one false track, now on another."

"And you have long ago given up all hope, I suppose?" I said, as he paused, walking up and down the room with a moody face.

"Given up all hope of seeing Laura Levison alive? Yes; but not of tracking her destroyer."

"Laura Levison! Then you think she married the Spanish merchant?"

"I am sure of it. I had been more than six months on the look-out for Mr. Daventry, and had begun to despair of finding him, when the man I employed came to me and told me that he had found the registry of a marriage between Michael Levison and Laura Daventry at an obscure church in the City, where he had occasion to make researches for another client. The date of the marriage was within a few days of Laura's departure from Sussex."

"Strange!"

"Yes, strange that a woman could be so fickle, you would say. I felt convinced that there had been something more than girlish inconstancy at work in this business—some motive power strong enough to induce this girl to sacrifice herself in a loveless marriage. I was confirmed in this belief when, within a very short time of the discovery of the registry, I came suddenly upon old Daventry in the street. He would willingly have avoided me; but I insisted on a conversation with him, and he reluctantly allowed me to accompany him to his lodging, a wretched place in Southwark. He was very ill, with the stamp of death upon his face, and had a craven look that convinced me it was to him I was indebted for my sorrow. I told him that I knew of his daughter's marriage, when and where it had taken place, and boldly accused him of having brought it about."

"How did he take your accusation?"

"Like a beaten hound. He whimpered piteously, and told me that the marriage had been no wish of his. But Levison had possession of secrets which made him the veriest slave. Little by little I wrung from him the nature of these secrets. They related to forged bills of exchange, in which the old man had made free with his kinsman's name. It was a transaction of many years ago; but Levison had used this power in order to induce Laura to marry him; and the girl, to save her father from disgrace and ruin, as she believed, had consented to become his wife. Levison had promised to do great things for the old man; but had left England immediately after his marriage, without settling a shilling on his father-in-law. It was altogether a dastardly business: the girl had been sacrificed to her father's weakness and folly. I asked him why he had not appealed to me, who could no doubt have extricated him from his difficulty; but he could give me no clear answer. He evidently had an overpowering dread of Michael Levison. I left him, utterly disgusted with his imbecility and selfishness; but, for Laura's sake, I took care that he wanted for nothing during the remainder of his life. He did not trouble me long."

"And Mrs. Levison?"

"The old man told me that the Levisons had gone to Switzerland. I followed post-haste, and traced them from place to place, closely questioning the people at all the hotels. The accounts I heard were by no means encouraging. The lady did not seem happy. The gentleman looked old enough to be her father, and was peevish and fretful in his manner, never letting his wife out of his sight, and evidently suffering agonies of jealousy on account of the admiration which her beauty won for her from every one they met. I traced them stage by stage, through Switzerland into Italy, and then suddenly lost the track. I concluded that they had returned to England by some other route; but all my attempts to discover traces of their return were useless. Neither by land nor by sea passage could I hear of the yellow-faced trader and his beautiful young wife. They were not a couple to be overlooked easily; and this puzzled me. Disheartened and dispirited, I halted in Paris, where I spent a couple of months in hopeless idleness—a state of utter stagnation, from which I was aroused abruptly by a communication from my agent, a private detective—a very clever fellow in his way, and well in with the police of civilised Europe. He sent me a cutting from a German newspaper, which described the discovery of a corpse in the Tyrol. It was supposed, from the style of the dress, to be the body of an Englishwoman; but no indication of a name or address had been found, to give a clue to identity. Whether the dead woman had been the victim of foul play, or whether she had met her death from an accidental fall no one had been able to decide. The body had been found at the bottom of a mountain gorge, the face disfigured by the fall from the height above. Had the victim been a native of the dis-

trict, it might have been easily supposed that she had lost her footing
on the mountain path; but that a stranger should have travelled alone
by so unfrequented a route seemed highly improbable. The spot at
which the body was found lay within a mile of a small village; but it
was a place rarely visited by travellers of any description."

"Had your agent any reason to identify this woman with Mrs.
Levison?"

"None; except the fact that Mrs. Levison was missing, and his
natural habit of suspecting the very worst. The paragraph was
nearly a month old when it reached me. I set off at once for the place
named; saw the village authorities, and visited the Englishwoman's
grave. They showed me the dress she had worn; a black silk, very
simply made. Her face had been too much disfigured by the fall, and
the passage of time that had occurred before the finding of the body,
for my informants to give me any minute description of her appearance. They could only tell me that her hair was dark auburn, the
colour of Laura's, thick and long; and that her figure was that of a
young woman.

"After exhausting every possible inquiry, I pushed on to the
next village, and there received confirmation of my worst fears. A
gentleman and his wife—the man of foreign appearance, but talking
English, the woman young and beautiful—had stopped for a night at
the chief inn of the place, and had left the next morning without a
guide. The gentleman, who talked German perfectly, told the landlady that his travelling carriage and servants were to meet him at the
nearest stage on the home journey. He knew every inch of the country, and wished to walk across the mountain, in order to show his
wife a prospect which had struck him particularly on his last expedition a few years before. The landlady remembered that, just before
setting out, he asked his wife some question about her watch, took it
from her to regulate it, and then, after some peevish exclamation
about her carelessness in leaving it unwound, put it into his waistcoat pocket. The lady was very pale and quiet, and seemed unhappy. The description which the landlady gave me was only too
like the woman I was looking for."

"And you believe there had been foul play?"

"As certainly as I believe in my own existence. This man Levison had grown tired of a wife whose affection had never been his;
nay, more, I have reason to know that his unresting jealousy had intensified into a kind of hatred of her some time before the end. From
the village in the Tyrol, which they left together on the bright October morning, I tracked their footsteps stage by stage back to the
point at which I had lost them on the Italian frontier. In the course
of my wanderings I met a young Austrian officer who had seen them

at Milan, and had ventured to pay the lady some harmless atten-
tions. He told me that he had never seen anything so appalling as
Levison's jealousy; not an open fury, but a concentrated silent rage,
which gave an almost devilish expression to the man's parchment
face. He watched his wife like a lynx, and did not allow her a
moment's freedom from his presence. Every one who met them
pitied the beautiful girlish wife, whose misery was so evident; every
one loathed her tyrant. I found that the story of the servants and the
travelling carriage was a lie. The Levisons had been attended by no
servants at any of the hotels where I heard of them, and had travelled always in public or in hired vehicles. The ultimate result of
my inquiries left me little doubt that the dead woman was Laura
Levison; and from that hour to this I have been employed, more or
less, in the endeavour to find the man who murdered her."

"And you have not been able to discover his whereabouts?"
asked Frank Lorrimore.

"Not yet. I am looking for him."

"A useless quest, Horace. What would be the result of your
finding him? you have no proof to offer of his guilt. You would not
take the law into your own hands?"

"By the heaven above me, I would!" answered the other fiercely. "I would shoot that man down with as little compunction as I
would kill a mad dog."

"I hope you may never meet him," said Frank solemnly.

Horace Wynward gave a short impatient sigh, and paced the
room for some time in silence. His share in the breakfast had been a
mere pretence. He had emptied his coffee-cup, but had eaten nothing.

"I am going back to London this afternoon, Frank."

"On the hunt for this man?"

"Yes. My agent sent me a description of a man calling himself
Lewis, a bill-discounter, who has lately set up an office in the City,
and whom I believe to be Michael Levison."

The office occupied by Mr. Lewis, the bill-discounter, was a
dismal place enough, consisting of a second floor in a narrow alley
called St. Guinevere's Lane. Horace Wynward presented himself at
this office about a week after his arrival in London, in the character
of a gentleman in difficulties.

He found Mr. Lewis exactly the kind of man he expected to see;
a man of about fifty, with small crafty black eyes shining out of a
sallow visage that was as dull and lifeless as a parchment mask, thin
lips, and a heavy jaw and bony chin that betokened no small amount
of power for evil.

Mr. Wynward presented himself under his own name; on hearing which the bill-discounter looked up at him suddenly with an exclamation of surprise.

"You know my name?" said Horace.

"Yes; I have heard your name before. I thought you were a rich man."

"I have a good estate, but I have been rather imprudent, and am short of ready money. Where and when did you hear my name, Mr. Lewis?"

"I don't remember that. The name sounds familiar to me, that is all."

"But you have heard of me as a rich man, you say?"

"I had an impression to that effect. But the circumstances under which I heard the name have quite escaped my memory."

Horace pushed the question no further. He played his cards very carefully, leading the usurer to believe that he had secured a profitable prey. The preliminaries of a loan were discussed, but nothing fully settled. Before leaving the money-lender's office, Horace Wynward invited Mr. Lewis to dine with him at his lodgings, in the neighbourhood of Piccadilly, on the following evening. After a few minutes' reflection Lewis accepted the invitation.

He made his appearance at the appointed hour, dressed in a suit of shabby black, in which his sallow complexion looked more than usually parchment like and ghastly. The door was opened by Horace Wynward in person, and the money-lender was surprised to find himself in an almost empty house. In the hall and on the staircase there were no signs of occupation whatever; but, in the dining-room, to which Horace immediately ushered his guest, there was a table ready laid for dinner, a couple of chairs, and a dumb waiter loaded with the appliances of the meal. The dishes and sauce tureens were on a hot plate in the fender. The room was dimly lighted by four wax candles in a tarnished candelabrum.

Mr. Lewis, the money-lender, looked round him with a shudder; there was something sinister in the aspect of the room.

"It's rather a dreary-looking place, I'm afraid," said Horace Wynward. "I've only just taken the house, you see, and have had in a few sticks of hired furniture to keep me going till I make arrangements with an upholsterer. But you'll excuse all shortcomings, I'm sure— bachelor fare, you know."

"I thought you said you were in lodgings, Mr. Wynward."

"Did I?" asked the other absently; "a mere slip of the tongue. I took this house on lease a week ago, and am going to furnish it as soon as I am in funds."

"And are you positively alone here?" inquired Mr. Lewis, rather suspiciously.

"Well, very nearly so. There is a charwoman somewhere in the depths below, as deaf as a post, and almost as useless. But you needn't be frightened about your dinner; I ordered it in from a confectioner in Picadilly. We must wait upon ourselves, you know, in a free and easy way, for that dirty old woman would take away our appetites."

He lifted the cover of the soup tureen as he spoke. The visitor seated himself at the table with rather a nervous air, and glanced more than once in the direction of the shutters, which were closely fastened with heavy bars. He began to think there was something alarmingly eccentric in the conduct and manner of his host, and was inclined to repent having accepted the invitation, profitable as his new client promised to be.

The dinner was excellent, the wines of the finest quality, and, after drinking somewhat freely, Mr. Lewis began to be better reconciled to his position. He was a little disconcerted, however, on perceiving that his host scarcely touched either the viands or the wine, and that those deep-set gray eyes were lifted every now and then to his face with a strangely observant look. When dinner was over, Mr. Wynward heaped the dishes on the dumb-waiter, wheeled it into the next room with his own hands, and came back to his seat at the table opposite the bill-discounter, who sat meditatively sipping his claret.

Horace filled his glass, but remained for some time silent, without once lifting it to his lips. His companion watched him nervously, every moment more impressed with the belief that there was something wrong in his new client's mind, and bent on making a speedy escape. He finished his claret, looked at his watch, and rose hastily.

"I think I must wish you good night, Mr. Wynward. I am a man of early habits, and have some distance to go. My lodgings are at Brompton, nearly an hour's ride from here."

"Stay," said Horace, "we have not begun business yet. It's only nine o'clock. I want an hour's quiet talk with you, Mr. Levison."

The bill-discounter's face changed. It was almost impossible for that pallid mask of parchment to grow paler, but a sudden ghastliness came over the man's evil countenance.

"My name is Lewis," he said, with an artificial grin.

"Lewis, or Levison. Men of your trade have as many names as they please. When you were travelling in Switzerland two years ago your name was Levison."

"You are under some absurd mistake, sir. The name of Levison is strange to me."

"Is the name of Daventry strange to you too? You recognised my name yesterday. When you first heard it I was a happy man, Michael Levison. The blight upon me is your work. Oh, I know you well enough, and am provided with ample means for your identification. I have followed you step by step upon your travels—tracked you to the inn from which you set out one October morning, nearly a year ago, with a companion who was never seen alive by mortal eyes after that date. You are a good German scholar, Mr. Levison. Read that."

Horace Wynward took out of his pocket-book the paragraph cut from the German paper, and laid it before his visitor. The bill-discounter pushed it away, after a hasty glance at its contents.

"What has this to do with me?" he asked.

"A great deal, Mr. Levison. The hapless woman described in that paragraph was once your wife—Laura Daventry, the girl I loved, and who returned my love; the girl whom you basely stole from me, by trading on her natural affection for a weak, unworthy father, and whose life you made wretched, until it was foully ended by your own cruel hand. If I had stood behind you upon that lonely mountain pathway in the Tyrol, and had seen you hurl your victim to destruction, I could not be more convinced than I am that your hand did the deed; but such crimes as these are difficult—in this case perhaps impossible—to prove, and I fear you will escape the gallows. There are other circumstances in your life, however, more easily brought to light; and by the aid of a clever detective I have made myself master of some curious secrets in your past existence. I know the name you bore some fifteen years ago, before you settled in Trinidad as a merchant. You were at that time called Michael Lucas, and you fled from this country with a large sum of money, embezzled from your employers, Messrs. Hardwell and Oliphant, sugar brokers in Nicholas Lane. You have been 'wanted' a long time, Mr. Levison; but you would most likely have gone scot-free to the end had I not set my agent to hunt you and your antecedents."

Michael Levison rose from his seat hastily, trembling in every limb. Horace rose at the same moment, and the two men stood face to face—one the very image of craven fear, the other cool and self-possessed.

"This is a tissue of lies!" gasped Levison, wiping his lips nervously with a handkerchief that fluttered in his tremulous fingers. "Have you brought me here to insult me with this madman's talk?"

"I have brought you here to your doom. There was a time when I thought that if you and I ever stood face to face, I should shoot you down like a dog; but I have changed my mind. Such carrion dogs as you are not worth the stain of blood upon an honest man's hand. It is useless to tell you how I loved the girl you murdered. Your savage nature would not comprehend any but the basest and most selfish passion. Don't stir another step—I have a loaded revolver within reach, and shall make an end of you if you attempt to quit this room.

The police are on the watch for you outside, and you will leave this place for a gaol. Hark! what is that?"

It was the sound of a footstep on the stairs outside, a woman's light footstep, and the rustling of a silk dress. The dining room door was ajar, and the sounds were distinctly audible in the empty house. Michael Levison made for the door, availing himself of this momentary diversion, with some vague hope of escape; but, within, a few paces of the threshold, he recoiled suddenly, with a hoarse gasping cry.

The door was pushed wide open by a light hand, and a figure stood upon the threshold—a girlish figure dressed in black silk, a pale sad face framed by dark auburn hair.

"The dead returned to life!" cried Levison. "Hide her, hide her! I can't face her! Let me go!"

He made for the other door leading into the inner room, but found it locked, and then sank cowering down into a chair, covering his eyes with his skinny hands. The girl came softly into the room and stood by Horace Wynward.

"You have forgotten me, Mr. Levison," she said; "and you take me for my sister's ghost. I was always like her, and they say I have grown more so within the last two years. We had a letter from you a month ago, posted from Trinidad, telling us that my sister Laura was well and happy there with you; yet you mistake me for the shadow of the dead!"

The frightened wretch did not look up. He had not yet recovered from the shock produced by his sister-in-law's sudden appearance. The handkerchief which he held to his lips was stained with blood. Horace Wynward went quietly to the outer door and opened it, returning presently with two men, who came softly into the room and approached Levison. He made no attempt to resist them as they slipped a pair of handcuffs on his bony wrists and led him away. There was a cab standing outside, ready to convey him to prison.

Emily Daventry sank into a chair as he was taken from the room.

"Oh, Mr. Wynward," she said, "I think there can be little doubt of my sister's wretched fate. The experiment which you proposed has succeeded only too well."

Horace had been down to Devonshire to question the two girls about their sister. He had been struck by Emily's likeness to his lost love, and had persuaded her aunt to bring her up to London, in order to identify Levison by her means, and to test the effect which her appearance might produce upon the nerves of the suspected assassin.

The police were furnished with a complicated mass of evidence

against Levison in his character of clerk, merchant, and bill-discounter; but the business was of a nature that entailed much delay, and
after several adjourned examinations the prisoner fell desperately ill
of heart disease, from which he had suffered for years, but which
grew much worse during his imprisonment. Finding his death certain, he sent for Horace Wynward, and to him confessed his crime,
boasting of his wife's death with a fiendish delight in the deed,
which he called an act of vengeance against his rival.

"I knew you well enough when you came home, Horace Wynward," he said, "and I thought it would be my happy lot to compass
your ruin. You trapped me, but to the last you have the worst of it.
The girl you loved is dead. She dared to tell me that she loved you;
defied my anger; told me that she had sold herself to me to save her
father from disgrace, and confessed that she hated me, and had
always hated me. From that hour she was doomed. Her white face
was a constant reproach to me. I was goaded to madness by her
tears. She used to mutter your name in her sleep. I wonder I did not
cut her throat as she lay there with the name upon her lips. But I
must have swung for that. So I was patient, and waited till I could
have her alone with me in the mountains. It was only a push, and
she was gone. I came home alone, free from the worry and fever of
her presence—except in my dreams. She has haunted those ever
since, with her pale face—yes, by heaven, I have hardly known what
it is to sleep, from that hour to this, without seeing her white face
and hearing the one long shriek that went up to the sky as she fell."

He died within a few days of this interview, and before his trial
could take place. Time, that heals almost all griefs, brought peace
by-and-by to Horace Wynward. He furnished the house in Mayfair,
and for some time led a misanthropical life there; but on paying a
second visit to Devonshire, where the two Daventry girls lived their
simple industrious life in their aunt's school, he discovered that
Emily's likeness to her sister made her very dear to him, and in the
following year he brought a mistress to Crofton in the person of that
young lady. Together they paid a mournful visit to that lonely spot
in the Tyrol where Laura Levison had perished, and stayed there
while a white marble cross was erected above her grave.

ÉMILE GABORIAU

(1832–1873) is the father of the detective novel. His L'Affaire Lerouge *(The Widow Lerouge) (1865–1866) was the first modern detective novel, and in it and several later novels he worked out many of the plot patterns and devices that have since become standard parts of the detective story. He considered Poe his master, while his own influence was quite strong on Wilkie Collins and A. Conan Doyle.*

Gaboriau was born near La Rochelle, France, into a patrician family. Destined to become a petty official, he ran away from home and joined the army. After his release he made his way to Paris, where he held a succession of menial jobs before becoming established as a journalist. He achieved fame and fortune almost overnight with L'Affaire *and followed this with a succession of other novels involving crime or detection. His best-known works are* The Mystery of Orcival *(1867),* File No. 113 *(1867),* Monsieur Lecoq *(1869), and* In Peril of His Life *(1873). His novels were translated into English within a decade or so after their French appearance and played an important part in the development of the popular detective literature of the 1880s and 1890s.*

"The Little Old Man of Batignolles"

I.

When I had finished my studies in order to become a health officer, a happy time it was. I was twenty-three years of age. I lived in the Rue Monsieur-le-Prince, almost at the corner of the Rue Racine.

There I had for thirty francs a month, service included, a fur-

nished room, which to-day would certainly be worth a hundred
francs; it was so spacious that I could easily put my arms in the
sleeves of my overcoat without opening the window.

Since I left early in the morning to make the calls for my hospital, and since I returned very late, because the Cafe Leroy had irresistible attractions for me, I scarcely knew by sight the tenants in my
house, peaceable people all; some living on their incomes, and some
small merchants.

There was one, however, to whom, little by little, I became attached.

He was a man of average size, insignificant, always scrupulously
shaved, who was pompously called "Monsieur Mechinet."

The doorkeeper treated him with a most particular regard, and
never omitted quickly to lift his cap as he passed the lodge.

As M. Mechinet's apartment opened on my landing, directly
opposite the door of my room, we repeatedly met face to face. On
such occasions we saluted one another.

One evening he came to ask me for some matches; another night
I borrowed tobacco of him; one morning it happened that we both
left at the same time, and walked side by side for a little stretch, talking.

Such were our first relations.

Without being curious or mistrusting—one is neither at the age
I was then—we like to know what to think about people to whom we
become attached.

Thus I naturally came to observe my neighbor's way of living,
and became interested in his actions and gestures.

He was married. Madame Caroline Mechinet, blonde and fair,
small, gay and plump, seemed to adore her husband.

But the husband's conduct was none too regular for that.
Frequently he decamped before daylight, and often the sun had set
before I heard him return to his domicile. At times he disappeared
for whole weeks.

That the pretty little Madame Mechinet should tolerate this is
what I could not understand.

Puzzled, I thought that our concierge, ordinarily as much a
babbler as a magpie, would give me some explanation.

Not so! Hardly had I pronounced Mechinet's name than, without ceremony, he sent me about my business, telling me, as he rolled
his eyes, that he was not in the habit of "spying" upon his tenants.

This reception doubled my curiosity to such an extent that,
banishing all shame, I began to watch my neighbor.

I discovered things.

Once I saw him coming home dressed in the latest fashion, his
buttonhole ornamented with five or six decorations; the next day I

noticed him on the stairway dressed in a sordid blouse, on his head a cloth rag, which gave him a sinister air.

Nor was that all. One beautiful afternoon, as he was going out, I saw his wife accompany him to the threshold of their apartment and there kiss him passionately, saying:

"I beg you, Mechinet, be prudent; think of your little wife."

Be prudent! Why? For what purpose? What did that mean? The wife must then be an accomplice.

It was not long before my astonishment was doubled.

One night, as I was sleeping soundly, some one knocked suddenly and rapidly at my door.

I arose and opened.

M. Mechinet entered, or rather rushed in, his clothing in disorder and torn, his necktie and the front of his shirt torn off, bareheaded, his face covered with blood.

"What has happened?" I exclaimed, frightened.

"Not so loud," said he; "you might be heard. Perhaps it is nothing, although I suffer devilishly. I said to myself that you, being a medical student would doubtless know how to help me."

Without saying a word, I made him sit down, and hastened to examine him and to do for him what was necessary.

Although he bled freely, the wound was a slight one—to tell the truth, it was only a superficial scratch, starting from the left ear and reaching to the corner of his mouth.

The dressing of the wound finished, "Well, here I am again healthy and safe for this time," M. Mechinet said to me. "Thousand thanks, dear Monsieur Godeuil. Above all, as a favor, do not speak to any one of this little accident, and—good night."

"Good night!" I had little thought of sleeping. When I remember all the absurd hypotheses and the romantic imaginations which passed through my brain, I can not help laughing.

In my mind, M. Mechinet took on fantastic proportions.

The next day he came to thank me again, and invited me to dinner.

That I was all eyes and ears when I entered my neighbor's home may be rightly guessed.

In vain did I concentrate my whole attention. I could not find out anything of a nature to dissipate the mystery which puzzled me so much.

However, from this dinner on, our relations became closer. M. Mechinet decidedly favored me with his friendship. Rarely a week passed without his taking me along, as he expressed it, to eat soup with him, and almost daily, at the time for absinthe, he came to meet me at the Cafe Leroy, where we played a game of dominoes.

Thus it was that on a certain evening in the month of July, on a

Friday, at about five o'clock, when he was just about to beat me at "full double-six," an ugly-looking bully abruptly entered, and, approaching him, murmured in his ears some words I could not hear.

M. Mechinet rose suddenly, looking troubled.

"I am coming," said he; "run and say that I am coming."

The man ran off as fast as his legs could carry him, and then M. Mechinet offered me his hand.

"Excuse me," added my old neighbor, "duty before everything; we shall continue our game to-morrow."

Consumed with curiosity, I showed great vexation, saying that I regretted very much not accompanying him.

"Well," grumbled he, "why not? Do you want to come? Perhaps it will be interesting."

For all answer, I took my hat and we left.

II.

I was certainly far from thinking that I was then venturing on one of those apparently insignificant steps which, nevertheless, have a deciding influence on one's whole life.

For once, I thought to myself, I am holding the solution of the enigma!

And full of a silly and childish satisfaction, I trotted, like a lean cat, at the side of M. Mechinet.

I say "trotted," because I had all I could do not to be left behind.

He rushed along, down the Rue Racine, running against the passers-by, as if his fortune depended on his legs.

Luckily, on the Place de l'Odeon a cab came in our way.

M. Mechinet stopped it, and, opening the door, "Get in, Monsieur Godeuil," said he to me.

I obeyed, and he seated himself at my side, after having called to the coachman in a commanding voice: "39 Rue Lecluse, at Batignolles, and drive fast!"

The distance drew from the coachman a string of oaths. Nevertheless he whipped up his broken-down horses and the carriage rolled off.

"Oh! it is to Batignolles we are going?" I asked with a courtier's smile.

But M. Mechinet did not answer me; I even doubt that he heard me.

A complete change took place in him. He did not seem exactly agitated but his set lips and the contraction of his heavy, brushwood-like eyebrows betrayed a keen preoccupation. His look, lost in space, seemed to be studying there the meaning of some insolvable problem.

He had pulled out his snuff-box and continually took from it enormous pinches of snuff, which he kneaded between the index and thumb, rolled into a ball, and raised it to his nose; but he did not actually snuff.

It was a habit which I had observed, and it amused me very much.

This worthy man, who abhorred tobacco, always carried a snuff-box as large as that of a vaudeville capitalist.

If anything unforeseen happened to him, either agreeable or vexatious, in a trice he had it out, and seemed to snuff furiously.

Often the snuff-box was empty, but his gestures remained the same.

I learned later that this was a system with him for the purpose of concealing his impressions and of diverting the attention of his questioners.

In the mean time we rolled on. The cab easily passed up the Rue de Clichy; it crossed the exterior boulevard, entered the Rue de Lecluse, and soon stopped at some distance from the address given.

It was materially impossible to go farther, as the street was obstructed by a compact crowd.

In front of No. 39, two or three hundred persons were standing, their necks craned, eyes gleaming breathless with curiosity, and with difficulty kept in bounds by half a dozen *sergents de ville*, who were everywhere repeating in vain and in their roughest voices: "Move on, gentlemen, move on!"

After alighting from the carriage, we approached, making our way with difficulty through the crowd of idlers.

We already had our hands on the door of No. 39, when a police officer rudely pushed us back.

"Keep back! You can not pass!"

My companion eyed him from head to foot, and straightening himself up, said:

"Well, don't you know me? I am Mechinet, and this young man," pointing to me, "is with me."

"I beg your pardon! Excuse me!" stammered the officer, carrying his hand to his three-cocked hat. "I did not know; please enter."

We entered.

In the hall, a powerful woman, evidently the concierge, more red than a peony, was holding forth and gesticulating in the midst of a group of house tenants.

"Where is it?" demanded M. Mechinet gruffly.

"Third floor, monsieur," she replied; "third floor, door to the right. Oh! my God! What a misfortune. In a house like this. Such a good man."

I did not hear more. M. Mechinet was rushing up the stairs, and I followed him, four steps at a time, my heart thumping.

On the third floor the door to the right was open. We entered, went through an anteroom, a dining-room, a parlor, and finally reached a bedroom.

If I live a thousand years I shall not forget the scene which struck my eyes. Even at this moment as I am writing, after many years, I still see it down to the smallest details.

At the fireplace opposite the door two men were leaning on their elbows: a police commissary, wearing his scarf of office, and an examining magistrate.

At the right, seated at a table a young man, the judge's clerk, was writing.

In the centre of the room, on the floor, in a pool of coagulated and black blood, lay the body of an old man with white hair. He was lying on his back, his arms folded crosswise.

Terrified, I stopped as if nailed to the threshold, so nearly fainting that I was compelled to lean against the door-frame.

My profession had accustomed me to death; I had long ago overcome repugnance to the amphitheatre, but this was the first time that I found myself face to face with a crime.

For it was evident that an abominable crime had been committed.

Less sensitive than I, my neighbor entered with a firm step.

"Oh, it is you, Mechinet," said the police commissary; "I am very sorry to have troubled you."

"Why?"

"Because we shall not need your services. We know the guilty one; I have given orders; by this time he must have been arrested."

How strange!

From M. Mechinet's gesture one might have believed that this assurance vexed him. He pulled out his snuff-box, took two or three of his fantastic pinches, and said:

"Ah! the guilty one is known?"

It was the examining magistrate who answered:

"Yes, and known in a certain and positive manner; yes, M. Mechinet, the crime once committed, the assassin escaped, believing that his victim had ceased living. He was mistaken. Providence was watching; this unfortunate old man was still breathing. Gathering all his energy, he dipped one of his fingers in the blood which was flowing in streams from his wound, and there, on the floor, he wrote in his blood his murderer's name. Now look for yourself."

Then I perceived what at first I had not seen.

On the inlaid floor, in large, badly shaped, but legible letters, was written in blood: MONIS.

"Well?" asked M. Mechinet.

"That," answered the police commissary, "is the beginning of the name of a nephew of the poor man; of a nephew for whom he had an affection, and whose name is Monistrol."

"The devil!" exclaimed my neighbor.

"I can not suppose," continued the investigating magistrate, "that the wretch would attempt denying. The five letters are an overwhelming accusation. Moreover, who would profit by this cowardly crime? He alone, as sole heir of this old man, who, they say, leaves a large fortune. There is more. It was last evening that the murder was committed. Well, last evening none other but his nephew called on this poor old man. The concierge saw him enter the house at about nine o'cock and leave again a little before midnight."

"It is clear," said M. Mechinet approvingly; "it is very clear, this Monistrol is nothing but an idiot." And, shrugging his shoulders, asked:

"But did he steal anything, break some piece of furniture, anything to give us an idea as to the motive for the crime?"

"Up to now nothing seems to have been disturbed," answered the commissary. "As you said, the wretch is not clever; as soon as he finds himself discovered, he will confess."

Whereupon the police commissary and M. Mechinet withdrew to the window, conversing in low tones, while the judge gave some instructions to his clerk.

III.

I had wanted to know exactly what my enigmatic neighbor was doing. Now I knew it. Now everything was explained. The looseness of his life, his absences, his late homecomings, his sudden disappearances, his young wife's fears and complicity; the wound I had cured. But what did I care now about that discovery?

I examined with curiosity everything around me.

From where I was standing, leaning against the door-frame, my eye took in the entire apartment.

Nothing, absolutely nothing, evidenced a scene of murder. On the contrary, everything betokened comfort, and at the same time habits parsimonious and methodical.

Everything was in its place; there was not one wrong fold in the curtains; the wood of the furniture was brilliantly polished, showing daily care.

It seemed evident that the conjectures of the examining magistrate and of the police commissary were correct, and that the poor old man had been murdered the evening before, when he was about to go to bed.

In fact, the bed was open, and on the blanket lay a shirt and a neckcloth.

On the table, at the head of the bed, I noticed a glass of sugared water, a box of safety matches, and an evening paper, the "Patrie."

On one corner of the mantelpiece a candlestick was shining brightly, a nice big, solid copper candlestick. But the candle which had illuminated the crime was burned out; the murderer had escaped without extinguishing it, and it had burned down to the end, blackening the alabaster save-all in which it was placed.

I noticed all these details at a glance, without any effort, without my will having anything to do with it. My eye had become a photographic objective; the stage of the murder had portrayed itself in my mind, as on a prepared plate, with such precision that no circumstance was lacking, and with such depth that to-day, even, I can sketch the apartment of the "little old man of Batignolles" without omitting anything, not even a cork, partly covered with green wax, which lay on the floor under the chair of the judge's clerk.

It was an extraordinary faculty, which had been bestowed upon me—my chief faculty, which as yet I had not occasion to exercise and which all at once revealed itself to me.

I was then too agitated to analyze my impressions. I had but one obstinate, burning, irresistible desire: to get close to the body, which was lying two yards from me.

At first I struggled against the temptation. But fatality had something to do with it. I approached. Had my presence been remembered? I do not believe it.

At any rate, nobody paid any attention to me. M. Mechinet and the police commissary were still talking near the window; the clerk was reading his report in an undertone to the investigating magistrate.

Thus nothing prevented me from carrying out my intention. And, besides, I must confess I was possessed with some kind of a fever, which rendered me insensible to exterior circumstances and absolutely isolated me. So much so that I dared to kneel close to the body, in order to see better.

Far from expecting any one to call out: "What are you doing there?" I acted slowly and deliberately, like a man who, having received a mission, executes it.

The unfortunate old man seemed to me to have been between seventy and seventy-five years old. He was small and very thin, but solid and built to pass the hundred-year mark. He still had considerable hair, yellowish white and curly, on the nape of the neck. His gray beard, strong and thick, looked as if he had not been shaven for five or six days; it must have grown after his death. This circumstance did not surprise me, as I had often noticed it on subjects in the amphitheatres.

What did surprise me was the expression of the face. It was calm; I should even say, smiling. His lips were parted, as for a friendly greeting. Death must have occurred then with terrible suddenness to preserve such a kindly expression! That was the first idea which came to my mind.

Yes, but how reconcile these two irreconcilable circumstances: a sudden death and those five letters—MONIS—which I saw in lines of blood on the floor? In order to write them, what effort must it have cost a dying man! Only the hope of revenge could have given him so much energy. And how great must his rage have been to feel himself expiring before being able to trace the entire name of his murderer! And yet the face of the dead seemed to smile at one.

The poor old man had been struck in the throat, and the weapon had gone right through the neck. The instrument must have been a dagger, or perhaps one of those terrible Catalan knives, as broad as the hand, which cut on both sides and are as pointed as a needle.

Never in my life before had I been agitated by such strange sensations. My temples throbbed with extraordinary violence, and my heart swelled as if it would break. What was I about to discover?

Driven by a mysterious and irresistible force, which annihilated my will-power, I took between my hands, for the purpose of examining them, the stiff and icy hands of the body.

The right hand was clean; it was one of the fingers of the left hand, the index, which was all blood-stained.

What! it was with the left hand that the old man had written? Impossible!

Seized with a kind of dizziness, with haggard eyes, my hair standing on end, paler than the dead lying at my feet, I rose with a terrible cry:

"Great God!"

At this cry all the others jumped up, surprised, frightened.

"What is it?" they asked me all together. "What has happened?"

I tried to answer, but the emotion was strangling me. All I could do was to show them the dead man's hands, stammering:

"There! There!"

Quick as lightning, M. Mechinet fell on his knees beside the body. What I had seen he saw, and my impression was also his, for, quickly rising, he said:

"It was not this poor old man who traced the letters there."

As the judge and the commissary looked at him with open

mouths, he explained to them the circumstance of the left hand alone
being blood-stained.

"And to think that I had not paid any attention to that," repeated the distressed commissary over and over again.

M. Mechinet was taking snuff furiously.

"So it is," he said, "the things that are not seen are those that
are near enough to put the eyes out. But no matter. Now the situation is devilishly changed. Since it is not the old man himself who
wrote, it must be the person who killed him."

"Evidently," approved the commissary.

"Now," continued my neighbor, "can any one imagine a murderer stupid enough to denounce himself by writing his own name
beside the body of his victim? No; is it not so? Now, conclude—"

The judge had become anxious.

"It is clear," he said, "appearances have deceived us. Monistrol
is not the guilty one. Who is it? It is your business, M. Mechinet, to
discover him."

He stopped; a police officer had entered, and, addressing the
commissary, said:

"Your orders have been carried out, sir. Monistrol has been arrested and locked up. He confessed everything."

IV.

It is impossible to describe our astonishment. What! While we were
there, exerting ourselves to find proofs of Monistrol's innocence, he
acknowledges himself guilty?

M. Mechinet was the first to recover.

Rapidly he raised his fingers from the snuff-box to his nose five
or six times, and advancing toward the officer, said:

"Either you are mistaken, or you are deceiving us; one or the
other."

"I'll take an oath, M. Mechinet."

"Hold your tongue. You either misunderstood what Monistrol
said or got intoxicated by the hope of astonishing us with the announcement that the affair was settled."

The officer, up to then humble and respectful, now became re-
fractory.

"Excuse me," he interrupted, "I am neither an idiot nor a liar,
and I know what I am talking about."

The discussion came so near being a quarrel that the investigating judge thought best to interfere.

"Calm yourself, Monsieur Mechinet," he said, "and before expressing an opinion, wait to be informed."

Then turning toward the officer, he continued:

"And you, my friend, tell us what you know, and give us reasons for your assurance."

Thus sustained, the officer crushed M. Mechinet with an ironical glance, and with a very marked trace of conceit he began:

"Well, this is what happened: Monsieur the Judge and Monsieur the Commissary, both here present, instructed us—Inspector Goulard, my colleague Poltin, and myself—to arrest Monistrol, dealer in imitation jewelry, living at 75 Rue Vivienne, the said Monistrol being accused of the murder of his uncle."

"Exactly so," approved the commissary in a low voice.

"Thereupon," continued the officer, "we took a cab and had him drive us to the address given. We arrived and found M. Monistrol in the back of his shop, about to sit down to dinner with his wife, a woman of twenty-five or thirty years, and very beautiful.

"Seeing the three of us stand like a string of onions, our man got up. 'What do you want?' he asked us. Sergeant Goulard drew from his pocket the warrant and answered: 'In the name of the law, I arrest you!' "

Here M. Mechinet behaved as if he were on a gridiron.

"Could you not hurry up?" he said to the officer.

But the latter, as if he had not heard, continued in the same calm tone:

"I have arrested many people during my life. Well! I never saw any of them go to pieces like this one.

" 'You are joking,' he said to us, 'or you are making a mistake.'

" 'No, we are not mistaken!'

" 'But, after all, what do you arrest me for?'

"Goulard shrugged his shoulders.

" 'Don't act like a child,' he said, 'what about your uncle? The body has been found, and we have overwhelming proofs against you.'

"Oh! that rascal, what a disagreeable shock! He tottered and finally dropped on a chair, sobbing and stammering I can not tell what answer.

"Goulard, seeing him thus, shook him by the coat collar and said:

" 'Believe me, the shortest way is to confess everything.'

"The man looked at us stupidly and murmured:

" 'Well, yes, I confess everything.' "

"Well maneuvred, Goulard," said the commissary approvingly. The officer looked triumphant.

"It was now a matter of cutting short our stay in the shop," he continued. "We had been instructed to avoid all commotion, and some idlers were already crowding around. Goulard seized the prisoner by the arm, shouting to him: 'Come on, let us start; they are waiting for us at headquarters.' Monistrol managed to get on his shaking legs, and in the voice of a man taking his courage in both hands, said: 'Let us go.'

"We were thinking that the worst was over; we did not count on the wife.

"Up to that moment she had remained in an armchair, as in a faint, without breathing a word, without seeming even to understand what was going on.

"But when she saw that we were taking away her husband, she sprang up like a lioness, and throwing herself in front of the door, shouted: 'You shall not pass.'

"On my word of honor she was superb; but Goulard, who had seen others before, said to her: 'Come, come, little woman, don't let us get angry; your husband will be brought back.'

"However, far from giving way to us, she clung more firmly to the door-frame, swearing that her husband was innocent; declaring that if he was taken to prison she would follow him, at times threatening us and crushing us with invectives, and then again entreating in her sweetest voice.

"When she understood that nothing would prevent us from doing our duty, she let go the door, and, throwing herself on her husband's neck, groaned: 'Oh, dearest beloved, is it possible that you are accused of a crime? You—you! Please tell them, these men, that you are innocent.'

"In truth, we were all affected, except the man, who pushed his poor wife back so brutally that she fell in a heap in a corner of the back shop.

"Fortunately that was the end.

"The woman had fainted; we took advantage of it to stow the husband away in the cab that had brought us.

"To stow away is the right word, because he had become like an inanimate thing; he could no longer stand up; he had to be carried. To omit nothing, I should add that his dog, a kind of black cur, wanted actually to jump into the carriage with us, and that we had the greatest trouble to get rid of it.

"On the way, as by right, Goulard tried to entertain our prisoner and to make him blab. But it was impossible to draw one word from him. It was only when we arrived at police headquarters that he seemed to come to his senses. When he was duly installed in one of the 'close confinement' cells, he threw himself headlong on the bed, repeating: 'What have I done to you, my God! What have I done to you!'

"At this moment Goulard approached him, and for the second time asked: 'Well, do you confess your guilt?' Monistrol motioned with his head: 'Yes, yes.' Then in a hoarse voice said: 'I beg you, leave me alone.'

"That is what we did, taking care, however, to place a keeper on watch at the window of the cell, in case the fellow should attempt suicide.

"Goulard and Poltin remained down there, and I, here I am."

"That is precise," grumbled the commissary; "It could not be more precise."

That was also the judge's opinion, for he murmured:

"How can we, after all this, doubt Monistrol's guilt?"

As for me, though I was confounded, my convictions were still firm. I was just about to open my mouth to venture an objection, when M. Mechinet forestalled me.

"All that is well and good," exclaimed he. "Only if we admit that Monistrol is the murderer, we are forced also to admit that it was he who wrote his name there on the floor—and—well, that's a hard nut."

'Bosh!" interrupted the commissary, "since the accused confessed, what is the use of bothering about a circumstance which will be explained at the trial?"

But my neighbor's remark had again roused perplexities in the mind of the judge, and without committing himself, he said:

"I am going to the Prefecture. I want to examine Monistrol this very evening."

And after telling the commissary to be sure and fulfil all formalities and to await the arrival of the physicians called for the autopsy of the body, he left, followed by his clerk and by the officer who had come to inform us of the successful arrest.

"Provided these devils of doctors do not keep me waiting too long," growled the commissary, who was thinking of his dinner.

Neither M. Mechinet nor I answered him. We remained standing, facing one another, evidently beset by the same thought.

"After all," murmured my neighbor, "perhaps it was the old man who wrote—"—"With the left hand, then? Is that possible? Without considering that this poor fellow must have died instantly."—"Are you certain of it?"—"Judging by his wound I would take an oath on it. Besides, the physicians will come; they will tell you whether I am right or wrong."

With veritable frenzy M. Mechinet pretended to take snuff.

"Perhaps there is some mystery beneath this," said he; "that remains to be seen."

"It is an examination to be gone over again."—"Be it so, let us do it over; and to begin, let us examine the concierge."

Running to the staircase, M. Mechinet leaned over the balustrade, calling: "Concierge! Hey! Concierge! Come up, please."

V.

While waiting for the concierge to come up, M. Mechinet proceeded with a rapid and able examination of the scene of the crime.

It was principally the lock of the main door to the apartment which attracted his attention; it was intact, and the key turned without difficulty. This circumstance absolutely discarded the thought that an evil-doer, a stranger, had entered during the night by means of false keys.

For my part, I had involuntarily, or rather inspired by the astonishing instinct which had revealed itself in me, picked up the cork, partly covered with green wax, which I had noticed on the floor.

It had been used, and on the side where the wax was showed traces of the corkscrew; but on the other end could be seen a kind of deepish notch, evidently produced by some sharp and pointed instrument.

Suspecting the importance of my discovery, I communicated it to M. Mechinet, and he could not avoid an exclamation of joy.

"At last," he exlaimed, "at last we have a clue! This cork, it's the murderer who dropped it here; he stuck in it the brittle point of the weapon he used. The conclusion is, that the instrument of the murder is a dagger with a fixed handle and not one of those knives which shut up. With this cork, I am certain to reach the guilty one, no matter who he is!"

The police commissary was just finishing his task in the room, M. Mechinet and I had remained in the parlor, when we were interrupted by the noise of heavy breathing.

Almost immediately appeared the powerful woman I had noticed holding forth in the hall in the midst of the tenants.

It was the concierge, if possible redder than at the time of our arrival.

"In what way can I serve you, monsieur?" she asked of M. Mechinet.

"Take a seat, madame," he answered.

"But, monsieur, I have people downstairs."

"They will wait for you. I tell you to sit down."

Nonplused by M. Mechinet's tone, she obeyed.

Then looking straight at her with his terrible, small, gray eyes, he began:

"I need certain information, and I'm going to question you. In your interest, I advise you to answer straightforwardly. Now, first of all, what is the name of this poor fellow who was murdered?"

"His name was Pigoreau, kind sir, but he was mostly known by the name of Antenor, which he had formerly taken as more suitable to his business."

"Did he live in this house a long time?"

"The last eight years."

"Where did he reside before?"

"Rue Richelieu, where he had his store; he had been a hairdresser, and it was in that business that he made his money."

"He was then considered rich?"

"I heard him say to his niece that he would not let his throat be cut for a million."

As to this, it must have been known to the investigating magistrate, as the papers of the poor old man had been included in the inventory made.

"Now," M. Mechinet continued, "what kind of a man was this M. Pigoreau, called Antenor?"

"Oh! the cream of men, my dear, kind sir," answered the concierge. "It is true he was cantankerous, queer, as miserly as possible, but he was not proud. And so funny with all that. One could have spent whole nights listening to him, when he was in the right mood. And the number of stories he knew! Just think, a former hairdresser, who, as he said, had dressed the hair of the most beautiful women in Paris!"

"How did he live?"

"As everybody else; as people do who have an income, you know, and who yet cling to their money."

"Can you give me some particulars?"

"Oh! As to that, I think so, since it was I who looked after his rooms, and that was no trouble at all for me, because he did almost everything himself—swept, dusted, and polished. Yes, it was his hobby. Well, every day at noon, I brought him up a cup of chocolate. He drank it; on top of that he took a large glass of water; that was his breakfast. Then he dressed and that took him until two o'clock, for he was a dandy, and careful of his person, more so than a newly married woman. As soon as he was dressed, he went out to take a walk through Paris. At six o'clock he went to dinner in a private boarding-house, the Mademoiselles Gomet, in the Rue de las Paix. After dinner he used to go to the Cafe Guerbois for his demitasse and to play his usual game, and at eleven he came home to go to bed. On the whole, the poor fellow had only one fault; he was fond of the other sex. I even told him often: 'At your age, are you not ashamed of yourself?' But no one is perfect, and after all it could be easily understood of a former perfumer, who in his life had had a great many good fortunes."

An obsequious smile strayed over the lips of the powerful concierge, but nothing could cheer up M. Mechinet.

"Did M. Pigoreau receive many calls?" he asked.

"Very few. I have hardly seen anybody call on him except his nephew, M. Monistrol, whom he invited every Sunday to dinner at Lathuile's."

"And how did they get along together, the uncle and the nephew?"

"Like two fingers of the same hand."

"Did they ever have any disputes?"

"Never, except that they were always wrangling about Madame Clara."

"Who is that Madame Clara?"

"Well, M. Monistrol's wife, a superb creature. The deceased, old Antenor, could not bear her. He said that his nephew loved that woman too much; that she was leading him by the end of his nose, and that she was fooling him in every way. He claimed that she did not love her husband; that she was too high and mighty for her position, and that finally she would do something foolish. Madame Clara and her uncle even had a falling out at the end of last year. She wanted the good fellow to lend a hundred thousand francs to M. Monistrol, to enable him to buy out a jeweler's stock at the Palais Royal. But he refused, saying that after his death they could do with his money whatever they wanted, but that until then, since he had earned it, he intended to keep and enjoy it."

I thought that M. Mechinet would dwell on this circumstance, which seemed to me very important. But no, in vain did I increase my signals; he continued:

"It remains now to be told by whom the crime was first discovered."

"By me, my kind monsieur, by me," moaned the concierge. "Oh! it is frightful! Just imagine, this morning, exactly at twelve, I brought up to old Antenor his chocolate, as usual. As I do the cleaning, I have a key to the apartment. I opened, I entered, and what did I see? Oh! my God!"

And she began to scream loudly.

"This grief proves that you have a good heart, madame," gravely said M. Mechinet. "Only, as I am in a great hurry, please try to overcome it. What did you think, seeing your tenant murdered?"

"I said to any one who wanted to hear: 'It is his nephew, the scoundrel, who has done it to inherit.' "

"What makes you so positive? Because after all to accuse a man of so great a crime, is to drive him to the scaffold."

"But, monsieur, who else would it be? M. Monistrol came to see his uncle last evening, and when he left it was nearly midnight. Besides, he nearly always speaks to me, but never said a word to me that night, neither when he came, nor when he left. And from that moment up to the time I discovered everything, I am sure nobody went up to M. Antenor's apartment."

I admit this evidence confused me. I would not have thought of continuing the examination. Fortunately, M. Mechinet's experience was great, and he was thoroughly master of the difficult art of drawing the whole truth from witnesses.

"Then, madame," he insisted, "you are certain that Monistrol came yesterday evening?"

"I am certain."

"Did you surely see him and recognize him?"

"Ah! wait. I did not look him in the face. He passed quickly, trying to hide himself, like the scoundrel he is, and the hallway is badly illuminated."

At this reply, of such incalculable importance, I jumped up and, approaching the concierge, exclaimed:

"If it is so, how dare you affirm that you recognized M. Monistrol?"

She looked me over from head to foot, and answered with an ironical smile:

"If I did not see the master's face, I did see the dog's nose. As I always pet him, he came into my lodge, and I was just going to give him a bone from a leg of mutton when his master whistled for him."

I looked at M. Mechinet, anxious to know what he thought of this, but his face faithfully kept the secret of his impressions.

He only added:

"Of what breed is M. Monistrol's dog?"

"It is a loulou, such as the drovers used formerly, all black, with a white spot over the ear; they call him "Pluton.""

M. Mechinet rose.

"You may retire," he said to the concierge; "I know all I want."

And when she had left, he remarked:

"It seems to me impossible that the nephew is not the guilty one."

During the time this long examination was taking place, the physicians had come. When they finished the autopsy they reached the following conclusion:

"M. Pigoreau's death had certainly been instantaneous." So it was not he who had lined out the five letters, Monis, which we saw on the floor near the body.

So I was not mistaken.

"But if it was not he," exclaimed M. Mechinet, "who was it then? Monistrol—that is what nobody will ever succeed in putting into my brain."

And the commissary, happy at being free to go to dinner at last, made fun of M. Mechinet's perplexities—ridiculous perplexities, since Monistrol had confessed. But M. Mechinet said:

"Perhaps I am really nothing but an idiot; the future will tell. In the mean time, come, my dear Monsieur Godeuil, come with me to Police Headquarters."

VI.

In like manner, as in going to Batignolles, we took a cab also to go to Police Headquarters.

M. Mechinet's preoccupation was great. His fingers continually traveled from the empty snuff-box to his nose, and I heard him grumbling between his teeth:

"I shall assure myself of the truth of this! I must find out the truth of this."

Then he took from his pocket the cork which I had given him, and turned it over and over like a monkey picking a nut, and murmured:

"This is evidence, however; there must be something gained by this green wax."

Buried in my corner, I did not breathe. My position was certainly one of the strangest, but I did not give it a thought. Whatever intelligence I had was absorbed in this affair; in my mind I went over its various and contradictory elements, and exhausted myself in trying to penetrate the secret of the tragedy, a secret of which I had a presentiment.

When our carriage stopped, it was night—dark.

The Quai des Orfevres was deserted and quiet; not a sound, not a passer-by. The stores in the neighborhood, few and far between, were closed. All the life of the district had hidden itself in the little restaurant which almost forms the corner of the Rue de Jerusalem, behind the red curtains, on which were outlined the shadows of the patrons.

"Will they let you see the accused?" I asked M. Mechinet.

"Certainly," he answered. "Am I not charged with the following up of this affair? Is it not necessary, in view of unforeseen requirements at the inquest, that I be allowed to examine the prisoner at any hour of the day or night?"

And with a quick step he entered under the arch, saying to me:

"Come, come, we have no time to lose."

I did not require any encouragement from him. I followed, agitated by indescribable emotions and trembling with vague curiosity.

It was the first time I had ever crossed the threshold of the

Police Headquarters, and God knows what my prejudices were then.

There, I said to myself, not without a certain terror, there is the secret of Paris!

I was so lost in thought, that, forgetting to look where I was going, I almost fell.

The shock brought me back to a sense of the situation.

We were going along an immense passageway, with damp walls and an uneven pavement. Soon my companion entered a small room where two men were playing cards, while three or four others, stretched on cots, were smoking pipes. M. Mechinet exchanged a few words with them—I could not hear, for I had remained outside. Then he came out again, and we continued our walk.

After crossing a court and entering another passageway, we soon came before an iron gate with heavy bolts and a formidable lock.

At a word from M. Mechinet, a watchman opened this gate for us; at the right we passed a spacious room, where it seemed to me I saw policemen and Paris guards; finally we climbed up a very steep stairway.

At the top of the stairs, at the entrance to a narrow passage with a number of small doors, was seated a stout man with a jovial face, that certainly had nothing of the classical jailer about it.

As soon as he noticed my companion, he exclaimed:

"Eh! it is M. Mechinet. Upon my word, I was expecting you. I bet you came for the murderer of the little old man of Batignolles."

"Precisely. Is there anything new?"

"No."

"But the investigating judge must have come."

"He has just gone."

"Well?"

"He did not stay more than three minutes with the accused, and when he left he seemed very much satisfied. At the bottom of the stairs he met the governor, and said to him: "This is a settled case; the murderer has not even attempted to deny.""

M. Mechinet jumped about three feet; but the jailer did not notice it, and continued:

"But then, that did not surprise me. At a mere glance at the individual as they brought him I said: 'Here is one who will not know how to hold out.'"

"And what is he doing now?"

"He moans. I have been instructed to watch him, for fear he should commit suicide, and as is my duty, I do watch him, but it is mere waste of time. He is another one of those fellows who care more for their own skin than for that of others."

"Let us go and see him," interrupted M. Mechinet; "and above all, no noise."

At once all three advanced on tiptoe till we reached a solid oak door, through which had been cut a little barred window about a man's height from the ground.

Through this little window could be seen everything that occurred in the cell, which was illuminated by a paltry gasburner.

The jailer glanced in first, M. Mechinet then looked, and at last my turn came.

On a narrow iron couch, covered with a gray woolen blanket with yellow stripes, I perceived a man lying flat, his head hidden between his partly folded arms.

He was crying; the smothered sound of his sobs reached me, and from time to time a convulsive trembling shook him from head to foot.

"Open now," ordered M. Mechinet of the watchman.

He obeyed, and we entered.

At the sound of the grating key, the prisoner had raised himself and, sitting on his pallet, his legs and arms hanging, his head inclined on his chest, he looked at us stupidly.

He was a man of thirty-five or thirty-eight years of age; his build a little above the average, but robust, with an apoplectic neck sunk between two broad shoulders. He was ugly; smallpox had disfigured him, and his long, straight nose and receding forehead gave him somewhat the stupid look of a sheep. However his blue eyes were very beautiful, and his teeth were of remarkable whiteness.

"Well! M. Monistrol," began M. Mechinet, "we are grieving, are we?"

As the unfortunate man did not answer, he continued:

"I admit that the situation is not enlivening. Nevertheless, if I were in your place, I would prove that I am a man. I would have common sense, and try to prove my innocence."

"I am not innocent."

This time there could not be any mistake, nor could the intelligence of the officer be doubted; it was from the very mouth of the accused that we gathered the terrible confession.

"What!" exclaimed M. Mechinet, "it was you who—"

The man stood up, staggering on his legs, his eyes bloodshot, his mouth foaming, prey to a veritable attack of rage.

"Yes, it was I," he interrupted; "I alone. How many times will I have to repeat it? Already, a while ago, a judge came; I confessed everything and signed my confession. What more do you ask? Go on, I know what awaits me, and I am not afraid. I killed, I must be killed! Well, cut my head off, the sooner the better."

Somewhat stunned at first, M. Mechinet soon recovered.

"One moment. You know," he said, "they do not cut people's heads off like that. First they must prove that they are guilty; after that the courts admit certain errors, certain fatalities, if you will, and it is for this very reason that they recognize 'extenuating circumstances.'"

An inarticulate moan was Monistrol's only answer. M. Mechinet continued:

"Did you have a terrible grudge against your uncle?"

"Oh, no."

"Then why?"

"To inherit; my affairs were in bad shape—you may make inquiry. I needed money; my uncle, who was very rich, refused me some."

"I understand; you hoped to escape from justice?"

"I was hoping to."

Until then I had been surprised at the way M. Mechinet was conducting this rapid examination, but now it became clear to me. I guessed rightly what followed; I saw what trap he was laying for the accused.

"Another thing," he continued suddenly, "where did you buy the revolver you used in committing the murder?"

No surprise appeared on Monistrol's face.

"I had it in my possession for a long time," he answered.

"What did you do with it after the crime?"

"I threw it outside on the boulevard."

"All right," spoke M. Mechinet gravely, "we will make search and will surely find it."

After a moment of silence he added:

"What I can not explain to myself is, why is it that you had your dog follow you?"

"What! How! My dog?"

"Yes, Pluton. The concierge recognized him."

Monistrol's fists moved convulsively; he opened his mouth as if to answer, but a sudden idea crossing his mind, he threw himself back on his bed, and said in a tone of firm determination:

"You have tortured me enough; you shall not draw another word from me."

It was clear that to insist would be taking trouble for nothing.

We then withdrew.

Once outside on the quay, grasping M. Mechinet's arm, I said:

"You heard it, that unfortunate man does not even know how his uncle died. Is it possible to still doubt his innocence?"

But he was a terrible skeptic, that old detective.

"Who knows?" he answered. "I have seen some famous actors in my life. But we have had enough of it for to-day. This evening I will take you to eat soup with me. To-morrow it will be daylight, and we shall see."

VII.

It was not far from ten o'clock when M. Mechinet, whom I was still accompanying, rang at the door of his apartment.

"I never carry any latch-key," he told me. "In our blessed business you can never know what may happen. There are many rascals who have a grudge against me, and even if I am not always careful for myself, I must be so for my wife."

My worthy neighbor's explanation was superfluous. I had understood. I even observed that he rang in a peculiar way, which must have been an agreed signal between his wife and himself.

It was the amiable Madame Mechinet who opened the door.

With a quick movement, as graceful as a kitten, she threw herself on her husband's neck, exclaiming:

"Here you are at last! I do not know why, but I was almost worried."

But she stopped suddenly; she had just noticed me. Her joyous expression darkened, and she drew back. Addressing both me and her husband:

"What!" she continued, "you come from the cafe at this hour? That is not common sense!"

M. Mechinet's lips wore the indulgent smile of the man who is sure of being loved, who knows how to appease by a word the quarrel picked with him.

"Do not scold us, Caroline," he answered; by this "us" associating me with his case. "We do not come from the cafe, and neither have we lost our time. They sent for me for an affair; for a murder committed at Batignolles."

With a suspicious look the young woman examined us—first her husband and then me; when she had persuaded herself that she was not being deceived, she said only:

"Ah!"

But it would take a whole page to give an inventory of all that was contained in that brief exclamation.

It was addressed to M. Mechinet, and clearly signified:

"What? you confided in this young man! You have revealed to him your position; you have initiated him into our secrets?"

Thus I interpreted that eloquent "Ah!" My worthy neighbor, too, must have interpreted it as I did, for he answered:

"Well, yes. Where is the wrong of it? I may have to dread the vengeance of wretches whom I give up to justice, but what have I to fear from honest people? Do you imagine perhaps that I hide myself; that I am ashamed of my trade?"

"You misunderstood me, my friend," objected the young woman.

M. Mechinet did not even hear her.

He had just mounted—I learned this detail later—on a favorite hobby that always carried the day.

"Upon my word," he continued, "you have some peculiar ideas, madame, my wife. What! I one of the sentinels of civilization! I, who assure society's safety at the price of my rest and at the risk of my life, and should I blush for it? That would be far too amusing. You will tell me that against us of the police there exist a number of absurd prejudices left behind by the past. What do I care? Yes, I know that there are some sensitive gentlemen who look down on us. But sacrebleu! How I should like to see their faces if tomorrow my colleagues and I should go on a strike, leaving the streets free to the army of rascals whom we hold in check."

Accustomed without doubt to explosions of this kind, Madame Mechinet did not say a word; she was right in doing so, for my good neighbor, meeting with no contradiction, calmed himself as if by magic.

"But enough of this," he said to his wife. "There is now a matter of far greater importance. We have not had any dinner yet; we are dying of hunger; have you anything to give us for supper?"

What happened that night must have happened too often for Madame Mechinet to be caught unprepared.

"In five minutes you gentlemen will be served," she answered with the most amiable smile.

In fact, a moment afterward we sat down at table before a fine cut of cold beef, served by Madame Mechinet, who did not stop filling our glasses with excellent Macon wine.

And while my worthy neighbor was conscientiously plying his fork I, looking at that peaceable home, which was his, that pretty, attentive little wife, which was his, kept asking myself whether I really saw before me one of those "savage" police agents who have been the heroes of so many absurd stories.

However, hunger soon satisfied, M. Mechinet started to tell his wife about our expedition. And he did not tell her about it lightly, but with the most minute details. She had taken a seat beside him, and by the way she listened and looked understandingly, asking for explanations when she had not well understood, one could recognize in her a plain "Egeria," accustomed to be consulted, and having a deliberative vote.

When M. Mechinet had finished, she said to him:

"You have made a great mistake, an irreparable mistake."

"Where?"

"It is not to Police Headquarters you should have gone, abandoning Batignolles."

"But Monistrol?"

"Yes, you wanted to examine him. What advantage did you get from that?"

"It was of use to me, my dear friend."

"For nothing. It was to the Rue Vivienne that you should have hurried, to the wife. You would have surprised her in a natural agitation caused by her husband's arrest, and if she is his accomplice, as we must suppose, with a little skill you would have made her confess."

At these words I jumped from my chair.

"What! madame," I exclaimed, "do you believe Monistrol guilty?"

After a moment's hesitation, she answered:

"Yes."

Then she added very vivaciously:

"But I am sure, do you hear, absolutely sure, that the murder was conceived by the woman. Of twenty crimes committed by men, fifteen have been conceived, planned and inspired by woman. Ask Mechinet. The concierge's deposition ought to have enlightened you. Who is that Madame Monistrol? They told you a remarkably beautiful person, coquettish, ambitious, affected with covetousness, and who was leading her husband by the end of his nose. Now what was her position? Wretched, tight, precarious. She suffered from it, and the proof of it is that she asked her uncle to loan her husband a hundred thousand francs. He refused them to her, thus shattering her hopes. Do you not think she had a deadly grudge against him? And when she kept seeing him in good health and sturdy as an oak, she must have said to herself fatally: 'He will live a hundred years; by the time he leaves us his inheritance we won't have any teeth left to munch it, and who knows even whether *he* will not bury *us!*' Is it so very far from this point to the conception of a crime? And the resolution once taken in her mind, she must have prepared her husband a long time before, she must have accustomed him to the thought of murder, she must have put, so to say, the knife in his hand. And he, one day, threatened with bankruptcy, crazed by his wife's lamentations, delivered the blow."

"All that is logical," approved M. Mechinet, "very logical, without a doubt, but what becomes of the circumstances brought to light by us?"

"Then, madame," I said, "you believe Monistrol stupid enough to denounce himself by writing down his name?"

She slightly shrugged her shoulders and answered:

"Is that stupidity? As for me, I maintain that it is not. Is not that point your strongest argument in favor of his innocence?"

This reasoning was so specious that for a moment I remained perplexed. Then recovering, I said, insisting:

"But he confesses his guilt, madame?"

"An excellent method of his for getting the authorities to prove him innocent."

"Oh!"

"You yourself are proof of its efficacy, dear M. Godeuil."

"Eh! madame, the unfortunate does not even know how his uncle was killed!"

"I beg your pardon; he *seemed* not to know it, which is not the same thing."

The discussion was becoming animated, and would have lasted much longer, had not M. Mechinet put an end to it.

"Come, come," he simply said to his wife, "you are too romantic this evening."

And addressing me, he continued:

"As for you, I shall come and get you to-morrow, and we shall go together to call on Madame Monistrol. And now, as I am dying for sleep, good night."

He may have slept. As for me, I could not close my eyes.

A secret voice within me seemed to say that Monistrol was innocent.

My imagination painted with painful liveliness the tortures of that unfortunate man, alone in his prison cell.

But why had he confessed?

VIII.

What I then lacked—I have had occasion to realize it hundreds of times since—was experience, business practise, and chiefly an exact knowledge of the means of action and of police investigation.

I felt vaguely that this particular investigation had been conducted wrongly, or rather superficially, but I would have been embarrassed to say why, and especially to say what should have been done.

None the less I was passionately interested in Monistrol.

It seemed to me that his cause was also mine, and it was only natural—my young vanity was at stake. Was it not one of my own remarks that had raised the first doubts as to the guilt of this unfortunate man?

I owed it to myself, I said, to prove his innocence.

Unfortunately the discussions of the evening troubled me to

such an extent that I did not know precisely on which fact to build up my system.

And, as always happens when the mind is for too long a time applied to the solution of a problem, my thoughts became tangled, like a skein in the hands of a child; I could no longer see clearly; it was chaos.

Buried in my armchair, I was torturing my brain, when, at about nine o'clock in the morning, M. Mechinet, faithful to his promise of the evening before, came for me.

"Come, let us go," he said, shaking me suddenly, for I had not heard him enter. "Let us start!"

"I am with you," I said, getting up.

We descended hurriedly, and I noticed then that my worthy neighbor was more carefully dressed than usual.

He had succeeded in giving himself that easy and well-to-do appearance which more than anything else impresses the Parisian shopkeeper.

His cheerfulness was that of a man sure of himself, marching toward certain victory.

We were soon in the street, and while walking he asked me:

"Well, what do you think of my wife? I pass for a clever man at police headquarters, and yet I consult her—even Moliere consulted his maid—and often I find it to my advantage. She has one weakness: for her, unreasonable crimes do not exist, and her imagination endows all scoundrels with diabolical plots. But as I have exactly the opposite fault, as I perhaps am a little too much matter-of-fact, it rarely happens that from our consultation the truth does not result somehow."

"What!" I exclaimed, "you think to have solved the mystery of the Monistrol case!"

He stopped short, drew out his snuff-box, inhaled three or four of his imaginary pinches, and in a tone of quiet vanity, answered:

"I have at least the means of solving it."

In the mean time we reached the upper end of the Rue Vivienne, not far from Monistrol's business place.

"Now look out," said M. Mechinet to me. "Follow me, and whatever happens do not be surprised."

He did well to warn me. Without the warning I would have been surprised at seeing him suddenly enter the store of an umbrella dealer.

Stiff and grave, like an Englishman, he made them show him everything there was in the shop, found nothing suitable, and finally inquired whether it was not possible for them to manufacture for him an umbrella according to a model which he would furnish.

They answered that it would be the easiest thing in the world, and he left, saying he would return the day following.

And most assuredly the half hour he spent in this store was not wasted.

While examining the objects submitted to him, he had artfully drawn from the dealers all they knew about the Monistrol couple.

Upon the whole, it was not a difficult task, as the affair of the "little old man of Batignolles" and the arrest of the imitation jeweler had deeply stirred the district and were the subject of all conversation.

"There, you see," he said to me, when we were outside, "how exact information is obtained. As soon as the people know with whom they are dealing, they pose, make long phrases, and then good-by to strict truth."

This comedy was repeated by Mr. Mechinet in seven or eight stores of the neighborhood.

In one of them, where the proprietors were disagreeable and not much inclined to talk, he even made a purchase amounting to twenty francs.

But after two hours of such practise, which amused me very much, we had gaged public opinion. We knew exactly what was thought of M. and Mme. Monistrol in the neighborhood, where they had lived since their marriage, that is, for the past four years.

As regards the husband, there was but one opinion—he was the most gentle and best of men, obliging, honest, intelligent, and hard-working. If he had not made a success in his business it was because luck does not always favor those who most deserve it. He did wrong in taking a shop doomed to bankruptcy, for, in the past fifteen years, four merchants had failed there.

Everybody knew and said that he adored his wife, but this great love had not exceeded the proper limits, and therefore no ridicule resulted for him.

Nobody could believe in his guilt.

His arrest, they said, must be a mistake made by the police.

As to Madame Monistrol, opinion was divided.

Some thought she was too stylish for her means; others claimed that a stylish dress was one of the requirements, one of the necessities, of a business dealing in luxuries.

In general, they were convinced that she loved her husband very much. For instance, they were unanimous in praising her modesty, the more meritorious, because she was remarkably beautiful, and because she was besieged by many admirers. But never had she given any occasion to be talked about, never had her immaculate reputation been glanced at by the lightest suspicion.

I noticed that this especially bewildered M. Mechinet.

"It is surprising," he said to me, "not one scandal, not one slander, not one calumny. Oh! this is not what Caroline thought. According to her, we were to find one of those lady shopkeepers, who occupy the principal place in the office, who display their beauty much more than their merchandise, and who banish to the back shop their husband—a blind idiot, or an indecent obliging scoundrel. But not at all."

I did not answer; I was not less disconcerted than my neighbor.

We were now far from the evidence the concierge of the Rue le Cluse had given; so greatly varies the point of view according to the location. What at Batignolles is considered to be a blamable coquetry, is in the Rue Vivienne nothing more than an unreasonable requirement of position.

But we had already employed too much time for our investigations to stop and exchange impressions and to discuss our conjectures.

"Now," said M. Mechinet, "before entering the place, let us study its approaches."

And trained in carrying out discreet investigations in the midst of Paris bustle, he motioned to me to follow him under a carriage entrance, exactly opposite Monistrol's store.

It was a modest shop, almost poor, compared with those around it. The front needed badly a painter's brush. Above, in letters which were formerly gilt, now smoky and blackened, Monistrol's name was displayed. On the plate-glass windows could be read: "Gold and Imitation."

Alas! it was principally imitation that was glistening in the show window. On the rods were hanging many plated chains, sets of jet jewelry, diadems studded with rhinestones, then imitation coral necklaces and brooches and rings; and cuff buttons set with imitation stones in all colors.

All in all, a poor display, it could never tempt gimlet thieves.

"Let us enter," I said to M. Mechinet.

He was less impatient than I, or knew better how to keep back his impatience, for he stopped me by the arm, saying:

"One moment. I should like at least to catch a glimpse of Madame Monistrol."

In vain did we continue to stand for more than twenty minutes on our observation post; the shop remained empty, Madame Monistrol did not appear.

"Come, Monsieur Godeuil, let us venture," exclaimed my worthy neighbor at last, "we have been standing in one place long enough."

IX.

In order to reach Monistrol's store we had only to cross the street.

At the noise of the door opening, a little servant girl, from fifteen to sixteen years old, dirty and ill combed, came out of the back shop.

"What can I serve the gentlemen with?" she asked.

"Madame Monistrol?"

"She is there, gentlemen; I am going to notify her, because you see—"

M. Mechinet did not give her time to finish. With a movement, rather brutal, I must confess, he pushed her out of the way and entered the back shop saying:

"All right, since she is there, I am going to speak to her."

As for me, I walked on the heels of my worthy neighbor, convinced that we would not leave without knowing the solution of the riddle.

That back shop was a miserable room, serving at the same time as parlor, dining-room, and bedroom. Disorder reigned supreme; moreover there was that incoherence we notice in the house of the poor who endeavor to appear rich.

In the back there was a bed with blue damask curtains and with pillows adorned with lace; in front of the mantelpiece stood a table all covered with the remains of a more than modest breakfast.

In a large armchair was seated, or rather lying, a very blond young woman, who was holding in her hand a sheet of stamped paper.

It was Madame Monistrol.

Surely in telling us of her beauty, all the neighbors had come far below the reality. I was dazzled.

Only one circumstance displeased me. She was in full mourning, and wore a crape dress, slightly decollete, which fitted her marvelously.

This showed too much presence of mind for so great a sorrow. Her attire seemed to me to be the contrivance of an actress dressing herself for the role she is to play.

As we entered, she stood up, like a frightened doe, and with a voice which seemed to be broken by tears, she asked:

"What do you want, gentlemen?"

M. Mechinet had also observed what I had noticed.

"Madame," he answered roughly, "I was sent by the Court; I am a police agent."

Hearing this, she fell back into her armchair with a moan that would have touched a tiger.

Then, all at once, seized by some kind of enthusiasm, with sparkling eyes and trembling lips, she exclaimed:

"So you have come to arrest me. God bless you. See! I am ready, take me. Thus I shall rejoin that honest man, arrested by you last evening. Whatever be his fate, I want to share it. He is as innocent as I am. No matter! If he is to be the victim of an error of human justice, it shall be for me a last joy to die with him."

She was interrupted by a low growl coming from one of the corners of the back shop.

I looked, and saw a black dog, with bristling hair and bloodshot eyes, showing his teeth, and ready to jump on us.

"Be quiet, Pluton!" called Madame Monistrol; "go and lie down; these gentlemen do not want to hurt me."

Slowly and without ceasing to glare at us furiously, the dog took refuge under the bed.

"You are right to say that we do not want to hurt you, madame," continued M. Mechinet, "we did not come to arrest you."

If she heard, she did not show it.

"This morning already," she said, "I received this paper here, commanding me to appear later in the day, at three o'clock, at the court-house, in the office of the investigating judge. What do they want of me? my God! What do they want of me?"

"To obtain explanations which will prove, I hope, your husband's innocence. So, madame, do not consider me an enemy. What I want is to get at the truth."

He produced his snuff-box, hastily poked his fingers therein, and in a solemn tone, which I did not recognize in him, he resumed:

"It is to tell you, madame, of what importance will be your answers to the questions which I shall have the honor of asking you. Will it be convenient for you to answer me frankly?"

For a long time she rested her large blue eyes, drowned in tears, on my worthy neighbor, and in a tone of painful resignation she said:

"Question me, monsieur."

For the third time I repeat it, I was absolutely without experience; I was troubled over the manner in which M. Mechinet had begun this examination.

It seemed to me that he betrayed his perplexity, and that, instead of pursuing an aim established in advance, he was delivering his blows at random.

Ah! if I were allowed to act! Ah! if I had dared.

He, impenetrable, had seated himself opposite Madame Monistrol.

"You must know, madame," he began, "that it was the night

before last, at eleven o'clock, that M. Pigoreau, called Antenor, your husband's uncle, was murdered."

"Alas!"

"Where was M. Monistrol at that hour?"

"My God! that is fatality."

M. Mechinet did not wince.

"I am asking you, madame," he insisted, "where your husband spent the evening of the day before yesterday?"

The young woman needed time to answer, because she sobbed so that it seemed to choke her. Finally mastering herself, she moaned:

"The day before yesterday my husband spent the evening out of the house."

"Do you know where he was?"

"Oh! as to that, yes. One of our workmen, who lives in Montrouge, had to deliver for us a set of false pearls, and did not deliver it. We were taking the risk of being obliged to keep the order on our account, which would have been a disaster, as we are not rich. That is why, at dinner, my husband told me: 'I am going to see that fellow.' And, in fact, toward nine o'clock, he went out, and I even went with him as far as the omnibus, where he got in in my presence, Rue Richelieu."

I was breathing more easily. This, perhaps, was an alibi after all.

M. Mechinet had the same thought, and, more gently, he resumed:

"If it is so, your workman will be able to affirm that he saw M. Monistrol at his house at eleven o'clock."

"Alas! no."

"How? Why?"

"Because he had gone out. My husband did not see him."

"That is indeed fatal. But it may be that the concierge noticed M. Monistrol."

"Our workman lives in a house where there is no concierge."

That may have been the truth; it was certainly a terrible charge against the unfortunate prisoner.

"And at what time did your husband return?" continued M. Mechinet.

"A little after midnight."

"Did you not find that he was absent a very long time?"

"Oh! yes. And I even reproved him for it. He told me as an excuse that he had taken the longest way, that he had sauntered on the road, and that he had stopped in a cafe to drink a glass of beer."

"How did he look when he came home?"

"It seemed to me that he was vexed; but that was natural."

"What clothes did he wear?"

"The same he had on when he was arrested."

"You did not observe in him anything out of the ordinary?"

"Nothing."

Standing a little behind M. Mechinet, I could, at my leisure, observe Madame Monistrol's face and catch the most fleeting signs of her emotion.

She seemed overwhelmed by an immense grief, large tears rolled down her pale cheeks; nevertheless, it seemed to me at times that I could discover in the depth of her large blue eyes something like a flash of joy.

Is it possible that she is guilty? And as this thought, which had already come to me before, presented itself more obstinately, I quickly stepped forward, and in a rough tone asked her:

"But you, madame, where were you on that fatal evening at the time your husband went uselessly to Montrouge, to look for his workman?"

She cast on me a long look, full of stupor, and softly answered:

"I was here, monsieur; witnesses will confirm it to you."

"Witnesses!"

"Yes, monsieur. It was so hot that evening that I had a longing for ice-cream, but it vexed me to eat it alone. So I sent my maid to invite my neighbors, Madame Dorstrich, the bootmaker's wife, whose store is next to ours, and Madame Rivaille, the glove manufacturer, opposite us. These two ladies accepted my invitation and remained here until half-past eleven. Ask them, they will tell you. In the midst of such cruel trials that I am suffering, this accidental circumstance is a blessing from God."

Was it really an accidental circumstance?

That is what we were asking ourselves, M. Mechinet and I, with glances more rapid than a flash.

When chance is so intelligent as that, when it serves a cause so directly, it is very hard not to suspect that it had been somewhat prepared and led on.

But the moment was badly chosen for this discovery of our bottom thoughts.

"You have never been suspected, you, madame," imprudently stated M. Mechinet. "The worst that may be supposed is that your husband perhaps told you something of the crime before he committed it."

"Monsieur—if you knew us."

"Wait. Your business is not going very well, we were told; you were embarrassed."

"Momentarily, yes; in fact—"

"Your husband must have been unhappy and worried about this precarious condition. He must have suffered especially for you, whom he adores; for you who are so young and beautiful; for you, more than for himself, he must have ardently desired the enjoyments of luxury and the satisfactions of self-esteem, procured by wealth."

"Monsieur, I repeat it, my husband is innocent."

With an air of reflection, M. Mechinet seemed to fill his nose with tobacco; then all at once he said:

"Then, by thunder! how do you explain his confessions? An innocent man does not declare himself to be guilty at the mere mentioning of the crime of which he is suspected; that is rare, madame; that is prodigious!"

A fugitive blush appeared on the cheeks of the young woman. Up to then her look had been straight and clear; now for the first time it became troubled and unsteady.

"I suppose," she answered in an indistinct voice and with increased tears, "I believe that my husband, seized by fright and stupor at finding himself accused of so great a crime, lost his head."

M. Mechinet shook his head.

"If absolutely necessary," he said, "a passing delirium might be admitted; but this morning, after a whole long night of reflection, M. Monistrol persists in his first confessions."

Was this true? Was my worthy neighbor talking at random, or else had he before coming to get me been at the prison to get news?

However it was, the young woman seemed almost to faint; hiding her head between her hands, she murmured:

"Lord God! My poor husband has become insane."

Convinced now that I was assisting at a comedy, and that the great despair of this young woman was nothing but falsehood, I was asking myself whether for certain reasons which were escaping me she had not shaped the terrible determination taken by her husband; and whether, he being innocent, she did not know the real guilty one.

But M. Mechinet did not have the air of a man looking so far ahead.

After having given the young woman a few words of consolation too common to compromise him in any way, he gave her to understand that she would forestall many prejudices by allowing a minute and strict search through her domicile.

This opening she seized with an eagerness which was not feigned.

"Search, gentlemen!" she told us; "examine, search everywhere. It is a service which you will render me. And it will not take long.

We have in our name nothing but the backshop where we are, our
maid's room on the sixth floor, and a little cellar. Here are the keys
for everything."

To my great surprise, M. Mechinet accepted; he seemed to
be starting on one of the most exact and painstaking investigations.

What was his object? It was not possible that he did not have in
view some secret aim, as his researches evidently had to end in
nothing.

As soon as he had apparently finished he said:

"There remains the cellar to be explored."

"I am going to take you down, monsieur," said Madame Monistrol.

And immediately taking a burning candle, she made us cross a
yard into which a door led from the back-shop, and took us across a
very slippery stairway to a door which she opened, saying:

"Here it is—enter, gentlemen."

I began to understand.

My worthy neighbor examined the cellar with a ready and
trained look. It was miserably kept, and more miserably fitted out.
In one corner was standing a small barrel of beer, and immediately
opposite, fastened on blocks, was a barrel of wine, with a wooden
tap to draw it. On the right side, on iron rods, were lined up about
fifty filled bottles. These bottles M. Mechinet did not lose sight of,
and found occasion to move them one by one.

And what I saw he noticed: not one of them was sealed with
green wax.

Thus the cork picked up by me, and which served to protect the
point of the murderer's weapon, did not come from the Monistrols'
cellar.

"Decidedly," M. Mechinet said, affecting some disappointment,
"I do not find anything; we can go up again."

We did so, but not in the same order in which we descended,
for in returning I was the first.

Thus it was I who opened the door of the back-shop. Immediately the dog of the Monistrol couple sprang at me, barking so
furiously that I jumped back.

"The devil! Your dog is vicious," M. Mechinet said to the
young woman.

She already called him off with a gesture of her hand.

"Certainly not, he is not vicious," she said, "but he is a good
watchdog. We are jewelers, exposed more than others to thieves; we
have trained him."

Involuntarily, as one always does after having been threatened
by a dog, I called him by his name, which I knew:

"Pluton! Pluton!"

But instead of coming near me, he retreated growling, showing his sharp teeth.

"Oh, it is useless for you to call him," thoughtlessly said Madame Monistrol. "He will not obey you."

"Indeed! And why?"

"Ah! because he is faithful, as all of his breed; he knows only his master and me."

This sentence apparently did not mean anything. For me it was like a flash of light. And without reflecting I asked:

"Where then, madame, was that faithful dog the evening of the crime?"

The effect produced on her by this direct question was such that she almost dropped the candlestick she was still holding.

"I do not know," she stammered; "I do not remember."

"Perhaps he followed your husband."

"In fact, yes, it seems to me now I remember."

"He must then have been trained to follow carriages, since you told us that you went with your husband as far as the Omnibus."

She remained silent, and I was going to continue when M. Mechinet interrupted me. Far from taking advantage of the young woman's troubled condition, he seemed to assume the task of reassuring her, and after having urged her to obey the summons of the investigating judge, he led me out.

Then when we were outside he said:

"Are you losing your head?"

The reproach hurt me.

"Is it losing one's head," I said, "to find the solution of the problem? Now I have it, that solution. Monistrol's dog shall guide us to the truth."

My hastiness made my worthy neighbor smile, and in a fatherly tone he said to me:

"You are right, and I have well understood you. Only if Madame Monistrol has penetrated into your suspicions, the dog before this evening will be dead or will have disappeared."

X.

I had committed an enormous imprudence, it was true. Nevertheless, I had found the weak point; that point by which the most solid system of defense may be broken down.

I, voluntary recruit, had seen clearly where the old stager was losing himself, groping about. Any other would, perhaps, have been jealous and would have had a grudge against me. But not he.

He did not think of anything else but of profiting by my fortunate discovery; and, as he said, everything was easy enough now, since the investigation rested on a positive point of departure.

We entered a neighboring restaurant to deliberate while lunching.

The problem, which an hour before seemed unsolvable, now stood as follows:

It had been proved to us, as much as could be by evidence, that Monistrol was innocent. Why had he confessed to being guilty? We thought we could guess why, but that was not the question of the moment. We were equally certain that Madame Monistrol had not budged from her home the night of the murder. But everything tended to show that she was morally an accomplice to the crime; that she had known of it, even if she did not advise and prepare it, and that, on the other hand, she knew the murderer very well.

Who was he, that murderer?

A man whom Monistrol's dog obeyed as well as his master, since he had him follow him when he went to the Batignolles.

Therefore, it was an intimate friend of the Monistrol household. He must have hated the husband, however, since he had arranged everything with an infernal skill, so that the suspicion of the crime should fall on that unfortunate.

On the other hand, he must have been very dear to the woman, since, knowing him, she did not give him up, and without hesitation sacrificed to him her husband.

Well!

Oh! my God! The conclusion was all in a definite shape. The murderer could only be a miserable hypocrite, who had taken advantage of the husband's affection and confidence to take possession of the wife.

In short, Madame Monistrol, belieing her reputation, certainly had a lover, and that lover necessarily was the culprit.

All filled by this certitude, I was torturing my mind to think of some infallible stratagem which would lead us to this wretch.

"And this," I said to M. Mechinet, "is how I think we ought to operate. Madame Monistrol and the murderer must have agreed that after the crime they would not see each other for some time; this is the most elementary prudence. But you may believe that it will not be long before impatience will conquer the woman, and that she will want to see her accomplice. Now place near her an observer who will follow her everywhere, and before twice forty-eight hours have passed the affair will be settled."

Furiously fumbling after his empty snuff-box, M. Mechinet remained a moment without answering, mumbling between his teeth I know not what unintelligible words.

Then suddenly, leaning toward me, he said:

"That isn't it. You have the professional genius, that is certain, but it is practise that you lack. Fortunately, I am here. What! a phrase regarding the crime puts you on the trail, and you do not follow it."

"How is that?"

"That faithful dog must be made use of."

"I do not quite catch on."

"Then know how to wait. Madame Monistrol will go out at about two o'clock, in order to be at the court-house at three; the little maid will be alone in the shop. You will see. I only tell you that."

I insisted in vain; he did not want to say anything more, taking revenge for his defeat by this innocent spite. Willing or unwilling, I had to follow him to the nearest cafe, where he forced me to play dominoes.

Preoccupied as I was, I played badly, and he, without shame, was taking advantage of it to beat me, when the clock struck two.

"Up, men of the post," he said to me, letting go of his dice.

He paid, we went out, and a moment later we were again on duty under the carriage entrance from which we had before studied the front of the Monistrol store.

We had not been there ten minutes, when Madame Monistrol appeared in the door of her shop, dressed in black, with a long crape veil, like a widow.

"A pretty dress to go to an examination," mumbled M. Mechinet.

She gave a few instructions to her little maid, and soon left.

My companion patiently waited for five long minutes, and when he thought the young woman was already far away, he said to me:

"It is time."

And for the second time we entered the jewelry store.

The little maid was there alone, sitting in the office, for pastime nibbling some pieces of sugar stolen from her mistress.

As soon as we appeared she recognized us, and reddening and somewhat frightened, she stood up. But without giving her time to open her mouth, M. Mechinet asked:

"Where is Madame Monistrol?"

"Gone out, monsieur."

"You are deceiving me. She is there in the back shop."

"I swear to you, gentlemen, that she is not. Look in, please."

With the most disappointed looks, M. Mechinet was striking his forehead, repeating:

"How disagreeable. My God! how distressed that poor Madame Monistrol will be." And as the little maid was looking at him with her mouth wide open and with big, astonished eyes, he continued:

"But, in fact, you, my pretty girl, you can perhaps take the place of your mistress. I came back because I lost the address of the gentleman on whom she asked me to call."

"What gentleman?"

"You know. Monsieur—well, I have forgotten his name now. Monsieur—upon my word! you know, only him—that gentleman whom your devilish dog obeys so well."

"Oh! M. Victor?"

"That's just it. What is that gentleman doing?"

"He is a jeweler's workman; he is a great friend of monsieur; they were working together when monsieur was a jeweler's workman, before becoming proprietor, and that is why he can do anything he wants with Pluton."

"Then you can tell me where this M. Victor resides?"

"Certainly. He lives in the Rue du Roi-Dore, No. 23."

She seemed so happy, the poor girl, to be so well informed; but as for me, I suffered in hearing her so unwittingly denounce her mistress.

M. Mechinet, more hardened, did not have any such scruples. And even after we had obtained our information, he ended the scene with a sad joke.

As I opened the door for us to go out, he said to the young girl:

"Thanks to you. You have just rendered a great service to Madame Monistrol, and she will be very pleased."

XI.

As soon as I was on the sidewalk I had but one thought: and that was to shake out our legs and to run to the Rue du Roi-Dore and arrest this Victor, evidently the real culprit.

One word from M. Mechinet fell on my enthusiasm like a shower-bath.

"And the court," he said to me. "Without a warrant by the investigating judge I can not do anything. It is to the court-house that we must run."

"But we shall meet there Madame Monistrol, and if she sees us she will have her accomplice warned."

"Be it so," answered M. Mechinet, with a badly disguised bitterness. "Be it so, the culprit will escape and formality will have been saved. However, I shall prevent that danger. Let us walk, let us walk faster."

And, in fact, the hope of success gave him deer legs. Reaching the court-house, he jumped, four steps at a time, up the steep stairway leading to the floor on which were the judges of investigation, and, addressing the chief bailiff, he inquired whether the magistrate in charge of the case of the "little old man of Batignolles" was in his room.

"He is there," answered the bailiff, "with a witness, a young lady in black."

"It is she!" said my companion to me. Then to the bailiff: "You know me," he continued. "Quick, give me something to write on, a few words which you will take to the judge."

The bailiff went off with the note, dragging his boots along the dusty floor, and was not long in returning with the announcement that the judge was awaiting us in No. 9.

In order to see M. Mechinet, the magistrate had left Madame Monistrol in his office, under his clerk's guard, and had borrowed the room of one of his colleagues.

"What has happened?" he asked in a tone which enabled me to measure the abyss separating a judge from a poor detective.

Briefly and clearly M. Mechinet described the steps taken by us, their results and our hopes.

Must we say it? The magistrate did not at all seem to share our convictions.

"But since Monistrol confesses," he repeated with an obstinacy which was exasperating to me.

However, after many explanations, he said:

"At any rate, I am going to sign a warrant."

The valuable paper once in his possession, M. Mechinet escaped so quickly that I nearly fell in precipitating myself after him down the stairs. I do not know whether it took us a quarter of an hour to reach the Rue du Roi-Dore. But once there: "Attention," said M. Mechinet to me.

And it was with the most composed air that he entered in the narrow passageway of the house bearing No. 23.

"M. Victor?" he asked of the concierge.

"On the fourth floor, the right-hand door in the hallway."

"Is he at home?"

"Yes."

M. Mechinet took a step toward the staircase, but seemed to change his mind, and said to the concierge:

"I must make a present of a good bottle of wine to that dear Victor. With which wine-merchant does he deal in this neighborhood?"

"With the one opposite."

We were there in a trice, and in the tone of a customer M. Mechinet ordered:

"One bottle, please, and of good wine—of that with the green seal."

Ah! upon my word! That thought would never have come to
me at that time. And yet it was very simple.

When the bottle was brought, my companion exhibited the cork
found at the home of M. Pigoreau, called Antenor, and we easily
identified the wax.

To our moral certainty was now added a material certainty, and
with a firm hand M. Mechinet knocked at Victor's door.

"Come in," cried a pleasant-sounding voice.

The key was in the door; we entered, and in a very neat room I
perceived a man of about thirty, slender, pale, and blond, who was
working in front of a bench.

Our presence did not seem to trouble him.

"What do you want?" he politely asked.

M. Mechinet advanced toward him, and, taking him by the
arm, said:

"In the name of the law, I arrest you."

The man became livid, but did not lower his eyes.

"Are you making fun of me?" he said with an insolent air.
"What have I done?"

M. Mechinet shrugged his shoulders.

"Do not act like a child," he answered; "your account is settled.
You were seen coming out from old man Antenor's home, and in my
pocket I have a cork which you made use of to prevent your dagger
from losing its point."

It was like a blow of a fist in the neck of the wretch. Overwhelmed, he dropped on his chair, stammering:

"I am innocent."

"You will tell that to the judge," said M. Mechinet good-
naturedly; "but I am afraid that he will not believe you. Your accomplice, the Monistrol woman, has confessed everything."

As if moved by a spring, Victor jumped up.

"That is impossible!" he exclaimed. "She did not know anything about it."

"Then you did the business all alone? Very well. There is at
least that much confessed."

Then addressing me in a tone of a man knowing what he is talking about, M. Mechinet continued:

"Will you please look in the drawers, my dear Monsieur
Godeuil; you will probably find there the dagger of this pretty fellow, and certainly also the love-letters and the picture of his sweetheart."

A flash of rage shone in the murderer's eyes, and he was gnashing his teeth, but M. Mechinet's broad shoulders and iron grip extinguished in him every desire for resistance.

I found in a drawer of the bureau all the articles my companion had mentioned. And twenty minutes later, Victor, "duly packed in," as the expression goes, in a cab, between M. Mechinet and myself, was driving toward Police Headquarters.

"What," I said to myself, astonished by the simplicity of the thing, "that is all there is to the arrest of a murderer; of a man destined for the scaffold!"

Later I had occasion to learn at my expense which of criminals is the most terrible.

This one, as soon as he found himself in the police cell, seeing that he was lost, gave up and told us all the details of his crime.

He knew for a long time, he said, the old man Pigoreau, and was known by him. His object in killing him was principally to cause the punishment of the crime to fall on Monistrol. That is why he dressed himself up like Monistrol and had Pluton follow him. The old man once murdered, he had had the terrible courage to dip in the blood a finger of the body, to trace these five letters, MONIS, which almost caused an innocent man to be lost.

"And that had been so nicely arranged," he said to us with cynic bragging. "If I had succeeded, I would have killed two birds with the same stone. I would have been rid of my friend Monistrol, whom I hate and of whom I am jealous, and I would have enriched the woman I love."

It was, in fact, simple and terrible.

"Unfortunately, my boy," M. Mechinet objected, "you lost your head at the last moment. Well, one is never perfect. It was the left hand of the body which you dipped in the blood."

With a jump, Victor stood up.

"What!" he exclaimed, "is that what betrayed me?"

"Exactly."

With a gesture of a misunderstood genius, the wretch raised his arm toward heaven.

"That is for being an artist," he exclaimed.

And looking us over with an air of pity, he added:

"Old man Pigoreau was left-handed!"

Thus it was due to a mistake made in the investigation that the culprit was discovered so promptly.

The day following Monistrol was released.

And when the investigating judge reproached him for his untrue confession, which had exposed the courts to a terrible error, he could not obtain any other answer than:

"I love my wife, and wanted to sacrifice myself for her. I thought she was guilty."

Was she guilty? I would have taken an oath on it. She was arrested, but was acquitted by the same judgment which sentenced Victor to forced labor for life.

M. and Mme. Monistrol to-day keep an ill-reputed wineshop on the Vincennes Road. Their uncle's inheritance has long ago disappeared; they live in terrible misery.

MRS. HENRY WOOD

née Ellen Price (1814–1887), was a leading British practitioner of both domestic and sensational fiction. Slightly crippled by a spinal malformation, she took to writing at an early age and soon was second only to Miss Braddon in popularity. Her most famous novel was East Lynne *(1861), which went through many editions in England and America and was enormously popular in stage versions. It is still occasionally revived. Many of her other novels also contained strong mystery and detective elements, the most important being* The Channings *(1862),* Trevlyn Hold *(1864),* Within the Maze *(1872), and* The Master of Greylands *(1873). The* Johnny Ludlow *stories first appeared anonymously in* The Argosy *magazine, which Mrs. Wood edited. A continued series based on the life and surroundings of a county family, they were often concerned with crime and detection.*

"Going through the Tunnel"

We had to make a rush for it. And making a rush did not suit the Squire, any more than it does other people who have come to an age when the body's heavy and the breath nowhere. He reached the train, pushed head-foremost into a carriage, and then remembered the tickets. "Bless my heart?" he exclaimed, as he jumped out again, and nearly upset a lady who had a little dog in her arms, and a mass of fashionable hair on her head, that the Squire, in his hurry, mistook for tow.

"Plenty of time, sir," said a guard who was passing. "Three minutes to spare."

Instead of saying he was obliged to the man for his civility, or

relieved to find the tickets might still be had, the Squire snatched out
his old watch, and began abusing the railway clocks for being slow.
Had Tod been there he would have told him to his face that the
watch was fast, braving all retort, for the Squire believed in his
watch as he did in himself, and would rather have been told that *he*
could go wrong than that the watch could. But there was only me:
and I wouldn't have said it for anything.

"Keep two back-seats there, Johnny," said the Squire.

I put my coat on the corner furthest from the door, and the rug
on the one next to it, and followed him into the station. When the
Squire was late in starting, he was apt to get into the greatest flurry
conceivable; and the first thing I saw was himself blocking up the
ticket-place, and undoing his pocket-book with nervous fingers. He
had some loose gold about him, silver too, but the pocket-book came
to his hand first, so he pulled it out. These flurried moments of the
Squire's amused Tod beyond everything; he was so cool himself.

"Can you change this?" said the Squire, drawing out one from a
roll of five-pound notes.

"No, I can't," was the answer, in the surly tones put on by
ticket-clerks.

How the Squire crumpled up the note again, and searched in
his breeches pocket for gold, and came away with the two tickets
and the change, I'm sure he never knew. A crowd had gathered
round, wanting to take their tickets in turn, and knowing that he was
keeping them flurried him all the more. He stood at the back a
moment, put the roll of notes into his case, fastened it and returned
it to the breast of his over-coat, sent the change down into another
pocket without counting it, and went out with the tickets in hand.
Not to the carriage; but to stare at the big clock in front.

"Don't you see, Johnny? exactly four minutes and a half difference," he cried, holding out his watch to me. "It is a strange thing
they can't keep these railway clocks in order."

"My watch keeps good time, sir, and mine is with the railway. I
think it is right."

"Hold your tongue, Johnny. How dare you! Right? You send
your watch to be regulated the first opportunity, sir; don't *you* get
into the habit of being too late or too early."

When we finally went to the carriage there were some people in
it, but our seats were left for us. Squire Todhetley sat down by the
further door, and settled himself and his coats and his things comfortably, which he had been too flurried to do before. Cool as a cu-
cumber was he, now the bustle was over; cool as Tod could have
been. At the other door, with his face to the engine, sat a dark,
gentleman-like man of forty, who had made room for us to pass as
we got in. He had a large signet-ring on one hand, and a lavender

glove on the other. The other three seats opposite to us were vacant. Next to me sat a little man with a fresh colour and gold spectacles, who was already reading; and beyond him, in the corner, face to face with the dark man, was a lunatic. That's to mention him politely. Of all the restless, fidgety, worrying, hot-tempered passengers that ever put themselves into a carriage to travel with people in their senses, he was the worst. In fifteen moments he had made as many darts; now after his hat-box and things above his head; now calling the guard and the porters to ask senseless questions about his luggage; now treading on our toes, and trying the corner seat opposite the Squire, and then darting back to his own. He wore a wig of a decided green tinge, the effect of keeping, perhaps, and his skin was dry and shrivelled as an Egyptian mummy's.

A servant, in undress livery, came to the door, and touched his hat, which had a cockade on it, as he spoke to the dark man.

"Your ticket, my lord."

Lords are not travelled with every day, and some of us looked up. The gentleman took the ticket from the man's hand and slipped it into his waistcoat pocket.

"You can get me a newspaper, Wilkins. The *Times*, if it is to be had."

"Yes, my lord."

"Yes, there's room here, ma'am," interrupted the guard, sending the door back for a lady who stood at it. "Make haste, please."

The lady who stepped in was the same the Squire had bolted against. She sat down in the seat opposite me, and looked at every one of us by turns. There was a sort of violet bloom on her face and some soft white powder, seen plain enough through her veil. She took the longest gaze at the dark gentleman, bending a little forward to do it, for, as he was in a line with her, and also had his head turned from her, her curiosity could only catch a view of his side-face. Mrs. Todhetley might have said she had not put on her company manners. In the midst of this, the man-servant came back again.

"The *Times* is not here yet, my lord. They are expecting the papers in by the next down-train."

"Never mind, then. You can get me one at the next station, Wilkins."

"Very well, my lord."

Wilkins must certainly have had to scramble for his carriage, for we started before he had well left the door. It was not an express-train, and we should have to stop at several stations. Where the Squire and I had been staying does not matter; it has nothing to do with what I have to tell. It was a long way from our own home, and that's saying enough.

"Would you mind changing seats with me, sir?"

I looked up, to find the lady's face close to mine; she had spoken in a half-whisper. The Squire, who carried his old-fashioned notions of politeness with him when he went travelling, at once got up to offer her the corner. But she declined it, saying she was subject to face-ache, and did not care to be next the window. So she took my seat, and I sat down on the one opposite Mr. Todhetley.

"Which of the peers is that?" I heard her ask him in a loud whisper, as the lord put his head out at his window.

"Don't know at all, ma'am," said the Squire. "Don't know many of the peers myself, except those of my own county: Lyttleton, and Beauchamp, and—"

Of all snarling barks, the worst was given that moment in the Squire's face, suddenly ending the list. The little dog, an ugly, hairy, vile-tempered Scotch terrier, had been kept concealed under the lady's jacket, and now struggled itself free. The Squire's look of consternation was good! He had not known any animal was there.

"Be quiet, Wasp. How dare you bark at the gentleman? He will not bite, sir: he—"

"Who has a dog in the carriage?" shrieked the lunatic, starting up in a passion. "Dogs don't travel with passengers. Here! Guard! Guard!"

To call out for the guard when a train is going at full speed is generally useless. The lunatic had to sit down again; and the lady defied him, so to say, coolly avowing that she had hidden the dog from the guard on purpose, staring him in the face while she said it.

After this there was a lull, and we went speeding along, the lady talking now and again to the Squire. She seemed to want to grow confidential with him; but the Squire did not seem to care for it, though he was quite civil. She held the dog huddled up in her lap, so that nothing but his head peeped out.

"Halloa! How dare they be so negligent? There's no lamp in this carriage."

It was the lunatic again, and we all looked at the lamp. It had no light in it; but that it *had* when we first reached the carriage was certain; for, as the Squire went stumbling in, his head nearly touched the lamp, and I had noticed the flame. It seems the Squire had also.

"They must have put it out while we were getting our tickets," he said.

"I'll know the reason why when we stop," cried the lunatic, fiercely. "After passing the next station, we dash into the long tunnel. The idea of going through it in pitch darkness! It would not be safe."

"Especially with a dog in the carriage," spoke the lord, in a chaffing kind of tone, but with a good-natured smile. "We will have the lamp lighted, however."

As if to reward him for interfering, the dog barked up loudly, and tried to make a spring at him; upon which the lady smothered the animal up, head and all.

Another minute or two, and the train began to slacken speed. It was only an insignificant station, one not likely to be halted at for above a minute. The lunatic twisted his body out of the window, and shouted for the guard long before we were at a standstill.

"Allow me to manage this," said the lord, quietly putting him down. "They know me on the line. Wilkins!"

The man came rushing up at the call. He must have been out already, though we were not quite at a standstill yet.

"Is it for the *Times*, my lord? I am going for it."

"Never mind the *Times*. This lamp is not lighted, Wilkins. See the guard, and *get it done*. At once."

"And ask him what the mischief he means by his carelessness," roared out the lunatic after Wilkins, who went flying off. "Sending us on our road without a light!—and that dangerous tunnel close at hand."

The authority laid upon the words "Get it done," seemed an earnest that the speaker was accustomed to be obeyed, and would be this time. For once the lunatic sat quiet, watching the lamp, and for the light that was to be dropped into it from the top; and so did I, and so did the lady. We were all deceived, however, and the train went puffing on. The lunatic shrieked, the lord put his head out of the carriage and shouted for Wilkins.

No good. Shouting after a train is off never is much good. The lord sat down on his seat again, an angry frown crossing his face, and the lunatic got up and danced with rage.

"I do not know where the blame lies," observed the lord. "Not with my servant, I think: he is attentive, and has been with me some years."

"I'll know where it lies," retorted the lunatic. "I am a director on the line, though I don't often travel on it. This *is* management, this is! A few minutes more and we shall be in the dark tunnel."

"Of course it would have been satisfactory to have a light; but it is not of so much consequence," said the nobleman, wishing to soothe him. "There's no danger in the dark."

"No danger! No danger, sir! I think there is danger. Who's to know that dog won't spring out and bite us? Who's to know there won't be an accident in the tunnel? A light is a protection against having our pockets picked, if it's a protection against nothing else."

"I fancy our pockets are pretty safe to-day," said the lord, glancing round at us with a good-natured smile; as much as to say that none of us looked like thieves. "And I certainly trust we shall get through the tunnel safely."

"And I'll take care the dog does not bite you in the dark," spoke up the lady, pushing her head forward to give the lunatic a nod or two that you'd hardly have matched for defying impudence. "You'll be good, won't you, Wasp? But I should like the lamp lighted myself. You will perhaps be so kind, my lord, as to see that there's no mistake made about it at the next station!"

He slightly raised his hat to her and bowed in answer, but did not speak. The lunatic buttoned up his coat with fingers that were either nervous or angry, and then disturbed the little gentleman next him, who had read his big book throughout the whole commotion without once lifting his eyes, by hunting everywhere for his pocket-handkerchief.

"Here's the tunnel!" he cried out resentfully, as we dashed with a shriek into pitch darkness.

It was all very well for her to say she would take care of the dog, but the first thing the young beast did was to make a spring at me and then at the Squire, barking and yelping frightfully. The Squire pushed it away in a commotion. Though well accustomed to dogs he always fought shy of strange ones. The lady chattered and laughed, and did not seem to try to get hold of him, but we couldn't see, you know; the Squire hissed at him, the dog snarled and growled, altogether there was noise enough to deafen anything but a tunnel.

"Pitch him out at the window," cried the lunatic.

"Pitch yourself out," answered the lady. And whether she propelled the dog, or whether he went of his own accord, the beast sprang to the other end of the carriage, and was seized upon by the nobleman.

"I think, madam, you had better put him under your mantle and keep him there," said he, bringing the dog back to her and speaking quite civilly, but in the same tone of authority he had used to his servant about the lamp. "I have not the slightest objection to dogs myself, but many people have, and it is not altogether pleasant to have them loose in a railway carriage. I beg your pardon; I cannot see; is this your hand?"

It was her hand, I suppose, for the dog was left with her, and he went back to his seat again. When we emerged out of the tunnel into daylight, the lunatic's face was blue.

"Ma'am, if that miserable brute had laid hold of me by so much as the corner of my great-coat tail, I'd have had the law of you. It is perfectly monstrous that any one, putting themselves into a first-class carriage, should attempt to outrage railway laws, and upset the comfort of travellers with impunity. I shall complain to the guard."

"He does not bite, sir; he never bites," she answered softly, as if sorry for the escapade, and wishing to conciliate him. "The poor little bijou is frightened at darkness, and leaped from my arms unawares. There! I'll promise that you shall neither see nor hear him again."

She had tucked the dog so completely out of sight, that no one could have suspected one was there, just as it had been on first entering. The train was drawn up to the next station; when it stopped, the servant came and opened the carriage-door for his master to get out.

"Did you understand me, Wilkins, when I told you to get this lamp lighted?"

"My lord, I'm very sorry; I understood your lordship perfectly, but I couldn't see the guard," answered Wilkins. "I caught sight of him running up to his van-door at the last moment, but the train began to move off, and I had to jump in myself, or else be left behind."

The guard passed as he was explaining this, and the nobleman drew his attention to the lamp, curtly ordering him to "light it instantly." Lifting his hat to us by way of farewell, he disappeared; and the lunatic began upon the guard as if he were commencing a lecture to a deaf audience. The guard seemed not to hear it, so lost was he in astonishment at there being no light.

"Why, what can have douted it?" he cried aloud, staring up at the lamp. And the Squire smiled at the familiar word, so common in our ears at home, and had a great mind to ask the guard where he came from.

"I lighted all these here lamps myself afore we started, and I see 'em all burning," said he. There was no mistaking the home accent now, and the Squire looked down the carriage with a beaming face.

"You are from Worcestershire, my man."

"From Worcester itself, sir. Leastways from St. John's, which is the same thing."

"Whether you are from Worcester, or whether you are from Jericho, I'll let you know that you can't put empty lamps into first-class carriages on this line without being made to answer for it!" roared the lunatic. "What's your name! I am a director."

"My name is Thomas Brooks, sir," replied the man, respectfully touching his cap. "But I declare to you, sir, that I've told the truth in saying the lamps were all right when we started: how this one can have got douted, I can't think. There's not a guard on the line, sir, more particular in seeing to the lamps than I am."

"Well, light it now; don't waste time excusing yourself,"
growled the lunatic. But he said nothing about the dog; which was
surprising.

In a twinkling the lamp was lighted, and we were off again.

The lady and her dog were quiet now: he was out of sight: she
leaned back to go to sleep. The Squire lodged his head against the
curtain, and shut his eyes to do the same; the little man, as before,
never looked off his book; and the lunatic frantically shifted himself
every two minutes between his own seat and that of the opposite
corner. There were no more tunnels, and we went smoothly on to
the next station. Five minutes allowed there.

The little man, putting his book in his pocket, took down a
black leather bag from above his head, and got out; the lady, her dog
hidden still, prepared to follow him, wishing the Squire and me, and
even the lunatic, with a forgiving smile, a polite good morning. I had
moved to that end, and was watching the lady's wonderful back hair
as she stepped out, when all in a moment the Squire sprang up with
a shout, and jumping out nearly upon her, called out that he had
been robbed. She dropped the dog, and I thought he must have
caught the lunatic's disorder and become frantic.

It is of no use attempting to describe exactly what followed.
The lady, snatching up her dog, shrieked out that perhaps she had
been robbed too; she laid hold of the Squire's arm, and went with
him into the station-master's room. And there we were: us three,
and the guard, and the station-master, and the lunatic, who had
come pouncing out too at the Squire's cry. The man in spectacles
had disappeared for good.

The Squire's pocket-book was gone. He gave his name and
address at once to the station-master: and the guard's face lighted
with intelligence when he heard it, for he knew Squire Todhetley by
reputation. The pocket-book had been safe just before we entered
the tunnel; the Squire was certain of that, having felt it. He had sat
in the carriage with his coat unbuttoned, rather thrown back; and
nothing could have been easier than for a clever thief to draw it out,
under cover of the darkness.

"I had fifty pounds in it," he said; "fifty pounds in five-pound
notes. And some memoranda besides."

"Fifty pounds!" cried the lady, quickly. "And you could travel
with all that about you, and not button up your coat! You ought to
be rich!"

"Have you been in the habit of meeting thieves, madam, when
travelling?" suddenly demanded the lunatic, turning upon her without warning, his coat whirling about on all sides with the rapidity of
his movements.

"No, sir, I have not," she answered, in indignant tones. "Have you?"

"I have not, madam. But, then, you perceive I see no risk in travelling with a coat unbuttoned, although it may have bank-notes in the pockets."

She made no reply: was too much occupied in turning out her own pockets and purse, to ascertain that they had not been rifled. Re-assured on the point, she sat down on a low box against the wall, nursing her dog; which had begun its snarling again.

"It must have been taken from me in the dark as we went through the tunnel," affirmed the Squire to the room in general and perhaps the station-master in particular. "I am a magistrate, and have some experience in these things. I sat completely off my guard, a prey for anybody, my hands stretched out before me, grappling with that dog, that seemed—why, goodness me! yes he *did*, now that I think of it—that seemed to be held about fifteen inches off my nose on purpose to attack me. That's when the thing must have been done. But now—which of them could it have been?"

He meant which of the passengers. As he looked hard at us in rotation, especially at the guard and station-master, who had not been in the carriage, the lady gave a shriek, and threw the dog into the middle of the room.

"I see it all," she said, faintly. "He has a habit of snatching at things with his mouth. He must have snatched the case out of your pocket, sir, and dropped it from the window. You will find it in the tunnel."

"Who has?" asked the lunatic, while the Squire stared in wonder.

"My poor little Wasp. Ah, villain! beast! it is he that has done all this mischief."

"He might have taken the pocket-book," I said, thinking it time to speak, "but he could not have dropped it out, for I put the window up as we went into the tunnel."

It seemed a nonplus for her, and her face fell again. "There was the other window," she said in a minute. "He might have dropped it there. I heard his bark quite close to it."

"*I* pulled up that window, madam," said the lunatic. "If the dog did take it out of the pocket it may be in the carriage now."

The guard rushed out to search it; the Squire followed, but the station-master remained where he was, and closed the door after them. A thought came over me that he was stopping to keep the two passengers in view.

No; the pocket-book could not be found in the carriage. As they came back, the Squire was asking the guard if he knew who the nobleman was who had got out at the last station with his servant. But the guard did not know.

"He said they knew him on the line."

"Very likely, sir. I have not been on this line above a month or two."

"Well, this is an unpleasant affair," said the lunatic impatiently; "and the question is—What's to be done? It appears pretty evident that your pocket-book was taken in the carriage, sir. Of the four passengers, I suppose the one who left us at the last station must be held exempt from suspicion, being a nobleman. Another got out here, and has disappeared; the other two are present. I propose that we should both be searched."

"I'm sure I am quite willing," said the lady, and she got up at once.

I think the Squire was about to disclaim any wish so to act; but the lunatic was resolute, and the station-master agreed with him. There was no time to be lost, for the train was ready to start again, her time being up, and the lunatic was turned out. The lady went into another room with two women, called by the station-master, and *she* was turned out. Neither of them had the pocket-book.

"Here's my card, sir," said the lunatic, handing one to Mr. Todhetley. "You know my name, I dare say. If I can be of any future assistance to you in this matter, you may command me."

"Bless my heart!" cried the Squire, as he read the name on the card. "How could you allow yourself to be searched, sir?"

"Because, in such a case as this, I think it only right and fair that every one who has the misfortune to be mixed up in it *should* be searched," replied the lunatic, as they went out together. "It is a satisfaction to both parties. Unless you offered to search me, you could not have offered to search that woman; and I suspected her."

"Suspected *her!*" cried the Squire, opening his eyes.

"If I didn't suspect, I doubted. Why on earth did she cause her dog to make all that row the moment we got into the tunnel? It must have been done then. I should not be startled out of my senses if I heard that that silent man by my side and hers was in league with her."

The Squire stood in a kind of amazement, trying to recall what he could of the little man in spectacles, and see if things would fit into one another.

"Don't you like her look?" he asked suddenly.

"No, I *don't*," said the lunatic, turning himself about. "I have a prejudice against painted women: they put me in mind of Jezebel. Look at her hair. It's awful."

He went out in a whirlwind, and took his seat in the carriage, not a moment before it puffed off.

"*Is* he a lunatic?" I whispered to the Squire.

"He a lunatic!" he roared. "You must be a lunatic for asking it, Johnny. Why, that's—that's——"

Instead of saying any more, he showed me the card, and the name nearly took my breath away. He is a well-known London man, of science, talent, and position, and of world-wide fame.

"Well, I thought him nothing better than an escaped maniac."

"*Did* you?" said the Squire. "Perhaps he returned the compliment on you, sir. But now—Johnny, who has got my pocket-book?"

As if it was any use asking me? As we turned back to the station-master's room, the lady came into it, evidently resenting the search, although she had seemed to acquiesce in it so readily.

"They were rude, those women. It is the first time I ever had the misfortune to travel with men who carry pocket-books to lose them, and I hope it will be the last," she pursued, in scornful passion, meant for the Squire. "One generally meets with *gentlemen* in a first-class carriage."

The emphasis came out with a shriek, and it told on him. Now that she was proved innocent, he was as vexed as she for having listened to the advice of the scientific man—but I can't help calling him a lunatic still. The Squire's apologies might have disarmed a cross-grained hyena; and she came round with a smile.

"If any one *has* got the pocket-book," she said, as she stroked her dog's ears, "it must be that silent man with the gold spectacles. There was no one else, sir, who could have reached you without getting up to do it. And I declare on my honour, that when that commotion first arose through my poor little dog, I felt for a moment something like a man's arm stretched across me. It could only have been his. I hope you have the numbers of the notes."

"But I have not," said the Squire.

The room was being invaded by this time. Two stray passengers, a friend of the station-master's, and the porter who took the tickets, had crept in. All thought the lady's opinion must be correct, and said the spectacled man had got clear off with the pocket-book. There was no one else to pitch upon. A nobleman travelling with his servant would not be likely to commit a robbery; the lunatic was really the man his card represented him to be, for the station-master's friend had seen and recognized him; and the lady was proved innocent by search. Wasn't the Squire in a passion!

"That close reading of his was all a blind," he said, in sudden conviction. "He kept his face down that we should not know him in future. He never looked at one of us! he never said a word! I shall go and find him."

Away went the Squire, as fast as he could hurry, but came back in a moment to know which was the way out, and where it led to.

There was quite a small crowd of us by this time. Some fields lay beyond the station at the back; and a boy affirmed that he had seen a little gentleman in spectacles, with a black bag in his hand, making over the first stile.

"Now look here, boy," said the Squire. "If you catch that same man, I'll give you five shillings."

Tod could not have flown faster than the boy did. He took the stile at a leap; and the Squire tumbled over it after him. Some boys and men joined in the chase; and a cow, grazing in the field, trotted after us and brought up the rear.

Such a shout from the boy. It came from behind the opposite hedge of the long field. I was over the gate first; the Squire came next.

On the hedge of the dry ditch sat the passenger, his legs dangling, his neck imprisoned in the boy's arms. I knew him at once. His hat and gold spectacles had fallen off in the scuffle; the black bag was wide open, and had a tall bunch of something green sticking up from it; some tools lay on the ground.

"Oh, you wicked hypocrite!" spluttered the Squire, not in the least knowing what he said in his passion. "Are you not ashamed to have played upon me such a vile trick? How dare you go about to commit robberies!"

"I have not robbed you, at any rate," said the man, his voice trembling a little and his face pale, while the boy loosed the neck but pinioned one of the arms.

"Not robbed me!" cried the Squire. "Good Heavens! Who do you suppose you have robbed, if not me? Here, Johnny, lad, you are a witness. He says he has not robbed me."

"I did not know it was yours," said the man meekly. "Loose me, boy; I'll not attempt to run away."

"Halloa! here! what's to do?" roared a big fellow, swinging himself over the gate. "Any tramp been trespassing?—anybody wanting to be took up? I'm the parish constable."

If he had said he was the parish engine, ready to let loose buckets of water on the offender, he could not have been more welcome. The Squire's face was rosy with satisfaction.

"Have you your handcuffs with you, my man?"

"I've not got them, sir; but I fancy I'm big enough and strong enough to take *him* without 'em. Something to spare, too."

"There's nothing like handcuffs for safety," said the Squire, rather damped, for he believed in them as one of the country's institutions. "Oh, you villain! Perhaps you can tie him with cords?"

The thief floundered out of the ditch and stood upon his feet. He did not look an ungentlemanly thief, now you came to see and hear him; and his face, though scared, might have been thought an honest one. He picked up his hat and glasses, and held them in his hand while he spoke, in tones of earnest remonstrance.

"Surely, sir, you would not have me taken up for this slight offence! I did not know I was doing wrong, and I doubt if the law would condemn me; I thought it was public property!"

"Public property!" cried the Squire, turning red at the words. "Of all the impudent brazen-faced rascals that are cheating the gallows, you must be the worst. My bank-notes public property!"

"Your what, sir?"

"My bank-notes, you villain. How dare you repeat your insolent questions?"

"But I don't know anything about your bank-notes, sir," said the man meekly. "I do not know what you mean."

They stood facing each other, a sight for a picture; the Squire with his hands under his coat, dancing a little in rage, his face crimson; the other quite still, holding his hat and gold spectacles, and looking at him in wonder.

"You don't know what I mean! When you confessed with your last breath that you had robbed me of my pocket-book!"

"I confessed—I have not sought to conceal—that I have robbed the ground of this rare fern," said the man, handling carefully the green stuff in the black bag. "I have not robbed you or any one of anything else."

The tone, simple, quiet, self-contained, threw the Squire in amazement. He stood staring.

"Are you a fool?" he asked. "What do you suppose I have to do with your rubbishing ferns?"

"Nay, I supposed you owned them; that is, owned the land. You led me to believe so, in saying I had robbed you."

"What I've lost is a pocket-book, with ten five-pound bank-notes in it; I lost it in the train; it must have been taken as we came through the tunnel; and you sat next but one to me," reiterated the Squire.

The man put on his hat and glasses. "I am a geologist and botanist, sir. I came here after this plant to-day—having seen it yesterday, but then I had not my tools with me. I don't know anything about the pocket-book and bank-notes."

So that was another mistake, for the botanist turned out of his pockets a heap of letters directed to him, and a big book he had been reading in the train, a treatise on botany, to prove who he was. And, as if to leave no loophole for doubt, one stepped up who knew him, and assured the Squire there was not a more learned man in his line, no, nor one more respected, in the three kingdoms. The Squire shook him by the hand in apologizing, and told him we had some valuable ferns near Dyke Manor, if he would come and see them.

Like Patience on a monument, when we got back, sat the lady, waiting to see the prisoner brought in. Her face would have made a picture too, when she heard the upshot, and saw the hot Squire and the gold spectacles walking side by side in friendly talk.

"I think still he must have got it," she said, sharply.

"No, madam," answered the Squire. "Whoever may have taken it, it was not he."

"Then there's only one man, and that is he whom you have let go on in the train," she returned decisively. "I thought his fidgety movements were not put on for nothing. He had secured the pocket-book somewhere, and then made a show of offering to be searched. Ah, ha!"

And the Squire veered round again at this suggestion, and began to suspect he had been doubly cheated. First, out of his money, next out of his suspicions. One only thing in the whole bother seemed clear; and that was, that the notes and case had gone for good. As, in point of fact, they had.

We were on the chain-pier at Brighton, Tod and I. It was about eight or nine months after. I had put my arms on the rails at the end, looking at a pleasure-party sailing by. Tod, next to me, was bewailing his ill-fortune in not possessing a yacht and opportunities of cruising in it.

"I tell you No. I don't want to be made sea-sick."

The words came from some one behind us. It seemed almost as though they were spoken in reference to Tod's wish for a yacht. But it was not *that* that made me turn round sharply; it was the sound of the voice, for I thought I recognized it.

Yes: there she was. The lady who had been with us in the carriage that day. The dog was not with her now, but her hair was more amazing than ever. She did not see me. As I turned, she turned, and began to walk slowly back, arm-in-arm with a gentleman. And to see him—that is, to see them together—made me open my eyes. For it was the lord who had travelled with us.

"Look, Tod!" I said, and told him in a word who they were.

"What the deuce do they know of each other?" cried Tod with a frown, for he felt angry every time the thing was referred to. Not for the loss of the money, but for what he called the stupidity of us all; saying always had *he* been there, he should have detected the thief at once.

I sauntered after them: why I wanted to learn which of the lords he was, I can't tell, for lords are numerous enough, but I had had a curiosity upon the point ever since. They encountered some people and were standing to speak to them; three ladies, and a fellow in a black glazed hat with a piece of green ribbon round it.

"I was trying to induce my wife to take a sail," the lord was saying, "but she won't. She is not a very good sailor, unless the sea has its best behaviour on."

"Will you go to-morrow, Mrs. Mowbray?" asked the man in the glazed hat, who spoke and looked like a gentleman. "I will promise you perfect calmness. I am weather-wise, and can assure you this little wind will have gone down before night, leaving us without a breath of air."

"I will go: on condition that your assurance proves correct."

"All right. You of course will come, Mowbray?"

The lord nodded. "Very happy."

"When do you leave Brighton, Mr. Mowbray?" asked one of the ladies.

"I don't know exactly. Not for some days."

"A muff as usual, Johnny," whispered Tod. "That man is no lord: he is a Mr. Mowbray."

"But, Tod, he *is* the lord. It is the one who travelled with us; there's no mistake about that. Lords can't put off their titles as parsons can: do you suppose his servant would have called him 'my lord,' if he had not been one?"

"At least there is no mistake that these people are calling him Mr. Mowbray now."

That was true. It was equally true that they were calling her Mrs. Mowbray. My ears had been as quick as Tod's, and I don't deny I was puzzled. They turned to come up the pier again with the people, and the lady saw me standing there with Tod. Saw me looking at her, too, and I think she did not relish it, for she took a step backward as one startled, and then stared me full in the face, as if asking who I might be. I lifted my hat.

There was no response. In another moment she and her husband were walking quickly down the pier together, and the other party went on to the end quietly. A man in a tweed suit and brown hat drawn low over his eyes, was standing with his arms folded, looking after the two with a queer smile upon his face. Tod marked it and spoke.

"Do you happen to know that gentleman?"

"Yes, I do," was the answer.

"Is he a peer?"

"On occasion."

"On occasion!" repeated Tod. "I have a reason for asking," he added; "do not think me impertinent."

"Been swindled out of anything?" asked the man, coolly.

"My father was, some months ago. He lost a pocket-book with fifty pounds in it in a railway carriage. Those people were both in it, but not then acquainted with each other."

"Oh, weren't they!" said the man.

"No, they were not," I put in, "for I was there. He was a lord then."

"Ah," said the man, "and had a servant in livery no doubt, who came up my-lording him unnecessarily every other minute, He is a member of the swell-mob; one of the cleverest of the *gentleman* fraternity, and the one who acts as servant is another of them."

"And the lady?" I asked.

"She is a third. They have been working in concert for two or three years now; and will give us trouble yet before their career is stopped. But for being singularly clever, we should have had them long ago. And so they did not know each other in the train! I dare say not!"

The man spoke with quiet authority. He was a detective come down from London to Brighton that morning; whether for a private trip, or on business, he did not say. I related to him what had passed in the train.

"Ay," said he, after listening. "They contrived to put the lamp out before starting. The lady took the pocket-book during the commotion she caused the dog to make, and the lord received it from her hand when he gave her back the dog. Cleverly done! He had it about him, young sir, when he got out at the next station. *She* waited to be searched, and to throw the scent off. Very ingenious. but they'll be a little too much so some fine day."

"Can't you take them up?" demanded Tod.

"No."

"I will accuse them of it," he haughtily said. "If I meet them again on this pier—"

"Which you won't do to-day," interrupted the man.

"I heard them say they were not going for some days."

"Ah, but they have seen you now. And I think—I'm not quite sure—that he saw me. They'll be off by the next train."

"Who are *they?*" asked Tod, pointing to the end of the pier.

"Unsuspecting people whose acquaintance they have casually made here. Yes, an hour or two will see Brighton quit of the pair."

And it was so. A train was starting within an hour, and Tod and I galloped to the station. There they were: in a first-class carriage: not apparently knowing each other, I verily believe, for he sat at one door and she at the other, passengers dividing them.

"Lambs between two wolves," remarked Tod. "I have a great mind to warn the people of the sort of company they are in. Would it be actionable, Johnny?"

The train moved off as he was speaking. And may I never write another word, if I did not catch sight of the man-servant and his cockade in the next carriage behind them!

WILKIE COLLINS

William Wilkie Collins (1824– 1889) is well known as the author of The Woman in White *(1860),* Armadale *(1866), and* The Moonstone *(1868), three of the classic Victorian mystery novels. Son of the painter William Collins, Wilkie Collins first thought of entering the tea business and later, law, before becoming a professional writer. For several years he was on the editorial staff of Dickens's magazine* All the Year Round, *and he became Dickens's close friend and collaborator. In addition to his long novels Collins wrote quite a few short stories, most of which involved either supernaturalism or crime. The present selection, "Mr. Policeman and the Cook," while showing obvious affinities to the pseudofactual stories written by Waters and his imitators, demonstrates Collins's great skill in fitting plots to credible human situations.*

"Mr. Policeman and the Cook"

A FIRST WORD FOR MYSELF

Before the doctor left me one evening, I asked him how much longer I was likely to live. He answered: "It's not easy to say; you may die before I can get back to you in the morning, or you may live to the end of the month."

I was alive enough on the next morning to think of the needs of my soul, and (being a member of the Roman Catholic Church) to send for the priest.

The history of my sins, related in confession, included blameworthy neglect of a duty which I owed to the laws of my country. In the priest's opinion—and I agreed with him—I was bound to make

189

public acknowledgment of my fault, as an act of penance becoming
to a Catholic Englishman. We concluded, thereupon, to try a division of labour. I related the circumstances, while his reverence took
the pen, and put the matter into shape.

Here follows what came of it:

1.   When I was a young man of five-and-twenty, I became a
member of the London police force. After nearly two year's ordinary
experience of the responsible and ill-paid duties of that vocation, I
found myself employed on my first serious and terrible case of official inquiry—relating to nothing less than the crime of Murder.

The circumstances were these:

I was then attached to a station in the northern district of
London—which I beg permission not to mention more particularly.
On a certain Monday in the week, I took my turn of night duty. Up
to four in the morning, nothing occurred at the station-house out of
the ordinary way. It was then spring time, and, between the gas and
the fire, the room became rather hot. I went to the door to get a
breath of fresh air—much to the surprise of our Inspector on duty,
who was constitutionally a chilly man. There was a fine rain falling;
and a nasty damp in the air sent me back to the fireside. I don't suppose I had sat down for more than a minute when the swinging-door
was violently pushed open. A frantic woman ran in with a scream,
and said: "Is this the station-house?"

Our Inspector (otherwise an excellent officer) had, by some perversity of nature, a hot temper in his chilly constitution. "Why, bless
the woman, can't you *see* it is?" he says. "What's the matter now?"

"Murder's the matter!" she burst out. "For God's sake come
back with me. It's at Mrs. Crosscapel's lodging-house, number 14,
Lehigh Street. A young woman has murdered her husband in the
night! With a knife, sir. She says she thinks she did it in her sleep."

I confess I was startled by this; and the third man on duty (a
sergeant) seemed to feel it too. She was a nice-looking young
woman, even in her terrified condition, just out of bed, with her
clothes huddled on anyhow. I was partial in those days to a tall
figure—and she was, as they say, my style. I put a chair for her; and
the sergeant poked the fire. As for the Inspector, nothing ever upset
him. He questioned her as coolly as if it had been a case of petty larceny.

"Have you seen the murdered man?" he asked.

"No, sir."

"Or the wife?"

"No sir. I didn't dare go into the room; I only heard about it!"

"Oh? And who are you? One of the lodgers?"

"No, sir. I'm the cook."

"Isn't there a master in the house?"

"Yes, sir. He's frightened out of his wits. And the housemaid's gone for the doctor. It all falls on the poor servants, of course. Oh, why did I ever set foot in that horrible house?"

The poor soul burst out crying, and shivered from head to foot. The Inspector made a note of her statement, and then asked her to read it, and sign it with her name. The object of this proceeding was to get her to come near enough to give him the opportunity of smelling her breath. "When people make extraordinary statements," he afterwards said to me, "it sometimes saves trouble to satisfy yourself that they are not drunk. I've known them to be mad—but not often. You will generally find *that* in their eyes."

She roused herself, and signed her name—"Priscilla Thurlby." The Inspector's own test proved her to be sober; and her eyes— a nice light blue colour, mild and pleasant, no doubt, when they were not staring with fear, and red with crying—satisfied him (as I supposed) that she was not mad. He turned the case over to me, in the first instance. I saw that he didn't believe in it, even yet.

"Go back with her to the house," he says. "This may be a stupid hoax, or a quarrel exaggerated. See to it yourself, and hear what the doctor says. If it *is* serious, send word back here directly, and let nobody enter the place or leave it till we come. Stop! You know the form if any statement is volunteered?"

"Yes, sir. I am to caution the persons that whatever they say will be taken down, and may be used against them."

"Quite right. You'll be an Inspector yourself one of these days. Now, miss!" With that he dismissed her, under my care.

Lehigh Street was not very far off—about twenty minutes' walk from the station. I confess I thought the Inspector had been rather hard on Priscilla. She was herself naturally angry with him. "What does he mean," she says, "by talking of a hoax? I wish he was as frightened as I am. This is the first time I have been out at service, sir—and I did think I had found a respectable place."

I said very little to her—feeling, if the truth must be told, rather anxious about the duty committed to me. On reaching the house the door was opened from within, before I could knock. A gentleman stepped out, who proved to be the doctor. He stopped the moment he saw me.

"You must be careful policeman," he says. "I found the man, lying on his back, in bed, dead—with the knife that had killed him left sticking in the wound."

Hearing this, I felt the necessity of sending at once to the station. Where could I find a trustworthy messenger? I took the liberty of asking the doctor if he would repeat to the police what he had already said to me. The station was not much out of his way home. He kindly granted my request.

The landlady (Mrs. Crosscapel) joined us while we were talking. She was still a young woman; not easily frightened, as far as I could see, even by a murder in the house. Her husband was in the passage behind her. He looked old enough to be her father; and he so trembled with terror that some people might have taken him for the guilty person. I removed the key from the street door, after locking it; and I said to the landlady: "Nobody must leave the house, or enter the house, till the Inspector comes. I must examine the premises to see if anyone has broken in."

"There is the key of the area gate," she said, in answer to me. "It's always kept locked. Come downstairs, and see for yourself." Priscilla went with us. Her mistress set her to work to light the kitchen fire. "Some of us," says Mrs. Crosscapel, "may be the better for a cup of tea." I remarked that she took things easy, under the circumstances. She answered that the landlady of a London lodging-house could not afford to lose her wits, no matter what might happen.

I found the gate locked, and the shutters of the kitchen window fastened. The back kitchen and back door were secured in the same way. No person was concealed anywhere. Returning upstairs, I examined the front parlour window. There again, the barred shutters answered for the security of that room. A cracked voice spoke through the door of the back parlour. "The policeman can come in," it said, "if he will promise not to look at me." I turned to the landlady for information. "It's my parlour lodger, Miss Mybus," she said, "a most respectable lady." Going into the room, I saw something rolled up perpendicularly in the bed curtains. Miss Mybus had made herself modestly invisible in that way. Having now satisfied my mind about the security of the lower part of the house, and having the keys safe in my pocket, I was ready to go upstairs.

On our way to the upper regions I asked if there had been any visitors on the previous day. There had been only two visitors, friends of the lodgers—and Mrs. Crosscapel herself had let them both out. My next inquiry related to the lodgers themselves. On the ground floor there was Miss Mybus. On the first floor (occupying both rooms) Mr. Barfield, an old bachelor, employed in a merchant's office. On the second floor, in the front room, Mr. John Zebedee, the murdered man, and his wife. In the back room, Mr. Deluc; described as a cigar agent, and supposed to be a Creole gentleman from Martinique. In the front garret, Mr. and Mrs. Crosscapel. In the back garret, the cook and the housemaid. These were the inhabitants, regularly accounted for. I asked about the servants. "Both ex-

cellent characters," says the landlady, "or they would not be in my
service."

We reached the second floor, and found the housemaid on the
watch outside the door of the front room. Not as nice a woman, personally, as the cook, and sadly frightened of course. Her mistress
had posted her, to give the alarm in the case of an outbreak on the
part of Mrs. Zebedee, kept locked up in the room. My arrival relieved the housemaid of further responsibility. She ran downstairs to
her fellow-servant in the kitchen.

I asked Mrs. Crosscapel how and when the alarm of the murder
had been given.

"Soon after three this morning," says she, "I was woke by the
screams of Mrs. Zebedee. I found her out here on the landing, and
Mr. Deluc, in great alarm, trying to quiet her. Sleeping in the next
room, he had only to open his door, when her screams woke him.
"My dear John's murdered! I am the miserable wretch—I did it in
my sleep!" She repeated those frantic words over and over again,
until she dropped in a swoon. Mr. Deluc and I carried her back into
the bedroom. We both thought the poor creature had been driven
distracted by some dreadful dream. But when we got to the bedside—don't ask me what we saw; the Doctor has told you about it
already. I was once a nurse in a hospital, and accustomed, as such,
to horrid sights. It turned me cold and giddy, notwithstanding. As
for Mr. Deluc, I thought *he* would have had a fainting fit next."

Hearing this, I inquired if Mrs. Zebedee had said or done any
strange things since she had been Mrs. Crosscapel's lodger.

"You think she's mad?" says the landlady. "And anybody
would be of your mind, when a woman accuses herself of murdering
her husband in her sleep. All I can say is that, up to this morning, a
more quiet, sensible, well-behaved little person than Mrs. Zebedee I
never met with. Only just married, mind, and as fond of her unfortunate husband as a woman could be. I should have called them a
pattern couple, in their own line of life."

There was no more to be said on the landing. We unlocked the
door and went into the room.

2.   He lay in bed on his back as the doctor had described him. On
the left side of his nightgown, just over his heart, the blood on the
linen told its terrible tale. As well as one could judge, looking un-
willingly at a dead face, he must have been a handsome young man
in his life-time. It was a sight to sadden anybody—but I think the
most painful sensation was when my eyes fell next on his miserable
wife.

She was down on the floor, crouched up in a corner—a dark
little woman, smartly dressed in gay colours. Her black hair and her

big brown eyes made the horrid paleness of her face look even more
deadly white than perhaps it really was. She stared straight at us
without appearing to see us. We spoke to her, and she never answered a word. She might have been dead—like her husband—except that she perpetually picked at her fingers, and shuddered every
now and then as if she was cold. I went to her and tried to lift her
up. She shrank back with a cry that wellnigh frightened me—not
because it was loud, but because it was more like the cry of some
animal than of a human being. However quietly she might have
behaved in the landlady's previous experience of her, she was beside
herself now. I might have been moved by a natural pity for her, or I
might have been completely upset in my mind—I only know this, I
could not persuade myself that she was guilty. I even said to Mrs.
Crosscapel, "I don't believe she did it."

While I spoke, there was a knock at the door. I went downstairs
at once, and admitted (to my great relief) the Inspector, accompanied by one of our men.

He waited downstairs to hear my report, and he approved of
what I had done. "It looks as if the murder had been committed by
somebody in the house." Saying this, he left the man below, and
went up with me to the second floor.

Before he had been a minute in the room, he discovered an object which had escaped my observation.

It was the knife that had done the deed.

The doctor had found it left in the body—had withdrawn it to
probe the wound—and had laid it on the bedside table. It was one of
those useful knives which contain a saw, a corkscrew, and other like
implements. The big blade fastened back, when open, with a spring.
Except where the blood was on it, it was as bright as when it had
been purchased. A small metal plate was fastened to the horn
handle, containing an inscription, only partly engraved, which ran
thus: "To John Zebedee, from——" There it stopped, strangely enough.

Who or what had interrupted the engraver's work? It was impossible even to guess. Nevertheless, the Inspector was encouraged.

"This ought to help us," he said—and then he gave an attentive
ear (looking all the while at the poor creature in the corner) to what
Mrs. Crosscapel had to tell him.

The landlady having done, he said he must now see the lodger
who slept in the next bedchamber.

Mr. Deluc made his appearance, standing at the door of the
room, and turning away his head with horror from the sight inside.

He was wrapped in a splendid blue dressing-gown, with a
golden girdle and trimmings. His scanty brownish hair curled
(whether artificially or not, I am unable to say) in little ringlets. His
complexion was yellow; his greenish-brown eyes were of the sort

called "goggle"—they looked as if they might drop out of his face, if you held a spoon under them. His moustache and goat's beard were beautifully oiled; and, to complete his equipment, he had a long black cigar in his mouth.

"It isn't insensibility to this terrible tragedy," he explained. "My nerves have been shattered, Mr. Policeman, and I can only repair the mischief in this way. Be pleased to excuse and feel for me."

The Inspector questioned this witness sharply and closely. He was not a man to be misled by appearances; but I could see that he was far from liking, or even trusting, Mr. Deluc. Nothing came of the examination, except what Mrs. Crosscapel had in substance already mentioned to me. Mr. Deluc returned to his room.

"How long has he been lodging with you?" the Inspector asked as soon as his back was turned.

"Nearly a year," the landlady answered.

"Did he give you a reference?"

"As good a reference as I could wish for." Thereupon, she mentioned the names of a well-known firm of cigar merchants in the City. The Inspector noted the information in his pocket-book.

I would rather not relate in detail what happened next: it is too distressing to be dwelt on. Let me only say that the poor demented woman was taken away in a cab to the station-house. The Inspector possessed himself of the knife, and of a book found on the floor, called *The World of Sleep*. The portmanteau containing the luggage was locked—and then the door of the room was secured, the keys in both cases being left in my charge. My instructions were to remain in the house, and allow nobody to leave it, until I heard again shortly from the Inspector.

3.   The coroner's inquest was adjourned; and the examination before the magistrate ended in a remand—Mrs. Zebedee being in no condition to understand the proceedings in either case. The surgeon reported her to be completely prostrated by a terrible nervous shock. When he was asked if he considered her to have been a sane woman before the murder took place, he refused to answer positively at that time.

A week passed. The murdered man was buried; his old father attending the funeral. I occasionally saw Mrs. Crosscapel, and the two servants, for the purpose of getting such further information as was thought desirable. Both the cook and the housemaid had given their month's notice to quit; declining, in the interest of their characters, to remain in a house which had been the scene of a murder. Mr. Deluc's nerves led also to his removal; his rest was now disturbed by frightful dreams. He paid the necessary forfeit-money, and left without notice. The first-floor lodger, Mr. Barfield, kept his rooms, but obtained leave of absence from his employers, and took refuge with some friends in the country. Miss Mybus alone remained in the parlours. "When I am comfortable," the old lady said, "nothing moves me, at my age. A murder up two pairs of stairs is nearly the same thing as a murder in the next house. Distance, you see, makes all the difference."

It mattered little to the police what the lodgers did. We had men in plain clothes watching the house night and day. Everybody who went away was privately followed; and the police in the district to which they retired were warned to keep an eye on them, after that. As long as we failed to put Mrs. Zebedee's extraordinary statement to any sort of test—to say nothing of having proved unsuccessful, thus far, in tracing the knife to its purchaser—we were bound to let no person living under Mr. Crosscapel's roof, on the night of the murder, slip through our fingers.

4. In a fortnight more, Mrs. Zebedee had sufficiently recovered to make the necessary statement—after the preliminary caution addressed to persons in such cases. The surgeon had no hesitation, now, in reporting her to be a sane woman.

Her station in life had been domestic service. She had lived for four years in her last place as lady's-maid, with a family residing in Dorsetshire. The one objection to her had been the occasional infirmity of sleep-walking, which made it necessary that one of the other female servants should sleep in the same room, with the door locked and the key under her pillow. In all other respects the lady's-maid was described by her mistress as "a perfect treasure."

In the last six months of her service, a young man named John Zebedee entered the house (with a written character) as a footman. He soon fell in love with the nice little lady's-maid, and she heartily returned the feeling. They might have waited for years before they were in a pecuniary position to marry, but for the death of Zebedee's uncle, who left him a little fortune of two thousand pounds. They were now, for persons in their station, rich enough to please themselves; and they were married from the house in which they had served together, the little daughters of the family showing their affection for Mrs. Zebedee, by acting as her bridesmaids.

The young husband was a careful man. He decided to employ his small capital to the best advantage, by sheep-farming in Australia. His wife made no objection; she was ready to go wherever John went.

Accordingly they spent their short honeymoon in London, so as to see for themselves the vessel in which their passage was to be taken. They went to Mrs. Crosscapel's lodging-house because Zebedee's uncle had always stayed there when in London. Ten days were to pass before the day of embarkation arrived. This gave the young couple a welcome holiday, and a prospect of amusing themselves to their hearts' content among the sights and shows of the great city.

On their first evening in London they went to the theatre. They were both accustomed to the fresh air of the country, and they felt half stifled by the heat and the gas. However, they were so pleased with an amusement which was new to them that they went to another theatre on the next evening. On this second occasion, John Zebedee found the heat unendurable. They left the theatre, and got back to their lodgings towards ten o'clock.

Let the rest be told in the words used by Mrs. Zebedee herself. She said:

"We sat talking for a while while in our room, and John's headache got worse and worse. I persuaded him to go to bed, and I put out the candle (the fire giving sufficient light to undress by), so that he might the sooner fall asleep. But he was too restless to sleep. He asked me to read him something. Books always made him drowsy at the best of times.

"I had not myself begun to undress. So I lit the candle again, and I opened the only book I had. John had noticed it at the railway bookstall by the name of *The World of Sleep*. He used to joke with me about my being a sleep-walker; and he said, 'Here's something that's sure to interest you'—and he made me a present of the book.

"Before I had read to him for more than half an hour he was fast asleep. Not feeling that way inclined, I went on reading to myself.

"The book did indeed interest me. There was one terrible story which took a hold on my mind—the story of a man who stabbed his own wife in a sleep-walking dream. I thought of putting down my book after that, and then changed my mind again and went on. The next chapters were not so interesting; they were full of learned acounts of why we fall asleep, and what our brains do in that state, and such like. It ended in my falling asleep, too, in my armchair by the fireside.

"I don't know what o'clock it was when I went to sleep. I don't know how long I slept, or whether I dreamed or not. The candle and and the fire had both burned out, and it was pitch dark when I woke. I can't even say why I woke—unless it was the coldness of the room.

"There was a spare candle on the chimney-piece. I found the match-box, and got a light. Then for the first time, I turned round towards the bed; and I saw——"

She had seen the dead body of her husband, murdered while she was unconsciously at his side—and she fainted, poor creature, at the bare remembrance of it.

The proceedings were adjourned. She received every possible

care and attention; the chaplain looking after her welfare as well as the surgeon.

I have said nothing of the evidence of the landlady and servants. It was taken as a mere formality. What little they knew proved nothing against Mrs. Zebedee. The police made no discoveries that supported her first frantic accusation of herself. Her master and mistress, where she had been last in service, spoke of her in the highest terms. We were at a complete deadlock.

It had been thought best not to surprise Mr. Deluc, as yet, by citing him as a witness. The action of the law was, however, hurried in this case by a private communication received from the chaplain.

After twice seeing, and speaking with, Mrs. Zebedee, the reverend gentleman was persuaded that she had no more to do than himself with the murder of her husband. He did not consider that he was justified in repeating a confidential communication—he would only recommend that Mr. Deluc should be summoned to appear at the next examination. This advice was followed.

The police had no evidence against Mrs. Zebedee when the inquiry was resumed. To assist the ends of justice she was now put into the witness-box. The discovery of her murdered husband, when she woke in the small hours of the morning was passed over as rapidly as possible. Only three questions of importance were put to her.

First, the knife was produced. Had she ever seen it in her husband's possession? Never. Did she know anything about it? Nothing whatever.

Secondly: Did she, or did her husband, lock the bedroom door when they returned from the theatre? No. Did she afterwards lock the door herself? No.

Thirdly: Had she any sort of reason to give for supposing that she had murdered her husband in a sleep-walking dream? No reason, except that she was beside herself at the time, and the book put the thought into her head.

After this the other witnesses were sent out of court. The motive for the chaplain's communication now appeared. Mrs. Zebedee was asked if anything unpleasant had occurred between Mr. Deluc and herself.

Yes. He had caught her alone on the stairs at the lodginghouse; had presumed to make love to her; and had carried the insult still further by attempting to kiss her. She had slapped his face, and had declared that her husband should know of it, if his misconduct was repeated. He was in a furious rage at having his face slapped; and he said to her: "Madam, you may live to regret this."

After consultation, and at the request of our Inspector, it was decided to keep Mr. Deluc in ignorance of Mrs. Zebedee's statement for the present. When the witnesses were recalled, he gave the same evidence which he had already given to the Inspector—and he was then asked if he knew anything of the knife. He looked at it without any guilty signs in his face, and swore that he had never seen it until that moment. The resumed inquiry ended, and still nothing had been discovered.

But we kept an eye on Mr. Deluc. Our next effort was to try if we could associate him with the purchase of the knife.

Here again (there really did seem to be a sort of fatality in this case) we reached no useful result. It was easy enough to find out the wholesale cutlers, who had manufactured the knife at Sheffield, by the mark on the blade. But they made tens of thousands of such knives, and disposed of them to retail dealers all over Great Britain—to say nothing of foreign parts. As to finding out the person who had engraved the imperfect inscription (without knowing where, or by whom, the knife had been purchased) we might as well have looked for the proverbial needle in the bundle of hay. Our last resource was to have the knife photographed, with the inscribed side uppermost, and to send copies to every police-station in the kingdom.

At the same time we reckoned up Mr. Deluc—I mean that we made investigations into his past life—on the chance that he and the murdered man might have known each other, and might have had a quarrel, or a rivalry about a woman, on some former occasion. No such discovery rewarded us.

We found Deluc to have led a dissipated life, and to have mixed with very bad company. But he had kept out of reach of the law. A man may be a profligate vagabond; may insult a lady; may say threatening things to her, in the first stinging sensation of having his face slapped—but it doesn't follow from these blots on his character that he has murdered her husband in the dead of the night.

Once more, then, when we were called upon to report ourselves, we had no evidence to produce. The photographs failed to discover the owner of the knife, and to explain its interrupted inscription. Poor Mrs. Zebedee was allowed to go back to her friends, on entering into her own recognizance to appear again if called upon. Articles in the newspapers began to inquire how many more murderers would succeed in baffling the police. The authorities at the Treasury offered a reward of a hundred pounds for the necessary information. And the weeks passed, and nobody claimed the reward.

Our Inspector was not a man to be easily beaten. More inquiries and examinations followed. It is needless to say anything about them. We were defeated—and there, so far as the police and the public were concerned, was an end of it.

The assassination of the poor young husband soon passed out of notice, like other undiscovered murders. One obscure person only was foolish enough, in his leisure hours, to persist in trying to solve the problem of Who Killed Zebedee? He felt that he might rise to the highest position in the police-force if he succeeded where his elders and betters had failed—and he held to his own little ambition, though everybody laughed at him. In plain English, I was the man.

5.   Without meaning it, I have told my story ungratefully. There were two persons who saw nothing ridiculous in my resolution to continue the investigation, single-handed. One of them was Miss Mybus, and the other was the cook, Priscilla Thurlby.

Mentioning the lady first, Miss Mybus was indignant at the resigned manner in which the police accepted their defeat. She was a little bright-eyed wiry woman; and she spoke her mind freely.

"This comes home to me," she said. "Just look back for a year or two. I can call to mind two cases of persons found murdered in London—and the assassins have never been traced. I am a person, too, and I ask myself if my turn is not coming next. You're a nice-looking fellow—and I like your pluck and perseverance. Come here as often as you think right; and say you are my visitor, if they make any difficulty about letting you in. One thing more! I have nothing particular to do, and I am no fool. Here, in the parlours, I see everybody who comes into the house or goes out of the house. Leave me your address—I may get some information for you yet."

With the best intentions, Miss Mybus found no opportunity of helping me. Of the two, Priscilla Thurlby seemed more likely to be of use.

In the first place, she was sharp and active, and (not having succeeded in getting another situation as yet) was mistress of her own movements.

In the second place, she was a woman I could trust. Before she had left home to try domestic service in London, the parson of her native parish gave her a written testimonial, of which I append a copy. Thus it ran:

I gladly recommend Priscilla Thurlby for any respectable employment which she may be competent to undertake. Her father and mother are infirm old people, who have lately suffered a diminution of their income; and they have a younger daughter to maintain. Rather than be a burden on her parents, Priscilla goes to London to find domestic employment, and to devote her earnings to the assistance of her father and mother. This circumstance speaks for itself. I have known the family many years; and I only regret that I have no vacant place in my own household which I can offer to this good girl.

(Signed) HENRY DERRINGTON, Rector of Roth

After reading those words, I could safely ask Priscilla to help me in reopening the mysterious murder case to some good purpose.

My notion was that the proceedings of the persons in Mrs. Crosscapel's house, had not been closely enough inquired into yet. By way of continuing the investigation, I asked Priscilla if she could tell me anything which associated the housemaid with Mr. Deluc. She was unwilling to answer. "I may be casting suspicion on an innocent person," she said. "Besides, I was for so short a time the housemaid's fellow servant——"

"You slept in the same room with her," I remarked; "and you had opportunities of observing her conduct towards the lodgers. If they had asked you, at the examination, what I now ask, you would have answered as an honest woman."

To this argument she yielded. I heard from her certain particulars which threw a new light on Mr. Deluc, and on the case generally. On that information I acted. It was slow work, owing to the claims on me of my regular duties; but with Priscilla's help, I steadily advanced towards the end I had in view.

Besides this, I owed another obligation to Mrs. Crosscapel's nice-looking cook. The confession must be made sooner or later—and I may as well make it now. I first knew what love was, thanks to Priscilla. I had delicious kisses, thanks to Priscilla. And, when I asked if she would marry me, she said: "How can two such poor people as we are ever hope to marry?" To this I answered: "It won't be long before I lay my hand on the clue which my Inspector has failed to find. I shall be in a position to marry you, my dear, when that time comes."

At our next meeting we spoke of her parents. I was now her promised husband. Judging by what I had heard of the proceedings of other people in my position, it seemed to be only right that I should be made known to her father and mother. She entirely agreed with me; and she wrote home that day to tell them to expect us at the end of the week.

I took my turn of night-duty, and so gained my liberty for the greater part of the next day. I dressed myself in plain clothes and we took our tickets on the railway for Yateland, being the nearest station to the village in which Priscilla's parents lived.

6.   The train stopped, as usual, at the big town of Waterbank. Supporting herself by her needle, while she was still unprovided with a situation, Priscilla had been at work late in the night—she was tired and thirsty. I left the carriage to get her some soda-water. The stupid girl in the refreshment room failed to pull the cork out of the bottle, and refused to let me help her. She took a corkscrew, and used it crookedly. I lost all patience, and snatched the bottle out of

her hand. Just as I drew the cork, the bell rang on the platform. I
only waited to pour the soda-water into a glass—but the train was
moving as I left the refreshment-room. The porters stopped me
when I tried to jump on to the step of the carriage. I was left behind.

As soon as I had recovered my temper, I looked at the time-
table. We had reached Waterbank at five minutes past one. By good
luck, the next train was due at forty-four minutes past one, and arrived at Yateland (the next station) ten minutes afterwards. I could
only hope that Priscilla would look at the timetable too, and wait for
me. If I had attempted to walk the distance between the two places,
I should have lost time instead of saving it. The interval before me
was not very long; I occupied it in looking over the town.

Speaking with all due respect to the inhabitants, Waterbank (to
other people) is a dull place. I went up one street and down another—and stopped to look at a shop which struck me; not from anything in itself, but because it was the only shop in the street with the
shutters closed.

A bill was posted on the shutters, announcing that the place was
to let. The out-going tradesman's name and business, announced in
the customary painted letters, ran thus:—*James Wycomb, Cutler, etc.*

For the first time, it occurred to me that we had forgotten an
obstacle in our way, when we distributed our photographs of the
knife. We had none of us remembered that a certain proportion of
cutlers might be placed, by circumstances, out of our reach—either
by retiring from business or by becoming bankrupt. I always carried
a copy of the photograph about me; and I thought to myself, "Here
is the ghost of a chance of tracing the knife to Mr. Deluc!"

The shop door was opened, after I had twice rung the bell, by
an old man, very dirty and very deaf. He said: "You had better go
upstairs and speak to Mr. Scorrier—top of the house."

I put my lips to the old fellow's ear-trumpet, and asked who
Mr. Scorrier was.

"Brother-in-law to Mr. Wycomb. Mr. Wycomb's dead. If you
want to buy the business apply to Mr. Scorrier."

Receiving that reply, I went upstairs, and found Mr. Scorrier
engaged in engraving a brass door-plate. He was a middle-aged man,
with a cadaverous face and dim eyes. After the necessary apologies, I
produced my photograph.

"May I ask, sir, if you know anything of the inscription on that
knife?" I said.

He took his magnifying glass to look at it.

"This is curious," he remarked quietly. "I remember the queer
name—Zebedee. Yes, sir; I did the engraving, as far as it goes. I
wonder what prevented me from finishing it?"

The name of Zebedee, and the unfinished inscription on the

knife had appeared in every English newspaper. He took the matter so coolly, that I was doubtful how to interpret his answer. Was it possible that he had not seen the account of the murder? Or was he an accomplice with prodigious powers of self-control?

"Excuse me," I said, "do you read the newspapers?"

"Never! My eyesight is failing me. I abstain from reading, in the interests of my occupation."

"Have you not heard the name of Zebedee mentioned—particularly by people who do read the newspapers?"

"Very likely; but I didn't attend to it. When the day's work is done, I take my walk. Then I have my supper, my drop of grog, and my pipe. Then I go to bed: A dull existence you think I dare say! I had a miserable life, sir, when I was young. A bare subsistence, and a little rest, before the last perfect rest in the grave—that is all I want. The world has gone by me long ago. So much the better."

The poor man spoke honestly. I was ashamed of having doubted him. I returned to the subject of the knife.

"Do you know where it was purchased, and by whom?" I asked.

"My memory is not so good as it was," he said; "but I have got something by me that helps it."

He took from a cupboard a dirty old scrap-book. Strips of paper, with writing on them, were pasted on the pages, as well as I could see. He turned to an index or table of contents, and, opened a page. Something like a flash of life showed itself on his dismal face.

"Ha! now I remember," he said. "The knife was bought of my late brother-in-law, in the shop downstairs. It all comes back to me, sir. A person in a state of frenzy burst into this very room, and snatched the knife away from me, when I was only half-way through the inscription!"

I felt that I was now close on discovery. "May I see what it is that has assisted your memory?" I asked.

"Oh yes. You must know, sir, I live by engraving inscriptions and addresses, and I paste in this book the manuscript instructions which I receive, with marks of my own on the margin. For one thing, they serve as a reference to new customers. And for another thing, they do certainly help my memory."

He turned the book towards me, and pointed to a slip of paper which occupied the lower half of a page.

I read the complete inscription, intended for the knife that killed Zebedee, and written as follows:

"To John Zebedee. From Priscilla Thurlby."

7.   I declare that it is impossible for me to describe what I felt when Priscilla's name confronted me like a written confession of guilt.

How long it was before I recovered myself in some degree, I cannot say. The only thing I can clearly call to mind is, that I frightened the poor engraver.

My first desire was to get possession of the manuscript inscription. I told him I was a policeman, and summoned him to assist me in the discovery of a crime. I even offered him money. He drew back from my hand. "You shall have it for nothing," he said, "if you will only go away and never come back here again." He tried to cut it out of the page—but his trembling hands were helpless. I cut it out myself, and attempted to thank him. He wouldn't hear me. "Go away!" he said, "I don't like the look of you."

It may be here objected that I ought not to have felt so sure as I did of the woman's guilt, until I had got more evidence against her. The knife might have been stolen from her, supposing she was the person who had snatched it out of the engraver's hands, and might have been afterwards used by the thief to commit the murder. All very true. But I never had a moment's doubt in my own mind, from the time when I read the damnable line in the engraver's book.

I went back to the railway without any plan in my head. The train by which I had proposed to follow her had left Waterbank. The next train that arrived was for London. I took my place in it— still without any plan in my head.

At Charing Cross a friend met me. He said, "You're looking miserably ill. Come and have a drink."

I went with him. The liquor was what I really wanted; it strung me up, and cleared my head. He went his way, and I went mine. In a little while more, I determined what I would do.

In the first place, I decided to resign my situation in the police, from a motive which will presently appear. In the second place, I took a bed at a public-house. She would no doubt return to London, and she would go to my lodgings to find out why I had broken my appointment. To bring to justice the one woman whom I had dearly loved was too cruel a duty for a poor creature like me. I preferred leaving the police force. On the other hand, if she and I met before time had helped me to control myself, I had a horrid fear that I might turn murderer next, and kill her then and there. The wretch had not only all but misled me into marrying her, but also into charging the innocent housemaid with being concerned in the murder.

The same night I hit on a way of clearing up such doubts as still harassed my mind. I wrote to the rector of Roth, informing him that I was engaged to marry her, and asking if he would tell me (in consideration of my position) what her former relations might have been with the person named John Zebedee.

By return of post I got this reply:

SIR,—Under the circumstances, I think I am bound to tell you confidentially what the friends and well-wishers of Priscilla have kept secret, for her sake.

Zebedee was in service in this neighborhood. I am sorry to say it, of a man who has come to such a miserable end—but his behaviour to Priscilla proves him to have been a vicious and heartless wretch. They were engaged—and, I add with indignation, he tried to seduce her under a promise of marriage. Her virtue resisted him, and he pretended to be ashamed of himself. The banns were published in my church. On the next day Zebedee disappeared, and cruelly deserted her. He was a capable servant; and I believe he got another place. I leave you to imagine what the poor girl suffered under the outrage inflicted on her. Going to London, with my recommendation, she answered the first advertisment that she saw, and was unfortunate enough to begin her career in domestic service in the very lodging-house, to which (as I gather from the newspaper report of the murder) the man Zebedee took the person whom he married, after deserting Priscilla. Be assured that you are about to unite yourself to an excellent girl, and accept my best wishes for your happiness.

It was plain from this that neither the rector nor the parents and friends knew anything of the purchase of the knife. The one miserable man who knew the truth was the man who had asked her to be his wife.

I owed it to myself—at least so it seemed to me—not to let it be supposed that I, too, had meanly deserted her. Dreadful as the prospect was, I felt that I must see her once more, and for the last time.

She was at work when I went into her room. As I opened the door she started to her feet. Her cheeks reddened, and her eyes flashed with anger. I stepped forward—and she saw my face. My face silenced her.

I spoke in the fewest words I could find.

"I have been to the cutler's shop at Waterbank," I said. "There is the unfinished inscription on the knife, completely in your handwriting. I could hang you by a word. God forgive me—I can't say the word."

Her bright complexion turned to a dreadful clay-colour. Her eyes were fixed and staring, like the eyes of a person in a fit. She stood before me, still and silent. Without saying more, I dropped the inscription into the fire. Without saying more, I left her.

I never saw her again.

8. But I heard from her a few days later.

The letter has long since burnt. I wish I could have forgotten it as well. It sticks to my memory. If I die with my senses about me, Priscilla's letter will be my last recollection on earth.

In substance it repeated what the rector had already told me. Further, it informed me that she had bought the knife as a keepsake for Zebedee, in place of a similar knife which he had lost. On the Saturday, she made the purchase, and left it to be engraved. On the Sunday, the banns were put up. On the Monday, she was deserted; and she snatched the knife from the table while the engraver was at work.

She only knew that Zebedee had added a new sting to the insult inflicted on her, when he arrived at the lodgings with his wife. Her duties as cook kept her in the kitchen—and Zebedee never discovered that she was in the house. I still remember the last lines of her confession:

"The devil entered into me when I tried their door, on my way up to bed, and found it unlocked, and listened awhile, and peeped in. I saw them by the dying light of the candle—one asleep on the bed, the other asleep by the fireside. I had the knife in my hand, and the thought came to me to do it, so that they might hang *her* for the murder. I couldn't take the knife out again, when I had done it. Mind this! I did really like you—I didn't say Yes, because you could hardly hang your own wife, if you found out who killed Zebedee."

Since the past time I have never heard again of Priscilla Thurlby; I don't know whether she is living or dead. Many people may think I deserve to be hanged myself for not having given her up to the gallows. They may, perhaps, be disappointed when they see this confession, and hear that I have died decently in my bed. I don't blame them. I am a penitent sinner. I wish all merciful Christians good-bye for ever.

MRS. J. H.
RIDDELL *née Charlotte Eliza Lawson Cowan (1832–1906), was born in Carrickfergus, near Belfast, Northern Ireland, but spent most of her adult life in and around London. She was known as the novelist of the City because her most successful novels, like* George Geith of Fen Court *(1864), were concerned with businessmen in the City of London. She was also a popular domestic novelist.*

Mrs. Riddell is highly regarded for her supernatural fiction, which in the Victorian period was second only to that of J. S. LeFanu. In addition to many short stories, she wrote four good supernatural novels.

"Dr. Varvill's Prescription" was written for a pharmacists' trade magazine when Mrs. Riddell was old, sick, and poor. A curious survival of fine, leisurely narrative techniques into a later age, it seems to be her only venture into detective fiction.

"Dr. Varvill's Prescription"

Chapter I.

One raw November evening, early in the Eighties, Mr. Isaac Hepplethorn, chemist, of 3, Beaufort Place, Upper Moor Road, London, W., sat alone in his shop doing—nothing.

He was doing nothing for the sufficient reason that he had nothing to do; and he sat alone because he had sent his son, besides whom he kept no assistant, upstairs, feeling he could contrive to be quite as miserable in solitude as in company.

Speaking quite dispassionately, it would have been difficult that evening to find in London, full of misery though the great city always is, a more wretched man than Mr. Hepplethorn.

Yet there was no deadly sin lying heavy on his conscience. He had not robbed a bank, or run away with his neighbour's wife, or done anything whatsoever which the law accounts a crime; but he had been foolish, and, as most of us know, folly is in this world generally much more severely punished than vice—perhaps because it will be easier to deal with vice than with folly in the next.

However this may be, Mr. Hepplethorn was, on the November evening when this story opens, bearing the punishment of his folly after a dogged, silent, stupid fashion, which some ill-natured persons attributed to drink, and others, more charitable, to the fact, as they believed, that the man was gone, or going, out of his mind.

Both theories were wrong as theories are ever apt to be. Mr. Hepplethorn did not drink, and he was not going out of his mind; but he was miserable, and with reason.

As he sat on a stool behind his desk idly turning over the leaves of a day-book, in which the entries were few and all for small amounts, his thoughts only left present anxieties in order to recall a time when he had no anxieties worth mentioning.

Often and often before they had travelled the same weary road, but on the evening in question he seemed to see with cruel distinctiveness the pleasant highway, shaded by trees and bordered with flowers, he might never, save in memory, traverse again.

Ruin is compassed more frequently than many worthy persons imagine by a fatal inability to let well alone.

Mr. Hepplethorn had brought all his misfortunes on himself by reason of a vaulting ambition which could not let well alone.

No one need have desired a better friend than the LUCK which had kept even step with him through many a prosperous year.

The principal chemist in an old-fashioned provincial town, where his father had been a chemist before him, he virtually enjoyed the confidence and custom of every one in a good position round about.

His was an ideal shop—cool in summer, warm in winter, artistic in its arrangement and appointments always—a shop ladies affected; where they arranged to meet their county sisters; where they left "dear little Algy" in charge of a devoted nurse, to have a first tooth tenderly removed; where they took Mr. Hepplethorn into confidence concerning the footman's sprain and the cook's neuralgia, the squire's curious illness and Sir George's most recent attack of gout— to all of which interesting details the chemist lent a sympathetic ear, and out of all of which he made a nice penny.

He had such pretty things, moreover, always so well displayed he never needed to say a word in their praise.

The articles sold themselves.

Ladies looked, and exclaimed, "Oh, Mr. Hepplethorn, how lovely!" or, "I really must take this home!" and such like.

If Mr. Hepplethorn had only understood in what safe and pleasant lines his lot was cast, this story concerning Dr. Varvill's prescription could never have been written.

As matters were, he grew tired of the ladies and their nurses, and dear little Algy, and the cooks and footmen, and squires and baronets—nay, even perhaps of uniform success. In a word, he lost his head; and who can conceive what follies under such circumstances a man may commit?

When any one begins to think too much of his own merits—to imagine good fortune attends all he attempts merely because he is so steady, or so clever, or so respectable—evil times are within appreciable distance; and the fact was that the kindness and esteem of his patrons and neighbours had so unduly puffed up poor Mr. Hepplethorn, and produced such an exaggerated idea of his own abilities, that at last he grew to believe the pleasant world in which he moved could but be regarded as unworthy of him.

Then the inevitable rule-of-three sum such a state of mind engenders was duly worked out from the usual inaccurate premises to the usual inaccurate result.

Given—that Isaac Hepplethorn, with his extraordinary knowledge of pharmacy, his general intelligence, his superior address, his attention to details, his grasp of many subjects seldom thoroughly understood save by manufacturing and analytical chemists, had in his native town—where, as is well known, no prophet is ever properly honoured—achieved a greatly-to-be-envied position and more than a fair amount of material prosperity, to what height might he not hope to climb if transplanted to some more congenial soil?

A very neat little sum indeed, the outcome of which nothing save experience, unhappily, could "prove."

It is scarcely necessary to add the "congenial soil" meant London—"the Capital of the World—the centre of modern civilization, the headquarters of genius—the city richer than Tyre—mightier than Babylon—the huge mental workshop wherein all the day long, week after week, and year after year, men employ themselves in sharpening the wits of men"!

Mr. Hepplethorn was so delighted with his own imaginings, and so satisfied of the correctness of his own calculations, that he at length decided to sell the excellent business his father had founded, to resign his appointment as churchwarden, as well as other appointments "thrust upon him" by appreciative and zealous friends, and bidding a not reluctant farewell to the accustomed streets filled with people he had known all his life, take railway ticket—the modern equivalent for staff and cockleshell—and start with his family for that terrible brick-and-mortar wilderness in which so many are defeated, and so comparatively few compass success; where so many fair and bright hopes find cruel burial, and broken hearts scarce to be numbered at last obtain rest.

There is no use in arguing with ignorance wise in its own esteem.

Mr. Hepplethorn, spite of his undoubted cleverness, was ignorant as a child of the thousand pitfalls London prepares for unsophisticated country folk, yet he would listen to no word of advice from those who knew more than he.

Bluff squires, gentle ladies, clergymen who had paced the stony-hearted pavements of Mr. Hepplethorn's dream city, travellers from the great wholesale houses who knew every in and out of London, and were aware of the horrible difficulties which often meet and overwhelm new-comers—all counselled delay and consideration, but Mr. Hepplethorn was as adamant.

He had entered into an interesting series of correspondence concerning the sale of his own business as well as the purchase of another, and never before in the whole of his experience had the post brought him such an amount of excitement and satisfaction.

"This is living," he thought. 'During all the previous years of my existence I have only been vegetating;" a remark we—you, my readers, and I—have heard many times from many people with sadness, or contempt, or indifference, or amusement, according to our respective temperaments.

In the quiet town where he had been born, people were almost unanimously of opinion Mr. Hepplethorn was doing a very foolish thing. "He will be a loss to the place," they said, "and the place will be a loss to him"—which last part of the sentence proved particularly true.

Ere Mr. Hepplethorn was very much older, the loss of his native town seemed to him a serious one.

"Aren't you doing a very good busines, then?" asked one rather plain-spoken traveller, when he heard of the proposed change. Wise travellers do not care to see valued customers playing at pitch-and-toss with fortune.

"A capital business," replied Mr. Hepplethorn; "but an opening now presents itself for making a change, and I feel I should be wrong not to avail myself of it. You see, I have sons coming on—and daughters too, for the matter of that."

"And can't they come on here?" suggested the traveller.

"Not so well. There are chances in London no one ever meets with in a place like this."

"There are chances of coming a cropper," said the other, with a sort of diabolical prescience which hurt Mr. Hepplethorn very much, though he answered bravely—

"I am not going to come a cropper. I have bought a splendid business in London."

"So I hear—Baynfleet's, in Upper Moor Road?"

"The same—been in his hands for nearly quarter of a century."

"No doubt of that."

"And he has made a fortune."

"So it is said."

"Do you not believe he has?"

"I? Wherefore should I disbelieve? The only thing that ever puzzled me was why he wanted to sell such a business."

"Just because he had made a fortune, and wished to go to Australia."

The other shook his head, but did not speak.

"What are you driving at?" asked Mr. Hepplethorn, impatiently.

"I am not driving at anything," was the reply; "only in my experience men like Baynfleet who have a good going concern, out of which a fortune has been made, and sons in the same line as themselves, don't, as a rule, sell or desire to emigrate."

"But if no one ever wanted to sell there would be no businesses in the market," returned Mr. Hepplethorn shrewdly, though with a slight increase of tone and temper; "and so far as Mr. Baynfleet having made a fortune goes, every one is aware of the fact."

"Precisely, and I am puzzled accordingly. However, I don't want to damp your enthusiasm, and I will only say I hope you may make your fortune too, and find London fulfil all your expectations." With which equivocal aspiration exit one traveller, who might be considered a fair sample of many more.

A few weeks later Mr. Hepplethorn was setled in Beaufort Place, where he felt—so he expressed himself—"as much at home as if he had lived there all his life."

Australia being a long way off, Mr. Baynfleet naturally decided it would be better not to transport his household furniture thither. "Therefore, if you like," he said to Mr. Hepplethorn, "I will hand you over the whole place as it stands. There need be no auction—no fuss. I go out; you come in. We won't quarrel about terms."

Nor did they. Mr. Hepplethorn, having already swallowed the Beaufort Place camel, never strained over the gnats subsequently offered to him. He took the stock, the fittings, the furniture, without a murmur, and paid for everything with an immediate cheque.

Under the best auspices, therefore, he entered upon his new life: the fame and glory of ready money preceded and shone around him like a halo.

Tradesmen touted for his custom; the local clergy soon found him out, and expressed in a breath their regret because Mr. Baynfleet was gone, and their pleasure because Mr. Hepplethorn was come.

It was under these delightful conditions the newcomer entered into possession of 3, Beaufort Place—no blinds to put up, no curtains to hang, no carpets to fit, no dark suspicions to allay, no hesitation about sending in goods to meet and overcome, no hateful requests for cash before delivery, no hanging back about the execution of orders—the cheeriest home-coming possible.

Mr. Hepplethorn enjoyed it thoroughly. He treated himself frequently to a little holiday, took his wife to see the sights, and his whole family more than once to the play. He welcomed London friends made in the provinces, and country friends who happened to be in London, and received their congratulations on the upward step he had taken; for was he not going to make his fortune?

There were pleasant days and doings at 3, Beaufort Place, during the August when a new chemist succeeded to Mr. Baynfleet's business. Every one worth mentioning was out of town, and trade consequently at a standstill; but Mr. Hepplethorn did not lament. Rather he felt he could be idle with a clear conscience.

He had plenty of money to go on with. A good time was coming; he could wait till that good time came.

Everything began well—everything went merry as a marriage-bell; there was not a cloud in the sky of his content.

Happy Mr. Hepplethorn!

Chapter II.

Mr. Hepplethorn's happiness was not of very long continuance, however.

Though he had done one extremely foolish thing, he was by no means lacking in common sense; and therefore the day came, as it was bound to come, when, after a series of enjoyable and rather expensive outings, it was borne in upon him that, even for the time of year, the "takings" in his new establishment were exceedingly small.

For this reason he deemed it prudent to curtail his amusements, and to devote the most of his time to business.

Whether he imagined his assistants were dishonest or indifferent is a matter of no importance, because he found the receipts did not increase when he was present to check them.

Doubtless he ought to have felt glad to know his people were blameless; but, after all, Mr. Hepplethorn was only human, and his humanity shrank back dismayed when he remembered the amount

handed over for good will, and beheld what the good will of Baynfleet's business promised to return for three months, at all events,
out of the twelve.

Meanwhile rent and taxes and salaries were going on just the
same as though money were rolling in!

It may be questioned, also, whether the customers who pa-
tronized Beaufort Place did not prove a greater trouble to Mr. Hepplethorn than the absence of others, who refrained.

Previous experience had made him fastidious, and he could not
help regarding with disfavour the persons who entered his establishment.

Was it to serve drabs who brought bottles he would not himself
have touched, for his assistants to fill with "stuff," he had sold his
good country connection, relinquished an enviable position, and sad-
dled himself with expenses that seemed never to end?

Was it to see his counters bombarded on Saturday evenings by
rough men, often incapable of articulating very distinctly, he had
turned his back on Algy and his nurse, on Lady This and the
Countess of That, who bought his latest novelties and raved concerning his newest perfumes?

He could not imagine where all the dreadful people came
from—the children with sore eyes and offensive skin-diseases, the
women who carried sickly babies and asked for outlandish drugs, the
men who bought boxes and boxes of a pill called by Mr. Baynfleet's
name, that appeared to be in great request, and partook of curious
medicines they liked to have mixed for them in tall glasses and drank
with relish in the shop.

The very coins in which they paid for these various confections
struck Mr. Hepplethorn as objectionable from a sanitary point of
view; and, truth to tell, of a "muggy" night there hung about the im-
maculately clean shop that "poor-peopley" odour which in no way
resembles that of Araby.

So matters went on till, Mr. Hepplethorn's anxiety over-master-
ing his reticence, he sarcastically asked Mr. Forwell, who had acted
as manager to the late proprietor of 3, Beaufort Place—

"Was it out of such custom as this Mr. Baynfleet amassed a fortune?"

"I do not think so, sir," was the answer; "Mr. Baynfleet had
made his pile before I came to him, at a time when the trade was
very different from what it is now."

"In what way?"

"Oh, in every way. Stores were in their infancy then. Doctors
did not make up their own prescriptions. 'Cutting' had not come in.
And, besides," went on Mr. Forwell, who thought, perhaps, the
time had arrived when Mr. Hepplethorn might be enlightened with

advantage, "Upper Moor Road is not the place it was once. It has been going to the bad ever since Park Station was opened."

"Where is Park Station?" inquired Mr. Hepplethorn.

"At the bottom of Albert Avenue—that fine road beyond Park Square. Park Terrace, Park Crescent, Park Gardens, Park Place, all run into it. Mr. Baynfleet owned several houses in that neighbourhood. The new station about doubled their value."

"Oh!" said Mr. Hepplethorn, on whom a glimmering of disagreeable light was dawning. "Park Station, I suppose, is now used by all the gentlemen who formerly passed up and down this road?" he suggested, after a pause.

"That is so," was the answer.

"And where do the people come from who honour us with their custom?" went on the chemist.

"From round and about; there is a regular rookery not a stone's throw from here."

"Do we get many orders from Park Square?"

"No; there are some good shops near the station. A chemist started in one of them about eighteen months ago, and he takes the cream of what business there is hereabouts."

"Ah!" remarked Mr. Hepplethorn, knowing he had been sold in the worst way possible—with a lie that was partly a truth and a truth which was more than half a lie.

And no redress could be obtained. Every statement Mr. Baynfleet had made was strictly true to the letter, if not in the spirit; the agents were not to blame; the accountants were not to blame; the lawyers were not to blame; no one was to blame, unless it might be the fortunate vendor, by that time far on his way to Australia, where, it may be stated, he did not intend to remain permanently.

Many persons advised Mr. Hepplethorn to sell—to transfer the fraud, if such a phrase be permissible—to get out of the matter as safely as he could. The suggested transaction was more euphoniously worded; but Mr. Hepplethorn was not the man to take in any one as he had been taken in.

Rather, with a courage worthy of all admiration, he resolved to try and retrieve his position.

That he failed was not his fault; that year by year he found himself going pecuniarily to the bad could not be imputed to him as a sin. He worked like a slave; he paid his way honestly; he did whatever his hand found to do; he managed to live and educate his children: but he knew matters were getting worse and worse—that he should not be able to hold on much longer, and that the inevitable end must come.

It had come very near on the November evening when he sat turning over the leaves of his daybook in that absent way which so little resembled his former manner. Neighbours hinted drink, or softening of the brain, or a stroke was the cause; whereas all that ailed the unfortunate chemist chanced to be that the waters of trouble had gone over his head.

He was considering, as usual, what he could do—to whom it would be possible for him to apply for advice and assistance—on that raw, chill night when, with many apologies for presenting so worn and harassed a man, Mr. Isaac Hepplethorn is introduced to the reader.

Matters were coming to a crisis. He knew he could not hold on much longer—honestly; and he certainly did not intend to hold on dishonestly.

For over seven years he had made as brave a fight as conqueror crowned with laurels ever waged.

Only the result in his case was not victory, wherein lay *all* the difference.

He had worked hard; he had denied himself; he had tried to retrieve his mistake by means of careful and persistent economy. He had hitherto managed to make two difficult ends meet; but now he understood—no work, no self-denial, no economy could delay the inevitable end. "I will go to my landlord to-morrow," he decided at last, digging the point of his steel pen deep into one of the pages of that day-book which contained so few entries.

There was nothing else to be done. Upper Moor Road had been going as steadily down as Mr. Hepplethorn, and with even greater rapidity. Some thoroughfares begin life with a great dash, only, as it would seem, that they may get to destruction all the quicker.

At its first start Upper Moor Road assumed great airs of respectability—many of the houses were let on long leases, and none for a shorter term than three years. There were but four shops in the street, and those pretentious edifices in Beaufort Place; the side paths were planted with trees, and the neighbourhood was considered select.

Before Upper Moor Road numbered more than thirty years, however, a change came o'er the spirit of its dream. Landlords were only too glad to secure annual tenants—nay, they did not disdain quarterly; then many of the houses were let out in tenements, and quite a number of bell-handles ornamented the hall-door lintels. After that, private dwellings transformed themselves into shops, which in their turn soon assumed the character of mere stalls, on which all sorts of goods—butcher's meat, grocery, china, greenstuff, boots and shoes, bacon and eggs, dress-stuffs, shirts, hats—were exposed for sale, and gradually spread in picturesque confusion to within a few feet of the kerbstone. Old tools, old furniture, old worthless books, soon followed suit. Carpets depended from the

irons intended for awnings; one cobbler in sight of the public pursued his calling down an area; finally, a fried-fish shop was opened,
which did a roaring trade, and poisoned the night air, by which time
the demoralization might have been considered complete.

Before that period, however, the last nail—figuratively speaking—was driven into the coffin containing the corpse of Mr. Hepplethorn's fortune by an audacious young chemist, who, opening a
shop near Moor Station, spirited away all those customers who had
once been regarded with disfavour in Beaufort Place.

The new light pharmacist—young, impudent, and vivacious—
soon established the most friendly relations with the working men
and women, the drabs, the children—those afflicted with sore eyes,
as well as their fellows who were the proud possessors of mysterious
internal complaints and loathsome skin-diseases.

How the new-comer raked in the pennies Mr. Hepplethorn had
formerly regarded with proud disdain!

Pills more powerful and draughts more potent than any Mr.
Baynfleet ever adventured upon were freely advertised by Mr. Runnicle in the local paper, and some broadcast in the shape of handbills.

Runnicle's Infallible Specifics were indeed things to fill the stout-
est heart with amazement, and having no fear of a coroner—or any
one else for that matter—the young gentleman prescribed his own
medicines for all the ills flesh is heir to with a cheerful confidence
that in itself went half-way towards effecting a cure.

He felt no doubt; he knew no hesitation. To hear him glibly dis-
coursing about disease any one might have imagined he had created
man, and that, consequently, man's internal economy held no secret
with which he was unacquainted. What chance had Mr. Hepplethorn against this unorthodox young fellow, who spoke of the elder
chemist as "a poor old chap"?

None whatever. Indeed, Mr. Runnicle had not been long in the
neighbourhood before the belief became general that Hepplethorn
was either out of his mind already or going out of it.

In simple justice it must be said Mr. Runnicle had no part in
starting this rumour, which came to him with the even more painful
suggestion that probably to drink alone could Mr. Hepplethorn's
"queerness" and "want of success" be attributed.

"He came here with lots of money, and stepped into a fine business," said the gossip who talked to Mr. Runnicle about the Beaufort
Place chemist.

"He was a first-rate man once on a time, so I am told," was the
answer. "Likely he has got softening of the brain." And then the
changes were rung so loud that Mr. Hepplethorn could not avoid
hearing some of their dismal music.

He knew he was growing old. He did not require any one to tell him trouble had wrought its bitter work. When a man is poor—as poor as Mr. Hepplethorn—he grows slow of speech, shy of his fellows, anxious to avoid notice. Mr. Hepplethorn had been a prosperous man, and was well-nigh a beggar. He might well seem "queer," "reticent," "odd."

Heaven help us! it needs a stout heart and great courage to carry the burden of poverty for seven long years without changing manner, or voice, or looks.

The end was coming very near for Isaac Hepplethorn, at any rate. How he had struggled, what he had endured, did not matter much on that chill November evening when he made up his mind to go to the man who had regularly been paid a preposterous rent through seven unprofitable years.

The end had drawn very near. As he came to that conclusion Mr. Hepplethorn got down from his stool, and advanced to meet a customer who had just opened the door and walked into the shop—a customer quite of a different stamp from any the chemist had met with for many a long day, and yet one whose face seemed not quite unfamiliar, though he failed to remember where he had seen it before.

Certainly he could but be considered what Mr. Runnicle in his airy way would have called a "toff."

"Good evening!" said the stranger courteously. He was a fine-looking man of forty or thereabouts—tall, and of a stately presence. "Seems as if it were going to be a nasty night."

"Do you think so, sir?" answered Mr. Hepplethorn, sensibly enough, though he had been sitting so long in company only with many troubles that the tones of his own voice sounded strange to him when he spoke, and he felt for the moment dazed, like one who had come out of darkness into a strong light.

"Yes, the wind seems to be blowing up for rain. However, we must expect that now, I suppose. I have a prescription I want you to make up for me," added the unwonted customer, unbuttoning his coat, and fumbling in his breast-pocket as he spoke.

"Certainly," said Mr. Hepplethorn, standing at ease, and trying to speak as he would have spoken years previously, before he ever so much as heard of Upper Moor Road, or had been tempted of the devil to sell his country practice, and yielded to the temptation.

He felt the stranger looked at him a little curiously. He knew he was somewhat confused, and strove to conceal his embarrassment the while he waited, till the gentleman, after turning over many letters and papers, at last found what he had been in search of.

"Ah, here we are," he exclaimed, handing an envelope across the counter with a smile.

Mr. Hepplethorn took it, and extracted a prescription that had been written by Dr. Varvill, of Chesham Place, and made up previously to that November evening by a well-known firm of chemists in Brompton.

Mr. Hepplethorn glanced it over half-carelessly, as one often does read a paper, likely to contain little of importance, for the first time. Then he read it again more carefully, doubting the evidence of his senses, and felt as if he had unexpectedly received a galvanic shock.

Chapter III.

Never before had Mr. Hepplethorn experienced such an awful shock—never even when it was borne in upon him that Mr. Baynflect's excellent business could only be regarded as a swindle. That knowledge had come upon him by degrees—but this terrible thing was unexpected as a pistol-shot.

The effect it produced, however, was strangely different from any which might have been anticipated.

Prompted by some vague instinct—even while his head reeled with astonishment—he turned a little aside, and holding the prescription under the gas-burner, affected to study it carefully, in order that he might regain command of himself.

Then almost in a moment the cobwebs of care that had for years been obscuring his brain were swept aside, his troubles dropped from his soul like a heavy garment, and, for the time, he stood a man free from the trammels of anxiety, able to think quickly and clearly as he had done in happier days, rather than after the uncertain nerveless fashion which of late caused so many people in and about Upper Moor Road to believe he was losing his wits.

The necessity for prompt and discreet action took him out of the cloudy atmosphere in which he had been for so long living. For the first time he was face to face with a danger he never conceived could menace any chemist, and its imminence steadied him.

One swift flash of that former intelligence on which he had been wont to pique himself seemed to make the position clear to his understanding, a short time previously befogged by care.

He recalled where and when he had seen the new customer. He remembered why that handsome face struck him as not pleasantly familiar; he suspected why to Isaac Hepplethorn, of 3, Beaufort Place, was accorded the honour of making up a prescription written by Dr. Varvill, of Chesham Place, and previously dispensed by a well-known firm in Brompton. He believed he partly grasped what the whole thing meant, and, though he recoiled from the conclusion forced upon him, felt so much might depend on how he dealt with the matter, that it behoved him to handle the dreadful difficulty with courage and wisdom.

"Can we send this for you, sir?" he asked after a pause, which was really very short.

The new customer, who had been intently examining the contents of a showcase, looked up at the question, while an expression almost of relief flitted across his face.

"No, thank you," he answered; "I will take it."

"I shall have to trouble you, then, to wait for a short time," returned Mr. Hepplethorn. "Will you not be seated?" And he indicated one of those uncomfortable, old-fashioned mahogany hall-chairs which are always to be found in chemist's shops.

The gentleman sat down and continued his investigation of scent-bottles, fancy soaps, combs, nail-trimmers, scissors, purses, and other such useful and refined trifles.

Mr. Hepplethorn, after touching a bell which rang upstairs to apprise his son that he was wanted, walked to the rear of the shop where all medicines were made up, taking Dr. Varvill's prescription with him.

When well out of sight behind a tall nest of shelves, which lent a dignity to the outer shop and screened the dispensing-counter from the profane gaze of customers, he again scanned that half-sheet of note-paper curiously, even examining it through a powerful microscope.

"Remarkably well done," he thought, planting both elbows on the counter, and resting his forehead on his hands. "An ignorant lad, now—or a careless assistant—or—a man in the state of health Runnicle hopes I am—might have—played the deuce."

He was right; and if Mr. Hepplethorn were not to play the deuce, only two courses were open; further, he had scarcely any time in which to make up his mind which to adopt.

He could refuse to dispense the prescription altogether, or he could dispense it, omitting one ingredient.

What he could not do was, make up the medicine as directed.

He argued the matter to the bitter end exhaustively—Isaac Hepplethorn, alone with Isaac Hepplethorn, in blissful forgetfulness that he was the most wretched fellow living.

For many a long day he had not stood so completely outside himself—so wholly absorbed in the peril of another human being, who appeared to be a certain J. Tercett, Esq. Who that gentleman was, where he lived, why any one desired his death, were mysteries to Mr. Hepplethorn—but mysteries he meant to solve ere he or his new customer were much older. He had not been grappling with the extraordinary prescription for three minutes, yet his mind was made up.

Pushing open a narrow door, which gave admittance into a
small room behind the inner shop, fitted with shelves, and furnished
with a deal table, a chair, plenty of bottles, phials, and empty boxes,
he said in those grave, slow tones anxiety had made habitual, to a lad
who was poring over some school-books—

"Hal, I want you to take a good look at the gentleman for whom
I am now making up a prescription. You can see him through the
window. When he leaves, follow him; if possible, ascertain his name
and address. Mind, not a word about this to any one till I give you
leave. Here is money; don't use a penny you can help, but spend
when needful. You quite understand the matter is of importance?"

The boy nodded assent, closed his books, took his coat and cap
from a peg, and, without a word, went out into the night. Mr.
Hepplethorn returned to his counter just in time to hear the new
customer ask his elder son—

"Do you think Mr. Hepplethorn will be much longer?"

"I cannot say, sir; it all depends," answered the young man,
beautifully unconscious of the drama in progress. "Some prescriptions are more troublesome to make up than others."

There ensued a dead silence. Mr. Hepplethorn selected his materials, made up the medicine, put it into a faultlessly bright bottle,
wrote on a label, bearing his name and address, the directions,
"One-sixth part to be taken three times a day: J. Tercett, Esq.,"
made up a neat little parcel wrapped in clean white paper, and, returning to the front of the shop, handed it to the stranger, with the
prescription, and the remark—

"Are you sure you would not like us to send it for you, sir?"

"Quite unnecessary, thank you. How much?"

Mr. Hepplethorn told him, and received the exact amount.

"Good evening," said the new customer.

"Good evening," answered Mr. Hepplethorn, holding open the
door. "It is raining. Should you not like a cab, sir?"

"I shan't hurt," was the reply; and the next instant he was gone,
followed at a safe distance, as Mr. Hepplethorn saw, by Hal.

The chemist breathed a sigh of relief, and walked back to his
desk, wiping his forehead as though he felt the night warm.

"That swell lives in Park Crescent," observed Mr. Hepplethorn,
junior, using the language of the period.

"Really?" observed his father.

"Yes; in the house with that lady who owns those two pretty
white dogs."

"It struck me his face was somewhat familiar," said the chemist.
"I thought I had seen it before."

"I wonder he did not go to Hanroyd's to get his prescription
made up. That would have been more in his way."

"He may have been coming from Moor Station; and, besides, the lady deals here," was the reply. "I have to go out, Ted, and I don't know how long I may be detained. Tell your mother not to wait supper for me or to sit up. Oh! and I have sent Hal an errand, so she need not be uneasy about him."

Mr. Hepplethorn was putting on his top-coat as he made these statements, and a minute later left Beaufort Place without vouchsafing any information as to his intended destination.

He walked briskly through the rain to Moor Station, where he took train for Victoria. Arrived there he made his way to Chesham Place, only to find Dr. Varvill out, and his servant unwilling to say where he was or when he would be in. Pressed very hard, the man said he thought he might be back by eleven; but even this was uncertain.

"I must see him to-night," said Mr. Hepplethorn, "so will return at eleven;" which he accordingly did, to meet the popular physician on his doorstep.

Dr. Varvill had been dining out, and after spending a most delightful evening, was returning home in excellent temper and spirits. If he had been asked to go and see a patient he might have demurred, but as Mr. Hepplethorn only craved a few minutes of his time, explained who he was, and said how well he remembered making up Dr. Varvill's prescriptions for one of his country patients, Sir George Montmorney, the chemist was accorded an interview at once.

"Dilworth, light the gas in my room. Walk in, Mr. Hepplethorn—pray walk in," said the genial physician, who had the most charming manners. "What can I do for you?" he went on, when Dilworth had closed the door upon prosperous Dr. Varvill and impecunious Mr. Hepplethorn. "What is this pressing matter about which you wish to consult me?"

"I will not waste your time, doctor," said Mr. Hepplethorn, in answer to the courteous question, which seemed like an echo of some pleasant melody long unheard, though once familiar, "so will come to the point at once. Did you write the prescription of which this is a facsimile?" And as he spoke he handed Dr. Varvill a fair copy he had made while the new customer waited.

Dr. Varvill took the paper and ran over the items.

"H—m! H—m! H—m!" he murmured. "J. Tercett, Esq.—that is all right. Poor dear fellow—a great friend of mine as well as patient." And he would have returned Mr. Hepplethorn his memorandum had that gentleman not said—

"Pardon me, but I do not think you have read the contents very carefully."

"Indeed! What have I overlooked?"

"The quantities—or, rather, one quantity. Please glance at the strychnine."

Dr. Varvill did as requested. Then he looked again, as if doubting the evidence of his eyes, and just as Mr. Hepplethorn had done, though not for the same reason, he held the copy-prescription where more light fell upon it. After that, springing to his feet, he exclaimed, in an access of dismay—

"I never wrote this prescription. I could not have done such a thing—why, there is enough poison in it to kill half-a-dozen people."

"Do not distress yourself, sir, pray," said Mr. Hepplethorn, who had risen also, infected by the physician's terrible agitation. "There would have been some one killed very soon had I made up the prescription as handed to me; but I did not. I omitted the strychnine altogether."

"Thank God!" said Dr. Varvill—"thank God!" And he walked to the fireplace and back striving to get over a shock which evidently was as great to him as it had been to Mr. Hepplethorn a few hours previously.

At last, signing to the chemist to do likewise, he resumed his seat, and began—

"All this is an utter mystery to me, and I must know what it means. Of course I need not say the prescription of which this professes to be a copy"—and he touched the paper Mr. Hepplethorn had handed him—"was never written by me. I could not—no man with the slightest knowledge of medicine could—have fallen into such an error."

"I am quite sure of that," was the reply; "but I feel equally confident the person who brought the prescription to me fell into no error either."

"What do you mean?"

"Exactly what I say. The prescription made up previously by Sawtell & Cowmeadow of Brompton, handed to me this evening, was evidently written originally by you. The quantity of strychnine had no doubt been altered with a purpose."

"What purpose?"

"Why, to speak plainly—I should imagine to put some one out of the way."

"But that would have been murder."

"I have no doubt murder was the object."

"Impossible!"

"It would not have been in the least impossible under certain conditions—no more impossible than fastening the guilt of the crime on *me*."

"Where is the original prescription?" asked Dr. Varvill, after a pause.

"I returned the original prescription with the medicine, as is customary."

"Surely it was your duty to keep it."

"I could not well have done anything of the kind unless I had been prepared to give the person who brought it into custody."

"Why not?" And the physician's tone was sharp as he asked the question.

"Put it to yourself, Dr. Varvill. Had I refused to return the prescription, my customer—a gentleman by birth and breeding, as the world accounts such things—would have made a disturbance, and it seemed to me a disturbance was the thing to avoid. Remember, the whole business was sprung upon me as a surprise, and I met a grave difficulty as best I could, almost at a moment's notice. I did not say the prescription struck me as extraordinary, but I made it up, omitting the one dangerous ingredient; and now, at considerable personal inconvenience, I have come to you to know what you consider ought to be done?"

"Indeed, Mr. Hepplethorn, I feel so bewildered that I am unable to make any suggestion. Like you, the whole thing has come upon me unawares. I do not know what to think about the business. Can you describe the appearance of the gentleman who asked you to dispense the prescription?"

"Certainly I can," was the answer, "and all the better because I had seen him before. He is a good deal at the house of a lady in our neighbourhood who calls herself Mrs. Osmond. He is known as Mr. Osmond, but his real name appears to be Tercett."

The doctor started. "Are you certain of this?" he asked.

"Perfectly certain. He went straight from Upper Moor Road this evening to Hans Place. Therefore if the medicine I made up contained what he believed it did, our patient would be a dead man to-morrow—or to-night, perhaps."

"Good heavens!"

"Has the gentleman who is not your patient any pecuniary interest in the death of the gentleman who is?"

"I do not know in the least—really I don't know. This is a terrible business, Mr. Hepplethorn, and one with which we are not equal to cope. What we had better do is this. Tomorrow I will see Mr. Steen, Mr. Tercett's solicitor, and put the whole thing before him. I am certain you will not object to my taking this course?"

"I? Not in the least."

"It would be better for you to see him also, perhaps," said Dr. Varvill, a little disconcerted by Mr. Hepplethorn's frank acceptance of his proposal.

"Much better, decidedly. I could explain matters more fully even than you."

"Then will you meet me to-morrow afternoon at Mr. Steen's office—four sharp?"

"Certainly. Where is his office?"

"New Square. I forget the number, but any one will tell you. Does my plan not suit you?" Dr. Varvill added, as the other hesitated ere replying.

"It suits me very well; but still I should like to propose an amendment."

"Which is?"

"In a case like this," began Mr. Hepplethorn, weighing his words carefully, "time seems to me of the utmost importance. Delay is proverbially dangerous. Suppose, instead of going to Mr. Steen at four o'clock to-morrow afternoon, you send him a telegram to come here as early as possible in the morning? I will run over about nine, and you can then let me know the hour Mr. Steen appoints."

"A very good thought!" exclaimed Dr. Varvill. "That will be better in every way."

Chapter IV.

As a matter of course—since time runs away very fast while talk is in progress—Mr. Hepplethorn missed the midnight train back to Moor Station, and had to tramp every step of the long way home.

On his arrival, wet and tired, at Beaufort Place, he lighted the gas-stove, and contentedly made a cup of cocoa, which, with some brown bread and butter, provided the poor fellow with what he called "a sumptuous repast."

All things are indeed comparative. Happy would Mr. Hepplethorn have been had he felt assured he should always possess a roof to cover him, and be able to count on that "dry morsel" which we are rightly told is better than "a house full of sacrifices."

And yet he had formerly enjoyed a good dinner as much as anybody. Truly circumstances alter cases!

Fatigued, he fell at once into the deep sleep of utter exhaustion; but this period of blessed forgetfulness did not last for long.

Ere four o'clock struck he was lying wide awake facing the usual difficulties, pondering the usual possibilities—or rather, impossibilities—oddly mixed up with the memory of his new customer and Dr. Varvill's prescription.

Before the first streak of daylight appeared in Upper Moor Road, Mr. Hepplethorn was so very weary of his miserable and tangled thoughts that he dressed and went down into that shop which had cost so dear and returned so little, only to ascertain the previous evening's business had, as usual, been almost *nil*.

There is nothing harder to change than a run of ill luck, and the chemist's run had been a long one!

A little before nine he found himself once more in Chesham Place, where Dr. Varvill showed him even greater courtesy than on the occasion of their first meeting—which courtesy, had Mr. Hepplethorn only understood its meaning, was the outward and visible token that the physician had altered his mind.

Always civil and gracious, Dr. Varvill was never half so civil or so gracious as when he intended to disappoint a man, or back out of a promise, or perform any other unpleasant act which needed soothing over to his conscience.

This was the reason exacting persons called Dr. Varvill a humbug, whereas he only did that pleasantly which his fellows as a rule do unpleasantly; nevertheless, the difference between his manners and his deeds often caused a sense of irritation which made many rude people say hard things concerning him.

As matters were, it chanced that he was in the morning not at all of the same opinion as he had been overnight.

Like Mr. Hepplethorn, sleep refused to remain with him. Through the long hours of darkness he had tossed and turned, and Dr. Varvill did not like lying awake. Again, when day dawned, rain was coming down in torrents, and Dr. Varvill did not like rain any better than he liked lying awake in the darkness.

Moreover, he did like to avoid disagreeable complications, and, so far as possible, to be all things to all men, more especially to those men who were rich and of a good standing; and how could he keep on agreeable terms with the Tercett family if he sprang a monstrous scandal upon one of the members composing it?

He had quite persuaded himself Mr. Hepplethorn's story could only be considered "a monstrous scandal"—whether a delusion or an invention, he was not called upon to decide. On the previous night he had been frightened! The idea that a prescription of his was wandering about the world, authorizing any chemist to deal out a subtle poison in quantity, seemed so terrible, he felt some one ought to be called in to stop the mischief; but upon reflection, he had arrived at the conclusion the whole thing was either a pure concoction, or that mere storm in a teacup busybodies have such a fancy for brewing.

He could have nothing further to do with the matter. Mr. Hepplethorn had not a tittle of evidence to support his assertion; his whole statement was absurd.

Why, Osmond and Jack Tercett were like brothers. They loved, had always loved each other. No better fellow lived than Jack Tercett; and if there had been stories about Osmond—a most agreeable person—was a man to be branded "poisoner" because a mere adventurer—and, according to his own confession, this chemist, this Hepplethorn, was an unsuccessful adventurer, who had sold one good business and let another go to the dogs—chose to tell a cock-and-bull story about his, Dr. Varvill's, own presciption having been tampered with?

He was sorry he had ever listened to such a rigmarole, but as he could not repair that error, he would get rid of the tiresome individual from Upper Moor Road as quietly as possible.

"What a morning, Mr. Hepplethorn!" he began in his suavest voice. "Pray be seated. I hope you are not very wet, because, if so, I shall feel a little guilty in having given you such a journey for nothing. I know I ought to have telegraphed to you, but the fact is I did not think of doing so till too late."

"Is Mr. Steen unable to come, then?" asked Mr. Hepplethorn.

"I have not sent for him," was the answer. "After a considerable amount of reflection, I have arrived at the conclusion I ought not to meddle in the affair."

If Dr. Varvill had expected Mr. Hepplethorn to utter some vehement expostulation, he ought to have been agreeably surprised, for the chemist spoke no word, bad or good—only sat like one stunned.

"I have been thinking the whole position over," went on Dr. Varvill, more disconcerted by the chemist's silence than he might have cared to confess, "and feel I could not possibly interfere. You see, even supposing you have made no mistake, we could not bring the smallest proof to support such a terrible accusation. Believe me, in saying this, I have no intention of casting a doubt upon your word, but I believe you are labouring under some great delusion. The first question any dispassionate person would ask we can easily imagine: 'Why did you not refuse to make up this extraordinary prescription?' and the next: 'Why in any case did you not retain the original document?' "

Mr. Varvill paused, but again Mr. Hepplethorn did not answer. If he had heard, he made no sign; only sat perfectly still, gazing straight before him at nothing.

With the pitiful daylight streaming full upon him, how ill and worn he looked! How poor!—how shabby!

"The man appears to me as if he were going mad," thought Dr. Varvill. "I am glad I did not send for Steen." Then he added aloud—

"After a few days, when you have had leisure to think the matter over quietly, I hope, Mr. Hepplethorn—nay, I am sure—you will come to the conclusion that I have acted rightly."

"Looking at it as you do, sir, I do not see that you could act differently," answered Mr. Hepplethorn, rising and terminating the interview with unexpected suddenness. "I must not occupy more of your time," he added nervously. "I beg to apologize for my intrusion, and to wish you good morning." And so, with "apologies and thanks," if one may be forgiven the phrase, exit Isaac Hepplethorn, chemist, leaving Dr. Varvill, on his direct way to a baronetcy, more puzzled and confused than he had ever felt before in the whole course of his successful life.

"Which is he, rogue or fool?" he asked himself—a question difficult to answer because the man was neither.

Meanwhile, straight up Grosvenor Place walked Mr. Hepplethorn—so astonished, so disappointed, so "thrown," that he scarcely knew where he was going. Not with any will of his own, but impelled by the vague instinct of a man seeking quiet, he turned along Piccadilly, and thence into the Green Park. The full bitterness of his position had never come so close home to him as when Dr. Varvill, speaking the world's words, explained precisely what the world would think of a story such as that he foolishly expected must be believed.

"I have fallen so low as to be unworthy of credit,—I, whose word would once have been received without question!" he thought, in a very agony of useless regret. "Is it I who am really changed," he went on, "or is it only because poverty has come upon me 'like an armed man,' I can now be of no use to myself or any one else?"

Grievous reflections to keep a man company through the pouring rain, and yet reflections which seemed not to have been quite without fruit; for, when close to St. James's Palace, he pulled up suddenly and considered himself. Then, all in a hurry, he said right out loud—where happily there was no one to hear, "I will! I will! I declare I will!"

It was but a step into Pall Mall. There he soon found an omnibus bound Cityward, which conveyed him and his fortunes to Chancery Lane, where, alighting and making his way to New Square, almost the first name he saw proved to be that of the person he sought.

To seek Mr. Steen was one thing, however, and to obtain an interview quite another. A young clerk—who might have been Cerberus himself, so jealously did he guard his employer from impertinent intruders—told the visitor Mr. Steen was engaged; that he would not be disengaged for hours; that when he was disengaged he had a particular appointment at the Law Courts. Yet still Mr. Hepplethorn stayed.

Almost pathetically the youth assured him it was of no use waiting. Mr. Hepplethorn held his ground. Any person might have supposed the last thing any member of the firm of Steen, Yarrow and Haine wanted to see was a client, but the chemist was not to be baulked. He felt it would be impossible to return home with that heavy secret burdening his heart. He must speak to Mr. Steen.

"Indeed, I cannot disturb him," explained the clerk. "You had better leave your name, and return some other day."

"What does the gentleman want?" asked a middle-aged individual, who entered the office at that moment.

"I want to see Mr. Steen," answered Mr. Hepplethorn for himself.

"Have you an appointment?"

"No."

"Then I am afraid——"

"I mean to see him, and that is all about it," interrupted Mr. Hepplethorn. "If he knew the nature of my business, he would not thank you for keeping me waiting."

"Perhaps our managing-clerk could attend to you. Shall I inquire?"

"No. I am obliged. If you will give me an envelope, however, I can explain the nature of my business to Mr. Steen."

It was wonderful the effect a line written in pencil on the back of one of Mr. Hepplethorn's business-cards produced. Almost, as it seemed, ere the message could have been delivered, the chemist was asked to "step this way," and in another minute found himself in the presence of Mr. Steen, a young-looking elderly man, who said—

"You come from Mr. Tercett?"

"No. I come on business which concerns Mr. Tercett."

"Ah! I thought," referring to the card. "I see;" and then Mr. Steen paused—waiting.

"I am here about a matter which seems to me of vital importance to your client."

"May I inquire how you know he is my client?"

"I know, because Dr. Varvill told me."

"Indeed. Pray proceed."

"There is one question I should like to put as a preliminary."

"And that is——"

"Has Mr. Osmond Tercett any interest in Mr. John Tercett's death?"

"What an extraordinary question! A most improper question— one I could not possibly think of answering."

"You have answered me. I will not offend again."

"May I request you to get to the point as quickly as possible? My time——"

"I quite understand," said Mr. Hepplethorn. "I will not detain you an instant longer than I can help. As my card states, I am a chemist carrying on business at 3, Beaufort Place, Upper Moor

Road. Seven years ago, last summer, I bought the lease and goodwill of 3, Beaufort Place, from a Mr. Baynfleet, who made his fortune there. I had no reason to suppose I was being taken in, but, practically, my purchase has ruined me. I came to London well-to-do. It is now a struggle, from day to day, for me to keep a roof over my head, and maintain my family."

"A very hard case, Mr. Hepplethorn. May I remind you, however, that you are here ostensibly about a matter which concerns Mr. Tercett, and Mr. Tercett only?"

"What I have said does concern Mr. Tercett, and Mr. Tercett only," was the reply. "Had I been a prosperous man, I should have known nothing of Mr. Tercett, of whom I never heard till last night, and wish to heaven I never had heard of him."

"I am sure Mr. Tercett cannot have injured you in any way," expostulated Mr. Steen, answering Mr. Hepplethorn's manner rather than his words.

"No; but, apparently, some one wants to injure *him*, and it is entirely owing to my misfortunes I chance to know anything about the matter," was the reply. "Though not through any complaint of mine, it is only too well understood in the neighborhood that affairs have gone very badly in Beaufort Place, and my neighbours generally believe the long strain has told upon me in a way and to an extent it has not done. I want you clearly to understand that, sir. Failure may have made me a little moody—somewhat over-inclined to brood; but I understand my business, and can make up a prescription as accurately as any man in England, let that man be who he will."

"I am very happy to hear you say so," returned Mr. Steen, politely; "but I would just venture to point out the question now is, not whether you can make up a prescription, but whether you have anything to tell which really relates to Mr. Tercett."

"You will soon be able to judge," answered the chemist. "Yesterday evening a gentleman brought me a prescription he wished to have made up."

"Indeed!"

"The prescription, signed by Dr. Varvill, and written on notepaper stamped with that gentleman's address, seemed to me so extraordinary that I took two fair copies, of which this is one."

Mr. Steen accepted the slip Mr. Hepplethorn handed to him, and glanced over the hieroglyphics written on it, which were, however, evidently Greek to him; for after trying to solve the enigma, he shook his head, and remarked—

"I am not a doctor."

"Allow me to explain. In the main this is quite an ordinary

prescription—one which might be written for any man a little out of health. There is nothing exceptional about it except the amount of poison ordered."

"*Poison!*" repeated Mr. Steen, in a manner which proved his interest was at last aroused.

"Yes."

"And do you mean to tell me Dr. Varvill wrote that prescription?"

"In its original form," answered the chemist; "but an addition has since been made to the quantity of strychnine ordered, so that had I dispensed the medicine, I should have been actually sending out DEATH. You follow my meaning?"

"I think so; I am trying to understand. Go on, please, with your story, which will be more intelligible if we have no break in the narrative. Just tell as shortly as you can exactly what took place. I can put any questions that occur to me later on."

Thus entreated, Mr. Hepplethorn repeated the same tale he had told on the previous night to Dr. Varvill. Beginning at the beginning, he led his hearer through the zigzag maze of every petty detail till he finished with his own resolve, come to in view of St. James's Park, of shifting his disagreeable burden upon the shoulders of some one better able to bear it than himself.

"I felt I *could* not go back home knowing I had done nothing really to warn Mr. Tercett of his danger; therefore I took the liberty of coming to you."

"Just so," observed Mr. Steen, which was rather a pet phrase of his, perhaps because it committed him to nothing. After that he lay back in his office chair looking up at the ceiling, and said nothing for a few minutes.

Mr. Steen was one of the most astute men in London, though any person might have been excused for not guessing the fact.

He had partners, but they merely attended to the ornamental portion of the business, for in his own person Mr. Steen was captain, mate, and boatswain of the New Square ship.

He it was who took the latitudes and longitudes of every abstruse case; it was he whose meridian observations always proved so accurate—to whom by common consent was entrusted the chart of every difficult suit—who was daily consulted by Messrs. Yarrow and Haine, both well versed in legal lore, but mere ignoramuses when compared with the head of the firm; and he who in his turn asked and took advice from no one.

A great man truly, and yet he lay back in his chair thinking over what Mr. Hepplethorn had told him just as anybody else might have done.

He was thinking, not because he doubted the story he had heard in the least.

At first he believed his visitor to be, if hardly a professional impostor, at all events one who, wanting money badly, had come to ask for it, making Mr. Tercett the pretext; but now he knew differently.

He had cast the chemist up like a column of figures, and found the result correct.

Moreover, he knew the Tercetts root and branch—knew John Tercett and his boundless liberality, Osmond Tercett and his shameless impecuniosity and unblushing appeals to the generous man who had never refused to help.

Osmond Tercett was a man who would have taken her mite from the poor widow, and stripped Dives of his purple and fine linen.

No; Mr. Steen could not say he felt surprised at the story, but he wanted to see his way, and, like Mr. Hepplethorn on the previous evening, he had not much time to see it in.

Whatever was done must be done soon. Already an idea was vaguely shaping itself in his mind, but its feasibility depended on a matter he did not quite understand.

"What is your reason for supposing Mr. Osmond Tercett went to Brighton last night?" he asked, taking up the thread of conversation as though Mr. Hepplethorn had that moment dropped it.

"I do not suppose—I know," the chemist answered. "As he stood on the doorstep, he said to the butler, 'Tell Mrs. Tercett that my address for a week will be Grand Hotel, Brighton. Don't forget.' "

"But he might not have gone for all that."

"He did go," was the reply; "my son followed to Victoria, and not merely heard him ask for a ticket, but saw him in the train."

"That lad of yours seems to be a sharp youth," remarked Mr. Steen.

"He is very sharp, though very quiet."

"Do you often employ him at detective work?"

"No; I never did before, and I am not likely to do so again."

Mr. Hepplethorn spoke as if aggrieved, and seemingly the lawyer felt he had reason, for he said—

"I beg your pardon," in a conciliatory manner, ere falling into another reverie.

"Dr. Varvill was quite shrewd enough to see the weak point in your story," he resumed at last, abruptly as before. "You ought to have kept the original prescription."

"Pardon me!" returned the chemist. "After thinking the matter out exhaustively, I am sure I ought to have done nothing of the kind.

In the first place, it was not my property. I had no more right to retain Dr. Varvill's prescription than to keep any other document
which did not belong to me. In the second, it seemed to me advisable, and I believe it was advisable, not to let my customer think I
suspected him; and in the third, we should have found ourselves in a
worse plight with the prescription than without it, because in that
case Mr. Osmond Tercett would certainly say *I* had altered it for my
own purposes."

"He will probably say that as it is. You had plenty of time to
stick in any number of marks you chose."

"I never thought of that. So I had," said Mr. Hepplethorn,
crestfallen—so utterly crestfallen that Mr. Steen could not refrain
from smiling.

"Never mind," he returned, speaking not unkindly. "*I* do not
believe you altered the prescription, and I do feel you have given us
information that may prove most valuable. I will consider what
ought to be done, and communicate with you later on. Oh, by-the-
by," he added, as the chemist rose to go, "there is one thing more I
want to ask. Supposing you—or any person for that matter—had
made up the prescription as handed in, how soon would a fatal effect
have ensued?"

"After taking one dose the patient would have been practically a
dead man."

"Really? One dose sufficient?"

"Quite."

"And how long would it be ere the end arrived?"

"That depends. Some people are not so susceptible to poison as
others."

"But what would be the longest time a man could live? Six
hours?"

"Less than that. With such a dose, two at the outside."

"I see. Then, whether Mr. Tercett took the medicine last night
or this morning, he would be dead in any case by now?"

"Yes."

"You are quite certain?"

"Perfectly."

"Thank you, Mr. Hepplethorn. I am very much obliged. I have
your address. You shall hear from me ere long. I think you said I
might keep this copy-prescription for the present. Good morning.
Thank you again."

Chapter V.

When Mr. Hepplethorn had departed Mr. Steen went into the next
office, where his managing clerk sat alone.

"Reford," he said, "did you not tell me the other day there was a writ out against Mr. Osmond Tercett at the suit of Tanna?"

"Yes, sir."

"Did you happen to hear the amount?"

"No; but it is heavy—very heavy."

"Just what I expected," commented Mr. Steen. "I am going out now. If Mr."—and he gave a number of instructions about people and things which, as they have nothing to do with this story, need not be repeated.

When he finished his directions the lawyer went his way to the Temple Station (calling *en route* at a dingy-looking house in Portugal Street), and from thence took train for Sloane Square. He did not immediately proceed to Hans Place, but repaired to the nearest post-office in order to despatch a telegram, brief but pregnant.

"That will fetch him," thought Mr. Steen, with a feeling of grim satisfaction.

He walked briskly to Hans Place, where the staid butler said Mr. Tercett was at home, and, in answer to inquiries, added that his master had not been very well, but seemed a little better.

"Nothing could be going more prosperously," Mr. Steen decided. "Mrs. Tercett was absent," her husband stated, while rejoicing over a visitor who came to break the tedium of his loneliness. "My sister-in-law met with an accident, so she is gone to see her, and won't return till late. What good wind has blown you here, Steen? I don't think you ever came to see me in the daytime before."

"I cannot remember that I ever did; but I am afraid the wind you speak of is not a very good one. It is your cousin."

"What! Is he in trouble again?"

"In very serious trouble, I fancy."

"Why, he was here yesterday, and told me he would soon be out of all his difficulties."

"No doubt he thought so."

"What is it now?"

"A writ, for one thing."

"How can we help him?"

"I do not know, unless you are prepared to pay all his debts, and that would only leave him free to incur fresh liabilities."

"You are always hard upon the poor fellow."

"Well, I won't say anything more about him till I can say what I mean before his face. I have telegraphed for him to meet me here."

"But he is at Brighton."

"He can come from Brighton, I suppose; there is a good service of trains. Now, will you give me some luncheon, and let me play at being master in this house just for one afternoon? I have a reason for the request."

"And a good one too, I am sure; so play at anything you like, so long as you will stay for dinner."

"Thank you;" and Mr. Steen took up a bottle which bore the name of I. Hepplethorn, 3, Beaufort Place, W., and, in addition, "To be taken three times a day." "Medicine as usual?" he said, with a laugh.

"Yes; I was feeling a little run down, and Osmond advised me to have Dr. Varvill's prescription made up again. I feel better for it already."

Mr. Steen did not laugh as he replaced the bottle; rather he shuddered as he thought of the grim "might have been."

Time went by. The butler had been sent on an errand likely to keep him absent for hours. Mr. Steen conferred with the upper housemaid, who, acting on his instructions, pulled down all the blinds in front. Though well trained, the woman was so amazed by this order that she ventured a remonstrance—

"People will think there is somebody dead, sir."

"Never mind," was the answer; "do as I tell you."

Shortly after that mystifying performance, a shabby and melancholy-looking individual made his appearance, and was told by Mr. Steen to sit down in the hall.

If such horrors had been possible in Mr. Tercett's house, he might have been taken for a man in possession!

After luncheon, Mr. Tercett himself was requested to remain in his study—a small back room on the second floor—till the arrival of his cousin, and Mr. Steen waited downstairs with no company save his thoughts and the dancing firelight.

At last there was a sound as of a hansom being driven at top speed; on and on it came; then the pace slackened, and the vehicle stopped opposite Mr. Tercett's door.

Out of it stepped Mr. Osmond Tercett, who threw one comprehensive glance over the house, and then rang the bell—not too loudly.

The melancholy man answered the summons. To the newcomer there was nothing unfit in the fact of his doing so—quite the contrary.

"When did my cousin die?" asked Mr. Osmond.

"I do not know, sir. I have not been here very long," was the reply.

Mr. Steen heard question and answer as he stood ready to receive the man who walked into the dining-room, confident that he was the owner of Templedale and its lordly income.

"This is very shocking, Mr. Steen," he said in a sad, subdued tone.

"Very, indeed."

"It must have been very sudden."

"Ill news is always sudden. Good news lags sometimes so long that it never comes at all."

Mr. Osmond Tercett reflected that one piece of good news had not tarried by the road, but as it would not have been seemly for him to say so, he sat down and covered his face with his hands, as though heart-broken.

Mr. Steen gave him ample opportunity to indulge his grief; indeed, it was not until many minutes had elapsed that he asked—

"Should you not like to see your cousin?"

Mr. Osmond Tercett uttered a constrained "Yes" softly. He could have dispensed with seeing his cousin; but, feeling under the circumstances it was the proper thing to do, followed Mr. Steen up the staircase, where their footsteps fell noiselessly.

They ascended to the second floor, but did not enter Mr. Tercett's bedchamber, Mr. Steen opening the door of that study to which his companion concluded "IT" had been removed.

The fire was low, the day dull and gloomy, and the room consequently dark. Mr. Osmond Tercett glanced around, but could see nothing of trestles—or—a coffin.

An armchair stood on the hearth, which seemed to be occupied. Perhaps his cousin had died in it, and could not be removed till after the inquest, which would, no doubt, have to be held.

Mr. Steen stooped over the something in the chair, and said, "Mr. Osmond Tercett!" and then a well-known voice exclaimed—

"I am so glad you have come. I think I must have been dozing, for I did not hear your ring. Why, what is the matter, Osmond?" he added, as the other, cowering, backed away from his outstretched hand.

He had come into the room sure of fourteen thousand a year, and now—THE MAN WAS NOT DEAD!

At that moment Mr. Steen lit the gas, and turned it up full, so that Mr. Tercett beheld, appalled, the look a lost angel might have worn when cast out of heaven.

"What has happened? What is wrong?" he asked, trembling under a shapeless horror which seemed overwhelming.

"This is some witless jest of yours, sir, I presume," said the younger man, addressing Mr. Steen in a voice choked with rage.

"If it were a jest it would indeed be a witless one," was the answer.

"You told me my cousin was dead, and brought me up here to see——"

"Him—not his corpse!" interrupted Mr. Steen. "And I never said your cousin was dead. I telegraphed I had bad news for you, and I have—in your opinion, doubtless—the worst of news: that Mr.

Tercett is, as you see, alive and well, and that your vile plot to poison him has failed utterly."

"To poison me?" exclaimed Mr. Tercett. "That can't be true. Why should he wish to poison me? I never did you any harm, Osmond."

"Harm!" with a mighty effort. "Of course not."

"Of course not!" repeated Mr. Steen, mocking the guilty man's tone. "Good only, by receiving the rent-roll he coveted—by standing between him and fourteen thousand a year!"

"It is an atrocious lie!" exclaimed Osmond Tercett, replying to Mr. Steen's accusation rather than to his later speech. "Why should I try to compass my cousin's death? Even had I wished to do so, how was I to give him poison?"

"By tampering with Dr. Varvill's prescription—by substituting for a harmless quantity of strychnine enough to kill half a dozen men!"

"Tampering with Dr. Varvill's prescription! My good sir, you have made a woeful mistake. If there be anything wrong with the medicine, you had better complain to the old imbecile who made it up instead of insulting *me!*"

"And may I ask why you went to an old imbecile for your cousin's medicine? It won't do, Mr. Osmond Tercett; to that 'imbecile' your cousin owes his life. Where is Dr. Varvill's prescription? Produce it, and we shall soon see whether what I have asserted be true or not."

"Do you suppose I carry prescriptions about with me? I tell you I know nothing about the matter. If anything were tampered with—which I don't credit—it must have been by that man in Moor Road."

"And what interest could he have in poisoning your cousin? No; as I said before, it won't do. You had every interest in committing such a crime. You are at your wit's end for money. There is one writ, at all events, out against you, and probably many more. You have failed to raise the smallest sum on your reversionary interest. Even the sixty per cent. men won't do any more of your paper. Your game is up, my friend. You had but one card left yesterday, when you played it and lost."

"Jack, to you I appeal. Stop Mr. Steen's slanders. There is not a word of truth in these calumnies. He always hated me, and has trumped up this horrible story to set the only real friend I possess in the world against me. We have always been like brothers—nearer than any brothers ever were. There is not a man on earth I love and trust as I do you. Won't you believe me?"

Mr. Tercett stood beside the chimney-piece, supporting his head with one hand—like one dazed—stricken.

"I want to believe no evil of you," he answered slowly, "but I can't get over the evidence of your own face when you saw me—alive!"

"I was startled——"

"And—disappointed. No; I can't get over that fact. If you had been glad—good heavens! if you had cared for me even a little—the joy of such a meeting would almost have sufficed to turn your brain. If you had been glad—but there is no use in talking about that, for you were sorry."

"I know Mr. Steen has prejudiced you against me," began the other.

"No one could have prejudiced me against you except yourself. The indictment is too true, and it has pierced me like a sword. Of course you must not starve. I will talk matters over with Mr. Steen, and see what we can arrange; but we cannot meet again. From this night our roads lie apart."

"You are unjust, Jack—you are condemning me without hearing my defence—you are treating me worse than if I were the greatest criminal that ever existed. I am poor, I admit, but is that a sin? I am in difficulties, no doubt"—Mr. Tercett winced, remembering—"but I shall get over all that—if—if only you will not cast me out utterly from your heart and your home. I want no more money from you— keep it; don't load me with any more favours—only never imagine I contemplated the awful wickedness of which Mr. Steen accuses me—and let me keep some place in your affections, my more than brother."

Mr. Tercett raised his head and looked at the speaker—looked at that false handsome face as if he would read the very soul of which it was a mask; then—

"Ah, Osmond!" he said, and let his head drop on his hand again.

There ensued a dead silence which no one broke—for something in the tone in which those two words were uttered made them sound like a funeral service read over a dead thing once full of beauty and vitality.

Twice the younger man opened his parched lips as if intending to speak, and twice he closed them again without carrying his intention into effect.

Mr. Tercett's love had been very great, his friendship very true, but there was no warmth or life in either any more: they were killed, and there was greater hope for a tree that is cut down than for them.

Realizing this, Mr. Osmond Tercett turned to the door, and, speaking no syllable, walked out of the room and down the stairs, closely followed by Mr. Steen.

"Good evening," said that gentleman, as they stood on the threshold; but Osmond Tercett made no reply—only passed forth—foiled—into the night.

When the lawyer's promised communication reached Mr. Isaac Hepplethorn that gentleman was ill in bed. He lay there for a long time hovering between life and death, but at last he returned from the borderland to find his affairs had been taken in hand by some one more competent than himself—some one with the Templedale rent-roll at his back, and all the knowledge of the (modern) Egyptians at his finger-ends.

He it was who induced the landlord to accept another tenant, and persuaded that tenant—not by any false pretences—to pay a moderate sum for the lease and good-will.

He it was who "arranged" that Mr. Hepplethorn should take over old Mr. Howard's business situate in Water Street, Temple Mills—a prosperous town distant about three miles from Templedale.

He it was who settled everything on the most favourable terms; and he it was, finally, who sent Mr. Hepplethorn the title-deeds of his new freehold premises, together with the most charming letter from his principal, stating, among other pleasant things, that a thousand pounds was lying to his credit at the Meadowshire Bank in Temple Mills, which Mr. Tercett hoped he would accept as a small evidence of his gratitude and respect.

Nearly eleven years have passed since then, but the chemist has not again been tempted by Satan. He has let well alone, and prospered exceedingly. His eldest son is a partner in the Temple Mills establishment, which is a very thriving concern. His second boy, having a taste for surgery, passed all his examinations with credit, and is now a rising man in London. Hal is in Mr. Steen's office, and the other members of a large family are doing equally well; but never to wife or son, or daughter has Mr. Hepplethorn, even in his most confidential moments, confided the story of "Dr. Varvill's Prescription."

GRANT ALLEN

*Charles Grant Blairfindie Allen (1848–1899), Canadian by birth, British resident in later life, was one of the outstanding popularizers of science in the last quarter of the century. His serious work—*Physiological Aesthetics *(1877),* The Colour Sense *(1879)—was praised by Darwin, Wallace, and Huxley; but he found it impossible to make a living at science and turned to journalism, where he was a frequent contributor to the periodicals. He is now remembered for* The Woman Who Did *(1895), the story of a woman who considered free love less degrading than marriage; and* The British Barbarians *(1896), in which a man from the future described British culture of the nineteenth century in terms of comparative anthropology. Allen's best-known mystery story is* An African Millionaire *(1897), an amusing episodic novel which relates the adventures and pranks of one Colonel Clay, an engaging confidence man.*

"The Great Ruby Robbery: A Detective Story"

I.

Persis Remanet was an American heiress. As she justly remarked, this was a commonplace profession for a young woman nowadays; for almost everybody of late years has been an American and an heiress. A poor Californian, indeed, would be a charming novelty in London society. But London society, so far, has had to go without one.

Persis Remanet was on her way back from the Wilcoxes' ball. She was stopping, of course, with Sir Everard and Lady Maclure at

their house at Hampstead. I say "of course" advisedly; because if
you or I go to see New York, we have to put up at our own expense
(five dollars a day, without wine or extras) at the Windsor or the
Fifth Avenue; but when the pretty American comes to London (and
every American girl is *ex officio* pretty, in Europe at least; I suppose
they keep their ugly ones at home for domestic consumption) she is
invariably the guest either of a dowager duchess or of a Royal
Academician, like Sir Everard, of the first distinction. Yankees visit
Europe, in fact, to see, among other things, our art and our old no-
bility; and by dint of native persistence they get into places that you
and I could never succeed in penetrating, unless we devoted all the
energies of a long and blameless life to securing an invitation.

Persis hadn't been to the Wilcoxes with Lady Maclure, however. The Maclures were too really great to know such people as the
Wilcoxes, who were something tremendous in the City, but didn't
buy pictures; and Academicians, you know, don't care to cultivate
City people—unless they're customers. ("Patrons," the Academicians
more usually call them; but I prefer the simple business word myself, as being a deal less patronizing.) So Persis had accepted an invitation from Mrs. Duncan Harrison, the wife of the well-known
member for the Hackness Division of Elmetshire, to take a seat in
her carriage to and from the Wilcoxes. Mrs. Harrison knew the
habits and manners of American heiresses too well to offer to chaperon Persis; and indeed, Persis, as a free-born American citizen, was
quite as well able to take care of herself, the wide world over, as any
three ordinary married Englishwomen.

Now, Mrs. Harrison had a brother, an Irish baronet, Sir Justin
O'Byrne, late of the Eighth Hussars, who had been with them to the
Wilcoxes, and who accompanied them home to Hampstead on the
back seat of the carriage. Sir Justin was one of those charming, inef-
fective, elusive Irishmen whom everybody likes and everybody dis-
approves of. He had been everywhere, and done everything—except
to earn an honest livelihood. The total absence of rents during the
sixties and seventies had never prevented his father, old Sir Terence
O'Byrne, who sat so long for Connemara in the unreformed Parliament, from sending his son Justin in state to Eton, and afterwards to
a fashionable college at Oxford. "He gave me the education of a gentleman," Sir Justin was wont regretfully to observe; "but he omitted
to give me also the income to keep it up with."

Nevertheless, society felt O'Byrne was the sort of man who
must be kept afloat somehow; and it kept him afloat accordingly in
those mysterious ways that only society understands, and that you
and I, who are not society, could never get to the bottom of if we
tried for a century. Sir Justin himself had essayed Parliament, too,
where he sat for a while behind the great Parnell without for a

moment forfeiting society's regard even in those earlier days when it was held as a prime article of faith by the world that no gentleman could possibly call himself a Home-Ruler. 'Twas only one of O'Byrne's wild Irish tricks, society said, complacently, with that singular indulgence it always extends to its special favourites, and which is, in fact, the correlative of that unsparing cruelty it shows in turn to those who happen to offend against its unwritten precepts. If Sir Justin had blown up a Czar or two in a fit of political exuberance, society would only have regarded the escapade as "one of O'Byrnes eccentricities." He had also held a commission for a while in a cavalry regiment, which he left, it was understood, owing to a difference of opinion about a lady with the colonel; and he was now a gentleman-at-large on London society, supposed by those who know more about everyone than one knows about oneself, to be on the lookout for a nice girl with a little money.

Sir Justin had paid Persis a great deal of attention that particular evening; in point of fact, he had paid her a great deal of attention from the very first, whenever he met her; and on the way home from the dance he had kept his eyes fixed on Persis' face to an extent that was almost embarrassing. The pretty Californian leaned back in her place in the carriage and surveyed him languidly. She was looking her level best that night, in her pale pink dress, with the famous Remanet rubies in a cascade of red light setting off that snowy neck of hers. 'Twas a neck for a painter. Sir Justin let his eyes fall regretfully more than once on the glittering rubies. He liked and admired Persis, oh! quite immensely. Your society man who has been through seven or eight London seasons could hardly be expected to go quite so far as falling in love with any woman; his habit is rather to look about him critically among all the nice girls trotted out by their mammas for his lordly inspection, and to reflect with a faint smile that this, that, or the other one might perhaps really suit him—if it were not for—and there comes in the inevitable *But* of all human commendation. Still, Sir Justin admitted with a sigh to himself that he liked Persis ever so much; she was so fresh and original! and she talked so cleverly! As for Persis, she would have given her eyes (like every other American girl) to be made "my lady"; and she had seen no man yet, with that auxiliary title in his gift, whom she liked half so well as this delightful wild Irishman.

At the Maclures' door the carriage stopped. Sir Justin jumped out and gave his hand to Persis. You know the house well, or course; Sir Everard Maclure's; it's one of those large new artistic mansions, in red brick and old oak, on the top of the hill; and it stands a little way back from the road, discreetly retired, with a big wooden porch, very convenient for leave-taking. Sir Justin ran up the steps with Persis to ring the bell for her; he had too much of the irrepressible Irish blood in his veins to leave that pleasant task to his sister's footman. But he didn't ring it at once; at the risk of keeping Mrs. Harrison waiting outside for nothing, he stopped and talked a minute or so with the pretty American. "You looked charming to-night, Miss Remanet," he said, as she threw back her light opera wrap for a moment in the porch and displayed a single flash of that snowy neck with the famous rubies; "those stones become you so."

Persis looked at him and smiled. "You think so?" she said, a little tremulous, for even your American heiress, after all, is a woman. "Well, I'm glad you do. But it's good-bye to-night, Sir Justin, for I go next week to Paris."

Even in the gloom of the porch, just lighted by an artistic red and blue lantern in wrought iron, she could see a shade of disappointment pass quickly over his handsome face as he answered, with a little gulp, "No! you don't mean that? Oh, Miss Remanet, I'm so sorry!" Then he paused and drew back: "And yet . . . after all," he continued, "perhaps——," and there he checked himself.

Persis looked up at him hastily. "Yet, after all, what?" she asked, with evident interest.

The young man drew an almost inaudible sigh. "Yet, after all— nothing," he answered, evasively.

"That might do for an Englishwoman," Persis put in, with American frankness, "but it won't do for me. You must tell me what you mean by it." For she reflected sagely that the happiness of two lives might depend upon those two minutes; and how foolish to throw away the chance of a man you really like (with a my-ladyship to boot), all for the sake of a pure convention!

Sir Justin leaned against the woodwork of that retiring porch. She was a beautiful girl. He had hot Irish blood. . . . Well, yes; just for once—he would say the plain truth to her.

"Miss Remanet," he began, leaning forward, and bringing his face close to hers, "Miss Remanet—Persis—shall I tell you the reason why? Because I like you so much. I almost think I love you!"

Persis felt the blood quiver in her tingling cheeks. How handsome he was—and a baronet! "And yet you're not altogether sorry," she said, reproachfully, "that I'm going to Paris!"

"No, not altogether sorry," he answered, sticking to it; "and I'll tell you why, too, Miss Remanet. I like you very much, and I think you like me. For a week or two, I've been saying to myself, 'I really believe I *must* ask her to marry me.' The temptation's been so strong I could hardly resist it."

"And why do you want to resist it?" Persis asked, all tremulous.

Sir Justin hesitated a second; then with a perfectly natural and instinctive movement (though only a gentleman would have ventured to make it) he lifted his hand and just touched with the tips of his

fingers the ruby pendants on her necklet. "*This* is why," he answered
simply, and with manly frankness. "Persis, you're so rich! I never
dare ask you."

"Perhaps you don't know what my answer would be," Persis
murmured very low, just to preserve her own dignity.

"Oh, yes; I think I do," the young man replied, gazing deeply
into her dark eyes. "It isn't that; if it were only that, I wouldn't so
much mind it. But I think you'd take me." There was moisture in
her eye. He went on more boldly: "I know you'd take me, Persis,
and that's why I don't ask you. You're a great deal too rich, and *these*
make it impossible."

"Sir Justin," Persis answered, removing his hand gently, but
with the moisture growing thicker, for she really liked him, "it's
most unkind of you to say so; either you oughtn't to have told me at
all, or else—if you did——" She stopped short. Womanly shame
overcame her.

The man leaned forward and spoke earnestly. "Oh, don't say
that!" he cried, from his heart. "I couldn't bear to offend you. But I
couldn't bear, either, to let you go away—well—without having ever
told you. In that case you might have thought I didn't care at all for
you, and was only flirting with you. But, Persis, I've cared a great
deal for you—a great, great deal—and had hard work many times to
prevent myself from asking you. And I'll tell you the plain reason
why I haven't asked you. I'm a man about town, not much good, I'm
afraid, for anybody or anything; and everybody says I'm on the
look-out for an heiress—which happens not to be true; and if I
married you, everybody'd say, 'Ah, there! I told you so!' Now, I
wouldn't mind that for myself; I'm a man, and I could snap my
fingers at them; but I'd mind it for *you*, Persis, for I'm enough in love
with you to be very, very jealous, indeed, for your honour. I
couldn't bear to think people should say, 'There's that pretty American girl, Persis Remanet that was, you know; she's thrown herself
away upon that good-for-nothing Irishman, Justin O'Byrne, a regular fortune-hunter, who's married her for her money.' So for your
sake, Persis, I'd rather not ask you; I'd rather leave you for some better man to marry."

"But *I* wouldn't," Persis cried aloud. "Oh, Sir Justin, you must
believe me. You must remember——"

At that precise point, Mrs. Harrison put her head out of the
carriage window and called out rather loudly:—

"Why, Justin, what's keeping you? The horses'll catch their
deaths of cold; and they were clipped this morning. Come back at
once, my dear boy. Besides, you know, *les convenances!*"

"All right, Nora," her brother answered; "I won't be a minute.
We can't get them to answer this precious bell. I believe it don't

ring! But I'll try again, anyhow." And half forgetting that his own words weren't strictly true, for he hadn't yet tried, he pressed the knob with a vengeance.

"Is that your room with the light burning, Miss Remanet?" he went on, in a fairly loud official voice, as the servant came to answer. "The one with the balcony, I mean? Quite Venetian, isn't it? Reminds one of Romeo and Juliet. But most convenient for a burglary, too! Such nice low rails! Mind you take good care of the Remanet rubies!"

"I don't want to take care of them," Persis answered, wiping her dim eyes hastily with her lace pocket-handkerchief, "if they make you feel as you say, Sir Justin. I don't mind if they go. Let the burglar take them!"

And even as she spoke, the Maclure footman, immutable, sphinx-like, opened the door for her.

II.

Persis sat long in her own room that night before she began undressing. Her head was full of Sir Justin and these mysterious hints of his. At last, however, she took her rubies off, and her pretty silk bodice. "I don't care for them at all," she thought, with a gulp, "if they keep from me the love of the man I'd like to marry."

It was late before she fell asleep; and when she did, her rest was troubled. She dreamt a great deal; in her dreams, Sir Justin, and dance music, and the rubies, and burglars were incongruously mingled. To make up for it, she slept late the next morning; and Lady Maclure let her sleep on, thinking she was probably wearied out with much dancing the previous evening—as though any amount of excitement could ever weary a pretty American! About ten o'clock she woke with a start. A vague feeling oppressed her that somebody had come in during the night and stolen her rubies. She rose hastily and went to her dressing-table to look for them. The case was there all right; she opened it and looked at it. Oh, prophetic soul! the rubies were gone, and the box was empty!

Now, Persis had honestly said the night before the burglar might take her rubies if he chose, and she wouldn't mind the loss of them. But that was last night, and the rubies hadn't then as yet been taken. This morning, somehow, things seemed quite different. It would be rough on us all (especially on politicians) if we must always be bound by what we said yesterday. Persis was an American, and no American is insensible to the charms of precious stones; 'tis a savage taste which the European immigrants seem to have inherited obliquely from their Red Indian predecessors. She rushed over to the bell and rang it with feminine violence. Lady Maclure's maid answered the summons, as usual. She was a clever, demure-looking girl, this maid of Lady Maclure's; and when Persis cried to her wildly, "Send for the police at once, and tell Sir Everard my jewels are stolen!" she answered "Yes, miss," with such sober acquiescence that Persis, who was American, and therefore a bundle of nerves, turned round and stared at her as an incomprehensible mystery. No Mahatma could have been more unmoved. She seemed quite to expect those rubies would be stolen, and to take no more notice of the incident than if Persis had told her she wanted hot water.

Lady Maclure, indeed, greatly prided herself on this cultivated imperturbability of Bertha's; she regarded it as the fine flower of English domestic service. But Persis was American, and saw things otherwise; to her, the calm repose with which Bertha answered, "Yes miss; certainly, miss; I'll go and tell Sir Everard," seemed nothing short of exasperating.

Bertha went off with the news, closing the door quite softly; and a few minutes later Lady Maclure herself appeared in the Californian's room, to console her visitor under this severe domestic affliction. She found Persis sitting up in bed, in her pretty French dressing jacket (pale blue with *revers* of fawn colour), reading a book of verses. "Why, my dear!" Lady Maclure exclaimed, "then you've found them again, I suppose? Bertha told us you'd lost your lovely rubies!"

"So I have, dear Lady Maclure," Persis answered, wiping her eyes; "they're gone. They've been stolen. I forgot to lock my door when I came home last night, and the window was open; somebody must have come in, this way or that, and taken them. But whenever I'm in trouble, I try a dose of Browning. He's splendid for the nerves. He's so consoling, you know; he brings one to anchor."

She breakfasted in bed; she wouldn't leave the room, she declared, till the police arrived. After breakfast she rose and put on her dainty Parisian morning wrap—Americans have always such pretty bedroom things for these informal receptions—and sat up in state to await the police officer. Sir Everard himself, much disturbed that such a mishap should have happened in his house, went round in person to fetch the official. While he was gone, Lady Maclure made a thorough search of the room, but couldn't find a trace of the missing rubies.

"Are you sure you put them in the case, dear?" she asked, for the honour of the household.

And Persis answered: "Quite confident, Lady Maclure; I always put them there the moment I take them off; and when I came to look for them this morning, the case was empty."

"They were *very* valuable, I believe?" Lady Maclure said, inquiringly.

"Six thousand pounds was the figure in your money, I guess," Persis answered, ruefully. "I don't know if you call that a lot of money in England, but we do in America."

There was a moment's pause, and then Persis spoke again:—

"Lady Maclure," she said, abruptly, "do you consider that maid of yours a Christian woman?"

Lady Maclure was startled. That was hardly the light in which she was accustomed to regard the lower classes.

"Well, I don't know about that," she said, slowly; "that's a great deal, you know, dear, to assert about *anybody*, especially one's maid. But I should think she was honest, quite decidedly honest."

"Well, that's the same thing, about, isn't it?" Persis answered, much relieved. "I'm glad you think that's so; for I was almost half afraid of her. She's too quiet for my taste, somehow; so silent, you know, and inscrutable."

"Oh, my dear," her hostess cried, "don't blame her for silence; that's just what I like about her. It's exactly what I chose her for. Such a nice, noiseless girl; moves about the room like a cat on tiptoe; knows her proper place, and never dreams of speaking unless she's spoken to."

"Well, you may like them that way in Europe," Persis responded, frankly; "but in America, we prefer them a little bit human."

Twenty minutes later the police officer arrived. He wasn't in uniform. The inspector, feeling at once the gravity of the case, and recognising that this was a Big Thing, in which there was glory to be won, and perhaps promotion, sent a detective at once, and advised that if possible nothing should be said to the household on the subject for the present, till the detective had taken a good look round the premises. That was useless, Sir Everard feared, for the lady's-maid knew; and the lady's-maid would be sure to go down, all agog with the news, to the servants' hall immediately. However, they might try; no harm in trying; and the sooner the detective got round to the house, of course, the better.

The detective accompanied him back—a keen-faced, close-shaven, irreproachable-looking man, like a vulgarized copy of Mr. John Morley. He was curt and business-like. His first question was, "Have the servants been told of this?"

Lady Maclure looked inquiringly across at Bertha. She herself had been sitting all the time with the bereaved Persis, to console her (with Browning) under this heavy affliction.

"No, my lady," Bertha answered, ever calm (invaluable servant, Bertha!), "I didn't mention it to anybody downstairs on purpose, thinking perhaps it might be decided to search the servants' boxes."

The detective pricked up his ears. He was engaged already in glancing casually round the room. He moved about it now, like a conjurer, with quiet steps and slow. "He doesn't get on one's nerves," Persis remarked, approvingly, in an undertone to her friend; then she added, aloud: "What's your name, please, Mr. Officer?"

The detective was lifting a lace handkerchief on the dressing-table at the side. He turned round softly. "Gregory, madam," he answered, hardly glancing at the girl, and going on with his occupation.

"The same as the powders!" Persis interposed, with a shudder. "I used to take them when I was a child. I never could bear them."

"We're useful, as remedies," the detective replied, with a quiet smile; "but nobody likes us." And he relapsed contentedly into his work once more, searching round the apartment.

"The first thing we have to do," he said, with a calm air of superiority, standing now by the window, with one hand in his pocket, "is to satisfy ourselves whether or not there has really, at all, been a robbery. We must look through the room well, and see you haven't left the rubies lying about loose somewhere. Such things often happen. We're constantly called in to investigate a case, when it's only a matter of a lady's carelessness."

At that Persis flared up. A daughter of the great republic isn't accustomed to be doubted like a mere European woman. "I'm quite sure I took them off," she said, "and put them back in the jewel case. Of that I'm just confident. There isn't a doubt possible."

Mr. Gregory redoubled his search in all likely and unlikely places. "I should say that settles the matter," he answered, blandly. "Our experience is that whenever a lady's perfectly certain, beyond the possibility of doubt, she put a thing away safely, it's absolutely sure to turn up where she says she didn't put it."

Persis answered him never a word. Her manners had not that repose that stamps the caste of Vere de Vere; so, to prevent an outbreak, she took refuge in Browning.

Mr. Gregory, nothing abashed, searched the room thoroughly, up and down, without the faintest regard to Persis's feelings; he was a detective, he said, and his business was first of all to unmask crime, irrespective of circumstances. Lady Maclure stood by, meanwhile, with the imperturbable Bertha. Mr. Gregory investigated every hole and cranny, like a man who wishes to let the world see for itself he performs a disagreeable duty with unflinching thoroughness. When he had finished, he turned to Lady Maclure. "And now, if you please," he said, blandly, "we'll proceed to investigate the servants' boxes."

Lady Maclure looked at her maid. "Bertha," she said, "go downstairs, and see that none of the other servants come up, meanwhile, to their bedrooms." Lady Maclure was not quite to the manner born, and had never acquired the hateful aristocratic habit of calling women servants by their surnames only.

But the detective interposed. "No, no," he said sharply. "This young woman had better stop here with Miss Remanet—strictly under her eye—till I've searched the boxes. For if I find nothing there, it may perhaps be my disagreeable duty, by-and-by, to call in a female detective to search her."

It was Lady Maclure's turn to flare up now. "Why, this is my own maid," she said, in a chilly tone, "and I've every confidence in her."

"Very sorry for that, my lady," Mr. Gregory responded, in a most official voice; "but our experience teaches us that if there's a person in the case whom nobody ever dreams of suspecting, that person's the one who has committed the robbery."

"Why, you'll be suspecting myself next!" Lady Maclure cried, with some disgust.

"Your ladyship's just the last person in the world I should think of suspecting," the detective answered, with a deferential bow— which, after his previous speech, was to say the least of it equivocal.

Persis began to get annoyed. She didn't half like the look of that girl Bertha, herself; but still, she was there as Lady Maclure's guest, and she couldn't expose her hostess to discomfort on her account.

"The girl shall *not* be searched," she put in, growing hot. "I don't care a cent whether I lose the wretched stones or not. Compared to human dignity, what are they worth? Not five minutes' consideration."

"They're worth just seven years," Mr. Gregory answered, with professional definiteness. "And as to searching, why, that's out of your hands now. This is a criminal case. I'm here to discharge a public duty."

"I don't in the least mind being searched," Bertha put in obligingly, with an air of indifference. "You can search me if you like— when you've got a warrant for it."

The detective looked up sharply; so also did Persis. This ready acquaintance with the liberty of the subject in criminal cases impressed her unfavourably. "Ah! we'll see about that," Mr. Gregory answered, with a cool smile. "Meanwhile, Lady Maclure, I'll have a look at the boxes."

III.

The search (strictly illegal) brought out nothing. Mr. Gregory returned to Persis's bedroom, disconsolate. "You can leave the room," he said to Bertha; and Bertha glided out. "I've set another man out-side to keep a constant eye on her," he added in explanation.

By this time Persis had almost made her mind up as to who was the culprit; but she said nothing overt, for Lady Maclure's sake, to the detective. As for that immovable official, he began asking ques-tions—some of them, on the personal. Where had she been last night? Was she sure she had really worn the rubies? How did she come home? Was she certain she took them off? Did the maid help her undress? Who came back with her in the carriage?

To all these questions, rapidly fired off with cross-examining acuteness, Persis answered in the direct American fashion. She was sure she had the rubies on when she came home to Hampstead, because Sir Justin O'Byrne, who came back with her in his sister's carriage, had noticed them the last thing, and had told her to take care of them.

At mention of that name the detective smiled meaningly. (A meaning smile is stock-in-trade to a detective.) "Oh, Sir Justin O'Byrne!" he repeated, with quiet self-constraint. "*He* came back with you in the carriage, then? And did he sit the same side with you?"

Lady Maclure grew indignant (that was Mr. Gregory's cue). "Really, sir," she said, angrily, "if you're going to suspect gentlemen in Sir Justin's position, we shall none of us be safe from you."

"The law," Mr. Gregory replied, with an air of profound defer-ence, "is no respecter of persons."

"But it ought to be of characters," Lady Maclure cried, warmly. "What's the good of having a blameless character, I should like to know, if—if——"

"If it doesn't allow you to commit a robbery with impunity?" the detective interposed, finishing her sentence his own way. "Well, well, that's true. That's per-fectly true—but Sir Justin's character, you see, can hardly be called blameless."

"He's a gentleman," Persis cried, with flashing eyes, turning round upon the officer; "and he's quite incapable of such a mean and despicable crime as you dare to suspect him of."

"Oh, I see," the officer answered, like one to whom a welcome ray of light breaks suddenly through a great darkness. "Sir Justin's a friend of yours! Did he come into the porch with you?"

"He did," Persis answered, flushing crimson; "and if you have the insolence to bring a charge against him——"

"Calm yourself, madam," the detective replied, coolly. "I do nothing of the sort—at this stage of the proceedings. It's possible there may have been no robbery in the case at all. We must keep our minds open for the present to every possible alternative. It's—it's a delicate matter to hint at; but before we go any further—do you think perhaps, Sir Justin may have carried the rubies away by mistake, entangled in his clothes? —say, for example, his coat-sleeve?"

It was a loophole of escape; but Persis didn't jump at it.

"He had never the opportunity," she answered, with a flash. "And I know quite well they were there on my neck when he left me, for the last thing he said to me was, looking up at this very window: 'That balcony's awfully convenient for a burglary. Mind you take good care of the Remanet rubies.' And I remembered what he'd said when I took them off last night; and that's what makes me so sure I really had them."

"*And* you slept with the window open!" the detective went on, still smiling to himself. "Well, here we have all the materials, to be sure, for a first-class mystery!"

IV.

For some days more, nothing further turned up of importance about the Great Ruby Robbery. It got into the papers, of course, as everything does nowadays, and all London was talking of it. Persis found herself quite famous as the American lady who had lost her jewels. People pointed her out in the park; people stared at her hard through their opera-glasses at the theatre. Indeed, the possession of the celebrated Remanet rubies had never made her half so conspicuous in the world as the loss of them made her. It was almost worth while losing them, Persis thought, to be so much made of as she was in society in consequence. All the world knows a young lady must be somebody when she can offer a reward of five hundred pounds for the recovery of gewgaws valued at six thousand.

Sir Justin met her in the Row one day. "Then you don't go to Paris for awhile yet—until you get them back?" he inquired very low.

And Persis answered, blushing, "No, Sir Justin; not yet; and—I'm almost glad of it."

"No, you don't mean that!" the young man cried, with perfect boyish ardour. "Well, I confess, Miss Remanet, the first thing I thought myself when I read in *The Times* was just the very same: 'Then, after all, she won't go yet to Paris!' "

Persis looked up at him from her pony with American frankness. "And I," she, said, quivering, "I found anchor in Browning. For what do you think I read?

'And learn to rate a true man's heart
Far above rubies.'

The book opened at the very place; and *there* I found anchor!"

But when Sir Justin went round to his rooms that same evening his servant said to him, "A gentleman was inquiring for you here this afternoon, sir. A close-shaven gentleman. Not very prepossessin'. And it seemed to me somehow, sir, as if he was trying to pump me."

Sir Justin's face was grave. He went to his bedroom at once. He knew what that man wanted; and he turned straight to his wardrobe, looking hard at the dress coat he had worn on the eventful evening. Things may cling to a sleeve, don't you know—or be entangled in a cuff—or get casually into a pocket! Or someone may put them there.

V.

For the next ten days or so Mr. Gregory was busy, constantly busy. Without doubt, he was the most active and energetic of detectives. He carried out so fully his own official principle of suspecting everybody, from China to Peru, that at last poor Persis got fairly mazed with his web of possibilities. Nobody was safe from his cultivated and highly-trained suspicion—not Sir Everard in his studio, nor Lady Maclure in her boudoir, not the butler in his pantry, nor Sir Justin O'Byrne in his rooms in St. James's. Mr. Gregory kept an open mind against everybody and everything. He even doubted the parrot, and had views as to the intervention of rats and terriers. Persis got rather tired at last of his perverse ingenuity; especially as she had a very shrewd idea herself who had stolen the rubies. When he suggested various doubts, however, which seemed remotely to implicate Sir Justin's honesty, the sensitive American girl "felt it go on her nerves," and refused to listen to him, though Mr. Gregory never ceased to enforce upon her, by precept and example, his own pet doctrine that the last person on earth one would be likely to suspect is always the one who turns out to have done it.

A morning or two later, Persis looked out of her window as she was dressing her hair. She dressed it herself now, though she was an American heiress, and, therefore, of course, the laziest of her kind; for she had taken an unaccountable dislike, somehow, to that quiet girl Bertha. On this particular morning, however, when Persis looked out, she saw Bertha engaged in close, and apparently very intimate, conversation with the Hampstead postman. This sight disturbed the unstable equilibrium of her equanimity not a little. Why should Bertha go to the door to the postman at all? Surely it was no part of the duty of Lady Maclure's maid to take in the letters! And why should she want to go prying into the question of who wrote to Miss Remanet? For Persis, intensely conscious herself that a note from Sir Justin lay on top of the postman's bundle—she recognised it at once, even at that distance below, by the peculiar shape of the broad rough envelope—jumped to the natural feminine conclusion that Bertha must needs be influenced by some abstruse motive of which she herself, Persis, was, to say the very least, a component element. 'Tis a human fallacy. We're all of us prone to see everything from a personal standpoint; indeed, the one quality which makes a man or woman into a possible novelist, good, bad, or indifferent, is just that special power of throwing himself or herself into a great many people's personalities alternately. And this is a power possessed on an average by not one in a thousand men or not one in ten thousand women.

Persis rang the bell violently. Bertha came up, all smiles: "Did you want anything, miss?" Persis could have choked her. "Yes," she answered, plainly, taking the bull by the horns; "I want to know what you were doing down there, prying into other people's letters with the postman?"

Bertha looked up at her, ever bland; she answered at once, without a second's hesitation; "The postman's my young man, miss; and we hope before very long now to get married."

"Odious thing!" Persis thought. "A glib lie always ready on the tip of her tongue for every emergency."

But Bertha's full heart was beating violently. Beating with love and hope and deferred anxiety.

A little later in the day Persis mentioned the incident casually to Lady Maclure—mainly in order to satisfy herself that the girl had been lying. Lady Maclure, however, gave a qualified assent:—

"I *believe* she's engaged to the postman," she said. "I *think* I've heard so; though I make it a rule, you see, my dear, to know as little as I can of these people's love affairs. They're so very uninteresting. But Bertha certainly told me she wouldn't leave me to get married for an indefinite period. That was only ten days ago. She said her young man wasn't just yet in a position to make a home for her."

"Perhaps," Persis suggested, grimly, "something has occurred meanwhile to better her position. Such strange things crop up. She may have come into a fortune!"

"Perhaps so," Lady Maclure replied, languidly. The subject bored her. "Though, if so, it must really have been very sudden; for I think it was the morning before you lost your jewels she told me so."

Persis thought that odd, but she made no comment.

Before dinner that evening she burst suddenly into Lady Maclure's room for a minute. Bertha was dressing her lady's hair. Friends were coming to dine—among them Sir Justin. "How do these pearls go with my complexion, Lady Maclure?" Persis asked rather anxiously; for she specially wished to look her best that evening, for one of the party.

"Oh, charming!" her hostess answered, with her society smile. "Never saw anything suit you better, Persis."

"Except my poor rubies!" Persis cried rather ruefully, for coloured gewgaws are dear to the savage and the woman. "I wish I could get them back! I wonder that man Gregory hasn't succeeded in finding them."

"Oh! my dear," Lady Maclure drawled out, "you may be sure by this time they're safe at Amsterdam. That's the only place in Europe now to look for them."

"Why to Amsterdam, my lady?" Bertha interposed suddenly, with a quick side-glance at Persis.

Lady Maclure threw her head back in surprise at so unwonted an intrusion. "What do you want to know that for, child?" she asked, somewhat curtly. "Why, to be cut, of course. All the diamond-cutters in the world are concentrated in Amsterdam; and the first thing a thief does when he steals big jewels is to send them across, and have them cut in new shapes so that they can't be identified."

"I shouldn't have thought," Bertha put in, calmly, "they'd have known who to send them to."

Lady Maclure turned to her sharply. "Why, these things," she said, with a calm air of knowledge, "are always done by experienced thieves, who know the ropes well, and are in league with receivers the whole world over. But Gregory has his eye on Amsterdam, I'm sure, and we'll soon hear something."

"Yes, my lady," Bertha answered in her acquiescent tone, and relapsed into silence.

VI.

Four days later, about nine at night, that hard-worked man, the posty on the beat, stood loitering outside Sir Everard Maclure's house, openly defying the rules of the department, in close conference with Bertha.

"Well, any news?" Bertha asked, trembling over with excitement, for she was a very different person outside with her lover from the demure and imperturbable model maid who waited on my lady.

"Why, yes," the posty answered, with a low laugh of triumph. "A letter from Amsterdam! And I think we've fixed it!"

Bertha almost flung herself upon him. "Oh, Harry!" she cried, all eagerness, "this is too good to be true! Then in just one other month we can really get married!"

There was a minute's pause, inarticulately filled up by sounds unrepresentable through the art of the type-founder. Then Harry spoke again. "It's an awful lot of money!" he said, musing. "A regular fortune! And what's more, Bertha, if it hadn't been for your cleverness we never should have got it!"

Bertha pressed his hand affectionately. Even ladies'-maids are human.

"Well, if I hadn't been so much in love with you," she answered, frankly, "I don't think I could ever have had the wit to manage it. But, oh! Harry, love makes one do or try anything!"

If Persis had heard those singular words, she would have felt no doubt was any longer possible.

VII.

Next morning, at ten o'clock, a policeman came round, post haste, to Sir Everard's. He asked to see Miss Remanet. When Persis came down, in her morning wrap, he had but a brief message from headquarters to give her: "Your jewels are found, Miss. Will you step round and identify them?"

Persis drove back with him, all trembling. Lady Maclure accompanied her. At the police-station they left their cab, and entered the ante-room.

A little group had assembled there. The first person Persis distinctly made out in it was Sir Justin. A great terror seized her. Gregory had so poisoned her mind by this time with suspicion of everybody and everything she came across, that she was afraid of her own shadow. But next moment she saw clearly he wasn't there as prisoner, or even as witness; merely as spectator. She acknowledged him with a hasty bow, and cast her eye round again. The next person she definitely distinguished was Bertha, as calm and cool as ever, but in the very centre of the group, occupying as it were the place of honour which naturally belongs to the prisoner on all similar occasions. Persis was not surprised at that; she had known it all along; she glanced meaningly at Gregory, who stood a little behind, looking by no means triumphant. Persis found his dejection odd; but he was a proud detective, and perhaps someone else had effected the capture!

"These are your jewels, I believe," the inspector said, holding them up; and Persis admitted it.

"This is a painful case," the inspector went on. "A very painful case. We grieve to have discovered such a clue against one of our own men; but as he owns to it himself, and intends to throw himself on the mercy of the Court, it's no use talking about it. He won't attempt to defend it; indeed, with such evidence, I think he's doing what's best and wisest."

Persis stood there, all dazed. "I—I don't understand," she cried, with a swimming brain. "Who on earth are you talking about?"

The inspector pointed mutely with one hand at Gregory; and then for the first time Persis saw he was guarded. She clapped her hand to her head. In a moment it all broke in upon her. When she had called in the police, the rubies had never been stolen at all. It was Gregory who stole them!

She understood it now, at once. The real facts came back to her. She had taken her necklet off at night, laid it carelessly down on the dressing-table (too full of Sir Justin), covered it accidentally with her lace pocket-handkerchief, and straightway forgotten all about it. Next day she missed it, and jumped at conclusions. When Gregory came, he spied the rubies askance under the corner of the handkerchief—of course, being a woman, she had naturally looked everywhere except in the place where she laid them—and knowing it was a safe case he had quietly pocketed them before her very eyes, all unsuspected. He felt sure nobody could accuse him of a robbery which was committed before he came, and which he had himself been called in to investigate.

"The worst of it is," the inspector went on, "he had woven a very ingenious case against Sir Justin O'Byrne, whom we were on the very point of arresting to-day, if this young woman hadn't come in at the eleventh hour, in the very nick of time, and earned the reward by giving us the clue that led to the discovery and recovery of the jewels. They were brought over this morning by an Amsterdam detective."

Persis looked hard at Bertha. Bertha answered her look. "My young man was the postman, miss," she explained, quite simply; "and after what my lady said, I put him up to watch Mr. Gregory's delivery for a letter from Amsterdam. I'd suspected him from the very first; and when the letter came, we had him arrested at once, and found out from it who were the people at Amsterdam who had the rubies."

Persis gasped with astonishment. Her brain was reeling. But Gregory in the background put in one last word:—

"Well, I was right, after all," he said, with professional pride. "I told you the very last person you'd dream of suspecting was sure to be the one that actually did it."

Lady O'Byrne's rubies were very much admired at Monte Carlo last season. Mr. Gregory has found permanent employment for the next seven years at Her Majesty's quarries on the Isle of Portland. Bertha and her postman have retired to Canada with five hundred pounds to buy a farm. And everybody says Sir Justin O'Byrne has beaten the record, after all, even for Irish baronets, by making a marriage at once of money and affection.

GUY
BOOTHBY

(1867–1905), Australian by birth, came to England in 1894 and was soon recognized as one of the better writers of thrillers. His life was short but prolific: more than fifty books were published under his name. Today he is remembered mostly for Pharos the Egyptian *(1899), a novel about a reanimated mummy who plots to wipe out Western civilization with a new plague, and for a series of novels about a Dr. Nikola, who is not quite a supervillain but skirts around occultism and high crime.*

Boothby's best work, however, was a little-known series of stories which appeared in Pearson's Magazine *in 1897. Titled* A Prince of Swindlers, *they described the exploits of Simon Carne, one of the earliest society thieves, a criminal of much more imagination and ingenuity than the more famous Raffles.*

"The Wedding Guest"

One bright summer morning Simon Carne sat in his study, and reflected on the slackness of things in general. Since he had rendered such a signal service to the State, as narrated in a previous story, he had done comparatively nothing to raise himself in his own estimation. He was thinking in this strain when his butler entered, and announced "Kelmare Sahib." The interruption was a welcome one, and Carne rose to greet his guest with every sign of pleasure on his face.

"Good morning, Kelmare," he said, as he took the other's outstretched hand; "I'm delighted to see you. How are you this morning?"

"As well as a man can hope to be under the circumstances," replied the new arrival, a somewhat *blasé* youth, dressed in the height of fashion. "You are going to the Greenthorpe wedding of course. I hear you have been invited."

"You are quite right; I have," said Carne, and presently produced a card from the basket, and tossed it across the table.

The other took it up with a groan.

"Yes," he said, "that's it, by Jove. And a nice-looking document it is. Carne, did you ever hate anybody so badly that it seemed as if it would be scarcely possible to discover anything you would not do to hurt them?"

"No," answered Carne, "I cannot say that I have. Fate has always found me some way or another in which I might get even with my enemies. But you seem very vindictive in this matter. What's the reason of it?"

"Vindictive?" said Kelmare, "of course I am; think how they have treated me. A year ago, this week, Sophie Greenthorpe and I were engaged. Old Greenthorpe had not then turned his business into a limited liability company, and my people were jolly angry with me for making a foolish match, but I did not care. I was in love, and Sophie Greenthorpe is as pretty a girl as can be found in the length and breadth of London. But there, you've seen her, so you know for yourself. Well, three months later, old Greenthorpe sold his business for upwards of three million sterling. On the strength of it he went into the House, gave thirty thousand to the funds of his party, and would have received a baronetcy for his generosity, had his party not been shunted out of power.

"Inside another month all the swells had taken them up; dukes and earls were as common at the old lady's receptions as they had been scarce before, and I began to understand that, instead of being everybody to them as I had once been, the old fellow was beginning to think his daughter might have done much better than become engaged to the third son of an impecunious earl.

"Then Kilbenham came upon the scene. He's a fine-looking fellow, and a marquis, but, as you know as well as I do, a real bad hat. He hasn't a red cent in the world to bless himself with, and he wanted money—well—just about as badly as a man *could* want it. What's the result? Within six weeks I am thrown over, and she has accepted Kilbenham's offer of marriage. Society says—'What a good match!' and, as if to endorse it, you received an invitation to the ceremony."

"Forgive me, but *you* are growing cynical now," said Carne, as he lit a fresh cigar.

"Haven't I good cause to be?" asked Kelmare. "Wait till you've been treated as I have, and then we'll see how you'll feel. When I think how every man you meet speaks of Kilbenham, and of the stories that are afloat concerning him, and hear the way old Greenthorpe and his pretensions are laughed at in the clubs, and sneered at in the papers, and am told that they are receiving presents of enormous value from all sorts and conditions of people, from Royalty to the poor devils of workmen he still under-pays, just because Kilbenham is a marquis and she is the daughter of a millionaire, why, I can tell you it is enough to make anyone cynical."

"In the main, I agree with you," said Carne. "But, as life is made up of just such contradictions, it seems to me absurd to butt your head against a stone wall, and then grumble because it hurts and you don't make any impression on it. Do you think the presents are as wonderful as they say? I want to know, because I've not given mine yet. In these days one gives as others give. If they have not received anything very good, then a pair of electro-plated entrée dishes will meet the case. If the reverse—well—diamonds, perhaps, or an old Master that the Americans are wild to buy, and can't."

"Who is cynical now, I should like to know?" said Kelmare. "I was told this morning that up to the present, with the superb diamonds given by the bride's father, they have totalled a value of something like twenty thousand pounds."

"You surprise me," answered Carne.

"I am surprised myself," said Kelmare, as he rose to go. "Now, I must be off. I came in to see if you felt inclined for a week's cruise in the Channel. Burgrave has lent me his yacht, and somehow I think a change of air will do me good."

"I am very sorry," said Carne, "but it would be quite impossible for me to get away just now. I have several important functions on hand that will keep me in town."

"I suppose this wedding is one of them?"

"To tell the honest truth, I had scarcely thought of it," replied Carne. "Must you be off? Well, then, good-bye, and a pleasant holiday to you."

When Kelmare had disappeared, Carne went back to his study, and seated himself at his writing-table. "Kelmare is a little over sensitive," he said, "and his pique is spoiling his judgment. He does not seem to realise that he has come very well out of a jolly bad business. I am not certain which I pity most—Miss Greenthorpe, who is a heartless little hussy, or the Marquis of Kilbenham, who is a thorough-paced scoundrel. The wedding, however, promises to be a fashionable one, and——"

He stopped midway, rose, and stood leaning against the mantelpiece, staring into the empty fireplace. Presently he flipped the ash off his cigar, and turned round, "It never struck me in that light before," he said, as he pressed the button of the electric bell in the wall beside him. When it was answered, he ordered his carriage, and a quarter of an hour later was rolling down Regent Street.

Reaching a well-known jeweller's shop, he pulled the check string, and, the door having been opened, descended, and went inside. It was not the first time he had had dealings with the firm, and as soon as he was recognised the proprietor hastened forward himself to wait upon him.

"I want a nice wedding present for a young lady," he said, when the other had asked what he could have the pleasure of showing him. "Diamonds, I think, for preference."

A tray containing hairpins, brooches, rings, and aigrettes set with stones was put before him, but Carne was not satisfied. He wanted something better, he said—something a little more imposing. When he left the shop a quarter of an hour later he had chosen a diamond bracelet, for which he had paid the sum of one thousand pounds. In consequence, the jeweller bowed him to his carriage with almost Oriental obsequiousness.

As Carne rolled down the street, he took the bracelet from its case and glanced at it. He had long since made up his mind as to his line of action, and having done so, was now prepared to start business without delay. On leaving the shop, he had ordered his coachman to drive home; but on second thoughts he changed his mind, and, once more pulling the check string, substituted Berkeley Square for Park Lane.

"I must be thoroughly convinced in my own mind," he said, "before I do anything, and the only way to do that will be to see old Greenthorpe himself without delay. I think I have a good and sufficient excuse in my pocket. At any rate, I'll try it."

On reaching the residence in question, he instructed his footman to inquire whether Mr. Greenthorpe was at home, and, if so, if he would see him. An answer in the affirmative was soon forthcoming, and a moment later Carne and Greenthorpe were greeting each other in the library.

"Delighted to see you, my dear sir," the latter said as he shook his guest warmly by the hand, at the same time hoping that old Sir Mowbray Mowbray next door, who was a gentleman of the old school, and looked down on the plutocracy, could see and recognise the magnificent equipage standing before his house. "This is most kind of you, and indeed I take it as most friendly too."

Carne's face was as smiling and fascinating as it was wont to be, but an acute observer might have read in the curves of his lips a little of the contempt he felt for the man before him. Matthew Greenthorpe's face and figure betrayed his origin as plainly as any words could have done. If this had not been sufficient, his dress and the profusion of jewellery—principally diamonds—that decked his person would have told the tale. In appearance he was short, stout, very red about the face, and made up what he lacked in breeding by an effusive familiarity that sometimes bordered on the offensive.

"I am afraid," said Carne, when his host had finished speaking, "that I ought to be ashamed of myself for intruding on you at such an early hour. I wanted, however, to thank you personally for the kind invitation you have sent me to be present at your daughter's wedding."

"I trust you will be able to come," replied Mr. Greenthorpe a little anxiously, for he was eager that the world should know that he and the now famous Simon Carne were on familiar terms.

"That is exactly what has brought me to see you," said Carne. "I regret to say I hardly know yet whether I shall be able to give myself that pleasure or not. An important complication has arisen in connection with some property in which I am interested, and it is just possible that I shall be called to the Continent within the next few days. My object in calling upon you this morning was to ask you to permit me to withhold my answer until I am at liberty to speak more definitely as to my arrangements."

"By all means, by all means," answered his host, placing himself with legs wide apart upon the hearthrug, and rattling the money in his trouser pockets. "Take just as long as you like so long as you don't say you can't come. Me and the missus—hem! I mean Mrs. Greenthorpe and I—are looking forward to the pleasure of your society, and I can tell you we shan't think our company complete if we don't have you with us."

"I am extremely flattered," said Carne sweetly, "and you may be sure it will not be my fault if I am *not* among your guests."

"Hear, hear, to that, sir," replied the old gentleman. "We shall be a merry party, and, I trust, a distinguished one. We *did* hope to have had Royalty present among us, but, unfortunately, there were special reasons, that I am hardly privileged to mention, which prevented it. However, the Duke of Rugby and his duchess, the father and mother of my future son-in-law, you know, are coming; the Earl of Boxmoor and his countess have accepted; Lord Southam and his lady, half-a-dozen baronets or so, and as many Members of Parliament and their wives as you can count on one hand. There'll be a ball the night before, given by the Mayor at the Assembly Rooms, a dinner to the tenants at the conclusion of the ceremony, and a ball in my own house after the young couple have gone away. You may take it from me, my dear sir, that nothing on a similar scale has ever been seen at Market Stopford before."

"I can quite believe it," said Carne. "It will mark an epoch in the history of the county."

"It will do more than that, sir. The festivities alone will cost me a cool five thousand pounds. At first *I* was all for having it in town, but I was persuaded out of it. After all, a country house is better suited to such jinks. And we mean to do it well."

He took Carne familiarly by the button of his coat, and, sinking his voice to an impressive whisper, asked him to hazard a guess how much he thought the whole affair, presents and all, would cost.

Carne shook his head. "I have not the remotest notion," he said. "But if you wish me to guess, I will put it at fifty thousand pounds."

"Not enough by half, sir—not enough by half. Why, I'll let you into a little secret that even my wife knows nothing about."

As he spoke, he crossed the room to a large safe in the wall. This he unlocked, and having done so took from it an oblong box, wrapped in tissue paper. This he placed on the table in the centre of the room, and then, having looked out into the hall to make sure that no one was about, shut and locked the door. Then, turning to Carne, he said:

"I don't know what you may think, sir, but there are some people I know as try to insinuate that if you have money you can't have taste. Now, I've got the money"—here he threw back his shoulders, and tapped himself proudly on the chest—"and I'm going to convince you, sir, that I've got as pretty an idea of taste as any man could wish to have. This box will prove it."

So saying, he unwrapped the tissue paper, and displayed to Carne's astonished gaze a large gilded casket, richly chased, standing upon four massive feet.

"There, sir, you see," he said, "an artistic bit of workmanship, and I'll ask you to guess what it's for."

Carne, however, shook his head. "I'm afraid I'm but a poor hand at guessing, but, if I must venture an opinion, I should say a jewel case."

Thereupon Mr. Greenthorpe lifted the lid.

"And you would be wrong, sir. I will tell you what it is for. That box has been constructed to contain exactly fifty thousand sovereigns, and on her wedding day it will be filled, and presented to the bride, as a token of her father's affection. Now, if that isn't in good taste, I shall have to ask you to tell me what is."

"I am astonished at your munificence," said Carne. "To be perfectly candid with you, I don't know that I have ever heard of such a present before."

"I thought you'd say so. I said to myself when I ordered that box, 'Mr. Carne is the best judge of what is artistic in England, and I'll take his opinion about it.'"

"I suppose your daughter has received some valuable presents?"

"Valuable, sir? Why, that's no name for it. I should put down what has come in up to the present at not a penny under twenty thousand pounds. Why, you may not believe it, sir, but Mrs. Greenthorpe has presented the young couple with a complete toilet set of solid gold. I doubt if such another has been seen in this country before."

"I should say it would be worth a burglar's while to pay a visit to your house on the wedding day," said Carne with a smile.

"He wouldn't get much for his pains," said the old gentleman warmly. "I have already provided for that contingency. The billiard room will be used as a treasure chamber for the time being, as there is a big safe like that over yonder in the wall. This week bars are being placed on all the windows, and on the night preceding, and also on the wedding day, one of my gardners will keep watch in the room itself, while one of the village policemen will mount guard at the door in the passage. Between them they ought to be sufficient to keep out any burglars who may wish to try their hands upon the presents. What do you think?"

At that moment the handle of the door turned, and an instant later the bride-elect entered the room. On seeing Simon Carne she paused upon the threshold with a gesture of embarrassment, and made as if she would retreat. Carne, however, was too quick for her. He advanced and held out his hand.

"How do you do, Miss Greenthorpe?" he said, looking her steadily in the face. "Your father has just been telling me of the many beautiful presents you have received. I am sure I congratulate you most heartily. With your permission I will add my mite to the list. Such as it is, I would beg your acceptance of it."

So saying, he took from his pocket the case containing the bracelet he had that morning purchased. Unfastening it, he withdrew the circlet and clasped it upon her wrist. So great was her surprise and delight that for some moments she was at a loss how to express her thanks. When she recovered her presence of mind and her speech, she attempted to do so, but Carne stopped her.

"You must not thank me too much," he said, "or I shall begin to think I have done a meritorious action. I trust Lord Kilbenham is well?"

"He was very well when I last saw him," answered the girl after a momentary pause, which Carne noticed, "but he is so busy just now that we see very little of each other. Good-bye."

All the way home Simon Carne sat wrapped in a brown study. On reaching his residence he went straight to his study, and to his writing-desk, where he engaged himself for some minutes jotting down certain memoranda on a sheet of note paper. When he had finished he rang the bell and ordered that Belton, his valet, should be sent to him.

"Belton," he said, when the person he wanted had arrived in answer to the summons, "on Thursday next I shall go down to Market Stopford to attend the wedding of the Marquis of Kilbenham with Miss Greenthorpe. You will, of course, accompany me. In the meantime (here he handed him the sheet of paper upon which he had been writing) I want you to attend to these few details. Some of the articles, I'm afraid, you will find rather difficult to obtain, but at any cost I must have them to take down to the country with me."

Belton took the paper and left the room with it, and for the time being Carne dismissed the matter from his head.

The sun was in the act of setting on the day immediately proceeding the wedding when Simon Carne and his faithful valet reached the wayside station of Market Stopford. As the train came to a standstill, a footman wearing the Greenthorpe livery opened the door of the reserved carriage and informed his master's guest that a brougham was waiting outside the station to convey him to his destination. Belton was to follow with the luggage in the servants' omnibus.

On arrival at Greenthorpe Park, Simon Carne was received by his host and hostess in the hall, the rearmost portion of which was furnished as a smoking-room. Judging from the number of guests passing, re-passing, and lolling about in the easy chairs, most of the company invited had already arrived. When he had greeted those with whom he was familiar, and had taken a cup of tea from the hands of the bride-elect, who was dispensing it at a small table near the great oak fireplace, he set himself to be agreeable to those about him for the space of a quarter of an hour, after which he was escorted to his bedroom, a pretty room situated in the main portion of the building at the head of the grand staircase. He found Belton awaiting him there. His luggage had been unpacked, and a glance at his watch told him that in a few minutes time it would be necessary for him to prepare for dinner.

"Well, Bolton," he said, as he threw himself into a chair beside the window that looked out over the rose garden, "here we are, and the next question is how are we going to succeed?"

"I have never known you fail yet, sir," replied the deferential valet, "and I don't suppose you'll do so on this occasion."

"You flatter me, Belton, but I will not be so falsely modest as to say that your praise is altogether undeserved. This, however, is a case of more than usual delicacy and danger, and it will be necessary for us to play our cards with considerable care. When I have examined this house I shall elaborate my plans more fully. We have none too much time, for the attempt must be made to-morrow night. You have brought down with you the things I mentioned on that list, I suppose?"

"They are in these chests, sir," said Belton. "They make a precious heavy load, and once or twice I was fearful lest they might arouse suspicion."

"You need have no fear, my good Belton," said Carne. "I have a very plausible excuse to account for their presence here. Everyone by this time knows that I am a great student, and also that I never travel without at least two cases of books. It is looked upon as a harmless fad. Here is my key. Open the box standing nearest to you."

Belton did as he was commanded, when it was seen that it was filled to its utmost holding capacity with books.

"No one would think," said Carne, with a smile at the astonishment depicted on the other's face, "that there are only two layers of volumes there, would they? If you lift out the tray upon which they rest, you will discover that the balance of the box is now occupied by the things you placed in it. Unknown to you, I had the trays fitted after you had packed the others. There is nothing like being prepared for all emergencies. Now, pay attention to what I am about to say to you. I have learned that the wedding presents, including the fifty thousand sovereigns presented by Mr. Greenthorpe to his daughter in that absurd casket, of which I spoke to you, will be on view to-morrow afternoon in the billiard room; to-night, and to-morrow before the ball commences, they will be placed in the safe. One of Mr. Greenthorpe's most trusted servants will keep watch over them in the room, while a constable will be on duty in the lobby outside. Bars have been placed on all the windows, and, as I understand, the village police will patrol the building at intervals during the night. The problem of how we are to get hold of them would seem rather a hard nut to crack, would it not?"

"I must confess I don't see how you are going to do it at all, sir," said Belton.

"Well, we'll see. I have a plan in my head now, but before I can adopt it. I must make a few inquiries. I believe there is a staircase leading from the end of this corridor down to the lobby outside the billiard and smoking-rooms. If this is so, we shall have to make use of it. It must be your business to discover at what time the custodians of the treasure have their last meal. When you have found that out let me know. Now you had better get me ready for dinner as soon as possible."

When Carne retired to rest that evening, his inimitable valet was in a position to report that the sentries were already installed, and that their supper had been taken to them, by Mr. Greenthorpe's orders, at ten o'clock precisely, by one of the under-footmen who had been instructed to look after them.

"Very good," said Carne, "I think I see my way now. I'll sleep on my scheme and let you know what decision I have come to in the morning. If we pull this little business off successfully there will be ten thousand pounds for you to pay into your credit, my friend."

Belton bowed and thanked his master without a sign of emotion upon his face. After which Simon Carne went to bed.

When he was called next morning, he discovered a perfect summer day. Brilliant sunshine streamed in at the windows, and the songs of birds came from the trees outside.

"An excellent augury," he said to himself as he jumped out of bed and donned the heavy dressing-gown his valet held open for him. "Miss Greenthorpe, my compliments to you. My lord Marquis is not the only man upon whom you are conferring happiness to-day."

His good humour did not leave him, for when he descended to the breakfast-room an hour later his face was radiant with smiles, and everyone admitted that it would be impossible to meet a more charming companion.

During the morning he was occupied in the library, writing letters.

At one he lunched with his fellow guests, none of the family being present, and at half-past went off to dress for the wedding ceremony. This important business completed, a move was made for the church; and in something less than a quarter of an hour the nuptial knot was tied, and Miss Sophie Greenthorpe, only daughter of Matthew Greenthorpe, erstwhile grocer and provision merchant, of Little Bexter Street, Tottenham Court Road, left the building, on her husband's arm, Marchioness of Kilbenham and future Duchess of Rugby.

Simon Carne and his fellow guests followed in her wake down the aisle, and, having entered their carriages, returned to the Park.

The ball that evening was an acknowledged success, but, though he was an excellent dancer, and had his choice of the prettiest women in the room, Carne was evidently ill at ease. The number of times he stealthily examined his watch said this as plainly as any words. As a matter of fact, the last-guest had scarcely arrived before he left the ballroom, and passed down the lobby towards the back staircase, stopping *en route* to glance at the billiard room door.

As he expected, it was closed, and a stalwart provincial policeman stood on guard before it.

He made a jocular reference about the treasure the constable was guarding, and, with a laugh at himself for forgetting the way to his bedroom, retraced his steps to the stairs, up which he passed to his own apartment. Belton was awaiting him there.

"It is ten minutes to ten, Belton," he said abruptly. "It must be now or never. Go down to the kitchen, and hang about there until the tray upon which the suppers of the guard are placed is prepared. When the footman starts with it for the billiard room, accompany him, and, as he opens the green baize door leading from the servants' quarters into the house, manage, by hook or crook, to hold him in conversation. Say something, and interrupt yourself by a severe fit

of coughing. That will give me my cue. If anything should happen
to me as I come down stairs, be sure that the man puts his tray down
on the slab at the foot of the stairs and renders me assistance. I will
manage the rest. Now be off."

Belton bowed respectfully, and left the room. As he did so,
Carne crossed to the dressing-table, and unlocked a small case standing upon it. From this he took a tiny silver-stoppered scent bottle,
containing, perhaps, half-an-ounce of white powder. This he slipped
into his waistcoat pocket, and then made for the door.

On the top of the back staircase he paused for a few moments to
listen. He heard the spring of the green baize door in the passage
below creak as it was pushed open. Next moment he distinguished
Belton's voice. "It's as true as that I'm standing here," he was saying.
"As I went up the stairs with the governor's hot water there she was
coming along the passage. I stood back to let her pass, and as I did
she——" (Here the narrative was interrupted by a violent fit of
coughing.) On hearing this Carne descended the stairs, and, when he
had got halfway down, saw the footman and his valet coming along
the passage below. At the same instant he must have caught his foot
in the stair carpet, for he tripped and fell headlong to the bottom.

"Heaven's alive!" cried Belton. "I do believe that's my governor,
and he's killed." At the same time he ran forward to the injured
man's assistance.

Carne lay at the foot of the stairs just as he had fallen, his head
thrown back, his eyes shut, and his body curled up and motionless.
Belton turned to the footman, who still stood holding the tray where
he had stopped on seeing the accident, and said: "Put down those
things and go and find Mr. Greenthorpe as quickly as you can. Tell
him Mr. Carne has fallen downstairs, and I'm afraid is seriously injured."

The footman immediately disappeared. His back was scarcely
turned, however, before Carne was on his feet.

"Excellent, my dear Belton," he whispered; and, as he spoke, he
slipped his fingers into his waistcoat pocket. "Hand me up that tray,
but be quiet, or the policeman round the corner will hear you."

Belton did as he was ordered, and Carne thereupon sprinkled
upon the suppers provided for the two men, some of the white
powder from the bottle he had taken from his dressing-case. This
done, he resumed his place at the foot of the stairs, while Belton,
kneeling over him and supporting his head, waited for assistance.
Very few minutes elapsed before Mr. Greenthorpe, with a scared
face, appeared upon the scene. At his direction Belton and the footman carried the unconscious gentleman to his bedroom, and placed
him upon his bed. Restoratives were administered, and in something
under ten minutes the injured man once more opened his eyes.

"What is the matter?" he asked feebly. "What has happened?"

"You have met with a slight accident, my dear sir," said the old gentleman, "but you are better now. You fell downstairs."

As if he scarcely comprehended what was said, Carne feebly repeated the last sentence after his host, and then closed his eyes again. When he opened them once more, it was to beg Mr. Greenthorpe to leave him and return to his guests downstairs. After a small amount of pressing, the latter consented to do so, and retired, taking the footman with him. The first use Carne made of their departure was to turn to Belton.

"The powder will take effect in five hours," he said. "See that you have all the things prepared."

"They are quite ready," replied Belton. "I arranged them this evening."

"Very good," said Carne. "Now, I am going to sleep in real earnest."

So saying, he closed his eyes, and resigned himself to slumber as composedly as if nothing out of the common had occurred. The clock on the stables had struck three when he woke again. Belton was still sleeping peacefully, and it was not until he had been repeatedly shaken that he became conscious that it was time to get up.

"Wake up," said Carne, "it is three o'clock, and time for us to be about our business. Unlock that box, and get out the things."

Belton did as he was ordered, placing the packets as he took them from the cases in small Gladstone bags. Having done this, he went to one of his master's trunks, and took from it two suits of clothes, a pair of wigs, two excellently contrived false beards, and a couple of soft felt hats. These he placed upon the bed. Ten minutes later he had assisted his master to change into one of the suits, and when this was done waited for further instructions.

"Before you dress, take a tumbler from that table, and go downstairs. If you should meet anyone, say that you are going to the butler's pantry in search of filtered water, as you have used all the drinking water in this room. The ball should be over by this time, and the guests in bed half-an-hour ago. Ascertain if this is the case, and as you return glance at the policeman on duty outside the billiard room door. Let me know his condition."

"Very good, sir," said Belton, and, taking a tumbler from the table in question, he left the room. In less than five minutes he had returned to report that, with the exception of the corridor outside the billiard room, the house was in darkness.

"And how is the guardian of the door?" Carne inquired.

"Fast asleep," said Belton, "and snoring like a pig, sir."

"That is right," said Carne. "The man inside should be the same, or that powder has failed me for the first time in my experience. We'll give them half-an-hour longer, however, and then get to work. You had better dress yourself."

While Belton was making himself up to resemble his master, Carne sat in an easy chair by his dressing-table, reading Ruskin's "Stones of Venice." It was one of the most important of his many peculiarities that he could withdraw his thoughts from any subject, however much it might hitherto have engrossed him, and fasten them upon another, without once allowing them to wander back to their original channel. As the stable clock chimed the half hour, he put the book aside, and sprang to his feet.

"If you're ready, Belton," he said. "Switch off the electric light and open that door."

When this had been done he bade his valet wait in the bedroom while he crept down the stairs on tip-toe. On turning into the billiard room lobby, he discovered the rural policeman propped up in the corner fast asleep. His heavy breathing echoed down the corridors, and one moment's inspection showed Carne that from him he had nothing to fear. Unlocking the door with a key which he took from his pocket, he entered the room, to find the gardener, like the policeman, fast asleep in an armchair by the window. He crossed to him, and, after a careful examination of his breathing, lifted one of his eyelids.

"Excellent," he said. "Nothing could be better. Now, when Belton comes, we shall be ready for business."

So saying, he left the room again, and went softly up the stairs to find his valet. The latter was awaiting him, and, before a witness, had there been one, could have counted twenty, they were standing in the billiard room together. It was a large apartment, luxuriously furnished, with a bow window at one end and an alcove, surrounded with seats, at the other. In this alcove, cleverly hidden by the wainscotting, as Mr. Greenthorpe had once been at some pains to point out to Simon Carne, there existed a large iron safe of the latest burglar-proof pattern and design.

The secret was an ingenious one, and would have baffled any ordinary craftsman. Carne, however, as has already been explained, was far from being a common-place member of his profession. Turning to Belton, he said: "Give me the tools." These being forthcoming, in something less than ten minutes he had picked the lock and was master of the safe's contents.

When these, including the fifty thousand sovereigns, had been safely carried upstairs and stowed away in the portmanteaux and chests, and the safe had been filled with the spurious jewellery he had brought with him for that purpose, he signed to Belton to bring him a long pair of steps which stood in a corner of the room, and which had been used for securing the sky-light above the billiard table. These he placed in such a position as would enable him to reach the window.

With a diamond-pointed instrument, and a hand as true as the eye that guided it, he quickly extracted a square of coloured glass, filed through the catch, and was soon standing on the leads outside. A few moments later, the ladder, which had already rendered him such signal service, had enabled him to descend into the garden on the other side.

There he arranged a succession of footsteps in the soft mould, and having done so, returned to the roof, carefully wiped the end of the ladder so that it should not betray him, and climbed down into the room below, pulling it after him.

"I think we have finished now," he said to Belton, as he took a last look at the recumbent guardians of the room. "These gentlemen sleep soundly, so we will not disturb them further. Come, let us re-tire to bed."

In less than half-an-hour he was in bed and fast asleep. Next morning he was still confined to his room by his accident, though he expressed himself as suffering but slight pain. Everyone was quick to sympathise with him, and numerous messages were conveyed to him expressive of sorrow that he should have met with his accident at such a time of general rejoicing. At ten o'clock the first batch of guests took their departure. It was arranged that the Duke and Duchess of Rugby, the Earl and Countess of Raxter, and Simon Carne, who was to be carried downstairs, should travel up to town together by the special train leaving immediately after lunch.

When they bade their host good-bye, the latter was nearly over-come.

"I'm sure it has been a real downright pleasure to me to enter-tain you, Mr. Carne," he said as he stood by the carriage door and shook his guest warmly by the hand. "There is only one thing bad about it, and that is your accident."

"You must not speak of that," said Carne with a little wave of his hand. "The pleasure I have derived from my visit to you amply compensates me for such a minor inconvenience."

So saying he shook hands and drove away to catch his train.

Next morning it was announced in all the Society papers that, owing to an unfortunate accident he had sustained while visiting Mr. Matthew Greenthorpe, at Greenthorpe Park, on the occasion of his daughter's marriage, Mr. Simon Carne would be unable to fulfil any of the engagements he might have entered into.

Any intelligent reader of the aforesaid papers might have been excused had he pictured the gentleman in question confined to his bed, tended by skilled nurses, and watched over by the most fash-ionable West End physicians obtainable for love or money. They

would doubtless, therefore, have been surprised could they have
seen him at a late hour on the following evening hard at work in the
laboratory he had constructed at the top of his house, as hale and
hearty a man as any to be found in the great Metropolis.

"Now those Apostle spoons," he was saying, as he turned from
the crucible at which he was engaged to Belton, who was busy at a
side table. "The diamonds are safely disposed of, their settings are
melted down, and, when these spoons have been added to the list,
he will be a wise man who can find in my possession any trace of the
famous Kilbenham-Greenthorpe wedding presents."

He was sitting before the fire in his study next morning, with
his left foot lying bound up upon a neighbouring chair, when Ram
Gafur announced "Kelmare Sahib."

"So sorry to hear that you are under the weather, Carne," said
the new comer as he shook hands. "I only heard of your accident
from Raxter last night, or I should have been round before. Beastly
hard luck, but you shouldn't have gone to the wedding, you know!"

"And, pray, why not?"

"You see for yourself you haven't profited by your visit, have
you?"

"That all depends upon what you consider profit," replied
Carne. "I was an actor in an interesting society spectacle. I was permitted an opportunity of observing my fellow creatures in many new
lights. Personally, I think I did very well. Besides that, to be laid up
just now is not altogether a thing to be despised, as you seem to
imagine."

"What do you mean?"

"It isn't everybody who can boast such a valid excuse for declining invitations as I now possess," said Carne. "When I tell you that I
had a dinner, a lecture at the Imperial Institute, two 'at homes,' and
three dances on my list for to-night, you will understand what I
mean. Now I am able to decline every one of them without risk of
giving offence or fear of hurting the susceptibilities of anyone. If you
don't call that luck, I do. And now tell me what has brought you
here, for I suppose you have some reason, other than friendship, for
this early call. When you came in I observed that you were bursting
with importance. You are not going to tell me that you have abandoned your yachting trip and are going to be married?"

"You need have no fear on that score. All the same, I have the
greatest and most glorious news for you. It isn't every day a man
finds Providence taking up his case and entering into judgment
against his enemies for him. That is my position. Haven't you heard
the news?"

"What news?" asked Carne innocently.

"The greatest of all possible news," answered Kelmare, "and

one which concerns you, my dear fellow. You may not believe it,
but it was discovered last evening that the Kilbenham-Greenthorpe
wedding presents have all been stolen, including the fifty thousand
sovereigns presented to the bride in the now famous jeweled casket.
What do you think of that?"

"Surely you must be joking," said Carne incredulously. "I cannot believe it."

"Nevertheless it's a fact," replied Kelmare.

"But when did it happen? and how did they discover it?" asked
Carne.

"When it took place nobody can tell, but they discovered it
when they came to put the presents together after the guests had
departed. On the morning after the wedding old Greenthorpe had
visited the safe himself, and glanced casually at its contents, just to
see that they were all right, you know; but it was not until the afternoon, when they began to do them up, that they discovered that
every single article of value the place contained had been abstracted,
and dummies substituted. Then investigation proved that the sky-
light had been tampered with, and one could see unmistakable foot-
marks on the flower beds outside.

"Good gracious!" said Carne. "This is news indeed. What a
haul the thieves must have had, to be sure! I can scarcely believe it
even now. But I thought they had a gardener in the room, a policeman at the door, and a patrol outside, and that old Greenthorpe
went to sleep with the keys of the room and safe under his pillow?"

"Quite right," said Kelmare, "so he did, that's the mysterious
part of it. The two chaps swear positively that they were wide awake
all night, and that nothing was tampered with while they were there.
Who the thieves were, and how they became so familiar with the
place, are the riddles that it would puzzle the Sphinx, or your friend
Klimo next door, to unravel."

"What an unfortunate thing," said Carne. "It's to be hoped the
police will catch them before they have time to dispose of their
booty."

"You are thinking of your bracelet, I suppose?"

"It may seem egotistical, but I must confess I was; and now I
suppose you'll stay to lunch?"

"I'm afraid that's impossible. There are at least five families who
have not heard the news, and I feel that it is my bounden duty to
enlighten them."

"You're quite right, it is not often a man has such glorious vengeance to chronicle. It behoves you to make the most of it."

The other looked at Carne as if to discover whether or not he
was laughing at him. Carne's face, however, was quite express-
ionless.

"Good-bye; I suppose you won't be at the Wilbringhams' to-night?"

"I'm afraid not. You evidently forget that, as I said just now, I have a very good and sufficient excuse."

When the front door had closed behind his guest, Carne lit a third cigar.

"I'm overstepping my allowance," he said reflectively, as he watched the smoke circle upward, "but it isn't every day a man gives a thousand pounds for a wedding present and gets upwards of seventy thousand back. I think I may congratulate myself on having brought off a very succesful little speculation."

A. CONAN DOYLE

Sir Arthur Conan Doyle (1859–1930) was the dominant figure in the late nineteenth-century detective story. A physician by profession, he found writing more profitable than medical practice and soon was highly regarded for his historical novels, topical novels, and, of course, detective stories. While Sherlock Holmes first appeared in A Study in Scarlet *(1887), it was not until 1891, when* The Adventures of Sherlock Holmes *began to run serially in* The Strand Magazine, *that Holmes suddenly became a figure of international importance. Doyle, as is well known, came to dislike the Sherlock Holmes stories intensely, since he felt that they kept him from more serious writing. Doyle was knighted in 1902 for his services as a propagandist for the British side of the Boer War, but his popularity with the government diminished greatly when he tried to correct the injustices done in the Edalji and Slater cases. During the First World War Doyle became converted to Spiritualism, and most of his later writings are apologetics.*

Doyle wrote some sixty stories about Sherlock Holmes and a scattering of isolated mystery and detective stories. "The Recollections of Captain Wilkie" is a little-known story that to my knowledge has never before been reprinted.

"The Recollections of Captain Wilkie"

'Who can he be?' thought I, as I watched my companion in the second-class carriage of the London and Dover Railway.

I had been so full of the fact that my long-expected holiday had come at last, and that for a few days at least the gaieties of Paris were about to supersede the dull routine of the hospital wards, that we were well out of London before I observed that I was not alone in the compartment. In these days we have all pretty well agreed that 'Three is company and two is none' upon the railway. At the time I write of, however, people were not so morbidly sensitive about their travelling companions. It was rather an agreeable surprise to me to find that there was some chance of whiling away the hours of a tedious journey. I therefore pulled my cap down over my eyes, took a good look from beneath it at my vis-à-vis, and repeated to myself, 'Who can he be?'

I used rather to pride myself on being able to spot a man's trade or profession by a good look at his exterior. I had the advantage of studying under a Professor at Edinburgh who was a master of the art, and used to electrify both his patients and his clinical classes by long shots, sometimes at the most unlikely of pursuits, and never very far from the mark. 'Well, my man,' I have heard him say, 'I can see by your fingers that you play some musical instrument for your livelihood, but it is a rather curious one—something quite out of my line.' The man afterwards informed us that he earned a few coppers by blowing *Rule Britannia* on a coffee-pot, the spout of which was pierced to form a rough flute. Though a novice in the art compared to the shrewd Professor, I was still able to astonish my ward companions on occasion, and I never lost an opportunity of practising myself. It was not mere curiosity, then, which led me to lean back on the cushions and analyse the quiet middle-aged man in front of me.

I used to do the thing systematically and my train of reflections ran somewhat in this wise: 'General appearance vulgar, fairly opulent, and extremely self-possessed—looks like a man who could out-chaff a bargee, and yet be at his ease in the best middle-class society. Eyes well set together, and nose rather prominent—would be a good long-range marksman. Cheeks flabby, but the softness of expression redeemed by a square-cut jaw and a well-set lower lip. On the whole, a powerful type. Now for the hands—rather disappointed there. Thought he was a self-made man by the look of him, but there is no callus in the palm, and no thickening at the joints. Has never been engaged in any real physical work, I should think. No tanning on the backs of the hands; on the contrary, they are very white, with blue projecting veins and long delicate fingers. Couldn't be an artist with that face, and yet he has the hands of a man engaged in delicate manipulations. No red acid spots upon his clothes, no ink-stains, no nitrate-of-silver marks upons the hands (this helps to negative my half-formed opinion that he was a photographer). Clothes not worn in any particular part. Coat made of tweed, and fairly old; but the left elbow, as far as I can see it, has as much of the fluff left on as the right, which is seldom the case with men who do much writing. Might be a commercial traveller, but the little pocket-book in the waistcoat is wanting, nor has he any of those handy valises suggestive of samples.'

I give these brief headings of my ideas merely to demonstrate my method of arriving at a conclusion. As yet I had obtained nothing but negative results; but now, to use a chemical metaphor, I was in a position to pour off this solution of dissolved possibilities and examine the residue. I found myself reduced to a very limited number of occupations. He was neither a lawyer nor a clergyman, in spite of a soft felt hat, and a somewhat clerical cut about the necktie. I was wavering now between pawnbroker and horse-dealer; but there was too much character about his face for the former; and he lacked that extraordinary equine atmosphere which hangs about the latter even in his hours of relaxation; so I formed a provisional diagnosis of betting man of methodistical proclivities, the latter clause being inserted in deference to his hat and necktie.

Pray, do not think that I reasoned it out like this in my own mind. It is only now, sitting down with pen and paper, that I can see the successive steps. As it was, I had formed my conclusion within sixty seconds of the time when I drew my hat down over my eyes and uttered the mental ejaculation with which my narrative begins.

I did not feel quite satisfied even then with my deduction. However, as a leading question would—to pursue my chemical analogy—act as my litmus paper, I determined to try one. There was a *Times* lying by my companion, and I thought the opportunity too good to be neglected.

'Do you mind my looking at your paper?' I asked.

'Certainly, sir, certainly,' said he most urbanely, handing it across.

I glanced down its columns until my eye rested upon the list of the latest betting.

'Hullo!' I said, 'they are laying odds upon the favorite for the Cambridgeshire.—But perhaps,' I added, looking up, 'you are not interested in these matters?'

'Snares, sir!' said he violently, 'wiles of the enemy! Mortals are but given a few years to live; how can they squander them so!— They have not even an eye to their poor worldly interests,' he added in a quieter tone, 'or they would never back a single horse at such short odds with a field of thirty.'

There was something in this speech of his which tickled me immensely. I suppose it was the odd way in which he blended religious intolerance with worldly wisdom. I laid the *Times* aside with the conviction that I should be able to spend the next two hours to better purpose than in its perusal.

'You speak as if you understood the matter, at any rate,' I remarked.

'Yes, sir,' he answered; 'few men in England understood these things better in the old days before I changed my profession. But that is all over now.'

'Changed your profession!' said I interrogatively.

'Yes; I changed my name too.'

'Indeed?' said I.

'Yes; you see, a man wants a real fresh start when his eyes become opened, so he has a new deal all round, so to speak. Then he gets a fair chance.'

There was a short pause here, as I seemed to be on delicate ground in touching on my companion's antecedents, and he did not volunteer any information. I broke the silence by offering him a cheroot.

'No; thanks,' said he; 'I have given up tobacco. It was the hardest wrench of all, was that. It does me good to smell the whiff of your weed.—Tell me,' he added suddenly, looking hard at me with his shrewd gray eyes, 'why did you take stock of me so carefully before you spoke?'

'It is a habit of mine,' said I. 'I am a medical man, and observation is everything in my profession. I had no idea you were looking.'

'I can see without looking,' he answered. 'I thought you were a detective, at first; but I couldn't recall your face at the time I knew the force.'

'Were you a detective, then?' said I.

'No,' he answered with a laugh; 'I was the other thing—the detected, you know. Old scores are wiped out now, and the law cannot touch me, so I don't mind confessing to a gentleman like yourself what a scoundrel I have been in my time.'

'We are none of us perfect,' said I.

'No; but I was a real out-and-outer. A "fake," you know, to start with, and afterwards a "cracksman." It is easy to talk of these things now, for I've changed my spirit. It's as if I was talking of some other man, you see.'

'Exactly so,' said I. Being a medical man I had none of that shrinking from crime and criminals which many men possess. I could make all allowances for congenital influence and the force of circumstances. No company, therefore, could have been more acceptable to me than that of the old malefactor; and as I sat puffing at my cigar, I was delighted to observe that my air of interest was gradually loosening his tongue.

'Yes; I'm a changed man now,' he continued, 'and of course I am a happier man for that. And yet,' he added wistfully, 'there are times when I long for the old trade again, and fancy myself strolling out on a cloudy night with my jemmy in my pocket. I left a name behind me in my profession, sir. I was one of the old school, you know. It was very seldom that we bungled a job. We used to begin at the foot of the ladder, in my younger days, and then work our way up through the successive grades, so that we were what you might call good men all round.'

'I see,' said I.

'I was always reckoned a hard-working, conscientious man, and had talent too—the very cleverest of them allowed that. I began as a blacksmith, and then did a little engineering and carpentering, and then I took to sleight-of-hand tricks, and then to picking pockets. I remember, when I was home on a visit, how my poor old father used to wonder why I was always hovering around him. He little knew that I used to clear everything out of his pockets a dozen times a day, and then replace them, just to keep my hand in. He believes to this day that I am in an office in the City. There are few of them could touch me in that particular line of business, though.'

'I suppose it is a matter of practice?' I remarked.

'To a great extent. Still, a man never quite loses it, if he has once been an adept.—Excuse me; you have dropped some cigar ash on your coat,' and he waved his hand politely in front of my breast, as if to brush it off.—'There,' he said, handing me my gold scarf pin, 'you see I have not forgot my old cunning yet.'

He had done it so quickly that I hardly saw the hand whisk over my bosom, nor did I feel his fingers touch me, and yet there was the pin glittering in his hand. 'It is wonderful!' I said as I fixed it again in its place.

'Oh, that's nothing! But I have been in some really smart jobs. I was in the gang that picked the new patent safe. You remember the case. It was guaranteed to resist anything; and we managed to open the first that was ever issued, within a week of its appearance. It was done with graduated wedges, sir, the first so small that you could hardly see it against the light, and the last strong enough to prise it open. It was a cleverly managed affair.'

'I remember it,' said I. 'But surely some one was convicted for that?'

'Yes, one was nabbed. But he didn't split, nor even let on how it was done. It would have been as much as his life was worth.—Perhaps I am boring you, talking about these old wicked days of mine?'

'On the contrary,' I said, 'you interest me extremely.'

'I like to get a listener I can trust. It's a sort of blow-off, you know, and I feel lighter after it. When I am among my new and highly respectable acquaintances, I dare hardly think of what has gone before.—Now, I'll tell you about another job I was in. To this day, I cannot think about it without laughing.'

I lit another cigar, and composed myself to listen.

'It was when I was a youngster,' said he. 'There was a big City man in those days who was known to have a very valuable gold watch. I followed him about for several days before I could get a chance; but when I did get one, you may be sure I did not throw it away. He found to his disgust, when he got home that day, that there was nothing in his fob. I hurried off with my prize, and got it stowed away in safety, intending to have it melted down next day. Now, it happened that this watch possessed a special value in the owner's eyes because it was a sort of ancestral possession—present to his father on coming of age, or something of that sort. I remember there was a long inscription on the back. He was determined not to lose it if he could help it, and accordingly he put an advertisement in an evening paper offering thirty pounds reward for its return, and promising that no questions should be asked. He gave the address of his house, 31 Caroline Square, at the end of the advertisement. The thing sounded good enough, so I set off for Caroline Square, leaving the watch in a parcel at a public-house which I passed on the way. When I got there, the gentleman was at dinner; but he came out quick enough when he heard that a young man wanted to see him. I suppose he guessed who the young man would prove to be. He was a genial-looking old fellow, and he led me away with him into his study.

"Well, my lad," said he, "what is it?"

"I've come about that watch of yours," said I. "I think I can lay my hands on it."

"Oh, it was you that took it!" said he.

"No," I answered; "I know nothing whatever about how you lost it. I have been sent by another party to see you about it. Even if you have me arrested, you will not find out anything."

"Well," he said, "I don't want to be hard on you. Hand it over, and here is my cheque for the amount."

"Cheques won't do," said I; "I must have it in gold."

"It will take me an hour or so to collect it in gold," said he.

"That will just suit," I answered, "for I have not got the watch with me. I'll go back and fetch it, while you raise the money."

'I started off, and got the watch where I had left it. When I came back, the old gentleman was sitting behind his study table, with the little heap of gold in front of him.

"Here is your money," he said, and pushed it over.

"Here is your watch," said I.

'He was evidently delighted to get it back; and after examining it carefully, and assuring himself that it was none the worse, he put it into the watch-pocket of his coat with a grunt of satisfaction.

"Now, my lad," he said, "I know it was you that took the watch. Tell me how you did it, and I don't mind giving you an extra five-pound note."

"I wouldn't tell you in any case," said I; "but especially I wouldn't tell you when you have a witness hid behind that curtain." You see, I had all my wits about me, and it didn't escape me that the curtain was drawn tighter than it had been before.

"You are too sharp for us," said he good-humouredly. "Well you have got your money, and that's an end of it. I'll take precious good care you don't get hold of my watch again in a hurry.—Good-night.—No; not that door," he added as I marched towards a cupboard. "This is the door," and he stood up and opened it. I brushed past him, opened the hall door, and was round the corner of the square in no time. I don't know how long the old gentleman took to find it out, but in passing him at the door, I managed to pick his pocket for the second time, and next morning the family heirloom was in the melting pot after all.—That wasn't bad, was it?'

The old war-horse was evidently getting his blood up now. There was a tone of triumph in the conclusion of his anecdote which showed that, sometimes at least, his pride in his smartness surpassed his repentance of his misdeeds. He seemed pleased at the astonishment and amusement I expressed at his adroitness.

'Yes,' he continued with a laugh, 'it was a capital joke. But sometimes the fun lies all the other way. Even the sharpest of us comes to grief at times. There was one rather curious incident which occurred in my career. You may possibly have seen the anecdote, for it got into print at the time.'

'Pray, let me hear it,' said I.

'Well, it is hard lines telling stories against one's self, but this was how it happened. I had made a rather good haul, and invested some of the swag in buying a very fine diamond ring. I thought it would be something to fall back upon when all the ready was gone and times were hard. I had just purchased it, and was going back to my lodgings in the omnibus, when, as luck would have it, a very stylishly dressed young lady came in and took her seat beside me. I didn't pay much attention to her at first; but after a time something hard in her dress knocked up against my hand, which my experienced touch soon made out to be a purse. It struck me that I could not pass the time more profitably or agreeably than by making this purse my own. I had to do it very carefully; but I managed at last to wriggle my hand into her rather tight pocket, and I thought the job was over. Just at this moment she rose abruptly to leave the 'bus, and I had hardly time to get my hand with the purse in it out of her pocket without detection. It was not until she had been gone some time that I found out that, in drawing out my hand in that hurried manner, the new and ill-fitting ring I wore had slipped over my finger and remained in the young lady's pocket. I sprang out, and ran in the direction in which she had gone, with the intention of picking her pocket once again. She had disappeared, however; and from that day till this I have never set eyes on her. To make the matter worse, there was only fourpence-halfpenny in coppers inside the purse. Serve me right for trying to rob such a pretty girl; still, if I had that two hundred quid now, I should not be reduced to—Good Heavens, forgive me! What am I saying?'

He seemed inclined to relapse into silence after this; but I was determined to draw him out a little more, if I could possibly manage it. 'There is less personal risk in the branch you have been talking of,' I remarked, 'than there is in burglary.'

'Ah!' he said, warming to his subject once again, 'it is the higher game which is best worth aiming at.—Talk about sport, sir, talk about fishing or hunting! why, it is tame in comparison! Think of the great country-house with its men-servants and its dogs and its firearms, and you with only your jemmy and your centre-bit, and your mother-wit, which is best of all. It is the triumph of intellect over brute-force, sir, as represented by bolts and bars.'

'People generally look upon it as quite the reverse,' I remarked.

'I was never one of those blundering life-preserver fellows,' said my companion. 'I did try my hand at garrotting once; but it was against my principles, and I gave it up. I have tried everything. I have been a bedridden widow with three young children; but I do object to physical force.'

'You have been what?' said I.

'A bedridden widow. Advertising, you know, and getting subscriptions. I have tried them all.—You seem interested in these experiences,' he continued; 'so I will tell you another anecdote. It was the narrowest escape from penal servitude that ever I had in my life. A pal and I had gone down on a country beat—it doesn't signify where it was—and taken up our headquarters in a little provincial town. Somehow it got noised abroad that we were there and householders were warned to be careful, as suspicious characters had been seen in the neighbourhood. We should have changed our plans when we saw the game was up; but my chum was a plucky fellow, and wouldn't consent to back down. Poor little Jim! He was only thirty-four round the chest, and about twelve at the biceps; but there is not a measuring tape in England could have given the size of his heart. He said we were in for it, and we must stick to it; so I agreed to stay, and we chose Morley Hall, the country-house of a certain Colonel Morley, to begin with.

'Now, this Colonel Morley was about the last man in the world that we should have meddled with. He was a shrewd, cool-headed fellow, who had knocked about and seen the world, and it seems that he took a special pride in the detection of criminals. However, we knew nothing of all this at that time; so we set forth hopefully to have a try at the house.

'The reason that made us pick him out among the rest was that he had a good-for-nothing groom, who was a tool in our hands. This fellow had drawn up a rough plan of the premises for us. The place was pretty well locked up and guarded, and the only weak point we could see was a certain trap-door, the padlock of which was broken, and which opened from the roof into one of the lumber-rooms. If we could only find any method of reaching the roof, we might force a way securely from above. We both thought the plan rather a good one, and it had a spice of originality about it which pleased us. It is not the mere jewels or plate, you know, that a good cracksman thinks about. The neatness of the job, and his reputation for smartness, are almost as important in his eyes.

'We had been very quiet for a day or two, just to let suspicion die away. Then we set out one dark night, Jim and I, and got over the avenue railings and up to the house without meeting a soul. It was blowing hard, I remember, and the clouds hurrying across the sky. We had a good look at the front of the house, and then Jim went round to the garden side. He came running back in a minute or two in a great state of delight. "Why, Bill," he said, gripping me by the arm, "there never was such a bit of luck! They've been repairing the roof or something, and they've left the ladder standing." We went round together, and there, sure enough, was the ladder towering above our heads, and one or two labourers' hods lying about, which showed that some work had been going on during the day. We had a good look round, to see that everything was quiet, and then we climbed up, Jim first, and I after him. We got to the top, and were sitting on the slates, having a bit of a breather, before beginning business, when you can fancy our feelings to see the ladder that we came up by suddenly stand straight up in the air, and then slowly descend until it rested in the garden below! At first, we hoped it might have slipped, though that was bad enough; but we soon had that idea put out of our head.

"Hullo, up there!" cried a voice from below.

We craned our heads over the edge, and there was a man, dressed, as far as we could make out, in evening dress, and standing in the middle of the grass plot. We kept quiet.

"Hullo!" he shouted again. "How do you feel yourselves? Pretty comfortable, eh? Ha! ha! You London rogues thought we were green in the country. What's your opinion now?"

'We both lay still, though feeling pretty considerably small, as you may imagine.

"It's all right; I see you," he continued. "Why, I have been waiting behind that lilac bush every night for the last week, expecting to see you. I knew you couldn't resist going up that ladder, when you found the windows were too much for you.—Joe! Joe!"

"Yes, sir," said a voice, and another man came from among the bushes.

"Just you keep your eye on the roof, will you, while I ride down to the station and fetch up a couple of constables?—*Au revoir*, gentlemen! You don't mind waiting, I suppose?" And Colonel Morley—for it was the owner of the house himself—strode off; and in a few minutes we heard the rattle of his horse's hoofs going down the avenue.

'Well, sir, we felt precious silly, as you may imagine. It wasn't so much having been nabbed that bothered us, as the feeling of being caught in such a simple trap. We looked at each other in blank disgust, and then, to save our lives, we couldn't help bursting into laughter at our own fix. However, it was no laughing matter; so we set to work going round the roof, and seeing if there was a likely water-pipe or anything that might give us a chance of escape. We had to give it up as a bad job; so we sat down again, and made up our minds to the worst. Suddenly an idea flashed into my head, and I groped my way over the roof until I felt wood under my feet. I bent down, and found that the Colonel had actually forgotten to secure the padlock! You will often notice, as you go through life, that it is the shrewdest and most cunning man who falls into the most absurd mistakes; and this was an example of it. You may guess that we did not lose much time, for we expected to hear the constables every moment. We dropped through into the lumber-room, slipped down-stairs, tore open the library shutters, and were out and away before the astonished groom could make out what had happened. There wasn't time enough to take any little souvenir with us, worse luck. I should have liked to have seen the Colonel's face when he came back with the constables and found that the birds were flown.'

'Did you ever come across the Colonel again?' I asked.

'Yes; we skinned him of every bit of plate he had, down to the salt-spoons, a few years later. It was partly out of revenge, you see, that we did it. It was a very well-managed and daring thing, one of the best I ever saw, and all done in open daylight too.'

'How in the world did you do it?' I asked.

'Well, there were three of us in it—Jim was one; and we set about it in this way. We wanted to begin by getting the Colonel out of the way, so I wrote him a note purporting to come from Squire Brotherwick, who lived about ten miles away, and was not always on the best of terms with the master of Morley Hall. I dressed myself up as a groom and delivered the note myself. It was to the effect that the Squire thought he was able to lay his hands on the scoundrels who had escaped from the Colonel a couple of years before, and that if the Colonel would ride over, they would have little difficulty in securing them. I was sure that this would have the desired effect; so, after handing it in, and remarking that I was the Squire's groom, I walked off again, as if on the way back to my master's.

'After getting out of sight of the house, I crouched down behind a hedge; and, as I expected, in less than a quarter of an hour the Colonel came swinging past me on his chestnut mare. Now, there is another accomplishment I possess which I have not mentioned to you yet, and that is, that I can copy any handwriting that I see. It is a very easy trick to pick up, if you only give your mind to it. I happened to have come across one of Colonel Morley's letters some days before, and I can write so that even now I defy an expert to detect a difference between the hands. This was a great assistance to me now, for I tore a leaf out of my pocket-book and wrote something to this effect:

"As Squire Brotherwick has seen some suspicious characters about, and the house may be attempted again, I have sent down to the bank, and ordered them to send up their bank-cart to convey the whole of the plate to a place of safety. It will save us a good deal of anxiety to know that it is in absolute security. Have it packed up and ready, and give the bearer a glass of beer."

'Having composed this precious epistle, I addressed it to the butler, and carried it back to the Hall, saying that their master had overtaken me on the way and asked me to deliver it. I was taken in and made much of down-stairs; while a great packing-case was dragged into the hall, and the plate stowed away among cotton-wool and stuffing. It was nearly ready, when I heard the sound of wheels upon the gravel, and sauntered round just in time to see a business-like closed car drive up to the door. One of my pals was sitting very demurely on the box; while Jim, with an official-looking hat, sprang out and bustled into the hall.

"Now, then," I heard him say, "look sharp! What's for the bank? Come on!"

"Wait a minute, sir," said the butler.

"Can't wait. There's a panic all over the country, and they are clamouring for us everywhere. Must drive on to Lord Blackbury's place, unless you are ready."

"Don't go, sir!" pleaded the butler. "There's only this one rope to tie.—There; it is ready now. You'll look after it, won't you?"

"That we will. You'll never have any more trouble with it now," said Jim, helping to push the great case into the car.

"I think I had better go with you and see it stowed away in the bank," said the butler.

"All right!" said Jim, nothing abashed. "You can't come in the car, though, for Lord Blackbury's box will take up all the spare room.—Let's see—it's twelve o'clock now. Well, you be waiting at the bank door at half-past one, and you will just catch us."

"All right—half past one," said the butler.

"Good-day!" cried my chum; and away went the car, while I made a bit of a short cut and caught it round a turn of the road. We drove right off into the next county, got a down-train to London; and before midnight, the Colonel's silver was fused into a solid lump.'

I could not help laughing at the versatility of the old scoundrel. 'It was a daring game to play,' I said.

'It is always the daring game which succeeds best,' he answered.

At this point the train began to show symptoms of slowing down, and my companion put on his overcoat and gave other signs of being near the end of his journey. 'You are going on to Dover?' he said.

'Yes.'

'For the Continent?'

'Yes.'

'How long do you intend to travel?'

'Only for a week or so.'

'Well, I must leave you here. You will remember my name, won't you? John Wilkie, I am pleased to have met you.—Is my umbrella behind you?' he added, stretching across.—'No; I beg your pardon. Here it is in the corner;' and with an affable smile, the ex-cracksman stepped out, bowed, and disappeared among the crowd upon the platform.

I lit another cigar, laughed as I thought of my late companion, and lifted up the *Times*, which he had left behind him. The bell had rung, the wheels were already revolving, when, to my astonishment, a pallid face looked in at me through the window. It was so contorted and agitated, that I hardly recognised the features which I had been gazing upon during the last couple of hours. 'Here, take it,' he said—'take it. It's hardly worth my while to rob you of seven pounds four shillings; but I couldn't resist once more trying my hand;' and he flung something into the carriage and disappeared.

It was my old leather purse, with my return ticket, and the

whole of my travelling expenses. How he had taken it he knows best himself; I suppose it was while he was bending over in search of an imaginary umbrella. His newly re-awakened conscience had then pricked him, so that he had been driven to instant restitution.

E. and H. HERON

Hesketh V. Prichard (1876–1922) was half of the pseudonym E. and H. Heron, the other half being his mother, Kate O'Brien Ryall Prichard. H. V. was well known as a big-game hunter and cricketeer, and was in government service in Great Britain. In 1907 he was aide to the Lord Lieutenant of Ireland. In World War I he was cited several times for heroism, but was often in disfavor for recommending sniper tactics rather than mass charges. His health ruined by the war, he died in 1922.

Prichard, with or without his mother, was a frequent contributor to the periodicals. His most successful work was a series of stories about Don Q, a sadistic Spanish bandit; they were eventually bowdlerized into a movie for Douglas Fairbanks, Sr. Prichard also wrote books about travel and big-game hunting, and detective literature, November Joe, Detective of the Woods *(1913).*

The adventures of Flaxman Low, written by both Prichards, are probably the first important stories based on an occult detective—that is, a detective who specializes in cases involving the supernatural. In the original periodical publications in Pearson's Magazine *in 1898 and 1899 each story was illustrated with a photograph of the haunted house featured in the story.*

"The Story of Baelbrow"

It is a matter for regret that so many of Mr. Flaxman Low's reminiscences should deal with the darker episodes of his career. Yet this is almost unavoidable, as the more purely scientific and less strongly marked cases would not, perhaps, contain the same elements of interest for the general public, however valuable and instructive they might be to the expert student. It has also been considered better to choose the completer cases, those that ended in something like satisfactory proof, rather than the many instances where the thread broke off abruptly amongst surmisings, which it was never possible to subject to convincing tests.

North of a low-lying strip of country on the East Anglian coast, the promontory of Bael Ness thrusts out a blunt nose into the sea. On the Ness, backed by pinewoods, stands a square, comfortable stone mansion, known to the countryside as Baelbrow. It has faced the east winds for close upon three hundred years, and during the whole period has been the home of the Swaffam family, who were never in any wise put out of conceit of their ancestral dwelling by the fact that it had always been haunted. Indeed, the Swaffams were proud of the Baelbrow Ghost, which enjoyed a wide notoriety, and no one dreamt of complaining of its behaviour until Professor Jungvort, of Nuremburg, laid information against it, and sent an urgent appeal for help to Mr. Flaxman Low.

The Professor, who was well acquainted with Mr. Low, detailed the circumstances of his tenancy of Baelbrow, and the unpleasant events that had followed thereupon.

It appeared that Mr. Swaffam, senior, who spent a large portion of his time abroad, had offered to lend his house to the Professor for the summer season. When the Jungvorts arrived at Baelbrow, they were charmed with the place. The prospect, though not very varied, was at least extensive, and the air exhilarating. Also the Professor's daughter enjoyed frequent visits from her betrothed—Harold Swaffam—and the Professor was delightfully employed in overhauling the Swaffam library.

The Jungvorts had been duly told of the ghost, which lent distinction to the old house, but never in any way interfered with the comfort of the inmates. For some time they found this description to be strictly true, but with the beginning of October came a change. Up to this time and as far back as the Swaffam annals reached, the ghost had been a shadow, a rustle, a passing sigh—nothing definite or troublesome. But early in October strange things began to occur, and the terror culminated when a housemaid was found dead in a corridor three weeks later. Upon this the Professor felt that it was time to send for Flaxman Low.

Mr. Low arrived upon a chilly evening when the house was already beginning to blur in the purple twilight, and the resinous scent of the pines came sweetly on the land breeze. Jungvort welcomed him in the spacious, firelit hall. He was a stout German with a quantity of white hair, round eyes emphasised by spectacles, and a kindly, dreamy face. His life-study was philology, and his two relaxations chess and the smoking of a big Bismarck-bowled meerschaum.

"Now, Professor," said Mr. Low when they had settled themselves in the smoking room, "how did it all begin?"

"I will tell you," replied Jungvort, thrusting out his chin, and tapping his broad chest, and speaking as if an unwarrantable liberty had been taken with him. "First of all, it has shown itself to me!"

Mr. Flaxman Low smiled and assured him that nothing could be more satisfactory.

"But not at all satisfactory!" exclaimed the Professor, "I was sitting here alone, it might have been midnight—when I hear something come creeping like a little dog with its nails, tick-tick, upon the oak flooring of the hall. I whistle, for I think it is the little 'Rags' of my daughter, and afterwards opened the door, and I saw"—he hesitated and looked hard at Low through his spectacles, "something that was just disappearing into the passage which connects the two wings of the house. It was a figure, not unlike the human figure, but narrow and straight. I fancied I saw a bunch of black hair, and a flutter of something detached, which may have been a handkerchief. I was overcome by a feeling of repulsion. I heard a few, clicking steps, then it stopped, as I thought, at the museum door. Come, I will show you the spot."

The Professor conducted Mr. Low into the hall. The main staircase, dark and massive, yawned above them, and directly behind it ran the passage referred to by the Professor. It was over twenty feet long, and about midway led past a deep arch containing a door reached by two steps. Jungvort explained that this door formed the entrance to a large room called the Museum, in which Mr. Swaffam, senior, who was something of a dilettante, stored the various curios he picked up during his excursions abroad. The Professor went on to say that he immediately followed the figure, which he believed had gone into the museum, but he found nothing there except the cases containing Swaffam's treasures.

"I mentioned my experience to no one. I concluded that I had seen the ghost. But two days after, one of the female servants coming through the passage in the dark, declared that a man leapt out at her from the embrasure of the Museum door, but she released herself and ran screaming into the servants' hall. We at once made a search but found nothing to substantiate her story.

"I took no notice of this, though it coincided pretty well with my own experience. The week after, my daughter Lena came down late one night for a book. As she was about to cross the hall, something leapt upon her from behind. Women are of little use in serious investigations—she fainted! Since then she has been ill and the doctor says 'Run down.' " Here the Professor spread out his hands. "So she leaves for a change to-morrow. Since then other members of the household have been attacked in much the same manner, with always the same result, they faint and are weak and useless when they recover.

"But, last Wednesday, the affair became a tragedy. By that time the servants had refused to come through the passage except in a crowd of three or four,—most of them preferring to go round by the terrace to reach this part of the house. But one maid, named Eliza Freeman, said she was not afraid of the Baelbrow Ghost, and undertook to put out the lights in the hall one night. When she had done so, and was returning through the passage past the Museum door, she appears to have been attacked, or at any rate frightened. In the grey of the morning they found her lying beside the steps dead. There was a little blood upon her sleeve but no mark upon her body except a small raised pustule under the ear. The doctor said the girl was extraordinarily anæmic, and that she probably died from fright, her heart being weak. I was surprised at this, for she had always seemed to be a particularly strong and active young woman."

"Can I see Miss Jungvort to-morrow before she goes?" asked Low, as the Professor signified he had nothing more to tell.

The Professor was rather unwilling that his daughter should be questioned, but he at last gave his permission, and next morning Low had a short talk with the girl before she left the house. He found her a very pretty girl, though listless and startlingly pale, and with a frightened stare in her light brown eyes. Mr. Low asked if she could describe her assailant.

"No," she answered, "I could not see him, for he was behind me. I only saw a dark, bony hand, with shining nails, and a bandaged arm pass just under my eyes before I fainted."

"Bandaged arm? I have heard nothing of this."

"Tut—tut, mere fancy!" put in the Professor impatiently.

"I saw the bandages on the arm," repeated the girl, turning her head wearily away, "and I smelt the antiseptics it was dressed with."

"You have hurt your neck," remarked Mr. Low, who noticed a small circular patch of pink under her ear.

She flushed and paled, raising her hand to her neck with a nervous jerk, as she said in a low voice:

"It has almost killed me. Before he touched me, I knew he was there! I felt it!"

When they left her the Professor apologised for the unreliability of her evidence, and pointed out the discrepancy between her statement and his own.

"She says she sees nothing but an arm, yet I tell you it had no arms! Preposterous! Conceive a wounded man entering this house to frighten the young women! I do not know what to make of it! Is it a man, or is it the Baelbrow Ghost?"

During the afternoon when Mr. Low and the Professor returned from a stroll on the shore, they found a dark-browed young man

290

with a bull neck, and strongly marked features, standing sullenly before the hall fire. The Professor presented him to Mr. Low as Harold Swaffam.

Swaffam seemed to be about thirty, but was already known as a far-seeing and successful member of the Stock Exchange.

"I am pleased to meet you, Mr. Low," he began, with a keen glance, "though you don't look sufficiently high-strung for one of your profession."

Mr. Low merely bowed.

"Come, you don't defend your craft against my insinuations?" went on Swaffam. "And so you have come to rout out our poor old ghost from Baelbrow? You forget that he is an heirloom, a family possession! What's this about his having turned rabid, eh, Professor?" he ended, wheeling round upon Jungvort in his brusque way.

The Professor told the story over again. It was plain that he stood rather in awe of his prospective son-in-law.

"I heard much the same from Lena, whom I met at the station," said Swaffam. "It is my opinion that the women in this house are suffering from an epidemic of hysteria. You agree with me, Mr. Low?"

"Possibly. Though hysteria could hardly account for Freeman's death."

"I can't say as to that until I have looked further into the particulars. I have not been idle since I arrived. I have examined the Museum. No one has entered it from the outside, and there is no other way of entrance except through the passage. The flooring is laid, I happen to know, on a thick layer of concrete. And there the case for the ghost stands at present." After a few moments of dogged reflection, he swung round on Mr. Low, in a manner that seemed peculiar to him when about to address any person. "What do you say to this plan, Mr. Low? I propose to drive the Professor over to Ferryvale, to stop there for a day or two at the hotel, and I will also dispose of the servants who still remain in the house for, say, forty-eight hours. Meanwhile you and I can try to go further into the secret of the ghost's new pranks?"

Flaxman Low replied that this scheme exactly met his views, but the Professor protested against being sent away. Harold Swaffam however was a man who liked to arrange things in his own fashion, and within forty-five minutes he and Jungvort departed in the dogcart.

The evening was lowering, and Baelbrow, like all houses built in exposed situations, was extremely susceptible to the changes of the weather. Therefore, before many hours were over, the place was full of creaking noises as the screaming gale battered at the shuttered windows, and the tree-branches tapped and groaned against the walls.

Harold Swaffam, on his way back, was caught in the storm and drenched to the skin. It was, therefore, settled that after he had changed his clothes he should have a couple of hours' rest on the smoking-room sofa, while Mr. Low kept watch in the hall.

The early part of the night passed over uneventfully. A light burned faintly in the great wainscotted hall, but the passage was dark. There was nothing to be heard but the wild moan and whistle of the wind coming in from the sea, and the squalls of rain dashing against the windows. As the hours advanced, Mr. Low lit a lantern that lay at hand, and, carrying it along the passage, tried the Museum door. It yielded, and the wind came muttering through to meet him. He looked round at the shutters and behind the big cases which held Mr. Swaffam's treasures, to make sure that the room contained no living occupant but himself.

Suddenly he fancied he heard a scraping noise behind him, and turned round, but discovered nothing to account for it. Finally, he laid the lantern on a bench so that its light should fall through the door into the passage, and returned again to the hall, where he put out the lamp, and then once more took up his station by the closed door of the smoking-room.

A long hour passed, during which the wind continued to roar down the wide hall chimney, and the old boards creaked as if furtive footsteps were gathering from every corner of the house. But Flaxman Low heeded none of these; he was waiting for a certain sound.

After a while, he heard it—the cautious scraping of wood on wood. He leant forward to watch the Museum door. Click, click, came the curious dog-like tread upon the tiled floor of the Museum, till the thing, whatever it was, paused and listened behind the open door. The wind lulled at the moment, and Low listened also, but no further sound was to be heard, only slowly across the broad ray of light falling through the door grew a stealthy shadow.

Again the wind rose, and blew in heavy gusts about the house, till even the flame in the lantern flickered; but when it steadied once more, Flaxman Low saw that the silent form had passed through the door, and was now on the steps outside. He could just make out a dim shadow in the dark angle of the embrasure.

Presently, from the shapeless shadow came a sound Mr. Low was not prepared to hear. The thing sniffed the air with the strong, audible inspiration of a bear, or some large animal. At the same moment, carried on the draughts of the hall, a faint, unfamiliar odour reached his nostrils. Lena Jungvort's words flashed back upon him—this, then, was the creature with the bandaged arm!

Again, as the storm shrieked and shook the windows, a darkness passed across the light. The thing had sprung out from the angle of the door, and Flaxman Low knew that it was making its way towards him through the illusive blackness of the hall. He hesitated for a second; then he opened the smoking-room door.

Harold Swaffam sat up on the sofa, dazed with sleep.

"What has happened? Has it come?"

Low told him what he had just seen. Swaffam listened half-smilingly.

"What do you make of it now?" he said.

"I must ask you to defer that question for a little," replied Low.

"Then you mean me to suppose that you have a theory to fit all these incongruous items?"

"I have a theory, which may be modified by further knowledge," said Low. "Meantime, am I right in concluding from the name of this house that it was built on a barrow or burying-place?"

"You are right, though that has nothing to do with the latest freaks of our ghost," returned Swaffam decidedly.

"I also gather that Mr. Swaffam has lately sent home one of the many cases now lying in the Museum?" went on Mr. Low.

"He sent one, certainly, last September."

"And you have opened it," asserted Low.

"Yes; though I flattered myself I had left no trace of my handiwork."

"I have not examined the cases," said Low. "I inferred that you had done so from other facts."

"Now, one thing more," went on Swaffam, still smiling. "Do you imagine there is any danger—I mean to men like ourselves? Hysterical women cannot be taken into serious account."

"Certainly; the gravest danger to any person who moves about this part of the house alone after dark," replied Low.

Harold Swaffam leant back and crossed his legs.

"To go back to the beginning of our conversation, Mr. Low, may I remind you of the various conflicting particulars you will have to reconcile before you can present any decent theory to the world?"

"I am quite aware of that."

"First of all, our original ghost was a mere misty presence, rather guessed at from vague sounds and shadows—now we have a something that is tangible, and that can, as we have proof, kill with fright. Next Jungvort declares the thing was a narrow, long and distinctly armless object, while Miss Jungvort has not only seen the arm and hand of a human being, but saw them clearly enough to tell us that the nails were gleaming and the arm bandaged. She also felt its strength. Jungvort, on the other hand, maintained that it clicked along like a dog—you bear out this description with the additional information that it sniffs like a wild beast. Now what can this thing be? It is capable of being seen, smelt, and felt, yet it hides itself successfully in a room where there is no cavity or space sufficient to afford covert to a cat! You still tell me that you believe that you can explain?"

"Most certainly," replied Flaxman Low with conviction.

"I have not the slightest intention or desire to be rude, but as a mere matter of common sense, I must express my opinion plainly. I believe the whole thing to be the result of excited imaginations, and I am about to prove it. Do you think there is any further danger to-night?"

"Very great danger to-night," replied Low.

"Very well; as I said, I am going to prove it. I will ask you to allow me to lock you up in one of the distant rooms, where I can get no help from you, and I will pass the remainder of the night walking about the passage and hall in the dark. That should give proof one way or the other."

"You can do so if you wish, but I must at least beg to be allowed to look on. I will leave the house and watch what goes on from the window in the passage, which I saw opposite the Museum door. You cannot, in any fairness, refuse to let me be a witness."

"I cannot, of course," returned Swaffam. "Still, the night is too bad to turn a dog out into, and I warn you that I shall lock you out."

"That will not matter. Lend me a macintosh, and leave the lantern lit in the Museum, where I placed it."

Swaffam agreed to this. Mr. Low gives a graphic account of what followed. He left the house and was duly locked out, and, after groping his way round the house, found himself at length outside the window of the passage, which was almost opposite to the door of the Museum. The door was still ajar and a thin band of light cut out into the gloom. Further down the hall gaped black and void. Low, sheltering himself as well as he could from the rain, waited for Swaffam's appearance. Was the terrible yellow watcher balancing itself upon its lean legs in the dim corner opposite, ready to spring out with its deadly strength upon the passer-by?

Presently Low heard a door bang inside the house, and the next moment Swaffam appeared with a candle in his hand, an isolated spread of weak rays against the vast darkness behind. He advanced steadily down the passage, his dark face grim and set, and as he came Mr. Low experienced that tingling sensation, which is so often the forerunner of some strange experience. Swaffam passed on towards the other end of the passage. There was a quick vibration of the Museum door as a lean shape with a shrunken head leapt out into the passage after him. Then all together came a hoarse shout, the noise of a fall and utter darkness.

In an instant, Mr. Low had broken the glass, opened the window, and swung himself into the passage. There he lit a match and as it flared he saw by its dim light a picture painted for a second upon the obscurity beyond.

Swaffam's big figure lay with outstretched arms, face downwards, and as Low looked a crouching shape extricated itself from the fallen man, raising a narrow vicious head from his shoulder.

The match spluttered feebly and went out, and Low heard a flying step click on the boards, before he could find the candle Swaffam had dropped. Lighting it, he stooped over Swaffam and turned him on his back. The man's strong colour had gone, and the wax-white face looked whiter still against the blackness of hair and brows, and upon his neck under the ear, was a little raised pustule, from which a thin line of blood was streaked up to the angle of his cheekbone.

Some instinctive feeling prompted Low to glance up at this moment. Half extended from the Museum doorway were a face and bony neck—a high-nosed, dull-eyed, malignant face, the eye-sockets hollow, and the darkened teeth showing. Low plunged his hand into his pocket, and a shot rang out in the echoing passage-way and hall. The wind sighed through the broken panes, a ribbon of stuff fluttered along the polished flooring, and that was all, as Flaxman Low half dragged, half carried Swaffam into the smoking-room.

It was some time before Swaffam recovered consciousness. He listened to Low's story of how he had found him with a red angry gleam in his sombre eyes.

"The ghost has scored off me," he said with an odd, sullen laugh, "but now I fancy it's my turn! But before we adjourn to the Museum to examine the place, I will ask you to let me hear your notion of things. You have been right in saying there was real danger. For myself I can only tell you that I felt something spring upon me, and I knew no more. Had this not happened I am afraid I should never have asked you a second time what your idea of the matter might be," he ended with a sort of sulky frankness.

"There are two main indications," replied Low. "This strip of yellow bandage, which I have just now picked up from the passage floor, and the mark on your neck."

"What's that you say?" Swaffam rose quickly and examined his neck in a small glass beside the mantelshelf.

"Connect those two, and I think I can leave you to work it out for yourself," said Low.

"Pray let us have your theory in full," requested Swaffam shortly.

"Very well," answered Low good-humouredly—he thought Swaffam's annoyance natural under the circumstances—"The long, narrow figure which seemed to the Professor to be armless is developed on the next occasion. For Miss Jungvort sees a bandaged arm and a dark hand with gleaming—which means, of course, gilded—nails. The clicking sound of the footstep coincides with these particulars, for we know that sandals made of strips of leather are not uncommon in company with gilt nails and bandages. Old and dry leather would naturally click upon your polished floors."

"Bravo, Mr. Low! So you mean to say that this house is haunted by a mummy!"

"That is my idea, and all I have seen confirms me in my opinion."

"To do you justice, you held this theory before to-night—before, in fact, you had seen anything for yourself. You gathered that my father had sent home a mummy, and you went on to conclude that I had opened the case?"

"Yes. I imagine you took off most of, or rather all, the outer bandages, thus leaving the limbs free, wrapped only in the inner bandages which were swathed round each separate limb. I fancy this mummy was preserved by the Theban method with aromatic spices, which left the skin olive-coloured, dry and flexible, like tanned leather, the features remaining distinct, and the hair, teeth and eyebrows perfect."

"So far, good," said Swaffam. "But now, how about the intermittent vitality? The pustule on the neck of those whom it attacks? And where is our old Baelbrow ghost to come in?"

Swaffam tried to speak in a rallying tone, but his excitement and lowering temper were visible enough, in spite of the attempts he made to suppress them.

"To begin at the beginning," said Flaxman Low, "everybody who, in a rational and honest manner, investigates the phenomena of spiritism will, sooner or later, meet in them some perplexing element, which is not to be explained by any of the ordinary theories. For reasons into which I need not now enter, this present case appears to me to be one of these. I am led to believe that the ghost which has for so many years given dim and vague manifestations of its existence in this house is a vampire."

Swaffam threw back his head with an incredulous gesture.

"We no longer live in the middle ages, Mr. Low! And besides, how could a vampire come here?" he said scoffingly.

"It is held by some authorities on these subjects that under certain conditions a vampire may be self-created. You tell me that this house is built upon an ancient barrow, in fact, on a spot where we might naturally expect to find such an elemental psychic germ. In those dead human systems were contained all the seeds for good and evil. The power which causes these psychic seeds or germs to grow is thought, and from being long dwelt on and indulged, a thought might finally gain a mysterious vitality, which could go increasing more and more by attracting to itself suitable and appropriate elements from its environment. For a long period this germ remained a helpless intelligence, awaiting the opportunity to assume some material form, by means of which to carry out its desires. The invisible is the real; the material only subserves its manifestation. The impalpable reality already existed, when you provided for it a physical medium for action by unwrapping the mummy's form. Now, we can only judge of the nature of the germ by its manifestation through matter. Here we have every indication of a vampire intelligence touching into life and energy the dead human frame. Hence the mark on the neck of its victims, and their bloodless and anæmic condition. For a vampire, as you know, sucks blood."

Swaffham rose, and took up the lamp.

"Now, for proof," he said bluntly. "Wait a second, Mr. Low. You say you fired at this appearance?" And he took up the pistol which Low had laid down on the table.

"Yes, I aimed at a small portion of its foot which I saw on the step."

Without more words, and with the pistol still in his hand, Swaffam led the way to the Museum.

The wind howled round the house, and the darkness, which precedes the dawn, lay upon the world, when the two men looked upon one of the strangest sights it has ever been given to men to shudder at.

Half in and half out of an oblong wooden box in a corner of the great room, lay a lean shape in its rotten yellow bandages, the scraggy neck surmounted by a mop of frizzled hair. The toe strap of a sandal and a portion of the right foot had been shot away.

Swaffam, with a working face, gazed down at it, then seizing it by its tearing bandages, he flung it into the box, where if fell into a life-like posture, its wide, moist-lipped mouth gaping up at them.

For a moment Swaffam stood over the thing; then with a curse he raised the revolver and shot into the grinning face again and again with a deliberate vindictiveness. Finally he rammed the thing down into the box, and, clubbing the weapon, smashed the head into fragments with a vicious energy that coloured the whole horrible scene with a suggestion of murder done.

Then, turning to Low, he said:

"Help me to fasten the cover on it."

"Are you going to bury it?"

"No, we must rid the earth of it," he answered savagely. "I'll put it into the old canoe and burn it."

The rain had ceased when in the daybreak they carried the old canoe down to the shore. In it they placed the mummy case with its ghastly occupant, and piled faggots about it. The sail was raised and the pile lighted, and Low and Swaffam watched it creep out on the ebb-tide, at first a twinkling spark, then a flare of waving fire, until far out to sea the history of that dead thing ended 3000 years after the priests of Amen had laid it to rest in its appointed pyramid.

CUTCLIFFE HYNE

Charles John Cutcliffe Hyne (1865–1944), after receiving his M.A. in the natural sciences from Cambridge, took to the sea for a time, serving as supercargo on a merchant ship. On his return to England he decided on journalism for a career and soon became a frequent contributor to the variety magazines. His specialties were popular scientific articles and adventure stories.

Hyne achieved fame with the creation of Captain Kettle, a crusty, jingoistic, somewhat unscrupulous little martinet in the merchant marine. For a time the Captain Kettle stories were second in popularity only to those about Sherlock Holmes, but today they are almost forgotten. Hyne also wrote a fair amount of science fiction, and his Atlantis novel, The Lost Continent *(1900), is still occasionally reprinted.*

"The Bank Note Forger"

A DETECTIVE STORY

We were running down to Aintree for Grand National day, and were taking it easy in a saloon.

O'Malley is a great man for making train journeys comfortable. We kept two rubbers of whist going for a couple of hours, and then, wearying of cards, lounged on the seats of the carriage and talked. Naturally we got on matters of sport, and discussed the varying size of Valentine's Brook, and the way Emperor had broken his neck on an in-and-out of fencing when dropped from the race, and kindred matters of parochial interest. And then we fell to chatting over heroes and idiots of the past, and with a reminiscent laugh Cope's name was chucked upon the carpet.

"There is no doubt," said Grayson, the Q.C., "that Master Willie Cope had been a young fool in the way of frittering away his money. He had been run with a very loose rein all his infancy, and at the age of twenty-two came into a property which yielded him at least nineteen thousand a year in hard cash. He started fair: he cleared away a prosperous crop of *post-obits;* and then he, so to speak, stripped off his coat and saw how much money a man could spend if he set his mind to it.

"His methods were large-minded and various. He took over a big racing stable, and ran at least one horse for every notable event on the turf. He had villas at Nice, Homburg, and Aix-les-Bains. He went in hot for yacht-racing, and on the strength of pulling off a few events for 10-raters, had a fling at the America Cup. He didn't bring that away with him, as you may recollect; but the attempt cost him something like fifty-four thousand. And, of course, in addition to these trifling expenses, he had to keep up the shooting lodge in Argyleshire, which was tacked on to the deer forest, and a big house near Hyde Park, as well as Castle Cope in Fermanagh, and Bordell Priory in Yorkshire.

"In fact, during the first four years of his reign, he purchased supreme popularity at the mild charge of nine-and-a-half times his income.

"The scandal papers very naturally got a nickname for him. They dubbed him 'The Flutterer.' He really had a jumpy, nervous manner about him; and so, as the sobriquet seemed happy, it stuck.

"He had got an agent fellow, by name Presse, to dry-nurse him; and I have reason to know that Presse was continually crying aloud against outrunning the constable. But Cope's domestic motto was, 'Whilst we live, don't let's have any doubt about it'; and as he thoroughly enjoyed the pace, he didn't feel in the least inclined to clap the brake on. So he got tighter and tighter nipped every rent day.

"Now, when a poor man commences ruining himself on a small scale, nobody out of his own parish pays any particular heed. But when a millionaire starts going a mucker, then proceedings get interesting to the mob at large. In Cope's case the aforesaid scandal papers made four long interesting paragraphs out of him every week. All the British Islanders watched with prim curiosity the pace at which he was going it. That's an amiable way they have. It makes them feel they aren't so bad as they might be; which is a pleasing sensation to anyone.

"It was when, in his own particular line, Cope had created himself the biggest celebrity in the country, that his earthquake arrived. He was accused of systematically uttering forged Bank of England thousand-pound notes. It seemed that he had negotiated at least fifty-four of them, and there might be others which had not yet come in.

"Now, as this is a crime which, in the British decalogue, comes very little short of brutal murder, Cope stood a very good chance of remaining in gaol from the first moment of his arrest; because, at the magistrate's inquiry, the case was proved against him up to the hilt. However, after they committed him for trial, great pressure was brought to bear, and he was released on bail that was simply enormous.

"Barnes was given the case, and he retained me for the defence; a pretty sick sort of defence it was. The principal argument I was bidden to use was, that Master Willie Cope felt quite convinced of his own innocence. It was his habit to make all his bets in thousand-pound notes. This avoided arithmetical calculations, which he was not good at, and also brought him fame. It is very easy to purchase notoriety of that brand in Great Britain—if only your purse is long enough to pay the price.

"The prosecution, on the other hand, could prove beyond argument that the last fifty of these trifling pieces of paper which Cope had drawn from various banks had been carefully and cunningly duplicated; that Cope, with his own fingers, had paid away the reproductions; and that the originals, after being saved up till their number amounted to some fifty odd, had been simultaneously cashed in Constantinople, Moscow, Berlin, Genoa, Monte Carlo, Marseilles, Lyons, and Paris. This pointed to an extensive organisation; but none of the confederates could be traced. Bank of England notes are good all the world over; and these which were passed on the Continent were genuine.

"The counterfeits, too, were, paper and all, so artfully made that they passed unchallenged through all the country banks, and for awhile even at the Bank of banks in the City; and it was not until the other pieces of crisp water-marked paper, bearing the signature of Mr. May, and the promise to pay bearer £1,000, began to dribble in from Europe, that the trouble commenced. Then it was observed that $\frac{E}{65}$ 16626 had been negotiated before, as had also $\frac{R}{16}$ 23360, and likewise $\frac{P}{84}$ 86162. The documents bore the blue impress of rubber stamps, and the scratchings of pens, which in part traced their circular tours; and the authorities easily collected other records of the hands passed through, because the majestic movements of thousand-pound notes are spied on with far more interest than the rambles of the commoner and more garden fiver.

"When they found that the last comers were undoubtedly orthodox, and the previous series superb forgeries, then there was one of the solidest rows inside that building ever known since Threadneedle Street was paved. The men at the top thundered at the carelessness of those immediately beneath them; the men at the bottom looked preternaturally grave, and hoped for their step; and the wretched tellers who passed the first batch of notes had to bear the brunt of all these bombardments. Most of the notes had been burnt; but enough were left to show—with the more glaring light of after-knowledge—that they were most accurate forgeries.

"Now, savaging your own underlings may, as sheer dissipation and amusement, be very pleasant in its way; but it isn't solid satisfactory vengeance, and it has no connection with the *lex talionis*, both of which are far more businesslike and to the point. So after the preliminary scratching and swearing match, the directors looked round them and demanded blood. Obviously the supply would have to come from Master Willie Cope; and, as no one else appeared to share the brunt, from him alone. He was a very fit and proper person to be made into an awful example, and so they set the mill of the law in motion, and it looked as though he would be mangled up very small indeed before he was done with. The *Morning Post* mentioned this in a most stately leader.

"Now, those are the outlines of the case, and Barnes quite agreed with me that matters for the defence looked very sick indeed. The prosecution would show that Cope was excessively hard up, that he had been losing very heavily on the turf, that he had drawn good thousand-pound notes from various banks, and then with his own fingers passed bogus notes on to the bookies. All this was absolutely true: we admitted it.

" 'Look here,' said I to Barnes, 'we must find how and by whom these spurious notes were manufactured.'

" 'Precisely,' said Barnes, 'that's obvious. The only trifle waiting to be discovered is the method of doing this. I confess that beats me, and what's more, it's too big an order for Cope. His inventive faculties are stimulated just now; he's got as good and solid a scare in him as a man can well carry amongst his ribs without tumbling down; but even that hasn't screwed him to the necessary pitch. He no more knows how those notes got into his pocket than Elk, your clerk, does.

" 'You see, the young fool was, in a way, most awfully slipshod about his money matters, though there was method in his madness. A thousand-pound Bank of England note isn't a thing an ordinary pickpocket can get rid of like a tenner. In consequence of this, Cope used to leave his money lying about anywhere, confident that it would not be stolen; and forty people might have had complete access to it. He says Presse was constantly blowing him up for his carelessness, and that he was always chaffing Presse for being a nervous old woman. Presse took a big interest in the fellow, there's no doubt about that.'

" 'Then, do you hint that this officious agent fellow forged the notes?'

" 'I hint nothing, Grayson; but I suspect everybody. I might remark, though, that Presse messes about with a hand camera, and photography certainly had something to do with the production of these forged notes.'

" 'Why on earth didn't you tell me this before?'

" 'Because I can add nothing to it. Between making bad amateur photographs with a half-plate camera and turning out perfect thousand-pound notes, there are many lengthy gaps which I can't fill in anyhow. I'm not exactly a fool, Grayson. You can bet your boots I've tried to father the job on Presse.'

" 'Yet it strikes me it's *aut Presse aut nullus*. Look here; from what you tell me, nearly all these forged notes were passed at Doncaster during the Leger week. Cope was then staying at Bordell Priory. Do you mind my sending Elk down there to see if he can hunt out anything?'

" 'You can send a whole menagerie if you like,' said Barnes. I could see he didn't like my trying further where he himself had failed; and if I had seen any other chance of bringing Cope off clear, I shouldn't have suggested the thing. But it seemed to me then that our only hope was to shift the blame on to Presse's shoulders, and if anyone could do that, I believed my queer head clerk to be the man.

"I told Elk what I wanted of him, and the fellow's eye brightened up at once.

" 'Think you can tear yourself away from the domestic hearth for a day or two?' I asked.

"Elk grinned like a fiend. He's a little man, and he has married into a nest of gaunt sisters. His home life is one continuous harlequinade, with himself as the bobby. When I send him off on any bit of business, he puts all his wits into it, and does it as well as possible in the hope of soon being packed off again on some other job. Of course, it isn't often that he comes into use; but I'll give him credit for working up some cases into a win which would otherwise have turned out an absolute fizzle.

"This matter of Cope's is a very good instance of Elk's nosing powers. He went down to Bordell Priory fully determined to shift the trouble on to Presse's shoulders, and he left no stone unturned to do it. Presse was away at Castle Cope in Fermanagh, and the coast was entirely clear.

"Cope was vastly civil to the little man. 'He treated me quite as the gentleman, sir,' said Elk, 'and gave me a most magnificent dinner. He had had a very bad scare given him that very morning. Some anonymous Fleet Street scoundrel had written an article about the bank-note scrape, giving the whole thing, chapter and verse. He gallantly disregarded the Court of Queen's Bench, and pronounced sentence on his own brazen hook. He pointed out that without the least doubt the whole bar could not argue Mr. Cope clear, and was kind enough to assure the young gentleman of fourteen years' toil on public works. He said that when a person of his record gets before a jury of upright tradesmen, they weren't in the habit of taking lenient views of his failings; nor is a judge, when passing sentence, able to restrain himself from making an example.

" 'Indeed, I think, sir,' said Elk, rubbing his hands, 'that it was owing to this scare that I banqueted with Mr. Cope in the dining-room. Otherwise I might have found myself taking high tea with the upper servants.'

" 'Yes, yes,' said I, 'but get to the point. Have you pinned the onus of this affair on Presse?'

"Elk grinned. 'I worked to do that, sir, from the very first moment I set foot in the house. Mr. Cope didn't like it, but I told him it was the only chance we saw of saving his own skin, and so he went away to his own room, and let me do as I pleased, without interfering. I started by overhauling Mr. Presse's photographic tackle.

" 'Ye know, sir, I'm a bit of an amateur in that line myself; got a quarter-plate, and do a touch of portrait work amongst friends against the rustic seat in my back garden; and so I could bring expert knowledge to bear on Mr. Presse's outfit.

" 'It was stowed in a hump-roofed attic which he used as a dark-room, and didn't seem to have been cared for recently. I took up the camera—an early Meagher—and examined it carefully. At first I thought the thing was sound enough, but on looking still more closely I found the bore-hole of a wood-worm barely an inch away from the lens. Now that, sir, would have formed a second superimposed picture of its own; and probably fogged everything as well. The wormhole was comparatively old, and I took it for certain that the camera had not been used since it was drilled.

" 'This, of course, didn't prove that Mr. Presse had no second camera somewhere stowed away. But I fancied he hadn't, for this reason: The developing bottles had not been used for a long time. Their shoulders were heavy with dust. The pyro. solution was black. The hypo. bottle had a cauliflower crust round its cork. Of course he might have had a second set of bottles, but that seemed rather far-fetched.

" 'The floor was swept, but on the shelves and in the sink there was evidence that the place hadn't been used as a dark-room for many a month. There was thick dust everywhere, except on one thing.

" 'Tilted by the side of the sink was an ebonite half-plate developing tray. The upper half was clean and shining: in the lower angle lay a drop or so of dark-brown liquid covered with a faintly opalescent scum. Now, that was pyrogallic developer, recently used; and I took the tray to the window to have a closer look.

" 'On one flange was a thumb-mark, faint indeed, but absolutely distinct in all its lines. Now, Mr. Presse has large hands as I have seen from his photograph, he being an enormous gentleman; and Mr. Cope has also "eights," as I noticed from himself. This thumb-mark could have been made by neither of them. It was small, and long, and delicately shaped. I fancied it was the mark of a woman's thumb, and a lady's at that.

" 'It puzzled me much. Mr. Cope is not a lady's man: he does not get on with the other sex. He told me himself that he has none but men friends to see him, and that the only women under the roof are the kitchen staff. And my thumb-mark seemed too delicate for anyone who could come from these last. But as I could think of no other way out of it, I went down to consult with Mrs. Jarrett, the housekeeper.

" 'I found Mrs. Jarrett a very nice lady, sir; much above her present station in life. She mentioned that before she had had her misfortune, she drove her own pair—'

" 'Bother Mrs. Jarrett, Elk,' said I, 'get along with your tale.'

" 'Certainly, sir. As I was saying, Mrs. Jarrett was very kind, and rendered all the information in her power. I wanted to know if she had noticed one of her staff who constantly had stained finger-ends. Mrs. Jarrett was on the point at once. There had been an under kitchen-maid whom she was always chiding at for this very fault; a nice, pleasant-spoken young woman she was, Mrs. Jarrett said, and—yes—her hands *were* small and nicely shaped, when she came to think about it. But I was rather knocked, sir, when Mrs. Jarrett told me she was gone away from the Priory. It seems that for no special cause, except a sudden spasm of temper, the young woman gave her sauce just two days before Mr. Cope's misfortune, and was bundled out of the house with a month's wages and no character, there and then. Her place had not been filled, and Mrs. Jarrett had no objection to my examining her bedroom, which had been undisturbed since she left. It was a plain enough attic room, sir—bed, chest of drawers, two cane-seated chairs, and the usual utensils; and for a good half-hour I stared about it without seeing anything suspicious. Then I trod on a drawing-pin, which was lying point uppermost on the floor, and on picking it out of my shoe, I noticed the white of plaster on the shank.'

"Elk paused, grinned, and then proceeded—

" 'There was nothing very remarkable in that, sir, you'll say. Perhaps not; but it made me stare over the walls more closely, and on one of them I saw three other pins driven into the plaster, and the hole where the fourth had been. Now, I didn't know the size of a thousand-pound Bank of England note, but I had with me the fiver you gave me for expenses, and, guessing it would be the same shape, I flattened that out over the drawing-pins on the wall. It fitted exactly. Each of the brass heads clamped a corner without the pins perforating the paper.

" 'So, thought I, that's all right. Now, where could it be photographed from? I looked round. The chest of drawers against the opposite wall would make a perfect camera stand; the gas bracket over them would give light in the right direction. I was prepared to stake a good deal that this was the first step in the process by which those fifty thousand-pound notes had been duplicated. But a lot more detailed proof was wanted before I could fill up a brief which you could handle. So I began to reason it out further.'

" 'I wish you would cut short your beautiful reasonings,' I said, 'and give me the bare result. To begin with, how are these things forged at all?'

" 'Photographed, sir,' said Elk, 'as I have shown you, from the original note on to a zinc plate covered with sensitised film. That is developed like an ordinary negative, and then placed in a bath of dilute nitric acid. The acid eats away what corresponds to the bare part of the note, leaving the lettering in bold relief. This is inked, placed in a press, and printed from on to specially watered paper in the usual way.'

" 'I see. Well, did you find the camera, and the press, and the negatives which these notes had been printed from?'

"The little man looked at me with a comical air of reproach. 'No, sir. Why, you'd hardly expect a woman who was clever enough to go through all these processes would be sufficiently green to leave the tackle behind. No, sir, when she had finished her job she sauced Mrs. Jarrett, and packed the outfit in her boxes, and went. But she did leave one or two mementos behind her. She used another attic at the end of the passage as her dark-room, a windowless, littered place which was never disturbed. Everything was well hidden even there; but, knowing what to look for, I found a good deal. She had developed on the top of a packing-case, which is all stained with her chemicals, and she poured her slops down into a hollow of the walls. She had also dropped into that niche another thing, a spoiled plate— under-exposed—of the note marked $\frac{P}{84}$ 86162. On the corner, over the drawing-pin head and a flower of the wall-paper, was a thumb mark, identically similar line for line with the thumb mark on the vulcanite developing tray.

" 'You have probably heard, sir, that the markings on the thumbs of no two individuals are the same; and on this matter——'

" 'Oh, confound you, do get on.'

" 'Yes, sir. Well, being able to do no more there just then, I ran up to town and gave at Scotland Yard an accurate description of the young person I wanted. They knew her at once—they've a remarkably wide acquaintance with a certain artistic set at the Yard, sir—and within half a dozen hours they'd got her. She was living in comfort in my own neighbourhood, Brixton; and they found in her house a light, handy lithographic press, an extremely good half-plate camera, with a rapid rectilinear lens, and several unexposed zinc plates coated with bromo-iodine emulsion. This property in itself was doubtless innocent, but in the light of what I could bring forward it was very damnatory. And, moreover, an impression of her right thumb taken in wax coincided line for line with the impressions in my possession. These facts were put before the young lady, Mr. Grayson, and I am pleased to inform you that she has owned up to making all those notes which Mr. Cope so unluckily fingered.'

"Elk rambled on a good deal more, because he wanted to go down to Bordell Priory again to gain further holiday from the gaunt sisters. His excuse was that he wished to complete the evidence. I knew that was rot, but I let him go out of gratitude. I'm afraid that's all he got out of the case, as I naturally gathered in the public *kudos* myself."

"Naturally. Then you got your man off all right?" queried O'Malley.

Grayson rubbed his hands. "Yes, and had a clinking trial of it, a regular *cause célèbre*. There were two counts, Forging and Uttering. There was no question about the Uttering, and we pleaded 'guilty as an unconscious instrument.' However, expert evidence from the Bank of England showed how marvellous had been the imitation, so I had little fear of sentence on that score. Still, we had a grand fight of it over the Forging, and some of the most head-aching inductive evidence ever heard in court. But we got a Not Guilty on it most triumphantly.

"Old Hawkins was on the Bench though, and you know his way. He couldn't resist reading Cope an improving lecture. It was, perhaps, unfair under the circumstances; but it certainly did that enterprising ass no violent harm. Master Willie Cope ripped out the old leaves and ranged himself most wonderfully afterwards; and, thanks to Presse, the estates are pretty nearly on their feet again by now."

"But what about the girl?"

"Oh, you see, she was a sinner much in request. She'd done time before for the same game, and came of a fine old criminal stock. Consequently she got it hot."

"Accomplices?"

"Were many, naturally. The whole thing was worked most scientifically by a large gang. But the girl was staunch, and she wouldn't tell. The rest of the crowd are at large to-day, and we shall probably meet some of them on the racecourse. If any of you chaps can spot one of them out, the Bank would give you more money than you're likely to make in the afternoon over backing gee-gees. Because, you see——"

The grinding of brakes made the Q.C. look out of window.

"Hullo! My faith, here we are at Aintree. How you fellows have kept me babbling. Here, tell me, someone, ought I still to get 25 to 1 about Canoptic for the National? I want him for a long shot."

L. T. MEADE and
ROBERT EUSTACE

Eliz-abeth Thomasina Meade (1854–1914), later Mrs. Smith, was born in Bandon, County Cork, Ireland. She came to London as a young woman, worked in the British Museum for a time, edited the magazine Atalanta, *and soon became one of the world's most prolific authors of girls' fiction. In addition to periodical literature, more than 250 books were published under her name, including stories built upon topical events, girls' gothics, school stories, and adventure stories. Probably none of her girls' books is read anymore, but L. T. Meade still has a large reputation in mystery story circles because of sensational episodic novels. These include (in collaboration with Robert Eustace)* A Master of Mysteries *(1898),* The Brotherhood of the Seven Kings *(1899),* The Sanctuary Club *(1900), and (in collaboration with Clifford Halifax)* Stories from the Diary of a Doctor, *which appeared in three series.*

Robert Eustace, the pseudonym of Robert Eustace Barton, M.D., made a practice of providing scientific background, ideas, and plots to other authors, who thereupon did the actual writing. His last known collaboration was with Dorothy Sayers in The Documents in the Case *(1930). His own original fiction was negligible. Almost nothing is known about Eustace, but according to Hugh Greene he lived for a time in Cornwall and was still alive in 1947.*

"The Outside Ledge"

A CABLEGRAM MYSTERY

I had not heard from my old friend Miss Cusack for some time, and was beginning to wonder whether anything was the matter with her, when on a certain Tuesday in the November of the year 1892 she called to see me.

"Dr. Lonsdale," she said, "I cannot stand defeat, and I am defeated now."

"Indeed," I replied, "this is interesting. You so seldom are defeated. What is it all about?"

"I have come here to tell you. You have heard, of course, of Oscar Hamilton, the great financier? He is the victim of a series of frauds that have been going on during the last two months and are still being perpetrated. So persistent and so unaccountable are they that the cleverest agents in London have been employed to detect them, but without result. His chief dealings are, as you know, in South African Gold Mines, and his income is, I believe, nearer fifty than thirty thousand a year. From time to time he receives private advices as to the gold crushings, and operates accordingly. You will say, of course, that he gambles, and that such gambling is not very scrupulous, but I assure you the matter is not at all looked at in that light on the Stock Exchange.

"Now, there is a dealer in the same market, a Mr. Gildford, who, by some means absolutely unknown, obtains the same advice in detail, and of course either forestalls Mr. Hamilton, or, on the other hand, discounts the profits he would make, by buying or selling exactly the same shares. The information, I am given to understand, is usually cabled to Oscar Hamilton in cipher by his confidential agent in South Africa, whose *bona fides* is unquestionable, since it is he who profits by Mr. Hamilton's gains.

"This important information arrives as a rule in the early morning about nine o'clock, and is put straight into my friend's hands in his office in Lennox Court. The details are discussed by him and his partner, Mr. Le Marchant, and he immediately afterwards goes to his broker to do whatever business is decided on. Now, this special broker's name is Edward Gregory, and time after time, not invariably, but very often, Mr. Gregory has gone into the house and found Mr. Gildford doing the identical deals that he was about to do."

"That is strange," I answered.

"It is; but you must listen further. To give you an idea of how every channel possible has been watched, I will tell you what has been done. In the first place it is practically certain that the information found its way from Mr. Hamilton's office to Mr. Gildford's, because no one knows the cipher except Mr. Hamilton and his partner, Mr. Le Marchant."

"Wireless telegraphy," I suggested.

Miss Cusack smiled, but shook her head.

"Listen," she said. "Mr. Gildford, the dealer, is a man who also has an office in Lennox Court, four doors from the office of Mr. Hamilton, also close to the Stock Exchange. He has one small room on the third floor back, and has no clerks. Now Mr. Gregory, Mr. Hamilton's broker, has his office in Draper's Gardens. Yesterday morning an important cable was expected, and extraordinary precautions were adopted. Two detectives were placed in the house of Mr. Gildford, of course unknown to him—one actually took up his position on the landing outside his door, so that no one could enter by the door without being seen. Another was at the telephone exchange to watch if any message went through that way. Thus you will see that telegrams and telephones were equally cut off.

"A detective was also in Mr. Hamilton's office when the cable arrived, the object of his presence being known to the clerks, who were not allowed to use the telephone or to leave the office. The cable was opened in the presence of the younger partner, Mr. Le Marchant, and also in the presence of the detective, by Mr. Hamilton himself. No one left the office, and no communication with the outside world took place. Thus, both at Mr. Gildford's office and at Mr. Hamilton's, had the information passed by any visible channel it must have been detected either leaving the former office or arriving at the latter."

"And what happened?" I inquired, beginning to be much interested in this strange story.

"You will soon know what happened. I call it witchery. In about ten minutes' time Mr. Hamilton left his office to visit his broker, Mr. Gregory, at the Stock Exchange, everyone else, including his partner, Mr. Le Marchant, remaining in the office. On his arrival at the Stock Exchange he told Mr. Gregory what he wanted done. The latter went to carry out his wishes, but came back after a few moments to say that the market was spoiled, Mr. Gildford having just arrived and dealt heavily in the very same shares and in the same manner. What do you make of it, Dr. Lonsdale?"

"There is only one conclusion for me to arrive at," I answered; "the information does not pass between the offices, but by some previously arranged channel."

"I should have agreed with you but for one circumstance, which I am now going to confide to you. Do you remember a pretty girl, a certain Evelyn Dudley, whom you once met at my house? She is the only daughter of Colonel Dudley of the Coldstream Guards, and at her father's death will be worth about seven thousand a year."

"Well, and what has she to do with the present state of things?"

"Only this: she is engaged to Mr. Le Marchant, and the wedding will take place next week. They are both going to dine with me to-night. I want you to join the party in order that you may meet them and let me know frankly afterwards what you think of him."

"But what has that to do with the frauds?" I asked.

"Everything, and this is why," She lowered her voice, and said in an emphatic whisper, "I have strong reasons for suspecting Mr. Le Marchant, Mr. Hamilton's young partner, of being in the plot."

"Good heavens!" I cried, "you cannot mean that. The frauds are to his own loss."

"Not at all. He has only at present a small share in the business. Yesterday from a very private source I learned that he was in great financial difficulties, and in the hands of some money-lenders; in short, I imagine—mind, I don't accuse him yet—that he is staving off his crash until he can marry Evelyn Dudley, when he hopes to right himself. If the crash came first, Colonel Dudley would not allow the marriage. But when it is a *fait accompli* he will be, as it were, forced to do something to prevent his son-in-law going under. Now I think you know about as much of the situation as I do myself. Evelyn is a dear friend of mine, and if I can prevent it I don't want her to marry a scoundrel. We dine at eight—it is now past seven, so if you will dress quickly I can drive you back in my brougham. Evelyn is to spend the night with me, and is already at my house. She will entertain you till I am ready. If nothing happens to prevent it, the wedding is to take place next Monday. You see, therefore, there is no time to lose in clearing up the mystery."

"There certainly is not," I replied, rising. "Well, if you will kindly wait here I will not keep you many minutes."

I went up to my room, dressed quickly, and returned in a very short time. We entered the brougham which was standing at the door, and at once drove off to Miss Cusack's house. She ushered me into the drawing-room, where a tall, dark-eyed girl was standing by the fire.

"Evelyn," said Miss Cusack, "you have often heard me talk of my great friend Dr. Lonsdale. I have just persuaded him to dine with us to-night. Dr. Lonsdale, may I introduce you to Miss Evelyn Dudley?"

I took the hand which Evelyn Dudley stretched out to me. She had an attractive, bright face, and during Miss Cusack's absence we each engaged the other in brisk conversation. I spoke about Miss Cusack, and the girl was warm in her admiration.

"She is my best friend," she said. "I lost my mother two years ago, and at that time I do not know what I should have done but for Florence Cusack. She took me to her house and kept me with her for some time, and taught me what the sin of rebellion meant. I loved my mother so passionately. I did not think when she was taken from me that I should ever know a happy hour again."

"And now, if report tells true, you are going to be very happy," I continued, "for Miss Cusack has confided some of your story to me. You are soon to be married?"

"Yes," she answered, and she looked thoughtful. After a moment she spoke again.

"You are right: I hope to be very happy in the future—happier than I have ever been before. I love Henry Le Marchant better than anyone else on earth."

I felt a certain pity for her as she spoke. After all, Miss Cusack's intuitions were wonderful, and she did not like Henry Le Marchant—nay, more, she suspected him of underhand dealings. Surely she must be wrong. I hoped when I saw this young man that I should be able to divert my friend's suspicions into another channel.

"I hope you will be happy," I said; "you have my best wishes."

"Thank you," she replied. She sat down near the fire as she spoke, and unfurled her fan.

"Ah! there is a ring," she said, the next moment. "He is coming. You know perhaps that he is dining here to-night. I shall be so pleased to introduce you."

At the same instant Miss Cusack entered the room.

"Our guest has arrived," she said, looking from Miss Dudley to me, and she had scarcely uttered the words before Henry Le Marchant was announced.

He was a tall, young-looking man, with a black, short moustache and very dark eyes. His manner was easy and self-possessed, and he looked with frank interest at me when his hostess introduced him.

The next moment dinner was announced. As the meal proceeded and I was considering in what words I could convey to Miss Cusack my impression that she was altogether on a wrong tack, something occurred which I thought very little of at the time, but yet was destined to lead to most important results presently.

The servant had just left the room when a slight whiff of some peculiar and rather disagreeable odour caught my nostrils. I was glancing across the table to see if it was due to any particular fruit, when I noticed that Miss Cusack had also caught the smell.

"What a curious sort of perfume!" she said, frowning slightly. "Evelyn, have you been buying any special new scent today?"

"Certainly not," replied Miss Dudley; "I hate scent, and never use it."

At the same moment Le Marchant, who had taken his handkerchief from his pocket, quickly replaced it, and a wave of blood suffused his swarthy cheeks, leaving them the next instant ashy pale. His embarrassment was so obvious that none of us could help noticing it.

"Surely that is the smell of valerian," I said, as the memory of what it was came to me.

"Yes, it is," he replied, recovering his composure and forcing a smile. "I must apologise to you all. I have been rather nervous lately, and have been ordered a few drops of valerian in water. I cannot think how it got on my handkerchief. My doctor prescribed it for me yesterday."

Miss Cusack made a common-place reply, and the conversation went on as before.

Perhaps my attitude of mind was preternaturally suspicious, but it occurred to me that Le Marchant's explanation was a very lame one. Valerian is not often ordered for a man of his evidently robust health, and I wondered if he were speaking the truth.

Having a case of some importance to attend, I took my departure shortly afterward.

During the three following days I heard nothing further from Miss Cusack, and made up my mind that her conjectures were all wrong and that the wedding would of course take place.

But on Saturday these hopes were destined to be rudely dispersed. I was awakened at an early hour by my servant, who entered with a note. I saw at once that it was in Miss Cusack's handwriting, and tore it open with some apprehension. The contents were certainly startling. It ran as follows—

"I want your help. Serious developments. Meet me on Royal Exchange steps at nine this morning. Do not fail."

After breakfast I sent for a cab, and drove at once to the city, alighting close to the Bank of England. The streets were thronged with the usual incoming flux of clerks hurrying to their different offices. I made my way across to the Royal Exchange, and the first person I saw was Miss Cusack standing just at the entrance. She turned to me eagerly.

"This is good of you, doctor; I shall not forget this kindness in a hurry. Come quickly, will you?"

We entered the throng, and moved rapidly down Bartholomew Lane into Throgmorton Street; then, turning round sharp to the left, found ourselves in Lennox Court.

I followed my guide with the greatest curiosity, wondering what could be her plans. The next moment we entered a house, and, threading our way up some bare, uncarpeted stairs, reached the top landing. Here Miss Cusack opened a door with a key which she had with her, pushed me into a small room, entered herself, and locked the door behind us both. I glanced around in some alarm.

The little room was quite bare, and here and there round the walls were the marks of where office furniture had once stood. The window looked out on to the backs of the houses in Lennox Court.

"Now we must act quickly," she said. "At 9.30 an important cable will reach Mr. Hamilton's office. This room in which we now find ourselves is next door to Mr. Gildford's office in the next house, and is between that and Mr. Hamilton's office two doors further down. I have rented this room—a quarter's rent for one morning's work. Well, if I am successful, the price will be cheap. It was great luck to get it at all."

"But what are you going to do?" I queried, as she proceeded to open the window and peep cautiously out.

"You will see directly," she answered; "keep back, and don't make a noise."

She leant out and drew the ends of her boa along the little ledge that ran outside just below the window. She then drew it in rapidly.

"Ah, ha! do you remember that, Dr. Lonsdale?" she cried softly, raising the boa to my face.

I started back and regarded her in amazement.

"Valerian!" I exclaimed. "Miss Cusack, what is this strange mystery?"

"Hush! not another word yet," she said. Her eyes sparkled with excitement. She rapidly produced a pair of very thick doeskin gloves, put them on, and stood by the window in an attitude of the utmost alertness. I stood still in the middle of the room, wondering whether I was in a dream, or whether Miss Cusack had taken leave of her senses.

The moments passed by, and still she stood rigid and tense as if expecting something. I watched her in wonderment, not attempting to say a word.

We must have remained in this extraordinary situation fully a quarter of an hour, when I saw her bend forward, her hand shot out of the window, and with an inconceivably rapid thrust she drew it back. She was now grasping by the back of the neck a large tabby cat; its four legs were drawn up with claws extended, and it was wriggling in evident dislike at being captured.

"A cat!" I cried, in the most utter and absolute bewilderment.

"Yes, a cat; a sweet pretty cat, too; aren't you, pussy?" She knelt down and began to stroke the creature, who changed its mind and rubbed itself against her in evident pleasure. The next moment it darted towards her fur boa and began sniffing at it greedily. As it did so Miss Cusack deftly stripped off a leather collar round its neck. A cry of delight broke from her lips as, unfastening a clasp that held an inner flap to the outer leather covering, she drew out a slip of paper.

"In Henry Le Marchant's handwriting," she cried. "What a scoundrel! We have him now."

"Henry Le Marchant's handwriting!" I exclaimed, bending over the slip as she held it in her hand.

"Yes," she answered; "see!"

I read with bated breath the brief communication which the tiny piece of paper contained. It was beyond doubt a replica of the telegram which must have arrived at Hamilton's office a few moments ago. Miss Cusack also read the words. She flung the piece of paper to the ground. I picked it up.

"We must keep this, it is evidence," I said.

"Yes," she answered, "but this has upset me. I have heard of some curious methods of communication, but never such a one as this before. It was the wildest chance, but thank God it has succeeded. We shall save Evelyn from marrying a man with whom her life would have been intolerable."

"But what could have led you to this extraordinary result?" I said.

"A chain of reasoning starting on the evening we dined together," she replied. "What puzzled me was this. What had Henry Le Marchant to do with valerian on his handkerchief? It was that fact which set me thinking. His explanation of using it as a nerve sedative was so obviously a lie on the face of it, and his embarrassment was so evident, that I did not trouble myself with this way out of the mystery for a single moment. I went through every conceivable hypothesis with regard to valerian, but it was not till I looked up its properties in a medical book that the first clue came to me. Valerian is, as you of course know, doctor, a plant which has a sort of intoxicating, almost maddening effect on cats, so much so that they will search out and follow the smell to the exclusion of any other desire. They are an independent race of creatures, and not easily trained like a dog. Then the amazing possibility suggested itself to me that the method employed by Mr. Le Marchant to communicate with Mr. Gildford, which has nonplussed every detective in London, was the very simple one of employing a cat.

"Come to the window and I will explain. You see that narrow ledge along which our friend pussy strolled so leisurely a moment ago. It runs, as you perceive, straight from Mr. Hamilton's office to that of Mr. Gildford. All Mr. Gildford had to do was to sprinkle some valerian along the ledge close to his own window. The peculiar smell would be detected by a cat quite as far off as the house where Mr. Hamilton's office is. I thought this all out, and, being pretty sure that my surmises were correct, I called yesterday on Henry Le Marchant at the office with the express purpose of seeing if there was a cat there.

"I went with a message from Evelyn. Nestling on his knee as he sat at his table writing in his private room was this very animal. Even then, of course, there was no certainty about my suspicions, but in view of the event which hung upon them—namely, his marriage to Evelyn—I was determined to spare no pains or trouble to put them to the test. I have done so, and, thank God, in time. But come, my course now is clear. I have a painful duty before me, and there is not a moment to lose."

As Miss Cusack spoke she took up her fur boa, flicked it slowly backwards and forwards to remove the taint of the valerian, and put it round her neck.

Five minutes later we were both communicating her extraordinary story to the ears of one of the sharpest detectives in London. Before that night Henry Le Marchant and James Gildford were both condemned to suffer the severest punishment that the law prescribes in such cases.

But why follow their careers any further? Evelyn's heart very nearly broke, but did not quite, and I am glad to be able to add that she has married a man in every respect worthy of her.

ARTHUR MORRISON

(1863–1945) was one of the leaders in the development of naturalistic fiction in England in the 1890s. His Tales of Mean Streets *(1894) and* A Child of the Jago *(1896) are still read as classic studies of the sordidness and hopelessness of slum life. In a different vein, however, were his detective stories about Martin Hewitt. They have been characterized as the second-best stories from the era of Sherlock Holmes, only Doyle's stories being superior. Morrison's stories are pleasantly written tales, well structured, and often very imaginative. They are gathered into book form as* Martin Hewitt, Investigator *(1894),* Chronicles of Martin Hewitt *(1895), and* Adventures of Martin Hewitt *(1896).*

About Morrison little biographical information is available, since he was a very secretive man. Born in the slums of London, the son of a steamfitter, self-educated, he eventually became one of the leading writers of his time. After the turn of the century he wrote little and devoted himself to the study of Oriental art, on which he became one of the world's authorities.

"The Case of the Late Mr. Rewse"

Of this case I personally saw nothing beyond the first advent in Hewitt's office of Mr. Horace Bowyer, who put the case in his hands, and then I merely saw Mr. Bowyer's back as I passed down stairs from my rooms. But I noted the case in full detail after Hewitt's return from Ireland, as it seemed to me one not entirely without interest, if only as an exemplar of the fatal case with which a man may unwittingly dig a pit for his own feet—a pit from which there is no climbing out.

A few moments after I had seen the stranger disappear into Hewitt's office, Kerrett brought to Hewitt in his inner room a visitor's slip announcing the arrival on urgent business of Mr. Horace Bowyer. That the visitor was in a hurry was plain from a hasty rattling of the closed wicket in the outer room where Mr. Bowyer was evidently making impatient attempts to follow his announcement in person. Hewitt showed himself at the door and invited Mr. Bowyer to enter, which he did, as soon as Kerrett had released the wicket, with much impetuosity. He was a stout, florid gentleman with a loud voice and a large stare.

"Mr. Hewitt," he said, "I must claim your immediate attention to a business of the utmost gravity. Will you please consider yourself commissioned, wholly regardless of expense, to set aside whatever you may have in hand and devote yourself to the case I shall put in your hands?"

"Certainly not," Hewitt replied with a slight smile. "What I have in hand are matters which I have engaged to attend to, and no mere compensation for loss of fees could persuade me to leave my clients in the lurch, else what would prevent some other gentleman coming here to-morrow with a bigger fee than yours and bribing me away from you?"

"But this—this is a most serious thing, Mr. Hewitt. A matter of life or death—it is indeed!"

"Quite so," Hewitt replied: "but there are a thousand such matters at this moment pending of which you and I know nothing, and there are also two or three more of which you know nothing but on which I am at work. So that it becomes a question of practicability. If you will tell me your business I can judge whether or not I may be able to accept your commission concurrently with those I have in hand. Some operations take months of constant attention; some can be conducted intermittently; others still are a mere matter of a few days—many of hours simply."

"I will tell you then," Mr. Bowyer replied. "In the first place, will you have the kindness to read that? It is a cutting from the *Standard*'s column of news from the provinces of two days ago."

Hewitt took the cutting and read as follows:—

"The epidemic of small-pox in County Mayo, Ireland, shows few signs of abating. The spread of the disease has been very remarkable considering the widely-scattered nature of the population, though there can be no doubt that the market towns are the centres of infection, and that it is from these that the germs of contagion are carried into the country by people from all parts who resort thither on market days. In many cases the disease has assumed a particularly malignant form, and deaths have been very rapid and numerous. The comparatively few medical men available are sadly overworked, owing largely to the distances separating their different patients. Among those who have succumbed within the last few days is Mr. Algernon Rewse, a young English gentleman who has been staying with a friend at a cottage a few miles from Cullanin, on a fishing excursion."

Hewitt placed the cutting on the table at his side. "Yes?" he said inquiringly. "It is to Mr. Algernon Rewse's death you wish to draw my attention?"

"It is," Mr. Bowyer answered; "and the reason I come to you is that I very much suspect—more than suspect, indeed—that Mr. Algernon Rewse has *not* died by smallpox, but has been murdered—murdered cold-bloodedly, and for the most sordid motives, by the friend who has been sharing his holiday."

"In what way do you suppose him to have been murdered?"

"That I cannot say—that, indeed, I want you to find out, among other things—chiefly perhaps, the murderer himself, who has made off."

"And your own status in the matter," queried Hewitt, "is that of ——?"

"I am trustee under a will by which Mr. Rewse would have benefited considerably had he lived but a month or two longer. That circumstance indeed lies rather near the root of the matter. The thing stood thus. Under the will I speak of—that of young Rewse's uncle, a very old friend of mine in his lifetime—the money lay in trust till the young fellow should attain twenty-five years of age. His younger sister, Miss Mary Rewse, was also benefited, but to a much smaller extent. She was to come into her property also on attaining the age of twenty-five, or on her marriage, whichever event happened first. It was further provided that in case either of these young people died before coming into the inheritance, his or her share should go to the survivor. I want you particularly to remember this. You will observe that now, in consequence of young Algernon Rewse's death, barely two months before his twenty-fifth birthday, the whole of the very large property—all personalty, and free from any tie or restriction—which would otherwise have been his, will, in the regular course, pass, on her twenty-fifth birthday, *or on her marriage*, to Miss Mary Rewse, whose own legacy was comparatively trifling. You will understand the importance of this when I tell you that the man whom I suspect of causing Algernon Rewse's death, and who has been his companion on his otherwise lonely holiday, is engaged to be married to Miss Rewse."

Mr. Bowyer paused at this, but Hewitt only raised his eyebrows and nodded.

"I have never particularly liked the man," Mr. Bowyer went on. "He never seemed to have much to say for himself. I like a man who holds up his head and opens his mouth. I don't believe in the sort of modesty that he showed so much of—it isn't genuine. A man can't afford to be genuinely meek and retiring who has his way to make in the world—and he was clever enough to know *that*."

"He is poor, then?" Hewitt asked.

"Oh yes, poor enough. His name, by-the-bye, is Main—Stanley Main—and he is a medical man. He hasn't been practising, except as assistant, since he became qualified, the reason being, I understand, that he couldn't afford to buy a good practice. He is the person who will profit by young Rewse's death—or at any rate who intended to; but we will see about that. As for Mary, poor girl, she wouldn't have lost her brother for fifty fortunes."

"As to the circumstances of the death, now?"

"Yes, yes, I am coming to that. Young Algernon Rewse, you must know, had rather run down in health, and Main persuaded him that he wanted a change. I don't know what it was altogether, but Rewse seemed to have been having his own little love troubles and that sort of thing, you know. He'd been engaged, I think, or very nearly so, and the young lady died, and so on. Well, as I said, he had run down and got into low health and spirits, and no doubt a change of some sort would have done him good. This Stanley Main always seemed to have a great influence over the poor boy—he was four or five years older than Rewse—and somehow he persuaded him to go away, the two together, to some outlandish wilderness of a place in the West of Ireland for salmon-fishing. It seemed to me at the time rather a ridiculous sort of place to go to, but Main had his way, and they went. There was a cottage—rather a good sort of cottage, I believe, for the district—which some friend of Main's, once a landowner in the district, had put up as a convenient box for salmon-fishing, and they rented it. Not long after they got there this epidemic of small-pox got about in the district—though that, I believe, has had little to do with poor young Rewse's death. All appeared to go well until a day over a week ago, when Mrs. Rewse received this letter from Main." Mr. Bowyer handed Martin Hewitt a letter, written in an irregular and broken hand, as though of a person writing under stress of extreme agitation. It ran thus:—

"My dear Mrs. Rewse,—"You will probably have heard through the newspapers—indeed I think Algernon has told you in his letters—that a very bad epidemic of small-pox is abroad in this district. I am deeply grieved to have to tell you that Algernon himself has taken the disease in a rather bad form. He showed the first symptoms to-day (Tuesday), and he is now in bed in the cottage. It is fortunate that I, as a medical man, happen to be on the spot, as the nearest local doctor is five miles off at Cullanin, and he is working and travelling night and day as it is. I have my little medicine chest with me, and can get whatever else is necessary from Cullanin, so that everything is being done for Algernon that is possible, and I hope to bring him up to scratch in good health soon, though of course the disease is a dangerous one. Pray don't unnecessarily alarm yourself, and don't think about coming over here, or anything of that sort. You can do no good, and will only run risk yourself. I will take care to let you know how things go on, so please don't attempt to come. The journey is long and would be very trying to you, and you would have no place to stay at nearer than Cullanin, which is quite a centre of infection. I will write again to-morrow.—Yours most sincerely,

STANLEY MAIN."

Not only did the handwriting of this letter show signs of agitation, but here and there words had been repeated, and sometimes a letter had been omitted. Hewitt placed the letter on the table by the newspaper cutting, and Mr. Bowyer proceeded.

"Another letter followed on the next day," he said, handing it to Hewitt as he spoke; "a short one, as you see; not written with quite such signs of agitation. It merely says that Rewse is very bad, and repeats the former entreaties that his mother will not think of going to him. Hewitt glanced at the letter and placed it with the other, while Mr. Bowyer continued: "Notwithstanding Main's persistent anxiety that she should stay at home, Mrs. Rewse, who was of course terribly worried about her only son, had almost made up her mind, in spite of her very delicate health, to start for Ireland, when she received a third letter announcing Algernon's death. Here it is. It is certainly the sort of letter that one might expect to be written in such circumstances, and yet there seems to me at least a certain air of disingenuousness about the wording. There are, as you see, the usual condolences, and so forth. The disease was of the malignant type, it says, which is terribly rapid in its action, often carrying off the patient even before the eruption has time to form. Then—and this is a thing I wish you especially to note—there is once more a repetition of his desire that neither the young man's mother nor his sister shall come to Ireland. The funeral must take place immediately, he says, under arrangements made by the local authorities, and before they could reach the spot. Now doesn't this obtrusive anxiety of his that no connection of young Rewse's should be near him during his illness, nor even at the funeral, strike you as rather singular?"

"Well, possibly it is: though it may easily be nothing but zeal for the health of Mrs. Rewse and her daughter. As a matter of fact what Main says is very plausible. They could do no sort of good in the circumstances, and might easily run into danger themselves, to say nothing of the fatigue of the journey and general nervous upset. Mrs. Rewse is in weak health, I think you said?"

"Yes, she's almost an invalid in fact; she is subject to heart disease. But tell me now, as an entirely impartial observer, doesn't it seem to you that there is a very forced, unreal sort of tone in all these letters?"

"Perhaps one may notice something of the sort, but fifty things may cause that. The case from the beginning may have been worse than he made it out. What ensued on the receipt of this letter?"

"Mrs. Rewse was prostrated, of course. Her daughter communicated with me as a friend of the family, and that is how I heard of the whole thing for the first time. I saw the letters, and it seemed to me, looking at all the circumstances of the case, that somebody at least ought to go over and make certain that everything was as it should be. Here was this poor young man, staying in a lonely cottage with the only man in the world who had any reason to desire his death, or any profit to gain by it, and he had a very great inducement indeed. Moreover he was a medical man, *carrying his medicine chest with him*, remember, as he says himself in his letter. In this situation Rewse suddenly dies, with nobody about him, so far as there is anything to show, but Main himself. As his medical attendant it would be Main who would certify and register the death, and no matter what foul play might have taken place he would be safe as long as nobody was on the spot to make searching inquiries—might easily escape even then, in fact. When one man is likely to profit much by the death of another a doctor's medicine chest is likely to supply but too easy a means to his end."

"Did you say anything of your suspicions to the ladies?"

"Well—well I hinted perhaps—no more than hinted, you know. But they wouldn't hear of it—got indignant, and 'took on' as people call it, worse than ever, so that I had to smooth them over. But since it seemed somebody's duty to see into the matter a little more closely, and there seemed to be nobody to do it but myself, I started off that very evening by the night mail. I was in Dublin early the next morning and spent that day getting across Ireland. The nearest station was ten miles from Cullanin, and that, as you remember, was five miles from the cottage, so that I drove over on the morning of the following day. I must say Main appeared very much taken aback at seeing me. His manner was nervous and apprehensive, and made me more suspicious than ever. The body had been buried, of course, a couple of days or more. I asked a few rather searching questions about the illness, and so forth, and his answers became positively confused. He had burned the clothes that Rewse was wearing at the time the disease first showed itself, he said, as well as all the bedclothes, since there was no really efficient means of disinfection at hand. His story in the main was that he had gone off to Cullanin one morning on foot to see about a top joint of a fishing-rod that was to be repaired. When he returned early in the afternoon he found Algernon Rewse sickening of small-pox, at once put him to bed, and there nursed him till he died. I wanted to know, of course, why no other medical man had been called in. He said that there was only one available, and it was doubtful if he could have been got at even a day's notice, so overworked was he; moreover he said this man, with his hurry and over-strain, could never have given the patient such efficient attention as he himself, who had nothing else to do. After a while I put it to him plainly that it would at any rate have been more prudent to have had the body at least inspected by some independent doctor, considering the fact that he was likely to profit so largely by young Rewse's death, and I suggested that with an exhumation order it might not be too late now, as a matter of justice to himself. The effect of that convinced me. The man gasped and turned blue with terror. It was a full minute, I should think, before he could collect himself sufficiently to attempt to dissuade me from doing what I had hinted at. He did so as soon as he could think of—entreated me in fact almost desperately. That decided me. I said that after what he had said, and particularly in view of his whole manner and bearing, I should insist, by every means in my power, on having the body properly examined, and I went off at once to Cullanin to set the telegraph going, and see whatever local authority might be proper. When I returned in the afternoon Stanley Main had packed his bag and vanished, and I have not heard nor seen anything of him since. I stayed in the neighbourhood that day and the next, and left for London in the evening. By the help of my solicitors proper representations were made at the Home Office, and, especially in view of Main's flight, a prompt order was made for exhumation and medical examination preliminary to an inquest. I am expecting to hear that the disinterment has been effected to-day. What I want you to do of course is chiefly to find Main. The Irish constabulary in that district are fine big men, and no doubt most excellent in quelling a faction fight or shutting up a shebeen, but I doubt their efficiency in anything requiring much more finesse. Perhaps also you may be able to find out something of the means by which the murder—it is plain it is one—was committed. It is quite possible that Main may have adopted some means to give the body the appearance, even to a medical man, of death from small-pox."

"That," Hewitt said, "is scarcely likely, else, indeed, why did he not take care that another doctor should see the body before the burial? That would have secured him. But that is not a thing one can deceive a doctor over. Of course in the circumstances exhumation is desirable, but if the case is one of small-pox, I don't envy the medical man who is to examine. At any rate the business is, I should imagine, not likely to be a very long one, and I can take it in hand at once. I will leave to-night for Ireland by the 6.30 train from Euston."

"Very good. I shall go over myself, of course. If anything comes to my knowledge in the meanwhile, of course I'll let you know."

An hour or two after this a cab stopped at the door, and a young lady dressed in black sent in her name and a minute later was shown into Hewitt's room. It was Miss Mary Rewse. She wore a heavy veil, and all she said she uttered in evidently deep distress of mind. Hewitt did what he could to calm her, and waited patiently.

At length, she said: "I felt that I must come to you, Mr. Hewitt, and yet now that I am here I don't know what to say. Is it the fact that Mr. Bowyer has commissioned you to investigate the circumstances of my poor brother's death, and to discover the whereabouts of Mr. Main?"

"Yes, Miss Rewse, that is the fact. Can you tell me anything that will help me?"

"No, no, Mr. Hewitt, I fear not. But it is such a dreadful thing, and Mr. Bowyer is—I'm afraid he is so much prejudiced against Mr. Main that I felt I ought to do something—to say something at least to prevent you entering on the case with your mind made up that he has been guilty of such an awful thing. He is really quite incapable of it, I assure you."

"Pray, Miss Rewse," Hewitt replied, "don't allow that apprehension to disturb you. If Mr. Main is, as you say, incapable of such an act as perhaps he is suspected of, you may rest assured no harm will come to him. So far as I am concerned at any rate I enter the case with a perfectly open mind. A man in my profession who accepted prejudices at the beginning of a case would have very poor results to show indeed. As yet I have no opinion, no theory, no prejudice, nothing indeed but a large outline of facts. I shall derive no opinion and no theory from anything but a consideration of the actual circumstances and evidences on the spot. I quite understand the relation in which Mr. Main stands in regard to yourself and your family. Have you heard from him lately?"

"Not since the letter informing us of my brother's death."

"Before then?"

Miss Rewse hesitated. "Yes," she said, "we corresponded. But—but there was really nothing—the letters were of a personal and private sort—they were——"

"Yes, yes, of course," Hewitt answered, with his eyes fixed keenly on the veil which Miss Rewse still kept down. "Of course I understand that. Then there is nothing else you can tell me?"

"No, I fear not. I can only implore you to remember that no matter what you may see and hear, no matter what the evidence may be, I am sure, sure, *sure* that poor Stanley could never do such a thing." And Miss Rewse buried her face in her hands.

Hewitt kept his eyes on the lady, though he smiled slightly, and asked, "How long have you known Mr. Main?"

"For some five or six years now. My poor brother knew him at school, though of course they were in different forms, Mr. Main being the elder."

"Were they always on good terms?"

"They were always like brothers."

Little more was said. Hewitt condoled with Miss Rewse as well as he might, and she presently took her departure. Even as she descended the stairs a messenger came with a short note for Mr. Bowyer enclosing a telegram just received from Cullanin. The telegram ran thus:—

Body exhumed. Death from shot-wound. No trace of small-pox. Nothing yet heard of Main. Have communicated with coroner.—O'Reilly.

II.

Hewitt and Mr. Bowyer travelled towards Mayo together, Mr. Bowyer restless and loquacious on the subject of the business in hand, and Hewitt rather bored thereby. He resolutely declined to offer an opinion on any single detail of the case till he had examined the available evidence, and his occasional remarks on matters of general interest, the scenery and so forth, struck his companion, unused to business of the sort which had occasioned the journey, as strangely cold-blooded and indifferent. Telegrams had been sent ordering that no disarrangement of the contents of the cottage was to be allowed pending their arrival, and Hewitt well knew that nothing more was practicable till the site was reached. At Ballymaine, where the train was left at last, they stayed for the night, and left early the next morning for Cullanin, where a meeting with Dr. O'Reilly at the mortuary had been appointed. There the body lay stripped of its shroud, calm and gray, and beginning to grow ugly, with a scarcely noticeable breach in the flesh of the left breast.

"The wound has been thoroughly cleansed, closed and stopped with a carbolic plug before interment," Dr. O'Reilly said. He was a middle-aged, grizzled man, with a face whereon many recent sleepless nights had left their traces. "I have not thought it necessary to do anything in the way of dissection. The bullet is not present, it has passed clean through the body, between the ribs both back and front, piercing the heart on its way. The death must have been instantaneous."

Hewitt quickly examined the two wounds, back and front, as

the doctor turned the body over, and then asked: "Perhaps, Dr. O'Reilly, you have some experience of a gunshot wound before this?"

The doctor smiled grimly. "I think so," he answered, with just enough of brogue in his words to hint his nationality and no more. "I was an army surgeon for a good many years before I came to Cullanin, and saw service in Ashanti and in India."

"Come then," Hewitt said, "you're an expert. Would it have been possible for the shot to have been fired from behind?"

"Oh, no. See! the bullet entering makes a wound of quite a different character from that of the bullet leaving."

"Have you any idea of the weapon used?"

"A large revolver, I should think; perhaps of the regulation size; that is, I should judge the bullet to have been a conical one of about the size fitted to such a weapon—smaller than that from a rifle."

"Can you form an idea of from what distance the shot was fired?"

Dr. O'Reilly shook his head. "The clothes have all been burned," he said, "and the wound has been washed, otherwise one might have looked for powder blackening."

"Did you know either the dead man or Dr. Main personally?"

"Only very slightly. I may say I saw just such a pistol as might cause that sort of wound in his hands the day before he gave out that Rewse had been attacked by small-pox. I drove past the cottage as he stood in the doorway with it in his hand. He had the breach opened, and seemed to be either loading or unloading it—which it was I couldn't say."

"Very good, doctor, that may be important. Now is there any single circumstance, incident or conjecture that you can tell me of in regard to this case that you have not already mentioned?"

Doctor O'Reilly thought for a moment, and replied in the negative. "I heard of course," he said, "of the reported new case of small-pox, and that Main had taken the case in hand himself. I was indeed relieved to hear it, for I had already more on my hands than one man can safely be expected to attend to. The cottage was fairly isolated, and there could have been nothing gained by removal to an asylum—indeed there was practically no accommodation. So far as I can make out nobody seems to have seen young Rewse, alive or dead, after Main had announced that he had the small-pox. He seems to have done everything himself, laying out the body and all, and you may be pretty sure that none of the strangers about was particularly anxious to have anything to do with it. The undertaker (there is only one here, and he is down with the small-pox himself now) was as much overworked as I was myself, and was glad enough to send off a coffin by a market cart and leave the laying out and screwing down to Main, since he had got those orders. Main made out the death certificate himself, and, since he was trebly qualified, everything seemed in order."

"The certificate merely attributed the death to small-pox, I take it, with no qualifying remarks?"

"Small-pox, simply."

Hewitt and Mr. Bowyer bade Dr. O'Reilly good morning, and their car was turned in the direction of the cottage where Algernon Rewse had met his death. At the Town Hall in the market place, however, Hewitt stopped the car and set his watch by the public clock. "This is more than half an hour before London time," he said, "and we mustn't be at odds with the natives about the time."

As he spoke, Dr. O'Reilly came running up breathlessly. "I've just heard something," he said. "Three men heard a shot in the cottage as they were passing, last Tuesday week."

"Where are the men?"

"I don't know at the moment; but they can be found. Shall I set about it?"

"If you possibly can," Hewitt said, "you will help us enormously. Can you send them messages to be at the cottage as soon as they can get there to-day? Tell them they shall have a half-a-sovereign apiece."

"Right, I will. Good-day."

"Tuesday week," said Mr. Bowyer as they drove off; "that was the date of Main's first letter, and the day on which, by his account, Rewse was taken ill. Then if that was the shot that killed Rewse he must have been lying dead in the place while Main was writing those letters reporting his sickness to his mother. The cold-blooded scoundrel!"

"Yes," Hewitt replied, "I think it probable in any case that Tuesday was the day that Rewse was shot. It wouldn't have been safe for Main to write the mother lying letters about the small-pox before. Rewse might have written home in the meantime, or something might have occurred to postpone Main's plans, and then there would be impossible explanations required."

Over a very bad road they jolted on and in the end arrived where the road, now become a mere path, passed a tumble-down old farmhouse.

"This is where the woman lives who cooked and cleaned house for Rewse and Main," Mr. Bowyer said. "There is the cottage, scarce a hundred yards off, a little to the right of the track."

"Well," replied Hewitt, "suppose we stop here and ask her a few questions? I like to get the evidence of all the witnesses as soon as possible. It simplifies subsequent work wonderfully."

They alighted, and Mr. Bowyer roared through the open door

and tapped with his stick. In reply to his summons a decent-looking woman of perhaps fifty, but wrinkled beyond her age, and better dressed than any woman Hewitt had seen since leaving Cullanin, appeared from the hinder buildings and curtesied pleasantly.

"Good morning, Mrs. Hurley, good morning," Mr. Bowyer said, "this is Mr. Martin Hewitt, a gentleman from London, who is going to look into this shocking murder of our young friend Mr. Rewse and sift it to the bottom. He would like you to tell him something, Mrs. Hurley."

The woman curtesied again. "An' it's the jintleman is welcome, sor, and doin's as ut is." She had a low, pleasing voice, much in contrast with her unattractive appearance, and characterised by the softest and broadest brogue imaginable. "Will ye not come in? Mother av Hiven! An' thim two livin' together, an' fishin' an' readin' an' all, like brothers! An' trut' ut is he was a foine young jintleman indade, indade!"

"I suppose, Mrs. Hurley," Hewitt said, "you've seen as much of the life of those two gentlemen here as anybody?"

"Treu ut is, sor; none more—nor as much."

"Did you ever hear of anybody being on bad terms with Mr. Rewse—anybody at all, Mr. Main or another?"

"Niver a soul in all Mayo. How could ye? Such a foine young jintleman, an' fair-spoken an' all."

"Tell me all that happened on the day that you heard that Mr. Rewse was ill—Tuesday week."

"In the mornin', sor, 'twas much as ord'nary. I was over there at half afther sivin, an' 'twas half an hour afther that I cud hear the jintlemen dhressin'. They tuk their breakfast—though Mr. Rewse's was a small wan. It was half afther nine that Mr. Main wint off walkin' to Cullanin, Mr. Rewse stayin' in, havin' letthers to write. Half an hour later I came away mesilf. Later than that (it was nigh elivin) I wint across for a pail from the yard, an' then, through the windy as I passed I saw the dear young jintleman sittin' writin' at the table calm an' peaceful—an' saw him no more in this warrl'."

"And after that?"

"Afther that, sor, I came back wid the pail, an' saw nor heard no more till two o'clock, whin Mr. Main came back from Cullanin."

"Did you see him as he came back?"

"That I did, sor, as I stud there nailin' the fence where the pig bruk ut. I'd been there an' had me oi down the road lookin' for him an hour past, expectin' he might be bringin' somethin' for me to cook for their dinner. An' more by token he gave me the toime from his watch, set by the Town Hall clock."

"And was it two o'clock?"

"It was that to the sthroke, an' me own ould clock was right too whin I wint to set ut. An'——"

"One moment; may I see your clock?"

Mrs. Hurley turned and shut an open door which had concealed an old hanging clock. Hewitt produced his watch and compared the time. "Still right I see, Mrs. Hurley," he said; "your clock keeps excellent time."

"It does that, sor, an' nivir more than claned twice by Rafferty since me own father (rest his soul!) lift ut here. 'Tis no bad clock, as Mr. Rewse himsilf said oft an' again; an' I always kape ut by the Town Hall toime. But as I was sayin', Mr. Main came back an' gave me the toime; thin he wint sthraight to his house, an' no more av him I saw till may be half afther three."

"And then?"

"An' thin, sor, he came across, in a sad takin', wid a letther. 'Take ut,' sez he, 'an' have ut posted at Cullanin by the first that can get there. Mr. Rewse has the sickness on him awful bad,' he sez, 'an' ye must not be near the place or ye'll take ut. I have him to bed, an' his clothes I shall burn behin' the cottage,' sez he, 'so if ye see smoke ye'll know what ut is. There'll be no docthor wanted. I'm wan mesilf, an' I'll do all for 'um. An' sure I knew him for a docthor ivir since he come. 'The cottage ye shall not come near,' he sez, 'till ut's over one way or another, an' yez can lave whativir av food an' dhrink we want midbetwixt the houses an' go back, an' I'll come and fetch ut. But have the letther posted,' he sez, 'at wanst. 'Tis not contagious,' he sez, 'bein' as I've dishinfected it mesilf. But kape yez away from the cottage.' An' I kept."

"And then did he go back to the cottage at once?"

"He did that, sor, an' a sore stew was he in to all seemin'— white as paper, and much need, too, the murtherin' scutt! An' him always so much the jintleman an' all. Well I saw no more av him that day. Next day he laves another letther wid the dirthy plates there mid-betwixt the houses, an' shouts for ut to be posted. 'Twas for the poor young jintleman's mother, sure, as was the other wan. An' the day afther there was another letther, an' wan for the undhertaker, too, for he tells me it's all over, an' he's dead. An' they buried him next day followin'."

"So that from the time you went for the pail and saw Mr. Rewse writing, till after the funeral, you were never at the cottage at all?"

"Nivir, sor; an' can ye blame me? Wid children an' Terence himself sick wid bronchitis in this house?"

"Of course, of course, you did quite right—indeed you only obeyed orders. But now think; do you remember on any one of those three days hearing a shot, or any other unusual noise in the cottage?"

"Nivir at all, sor. 'Tis that I've been thryin' to bring to mind these four days. Such may have been, but not that I heard."

"After you went for the pail, and before Mr. Main returned to the house, did Mr. Rewse leave the cottage at all, or might he have done so?"

"He did not lave at all, to my knowledge. Sure he *might* have gone an' he might have come back widout my knowin'. But see him I did not."

"Thank you, Mrs. Hurley. I think we'll go across to the cottage now. If any people come will you send them after us? I suppose a policeman is there?"

"He is, sor. An' the serjint is not far away. They've been in chyarge since Mr. Bowyer wint away last—but shlapin' here."

Hewitt and Mr. Bowyer walked towards the cottage. "Did you notice," said Mr. Bowyer, "that the woman saw Rewse *writing letters?* Now what were those letters, and where are they? He has no correspondents that I know of but his mother and sister, and they heard nothing from him. Is this something else?—some other plot? There is something very deep here."

"Yes," Hewitt replied thoughtfully, "I think our inquiries may take us deeper than we have expected; and in the matter of those letters—yes, I think they may lie near the kernel of the mystery."

Here they arrived at the cottage—an uncommonly substantial structure for the district. It was square, of plain, solid brick, with a slated roof. On the patch of ground behind it there were still signs of the fires, wherein Main had burnt Rewse's clothes and other belongings. And sitting on the window-sill in front was a big member of the R.I.C., soldierly and broad, who rose as they came and saluted Mr. Bowyer.

"Good-day constable," Mr. Bowyer said. "I hope nothing has been disturbed?"

"Not a shtick, sor. Nobody's as much as gone in."

"Have any of the windows been opened or shut?" Hewitt asked.

"This wan was, sor," the policeman said, indicating the one behind him, "when they took away the corrpse, an' so was the next round the corrner. 'Tis the bedroom windies they are, an' they opened thim to give ut a bit av air. The other windy behin'—sittin'-room windy—has not been opened."

"Very well," Hewitt answered, "we'll take a look at that unopened window from the inside."

The door was opened and they passed inside. There was a small lobby, and on the left of this was the bedroom with two single beds. The only other room of consequence was the sitting-room, the cottage consisting merely of these, a small scullery and a narrow closet

used as a bath-room, wedged between the bedroom and the sitting-
room. They made for the single window of the sitting-room at the
back. It was an ordinary sash window, and was shut, but the catch
was not fastened. Hewitt examined the catch, drawing Mr. Bowyer's
attention to a bright scratch on the grimy brass. "See," he said, "that
nick in the catch exactly corresponds with the narrow space between
the two frames of the window. And look"—he lifted the bottom sash
a little as he spoke—"there is the mark of a knife on the frame of the
top sash. Somebody has come in by that window, forcing the catch
with a knife."

"Yes, yes!" cried Mr. Bowyer, greatly excited, "and he has gone
out that way too, else why is the window shut and the catch not fastened? Why should he do that? What in the world does *this* thing
mean?"

Before Hewitt could reply the constable put his head into the
room and announced that one Larry Shanahan was at the door, and
had been promised half-a-sovereign.

"One of the men who heard a shot," Hewitt said to Mr. Bowyer. "Bring him in, constable."

The constable brought in Larry Shanahan, and Larry Shanahan
brought in a strong smell of whisky. He was an extremely ragged
person, with only one eye, which caused him to hold his head aside
as he regarded Hewitt, much as a parrot does. On his face
sun-scorched brown and fiery red struggled for mastery, and his
voice was none of the clearest. He held his hat against his stomach
with one hand and with the other pulled his forelock.

"An' which is the honourable jintleman," he said, "as do be
burrnin' to prisint me wid a bit o' goold?"

"Here I am," said Hewitt, jingling money in his pocket, "and
here is the half-sovereign. It's only waiting where it is till you have
answered a few questions. They say you heard a shot fired here-
about?"

"Faith, an' that I did, sor. 'Twas a shot in this house, indade, no
other."

"And when was it?"

"Sure, 'twas in the afthernoon."

"But on what day?"

"Last Tuesday sivin-noight, sor, as I know by rayson av Ballyshiel fair that I wint to."

"Tell me all about it."

"I will, sor. 'Twas pigs I was dhrivin' that day, sor, to Ballyshiel fair from just beyond Cullanin. At Cullanin, sor, I dhropped in
wid Danny Mulcahy, that intintioned thravellin' the same way, an'
while we tuk a thrifle av a dhrink in comes Dennis Grady, that was
to go to Ballyshiel similiarously. An' so we had another thrifle av a

dhrink, or maybe a thrifle more, an' we wint togedther, passin' this way, sor, as ye may not know, bein' likely a shtranger. Well, sor, ut was as we were just forninst this place that there came a divil av a bang that makes us shtop simultaneous. 'What's that?' sez Dan. ' 'Tis a gunshot,' sez I, 'an' 'tis in the brick house too.' 'That is so,' sez Dennis; 'nowhere else.' And we lukt at wan another. 'An' what'll we do?' sez I. 'What would yez?' sez Dan; ' 'tis non av our business.' 'That is so,' sez Dennis again, and we wint on. Ut was quare, maybe, but it might aisily be wan av the jintlemen emptyin' a barr'l out o' windy or what not. An'—an' so—an' so——" Mr. Shanahan scratched his ear, "an' so—we wint."

"And do you know at what time this was?"

Larry Shanahan ceased scratching, and seized his ear between thumb and forefinger, gazing severely at the floor with his one eye as he did so, plunged in computation. "Sure," he said, " 'twould be— 'twould be—let's see—'twould be—" he looked up, " 'twould be half-past two maybe, or maybe a thrifle nearer three."

"And Main was in the place all the time after two," Mr. Bowyer said, bringing down his fist on his open hand. "That finishes it. We've nailed him to the minute."

"Had you a watch with you?" asked Hewitt.

"Divil of a watch in the company, sor. I made an internal calculation. 'Tis foive mile from Cullanin, and we never lift till near half an hour after the Town Hall clock had struck twelve. 'Twould take us two hours and a thrifle more, considherin' the pigs an' the rough road, an' the distance, an'—an' the thrifle of dhrink." His eye rolled slyly as he said it. "That was my calculation, sor."

Here the constable appeared with two more men. Each had the usual number of eyes, but in other respects they were very good copies of Mr. Shanahan. They were both ragged, and neither bore any violent likeness to a teetotaler. "Dan Mulcahy and Dennis Grady," announced the constable.

Mr. Dan Mulcahy's tale was of a piece with Mr. Larry Shanahan's, and Mr. Dennis Grady's was the same. They had all heard the shot it was plain. What Dan had said to Dennis and what Dennis had said to Larry mattered little. Also they were all agreed that the day was Tuesday by token of the fair. But as to the time of day there arose a disagreement.

" 'Twas nigh soon afther wan o'clock," said Dan Mulcahy.

"Soon afther wan!" exclaimed Larry Shanahan with scorn. "Soon afther your grandmother's pig! 'Twas half afther two at laste. Ut struck twelve nigh 'alf an hour before we lift Cullanin. Why, yez heard ut!"

"That I did not. Ut struck eleven, an' we wint in foive minutes."

"What fool-talk ye shpake Dan Mulcahy. 'Twas twelve sthruck; I counted ut."

"Thin ye counted wrong. I counted ut, an' 'twas elivin."

"Yez nayther av yez right," interposed Dennis Grady. " 'Twas not elivin when we lift; 'twas not, be the mother av Moses!"

"I wondher at ye, Dennis Grady; ye must have been dhrunk as a Kerry cow," and both Mulcahy and Shanahan turned upon the obstinate Grady, and the dispute waxed clamorous till Hewitt stopped it.

"Come, come," he said, "never mind the time then. Settle that between you after you've gone. Does either of you remember—not calculate, you know, but *remember*—the time you got to Ballyshiel?—the actual time by a clock—not a guess."

Not one of the three had looked at a clock at Ballyshiel.

"Do you remember anything about coming home again?"

They did not. They looked furtively at one another and presently broke into a grin.

"Ah! I see how *that* was," Hewitt said good-humouredly. "That's all now, I think. Come, it's ten shillings each, I think." And he handed over the money. The men touched their forelocks again, stowed away the money and prepared to depart. As they went Larry Shanahan stepped mysteriously back again and said in a whisper, "Maybe the jintlemen wud like me to kiss the book on ut? An' as to the toime——"

"Oh, no thank you," Hewitt laughed. "We take your word for it Mr. Shanahan." And Mr. Shanahan pulled his forelock again and vanished.

"There's nothing but confusion to be got from them," Mr. Bowyer remarked testily. "It's a mere waste of time."

"No, no, not a waste of time," Hewitt replied, "nor a waste of money. One thing is made pretty plain. That is that the shot was fired on Tuesday. Mrs. Hurley never noticed the report, but these three men were close by, and there is no doubt that they heard it. It's the only single thing they agree about at all. They contradict one another over everything else, but they agree completely in that. Of course I wish we could have got the exact time; but that can't be helped. As it is it is rather fortunate that they disagreed so entirely. Two of them are certainly wrong, and perhaps all three. In any case it wouldn't have been safe to trust to mere computation of time by three men just beginning to get drunk, who had no particular reason for remembering. But if by any chance they had agreed on the time we might have been led into a wrong track altogether by taking the thing as fact. But a gunshot is not such a doubtful thing. When three independent witnesses hear a gunshot together there can be little doubt that a shot has been fired. Now I think you'd better sit down.

Perhaps you can find something to read. I'm about to make a very minute examination of this place, and it will probably bore you if you've nothing else to do."

But Mr. Bowyer would think of nothing but the business in hand. "I don't understand that window," he said, shaking his finger towards it as he spoke. "Not at all. Why should Main want to get in and out by a window? He wasn't a stranger."

Hewitt began a most careful inspection of the whole surface of floor, ceiling, walls and furniture of the sitting-room. At the fire-place he stooped and lifted with great care a few sheets of charred paper from the grate. These he put on the window-ledge. "Will you just bring over that little screen," he asked, "to keep the draught from this burnt paper? Thank you. It looks like letter paper, and thick letter paper, since the ashes are very little broken. The weather has been fine, and there has been no fire in that grate for a long time. These papers have been carefully burned with a match or a candle."

"Ah! perhaps the letters poor young Rewse was writing in the morning. But what can they tell us?"

"Perhaps nothing—perhaps a great deal." Hewitt was examining the cinders keenly, holding the surface sidways to the light. "Come," he said, "see if I can guess Rewse's address in London. 17 Mountjoy Gardens, Hampstead. Is that it?"

"Yes. Is it there? Can you read it? Show me." Mr. Bowyer hurried across the room, eager and excited.

"You can sometimes read words on charred paper," Hewitt replied, "as you may have noticed. This has curled and crinkled rather too much in the burning, but it is plainly notepaper with an embossed heading, which stands out rather clearly. He has evidently brought some notepaper with him from home in his trunk. See, you can just see the ink lines crossing out the address; but there's little else. At the beginning of the letter there is 'My d——' then a gap, and then the last stroke of 'M' and the rest of the word 'mother.' 'My dear Mother,' or My dearest Mother' evidently. Something follows too in the same line, but that is unreadable. 'My dear Mother and Sister' perhaps. After that there is nothing recognisable. The first letter looks rather like 'W,' but even that is indistinct. It seems to be a longish letter—several sheets, but they are stuck together in the charring. Perhaps more than one letter."

"The thing is plain," Mr. Bowyer said. "The poor lad was writing home, and perhaps to other places, and Main, after his crime, burned the letters, because they would have stultified his own with the lying tale about small-pox."

Hewitt said nothing, but resumed his general search. He passed his hand rapidly over every inch of the surface of everything in the room. Then he entered the bedroom and began an inspection of the same sort there. There were two beds, one at each end of the room, and each inch of each piece of bed linen passed rapidly under his sharp eye. After the bedroom he betook himself to the little bath-room, and then to the scullery. Finally he went outside and exam-ined every board of a close fence that stood a few feet from the sit-ting-room window, and the brick-paved path lying between.

When it was all over he returned to Mr. Bowyer. "Here is a strange thing," he said. "The shot passed clean through Rewse's body, striking no bones, and meeting no solid resistance. It was a good-sized bullet, as Dr. O'Reilly testifies, and therefore must have had a large charge of powder behind it in the cartridge. After emerg-ing from Rewse's back it *must* have struck something else in this con-fined place. Yet on nowhere—ceiling, floor, wall nor furniture, can I find the mark of a bullet nor the bullet itself."

"The bullet itself Main might easily have got rid of."

"Yes, but not the mark. Indeed, the bullet would scarcely be easy to get at if it had struck anything I have seen about here; it would have buried itself. Just look round now. Where could a bullet strike in this place without leaving its mark?"

Mr. Bowyer looked round. "Well, no," he said, "nowhere. Unless the window was open and it went out that way."

"Then it must have hit the fence or the brick paving between, and there is no sign of a bullet there," Hewitt replied. "Push the sash, as high as you please, the shot couldn't have passed *over* the fence without hitting the window first. As to the bedroom windows, that's impossible. Mr. Shanahan and his friends would not only have heard the shot, they would have seen it—which they didn't."

"Then what's the meaning of it?"

"The meaning of it is simply this: either Rewse was shot some-where else and his body brought here afterwards, or the article, whatever it was, that the bullet struck must have been taken away."

"Yes, of course. It's just another piece of evidence destroyed by Main, that's all. Every step we go we see the diabolical completeness of his plans. But now every piece of evidence missing only tells the more against him. The body alone condemns him past all redemp-tion."

Hewitt was gazing about the room thoughtfully. "I think we'll have Mrs. Hurley over here," he said; "she should tell us if anything is missing. Constable, will you ask Mrs. Hurley to step over here?"

Mrs. Hurley came at once and was brought into the sitting-room. "Just look about you, Mrs. Hurley," Hewitt said, "in this room and everywhere else, and tell me if anything is missing that you can remember was here on the morning of the day you last saw Mr. Rewse."

She looked thoughtfully up and down the room. "Sure, sor,"

she said, " 'tis all there as ord'nary." Her eyes rested on the mantelpiece and she added at once, "Except the clock, indade."

"Except the clock?"

"The clock ut is, sure. Ut stud on that same mantelpiece on that mornin' as ut always did."

"What sort of clock was it?"

"Just a plain round wan wid a metal case—an American clock they said ut was. But ut kept nigh as good time as me own."

"It *did* keep good time, you say?"

"Faith an' ut did, sor. Mine an' this ran together for weeks wid nivir a minute betune thim."

"Thank you, Mrs. Hurley, thank you; that will do," Hewitt exclaimed, with some excitement in his voice. He turned to Mr. Bowyer. "We must find that clock," he said. "And there's the pistol; nothing has been seen of that. Come, help me search. Look for a loose board."

"But he'll have taken them away with him probably."

"The pistol perhaps—although that isn't likely. The clock, no. It's evidence, man, evidence!" Hewitt darted outside and walked hurriedly round the cottage, looking this way and that about the country adjacent.

Presently he returned. "No," he said, "I think it's more likely in the house." He stood for a moment and thought. Then he made for the fireplace and flung the fender across the floor. All round the hearthstone an open crack extended. "See there!" he exclaimed as he pointed to it. He took the tongs, and with one leg levered the stone up till he could seize it in his fingers. Then he dragged it out and pushed it across the linoleum that covered the floor. In the space beneath lay a large revolver and a common American round nickel-plated clock. "See here!" he cried, "see here!" and he rose and placed the articles on the mantelpiece. The glass before the clock-face was smashed to atoms, and there was a gaping rent in the face itself. For a few seconds Hewitt regarded it as it stood, and then he turned to Mr. Bowyer. "Mr. Bowyer," he said, "we have done Mr. Stanley Main a sad injustice. Poor young Rewse committed suicide. There is proof undeniable," and he pointed to the clock.

"Proof? How? Where? Nonsense, man. Pooh! Ridiculous! If Rewse committed suicide why should Main go to all that trouble and tell all those lies to prove that he died of small-pox? More even that that, what has he run away for?"

"I'll tell you, Mr. Bowyer, in a moment. But first as to this clock. Remember, Main set his watch by the Cullanin Town Hall clock, and Mrs. Hurley's clock agreed exactly. That we have proved ourselves to-day by my own watch. Mrs. Hurley's clock still agrees. *This* clock was always kept in time with Mrs. Hurley's. Main returned at two exactly. Look at the time by that clock—the time when the bullet crashed into and stopped it."

The time was three minutes to one.

Hewitt took the clock, unscrewed the winder and quickly stripped off the back, exposing the works. "See," he said, "the bullet is lodged firmly among the wheels, and has been torn into snags and strips by the impact. The wheels themselves are ruined altogether. The central axle which carries the hands is bent. See there! Neither hand will move in the slightest. That bullet struck the axle and fixed those hands immovably at the moment of the time when Algernon Rewse died. Look at the mainspring. It is less than half run out. Proof that the clock was going when the shot struck it. Main left Rewse alive and well at half-past nine. He did not return till two— when Rewse had been dead more than an hour."

"But then, hang it all! How about the lies and the false certificate, and the bolting?"

"Let me tell you the whole tale, Mr. Bowyer, as I conjecture it to have been. Poor young Rewse was, as you told me, in a bad state of health—thoroughly run down, I think you said. You said something of his engagement and the death of the lady. This pointed clearly to a nervous—a mental upset. Very well. He broods, and so forth. He must go away and find change of scene and occupation. His intimate friend Main brings him here. The holiday has its good effect perhaps, at first, but after a while it gets monotonous, and brooding sets in again. I do not know whether or not you happen to know it, but it is a fact that four-fifths of all persons suffering from melancholia have suicidal tendencies. This may never have been suspected by Main, who otherwise might not have left him so long alone. At any rate he *is* left alone, and he takes the opportunity. He writes a note to Main and a long letter to his mother—an awful, heartbreaking letter, with a terrible picture of the mental agony wherein he was to die—perhaps with a tincture of religious mania in it, and prophesying merited hell for himself in the hereafter. This done, he simply stands up from the table, at which he has been writing, and with his back to the fireplace shoots himself. There he lies till Main returns an hour later. Main finds the door shut and nobody answers his knock. He goes round to the sitting-room window, looks through, and perhaps he sees the body. Anyway he pushes back the catch with his knife, opens the window and gets in, and *then* he sees. He is completely knocked out of time. The thing is terrible. What shall he—what can he do? Poor Rewse's mother and sister dote on him, and his mother is an invalid—heart disease. To let her see that awful letter would be to kill her. He burns the letter, also the note to himself. Then an idea strikes him. Even without the letter the news of her boy's suicide will probably kill the poor old lady. Can she be prevented hearing of it? Of his death she must know—that's inevitable. But as to the manner? Would it not be possible to concoct some kind lie? And then the opportunities of the situation occur to him. Nobody but himself knows of it. He is a medical man, fully qualified, and empowered to give certificates of death. More, there is an epidemic of small-pox in the neighbourhood. What easier, with a little management, than to call the death one by small-pox? Nobody would be anxious to examine too closely the corpse of a small-pox patient. He decides that he will do it. He writes the letter to Mrs. Rewse announcing that her son has the disease, and he forbids Mrs. Hurley to come near the place for fear of infection. He cleans the floor—it is linoleum here, you see, and the stains were fresh—burns the clothes, cleans and stops the wound. At every turn his medical knowledge is of use. He puts the smashed clock and the pistol out of sight under the hearth. In a word he carries out the whole thing rather cleverly, and a terrible few days he must have passed. It never strikes him that he has dug a frightful pit for his own feet. You are suspicious, and you come across. In a perhaps rather peremptory manner you tell him how suspicious his conduct has been. And then a sense of his terrible position comes upon him like a thunderclap. He sees it all. He has deliberately of his own motion destroyed every evidence of the suicide. There is no evidence in the world that Rewse did not die a natural death, except the body, and that you are going to dig up. He sees now (you remind him of it in fact) that *he* is the one man alive who can profit by Rewse's death. And there is the shot body, and there is the false death certificate, and there are the lying letters, and the tales to the neighbours and everything. He has himself destroyed everything that proves suicide. All that remains points to a foul murder and to him as the murderer. Can you wonder at his complete breakdown and his flight? What else in the world could the poor fellow do?"

"Well, well—yes, yes," Mr. Bowyer replied thoughtfully, "it seems very plausible of course. But still, look at probabilities, my dear sir, look at probabilities."

"No, but look at *possibilities*. There is that clock. Get over it if you can. Was there ever a more insurmountable alibi? Could Main possibly be here shooting Rewse and half way between here and Cullanin at the same time? Remember, Mrs. Hurley saw him come back at two, and she had been watching for an hour, and could see more than half a mile up the road."

"Well, yes, I suppose you're right. And what must we do now?"

"Bring Main back. I think we should advertise to begin with. Say, 'Rewse is proved to have died over an hour before you came. All safe. Your evidence is wanted,' or something of that sort. And we must set the telegraph going. The police already are looking for him, no doubt. Meanwhile I will look here for a clue myself."

The advertisement was successful in two days. Indeed Main afterwards said that he was at the time, once the first terror was over, in doubt whether or not it would be best to go back and face the thing out, trusting to his innocence. He could not venture home for money, nor to his bank, for fear of the police. He chanced upon the advertisement as he searched the paper for news of the case, and that decided him. His explanation of the matter was precisely as Hewitt had expected. His only thought till Mr. Bowyer first arrived at the cottage had been to smother the real facts and to spare the feelings of Mrs. Rewse and her daughter, and it was not till that gentleman put them so plainly before him that he in the least realised the dangers of his position. That his fears for Mrs. Rewse were only too well grounded was proved by events, for the poor old lady only survived her son by a month.

These events took place some little while ago, as may be gathered from the fact that Miss Rewse has now been Mrs. Stanley Main for nearly three years.

C. L. PIRKIS

Mrs. Catherine Louisa Pirkis (?–1910) was a fairly prolific British ladies' novelist of the late nineteenth century, with some fourteen books and considerable periodical material to her credit. Her most popular novels were A Dateless Bargain *(1877) and* Lady Lovelace *(1884), both of which are now forgotten. Today, however, she is remembered for her short detective stories about Loveday Brooke, which first appeared in* The Ludgate Monthly *in 1893, and then were reprinted in book form as* The Experiences of Loveday Brooke: Lady Detective *(1894). They are generally considered to be the best premodern stories about a female detective.*

In her later life Mrs. Pirkis concerned herself with various social and humanitarian causes and became one of the founders of the National Canine Defense League, an antivivisection organization.

"The Black Bag Left on a Door-Step"

"It's a big thing," said Loveday Brooke, addressing Ebenezer Dyer, chief of the well-known detective agency in Lynch Court, Fleet Street; "Lady Cathrow has lost £30,000 worth of jewellery, if the newspaper accounts are to be trusted."

"They are fairly accurate this time. The robbery differs in few respects from the usual run of country-house robberies. The time chosen, of course, was the dinner-hour, when the family and guests were at table and the servants not on duty were amusing themselves in their own quarters. The fact of its being Christmas Eve would also of necessity add to the business and consequent distraction of the household. The entry to the house, however, in this case was not effected in the usual manner by a ladder to the dressing-room window, but through the window of a room on the ground floor—a small room with one window and two doors, one of which opens into the hall, and the other into a passage that leads by the back stairs to the bedroom floor. It is used, I believe, as a sort of hat and coat room by the gentlemen of the house."

"It was, I suppose, the weak point of the house?"

"Quite so. A very weak point indeed. Craigen Court, the residence of Sir George and Lady Cathrow, is an oddly-built old place, jutting out in all directions, and as this window looked out upon a blank wall, it was filled in with stained glass, kept fastened by a strong brass catch, and never opened, day or night, ventilation being obtained by means of a glass ventilator fitted in the upper panes. It seems absurd to think that this window, being only about four feet from the ground, should have had neither iron bars nor shutters added to it; such, however, was the case. On the night of the robbery, someone within the house must have deliberately, and of intention, unfastened its only protection, the brass catch, and thus given the thieves easy entrance to the house."

"Your suspicions, I suppose, centre upon the servants?"

"Undoubtedly; and it is in the servants' hall that your services will be required. The thieves, whoever they were, were perfectly cognizant of the ways of the house. Lady Cathrow's jewellery was kept in a safe in her dressing room, and as the dressing-room was over the dining-room, Sir George was in the habit of saying that it was the 'safest' room in the house. (Note the pun, please, Sir George is rather proud of it.) By his orders the window of the dining-room immediately under the dressing-room window was always left unshuttered and without blind during dinner, and as a full stream of light thus fell through it on to the outside terrace, it would have been impossible for anyone to have placed a ladder there unseen."

"I see from the newspapers that it was Sir George's invariable custom to fill his house and give a large dinner on Christmas Eve."

"Yes. Sir George and Lady Cathrow are elderly people, with no family and few relatives, and have consequently a large amount of time to spend on their friends."

"I suppose the key of the safe was frequently left in the possession of Lady Cathrow's maid?"

"Yes. She is a young French girl, Stephanie Delcroix by name. It was her duty to clear the dressing-room directly after her mistress left it: put away any jewellery that might be lying about, lock the safe, and keep the key till her mistress came up to bed. On the night of the robbery, however, she admits that, instead of so doing, directly her mistress left the dressing-room, she ran down to the housekeeper's room to see if any letters had come for her, and remained chatting with the other servants for some time—she could not say for how long. It was by the half-past-seven post that her letters generally arrived from St. Omer, where her home is."

"Oh, then, she was in the habit of thus running down to enquire for her letters, no doubt, and the thieves, who appear to be so thoroughly cognizant of the house, would know this also."

"Perhaps; though at the present moment I must say things look very black against the girl. Her manner, too, when questioned, is not calculated to remove suspicion. She goes from one fit of hysterics into another; contradicts herself nearly every time she opens her mouth, then lays it to the charge of her ignorance of our language; breaks into voluble French; becomes theatrical in action, and then goes off into hysterics once more."

"All that is quite Français, you know," said Loveday. "Do the authorities at Scotland Yard lay much stress on the safe being left unlocked that night?"

"They do, and they are instituting a keen enquiry as to the possible lovers the girl may have. For this purpose they have sent Bates down to stay in the village and collect all the information he can outside the house. But they want someone within the walls to hob-nob with the maids generally, and to find out if she has taken any of them into her confidence respecting her lovers. So they sent to me to know if I would send down for this purpose one of the shrewdest and most clear-headed of my female detectives. I, in my turn, Miss Brooke, have sent for you—you may take it as a compliment if you like. So please now get out your note-book, and I'll give you sailing orders."

Loveday Brooke, at this period of her career, was a little over thirty years of age, and could be best described in a series of negations.

She was not tall, she was not short; she was not dark, she was not fair; she was neither handsome nor ugly. Her features were altogether nondescript; her one noticeable trait was a habit she had, when absorbed in thought, of dropping her eyelids over her eyes till only a line of eyeball showed, and she appeared to be looking out at the world through a slit, instead of through a window.

Her dress was invariably black, and was almost Quaker-like in its neat primness.

Some five or six years previously, by a jerk of Fortune's wheel, Loveday had been thrown upon the world penniless and all but friendless. Marketable accomplishments she had found she had none, so she had forthwith defied convention, and had chosen for herself a career that had cut her off sharply from her former associates and her position in society. For five or six years she drudged away patiently in the lower walks of her profession; then chance, or, to speak more precisely, an intricate criminal case, threw her in the way of the experienced head of the flourishing detective agency in Lynch Court. He quickly enough found out the stuff she was made of, and threw her in the way of better-class work—work, indeed, that brought increase of pay and of reputation alike to him and to Loveday.

Ebenezer Dyer was not, as a rule, given to enthusiasm; but he would at times wax eloquent over Miss Brooke's qualifications for the profession she had chosen.

"Too much of a lady, do you say?" he would say to anyone who chanced to call in question those qualifications. "I don't care twopence-halfpenny whether she is or is not a lady. I only know she is the most sensible and practical woman I ever met. In the first place, she has the faculty—so rare among women—of carrying out orders to the very letter; in the second place, she has a clear, shrewd brain, unhampered by any hard-and-fast theories; thirdly, and most important item of all, she has so much common sense that it amounts to genius—positively to genius, sir."

But although Loveday and her chief as a rule, worked together upon an easy and friendly footing, there were occasions on which they were wont, so to speak, to snarl at each other.

Such an occasion was at hand now.

Loveday showed no disposition to take out her note-book and receive her "sailing orders."

"I want to know," she said, "if what I saw in one newspaper is true—that one of the thieves before leaving, took the trouble to close the safe-door, and to write across it in chalk: 'To be let, unfurnished'?"

"Perfectly true; but I do not see that stress need be laid on the fact. The scoundrels often do that sort of thing out of insolence or bravado. In that robbery at Reigate, the other day, they went to a lady's Davenport, took a sheet of her note-paper, and wrote their thanks on it for her kindness in not having had the lock of her safe repaired. Now, if you will get out your note-book——"

"Don't be in such a hurry," said Loveday calmly; "I want to know if you have seen this?" She leaned across the writing-table at which they sat, one either side, and handed to him a newspaper cutting which she took from her letter-case.

Mr. Dyer was a tall, powerfully-built man with a large head, benevolent bald forehead and a genial smile. That smile, however, often proved a trap to the unwary, for he owned a temper so irritable that a child with a chance word might ruffle it.

The genial smile vanished as he took the newspaper cutting from Loveday's hand.

"I would have you to remember, Miss Brooke," he said severely, "that although I am in the habit of using despatch in my business, I am never known to be in a hurry; hurry in affairs I take to be the especial mark of the slovenly and unpunctual."

Then, as if still further to give contradiction to her words, he very deliberately unfolded her slip of newspaper and slowly, accentuating each word and syllable, read as follows:—

"Singular Discovery.

"A black leather bag, or portmanteau, was found early yesterday morning by one of Smith's newspaper boys on the doorstep of a house in the road running between Easterbrook and Wreford, and inhabited by an elderly spinster lady. The contents of the bag include a clerical collar and necktie, a Church Service, a book of sermons, a copy of the works of Virgil, a *facsimile* of Magna Charta, with translations, a pair of black kid gloves, a brush and comb, some newspapers, and several small articles suggesting clerical ownership. On the top of the bag the following extraordinary letter, written in pencil on a long slip of paper, was found:

'The fatal day has arrived. I can exist no longer. I go hence and shall be no more seen. But I would have Coroner and Jury know that I am a sane man, and a verdict of temporary insanity in my case would be an error most gross after this intimation. I care not if it is *felo de se*, as I shall have passed all suffering. Search diligently for my poor lifeless body in the immediate neighbourhood—on the cold heath, the rail, or the river by yonder bridge—a few moments will decide how I shall depart. If I had walked aright I might have been a power in the Church of which I am now an unworthy member and priest; but the damnable sin of gambling got hold on me, and betting has been my ruin, as it has been the ruin of thousands who have preceded me. Young man, shun the bookmaker and the race-course as you would shun the devil and hell. Farewell, chums of Magdalen. Farewell, and take warning. Though I can claim relationship with a Duke, a Marquess, and a Bishop, and though I am the son of a noble woman, yet am I a tramp and an outcast, verily and indeed. Sweet death, I greet thee. I dare not sign my name. To one and all, farewell. O, my poor Marchioness mother, a dying kiss to thee. R.I.P.'

"The police and some of the railway officials have made a 'diligent search' in the neighbourhood of the railway station, but no 'poor lifeless body' has been found. The police authorities are inclined to the belief that the letter is a hoax, though they are still investigating the matter."

In the same deliberate fashion as he had opened and read the cutting, Mr. Dyer folded and returned it to Loveday.

"May I ask," he said sarcastically, "what you see in that silly hoax to waste your and my valuable time over?"

"I wanted to know," said Loveday, in the same level tones as before, "if you saw anything in it that might in some way connect this discovery with the robbery at Craigen Court?"

Mr. Dyer stared at her in utter, blank astonishment.

"When I was a boy," he said sarcastically as before, "I used to play at a game called 'what is my thought like?' Someone would think of something absurd—say the top of the monument—and someone else would hazard a guess that his thought might be—say the toe of his left boot, and that unfortunate individual would have to show the connection between the toe of his left boot and the top of the monument. Miss Brooke, I have no wish to repeat the silly game this evening for your benefit and mine."

"Oh, very well," said Loveday, calmly; "I fancied you might like to talk it over, that was all. Give me my 'sailing orders,' as you call them, and I'll endeavour to concentrate my attention on the little French maid and her various lovers."

Mr. Dyer grew amiable again.

"That's the point on which I wish you to fix your thoughts," he said; "you had better start for Craigen Court by the first train to-morrow—it's about sixty miles down the Great Eastern line. Huxwell is the station you must land at. There one of the grooms from the Court will meet you, and drive you to the house. I have arranged with the housekeeper there—Mrs. Williams, a very worthy and discreet person—that you shall pass in the house for a niece of hers, on a visit to recruit, after severe study in order to pass board-school teachers' exams. Naturally you have injured your eyes as well as your health with overwork; and so you can wear your blue spectacles. Your name, by the way, will be Jane Smith—better write it down. All your work will lie among the servants of the establishment, and there will be no necessity for you to see either Sir George or Lady Cathrow—in fact, neither of them have been apprised of your intended visit—the fewer we take into our confidence the better. I've no doubt, however, that Bates will hear from Scotland Yard that you are in the house, and will make a point of seeing you."

"Has Bates unearthed anything of importance?"

"Not as yet. He has discovered one of the girl's lovers, a young farmer of the name of Holt; but as he seems to be an honest, respectable young fellow, and entirely above suspicion, the discovery does not count for much."

"I think there's nothing else to ask," said Loveday, rising to take her departure. "Of course, I'll telegraph, should need arise, in our usual cipher."

The first train that left Bishopsgate for Huxwell on the following morning included, among its passengers, Loveday Brooke, dressed in the neat black supposed to be appropriate to servants of the upper class. The only literature with which she had provided herself in order to beguile the tedium of her journey was a small volume bound in paper boards, and entitled, "The Reciter's Treasury." It was published at the low price of one shilling, and seemed spe-

cially designed to meet the requirements of third-rate amateur reciters at penny readings.

Miss Brooke appeared to be all-absorbed in the contents of this
book during the first half of her journey. During the second, she lay
back in the carriage with closed eyes, and motionless as if asleep or
lost in deep thought.

The stopping of the train at Huxwell aroused her, and set her
collecting together her wraps.

It was easy to single out the trim groom from Craigen Court
from among the country loafers on the platform. Someone else beside the trim groom at the same moment caught her eye—Bates,
from Scotland Yard, got up in the style of a commercial traveller,
and carrying the orthodox "commercial bag" in his hand. He was a
small, wiry man, with red hair and whiskers, and an eager, hungry
expression of countenance.

"I am half-frozen with cold," said Loveday, addressing Sir
George's groom; "if you'll kindly take charge of my portmanteau, I'd
prefer walking to driving to the Court."

The man gave her a few directions as to the road she was to
follow, and then drove off with her box, leaving her free to indulge
Mr. Bates's evident wish for a walk and confidential talk along the
country road.

Bates seemed to be in a happy frame of mind that morning.

"Quite a simple affair, this, Miss Brooke," he said; "a walk over
the course, I take it, with you working inside the castle walls and I
unearthing without. No complications as yet have arisen, and if that
girl does not find herself in jail before another week is over her head,
my name is not Jeremiah Bates."

"You mean the French maid?"

"Why, yes, of course. I take it there's little doubt but what she
performed the double duty of unlocking the safe and the window
too. You see I look at it this way, Miss Brooke: all girls have lovers, I
say to myself, but a pretty girl like that French maid, is bound to
have double the number of lovers than the plain ones. Now, of
course, the greater the number of lovers, the greater chance there is
of a criminal being found among them. That's plain as a pikestaff,
isn't it?"

"Just as plain."

Bates felt encouraged to proceed.

"Well, then arguing on the same lines, I say to myself, this girl
is only a pretty, silly thing, not an accomplished criminal, or she
wouldn't have admitted leaving open the safe door; give her rope
enough and she'll hang herself. In a day or two, if we let her alone,
she'll be bolting off to join the fellow whose nest she has helped to
feather, and we shall catch the pair of them 'twixt here and Dover

Straits, and also possibly get a clue that will bring us on the traces of their accomplices. Eh, Miss Brooke, that'll be a thing worth doing?"

"Undoubtedly. Who is this coming along in this buggy at such a good pace?"

The question was added as the sound of wheels behind them made her look round.

Bates turned also. "Oh, this is young Holt; his father farms land about a couple of miles from here. He is one of Stephanie's lovers, and I should imagine about the best of the lot. But he does not appear to be first favourite; from what I hear someone else must have made the running on the sly. Ever since the robbery I'm told the young woman has given him the cold shoulder."

As the young man came nearer in his buggy he slackened his pace, and Loveday could not but admire his frank, honest expression of countenance.

"Room for one—can I give you a lift?" he said, as he came alongside of them.

And to the ineffable disgust of Bates, who had counted upon at least an hour's confidential talk with her, Miss Brooke accepted the young farmer's offer, and mounted beside him in his buggy.

As they went swifty along the country road, Loveday explained to the young man that her destination was Craigen Court, and that as she was a stranger to the place, she must trust to him to put her down at the nearest point to it that he would pass.

At the mention of Craigen Court his face clouded.

"They're in trouble there, and their trouble has brought trouble on others," he said a little bitterly.

"I know," said Loveday sympathetically; "it is often so. In such circumstances as these suspicion frequently fastens on an entirely innocent person."

"That's it! that's it!" he cried excitedly; "if you go into that house you'll hear all sorts of wicked things said of her, and see everything setting in dead against her. But she's innocent. I swear to you she is as innocent as you or I are."

His voice rang out above the clatter of his horse's hoofs. He seemed to forget that he had mentioned no name, and that Loveday, as a stranger, might be at a loss to know to whom he referred.

"Who is guilty Heaven only knows," he went on after a moment's pause; "it isn't for me to give an ill name to anyone in that house; but I only say she is innocent, and that I'll stake my life on."

"She is a lucky girl to have found one to believe in her, and trust her as you do," said Loveday, even more sympathetically than before.

"Is she? I wish she'd take advantage of her luck, then," he answered bitterly. "Most girls in her position would be glad to have a

man to stand by them through thick and thin. But not she! Ever
since the night of that accursed robbery she has refused to see me—
won't answer my letters—won't even send me a message. And, great
Heavens! I'd marry her tomorrow, if I had the chance, and dare the
world to say a word against her."

He whipped up his pony. The hedges seemed to fly on either
side of them, and before Loveday realised that half her drive was
over, he had drawn rein, and was helping her to alight at the servants' entrance to Craigen Court.

"You'll tell her what I've said to you, if you get the opportunity,
and beg her to see me, if only for five minutes?" he petitioned before
he re-mounted his buggy. And Loveday, as she thanked the young
man for his kind attention, promised to make an opportunity to give
his message to the girl.

Mrs. Williams, the housekeeper, welcomed Loveday in the servants' hall, and then took her to her own room to pull off her wraps.
Mrs. Williams was the widow of a London tradesman, and a little
beyond the average housekeeper in speech and manner.

She was a genial, pleasant woman, and readily entered into conversation with Loveday. Tea was brought in, and each seemed to
feel at home with the other. Loveday in the course of this easy,
pleasant talk, elicited from her the whole history of the events of the
day of the robbery, the number and names of the guests who sat
down to dinner that night, together with some other apparently trivial details.

The housekeeper made no attempt to disguise the painful position in which she and every one of the servants of the house felt
themselves to be at the present moment.

"We are none of us at our ease with each other now," she said,
as she poured out hot tea for Loveday, and piled up a blazing fire.
"Everyone fancies that everyone else is suspecting him or her, and
trying to rake up past words or deeds to bring in as evidence. The
whole house seems under a cloud. And at this time of year, too; just
when everything as a rule is at its merriest!" and here she gave a
doleful glance to the big bunch of holly and mistletoe hanging from
the ceiling.

"I suppose you are generally very merry downstairs at
Christmas time?" said Loveday. "Servants' balls, theatricals, and all
that sort of thing?"

"I should think we were! When I think of this time last year and
the fun we all had, I can scarcely believe it is the same house. Our
ball always follows my lady's ball, and we have permission to ask
our friends to it, and we keep it up as late as ever we please. We
begin our evening with a concert and recitations in character, then
we have a supper and then we dance right on till morning; but this

year!"—she broke off, giving a long, melancholy shake of her head that spoke volumes.

"I suppose," said Loveday, "some of your friends are very clever as musicians or reciters?"

"Very clever indeed. Sir George and my lady are always present during the early part of the evening, and I should like you to have seen Sir George last year laughing fit to kill himself at Harry Emmett dressed in prison dress with a bit of oakum in his hand, reciting the "Noble Convict!" Sir George said if the young man had gone on the stage, he would have been bound to make his fortune."

"Half a cup, please," said Loveday, presenting her cup. "Who was this Harry Emmett then—a sweetheart of one of the maids?"

"Oh, he would flirt with them all, but he was sweetheart to none. He was footman to Colonel James, who is a great friend of Sir George's, and Harry was constantly backwards and forwards bringing messages from his master. His father, I think, drove a cab in London, and Harry for a time did so also; then he took it into his head to be a gentleman's servant, and great satisfaction he gave as such. He was always such a bright, handsome young fellow and so full of fun, that everyone liked him. But I shall tire you with all this; and you, of course, want to talk about something so different;" and the housekeeper sighed again, as the thought of the dreadful robbery entered her brain once more.

"Not at all. I am greatly interested in you and your festivities. Is Emmett still in the neighbourhood? I should amazingly like to hear him recite myself."

"I'm sorry to say he left Colonel James about six months ago. We all missed him very much at first. He was a good, kind-hearted young man, and I remember he told me he was going away to look after his dear old grandmother, who had a sweetstuff shop somewhere or other, but where I can't remember."

Loveday was leaning back in her chair now, with eyelids drooped so low that she literally looked out through "slits" instead of eyes.

Suddenly and abruptly she changed the conversation.

"When will it be convenient for me to see Lady Cathrow's dressing-room?" she asked.

The housekeeper looked at her watch. "Now, at once," she answered; "it's a quarter to five now and my lady sometimes goes up to her room to rest for half an hour before she dresses for dinner."

"Is Stephanie still in attendance on Lady Cathrow?" Miss Brooke asked as she followed the housekeeper up the back stairs to the bedroom floor.

"Yes. Sir George and my lady have been goodness itself to us through this trying time, and they say we are all innocent till we are proved guilty, and will have it that none of our duties are to be in any way altered."

"Stephanie is scarcely fit to perform hers, I should imagine?"

"Scarcely. She was in hysterics nearly from morning till night for the first two or three days after the detectives came down, but now she has grown sullen, eats nothing and never speaks a word to any of us except when she is obliged. This is my lady's dressing-room, walk in please."

Loveday entered a large, luxuriously furnished room, and naturally made her way straight to the chief point of attraction in it—the iron safe fitted into the wall that separated the dressing-room from the bedroom.

It was a safe of the ordinary description, fitted with a strong iron door and Chubb lock. And across this door was written with chalk in characters that seemed defiant in their size and boldness, the words: "To be let, unfurnished."

Loveday spent about five minutes in front of this safe, all her attention concentrated upon the big, bold writing.

She took from her pocket-book a narrow strip of tracing-paper and compared the writing on it, letter by letter, with that on the safe door. This done she turned to Mrs. Williams and professed herself ready to follow her to the room below.

Mrs. Williams looked surprised. Her opinion of Miss Brooke's professional capabilities suffered considerable diminution.

"The gentlemen detectives," she said, "spent over an hour in this room; they paced the floor, they measured the candles, they——"

"Mrs. Williams," interrupted Loveday, "I am quite ready to look at the room below." Her manner had changed from gossiping friendliness to that of the business woman hard at work at her profession.

Without another word, Mrs. Williams led the way to the little room which had proved itself to be the "weak point" of the house.

They entered it by the door which opened into a passage leading to the back-stairs of the house. Loveday found the room exactly what it had been described to her by Mr. Dyer. It needed no second glance at the window to see the ease with which anyone could open it from the outside, and swing themselves into the room, when once the brass catch had been unfastened.

Loveday wasted no time here. In fact, much to Mrs. Williams's surprise and disappointment, she merely walked across the room, in at one door and out at the opposite one, which opened into the large inner hall of the house.

Here, however, she paused to ask a question:

"Is that chair always placed exactly in that position?" she said, pointing to an oak chair that stood immediately outside the room they had just quitted.

The housekeeper answered in the affirmative. It was a warm corner. "My lady" was particular that everyone who came to the house on messages should have a comfortable place to wait in.

"I shall be glad if you will show me to my room now," said Loveday, a little abruptly; "and will you kindly send up to me a county trade directory, if, that is, you have such a thing in the house?"

Mrs. Williams, with an air of offended dignity, led the way to the bedroom quarters once more. The worthy housekeeper felt as if her own dignity had, in some sort, been injured by the want of interest Miss Brooke had evinced in the rooms which, at the present moment, she considered the "show" rooms of the house.

"Shall I send someone to help you unpack?" she asked, a little stiffly, at the door of Loveday's room.

"No, thank you; there will not be much unpacking to do. I must leave here by the first up-train to-morrow morning."

"To-morrow morning! Why, I have told everyone you will be here at least a fortnight!"

"Ah, then you must explain that I have been suddenly summoned home by telegram. I'm sure I can trust you to make excuses for me. Do not, however, make them before supper-time. I shall like to sit down to that meal with you. I suppose I shall see Stephanie then?"

The housekeeper answered in the affirmative, and went her way, wondering over the strange manners of the lady whom, at first, she had been disposed to consider "such a nice, pleasant, conversable person!"

At supper-time, however, when the upper-servants assembled at what was, to them, the pleasantest meal of the day, a great surprise was to greet them.

Stephanie did not take her usual place at table, and a fellow-servant, sent to her room to summon her, returned, saying that the room was empty, and Stephanie was nowhere to be found.

Loveday and Mrs. Williams together went to the girl's bedroom. It bore its usual appearance: no packing had been done in it, and, beyond her hat and jacket, the girl appeared to have taken nothing away with her.

On enquiry, it transpired that Stephanie had, as usual, assisted Lady Cathrow to dress for dinner; but after that not a soul in the house appeared to have seen her.

Mrs. Williams thought the matter of sufficient importance to be at once reported to her master and mistress; and Sir George, in his turn, promptly despatched a messenger to Mr. Bates, at the "King's Head," to summon him to an immediate consultation.

Loveday despatched a messenger in another direction—to young Mr. Holt, at his farm, giving him particulars of the girl's disappearance.

Mr. Bates had a brief interview with Sir George in his study, from which he emerged radiant. He made a point of seeing Loveday before he left the Court, sending a special request to her that she would speak to him for a minute in the outside drive.

Loveday put her hat on, and went out to him. She found him almost dancing for glee.

"Told you so! told you so! told you so! Now, didn't I, Miss Brooke?" he exclaimed. "We'll come upon her traces before morning, never fear. I'm quite prepared. I knew what was in her mind all along. I said to myself, when that girl bolts it will be after she has dressed my lady for dinner—when she has two good clear hours all to herself, and her absence from the house won't be noticed, and when, without much difficulty, she can catch a train leaving Huxwell for Wreford. Well, she'll get to Wreford safe enough; but from Wreford she'll be followed every step of the way she goes. Only yesterday I set a man on there—a keen fellow at this sort of thing—and gave him full directions; and he'll hunt her down to her hole properly. Taken nothing with her, do you say? What does that matter? She thinks she'll find all she wants where she's going—'the feathered nest' I spoke to you about this morning. Ha! ha! Well, instead of stepping into it, as she fancies she will, she'll walk straight into a detective's arms, and land her pal there into the bargain. There'll be two of them netted before another forty-eight hours are over our heads, or my name's not Jeremiah Bates."

"What are you going to do now?" asked Loveday, as the man finished his long speech.

"Now! I'm back to the "King's Head" to wait for a telegram from my colleague at Wreford. Once he's got her in front of him he'll give me instructions at what point to meet him. You see, Huxwell being such an out-of-the-way place, and only one train leaving between 7.30 and 10.15, makes us really positive that Wreford must be the girl's destination and relieves my mind from all anxiety on the matter."

"Does it?" answered Loveday gravely. "I can see another possible destination for the girl—the stream that runs through the wood we drove past this morning. Good night, Mr. Bates, it's cold out here. Of course so soon as you have any news you'll send it up to Sir George."

The household sat up late that night, but no news was received of Stephanie from any quarter. Mr. Bates had impressed upon Sir George the ill-advisability of setting up a hue and cry after the girl that might possibly reach her ears and scare her from joining the person whom he was pleased to designate as her "pal."

"We want to follow her silently, Sir George, silently as, the shadow follows the man," he had said grandiloquently, "and then we shall come upon the two, and I trust upon their booty also." Sir George in his turn had impressed Mr. Bates's wishes upon his household, and if it had not been for Loveday's message, despatched early in the evening to young Holt, not a soul outside the house would have known of Stephanie's disappearance.

Loveday was stirring early the next morning, and the eight o'clock train for Wreford numbered her among its passengers. Before starting, she despatched a telegram to her chief in Lynch Court. It read rather oddly, as follows:—

"Cracker fired. Am just starting for Wreford. Will wire to you from there. L.B."

Oddly though it might read, Mr. Dyer did not need to refer to his cipher book to interpret it. "Cracker fired" was the easily remembered equivalent for "clue found" in the detective phraseology of the office.

"Well, she has been quick enough about it this time!" he soliloquised as he speculated in his own mind over what the purport of the next telegram might be.

Half an hour later there came to him a constable from Scotland Yard to tell him of Stephanie's disappearance and the conjectures that were rife on the matter, and he then, not unnaturally, read Loveday's telegram by the light of this information, and concluded that the clue in her hands related to the discovery of Stephanie's whereabouts as well as to that of her guilt.

A telegram received a little later on, however, was to turn this theory upside down. It was, like the former one, worded in the enigmatic language current in the Lynch Court establishment, but as it was a lengthier and more intricate message, it sent Mr. Dyer at once to his cipher book.

"Wonderful! She has cut them all out this time!" was Mr. Dyer's exclamation as he read and interpreted the final word.

In another ten minutes he had given over his office to the charge of his head clerk for the day, and was rattling along the streets in a hansom in the direction of Bishopsgate Station.

There he was lucky enough to catch a train just starting for Wreford.

"The event of the day," he muttered, as he settled himself comfortably in a corner seat, "will be the return journey when she tells me, bit by bit, how she has worked it all out."

It was not until close upon three o'clock in the afternoon that he arrived at the old-fashioned market town of Wreford. It chanced to be cattle-market day, and the station was crowded with drovers and farmers. Outside the station Loveday was waiting for him, as she had told him in her telegram that she would, in a four-wheeler.

"It's all right," she said to him as he got in; "he can't get away, even if he had an idea that we were after him. Two of the local police are waiting outside the house door with a warrant for his arrest, signed by a magistrate. I did not, however, see why the Lynch Court office should not have the credit of the thing, and so telegraphed to you to conduct the arrest."

They drove through the High Street to the outskirts of the town, where the shops became intermixed with private houses let out in offices. The cab pulled up outside one of these, and two policemen in plain clothes came forward, and touched their hats to Mr. Dyer.

"He's in there now, sir, doing his office work," said one of the men pointing to a door, just within the entrance, on which was painted in black letters, "The United Kingdom Cab-drivers' Beneficent Association." "I hear, however, that this is the last time he will be found there, as a week ago he gave notice to leave."

As the man finished speaking, a man, evidently of the cab-driving fraternity, came up the steps. He stared curiously at the little group just within the entrance, and then chinking his money in his hand, passed on to the office as if to pay his subscription.

"Will you be good enough to tell Mr. Emmett in there," said Mr. Dyer, addressing the man, "that a gentleman outside wishes to speak with him."

The man nodded and passed into the office. As the door opened, it disclosed to view an old gentleman seated at a desk apparently writing receipts for money. A little in his rear at his right hand, sat a young and decidedly good-looking man, at a table on which were placed various little piles of silver and pence. The get-up of this young man was gentleman-like, and his manner was affable and pleasant as he responded, with a nod and a smile, to the cab-driver's message.

"I sha'n't be a minute," he said to his colleague at the other desk, as he rose and crossed the room towards the door.

But once outside that door it was closed firmly behind him, and he found himself in the centre of three stalwart individuals, one of whom informed him that he held in his hand a warrant for the arrest of Harry Emmett on the charge of complicity in the Craigen Court robbery, and that he had "better come along quietly, for resistance would be useless."

Emmett seemed convinced of the latter fact. He grew deadly white for a moment, then recovered himself.

"Will someone have the kindness to fetch my hat and coat," he said in a lofty manner. "I don't see why I should be made to catch my death of cold because some other people have seen fit to make asses of themselves."

His hat and coat were fetched, and he was handed into the cab between the two officials.

"Let me give you a word of warning, young man," said Mr. Dyer, closing the cab door and looking in for a moment through the window at Emmett. "I don't suppose it's a punishable offence to leave a black bag on an old maid's doorstep, but let me tell you, if it had not been for that black bag you might have got clean off with your spoil."

Emmett, the irrepressible, had his answer ready. He lifted his hat ironically to Mr. Dyer; "You might have put it more neatly, guv'nor," he said; "if I had been in your place I would have said: 'Young man, you are being justly punished for your misdeeds; you have been taking off your fellow-creatures all your life long, and now they are taking off you.'"

Mr. Dyer's duty that day did not end with the depositing of Harry Emmett in the local jail. The search through Emmett's lodgings and effects had to be made, and at this he was naturally present. About a third of the lost jewellery was found there, and from this it was consequently concluded that his accomplices in the crime had considered that he had borne a third of the risk and of the danger of it.

Letters and various memoranda discovered in the rooms, eventually led to the detection of those accomplices, and although Lady Cathrow was doomed to lose the greater part of her valuable property, she had ultimately the satisfaction of knowing that each one of the thieves received a sentence proportionate to his crime.

It was not until close upon midnight that Mr. Dyer found himself seated in the train, facing Miss Brooke, and had leisure to ask for the links in the chain of reasoning that had led her in so remarkable a manner to connect the finding of a black bag, with insignificant contents, with an extensive robbery of valuable jewellery.

Loveday explained the whole thing, easily, naturally, step by step in her usual methodical manner.

"I read," she said, "as I dare say a great many other people did, the account of the two things in the same newspaper, on the same day, and I detected, as I dare say a great many other people did not, a sense of fun in the principal actor in each incident. I notice while all people are agreed as to the variety of motives that instigate crime, very few allow sufficient margin for variety of character in the criminal. We are apt to imagine that he stalks about the world with a bundle of deadly motives under his arm, and cannot picture him at his work with a twinkle in his eye and a keen sense of fun, such as honest folk have sometimes when at work at their calling."

Here Mr. Dyer gave a little grunt; it might have been either of assent or dissent.

Loveday went on:

"Of course, the ludicrousness of the diction of the letter found in the bag would be apparent to the most casual reader; to me the high falutin sentences sounded in addition strangely familiar; I had heard or read them somewhere I felt sure, although where I could not at first remember. They rang in my ears, and it was not altogether out of idle curiosity that I went to Scotland Yard to see the bag and its contents, and to copy, with a slip of tracing paper, a line or two of the letter. When I found that the handwriting of this letter was not identical with that of the translations found in the bag, I was confirmed in my impression that the owner of the bag was not the writer of the letter; that possibly the bag and its contents had been appropriated from some railway station for some distinct purpose; and, that purpose accomplished, the appropriator no longer wished to be burdened with it, and disposed of it in the readiest fashion that suggested itself. The letter, it seemed to me, had been begun with the intention of throwing the police off the scent, but the irrepressible spirit of fun that had induced the writer to deposit his clerical adjuncts upon the old maid's doorstep had proved too strong for him here, and had carried him away, and the letter that was intended to be pathetic ended in being comic."

"Very ingenious, so far," murmured Mr. Dyer: "I've no doubt when the contents of the bag are widely made known through advertisements a claimant will come forward, and your theory be found correct."

"When I returned from Scotland Yard," Loveday continued, "I found your note, asking me to go round and see you respecting the big jewel robbery. Before I did so I thought it best to read once more the newspaper account of the case, so that I might be well up in its details. When I came to the words that the thief had written across the door of the safe, 'To be Let, Unfurnished,' they at once connected themselves in my mind with the 'dying kiss to my Marchioness Mother,' and the solemn warning against the race-course and the book-maker, of the black-bag letter-writer. Then, all in a flash, the whole thing became clear to me. Some two or three years back my professional duties necessitated my frequent attendance at certain low class penny-readings, given in the South London slums. At these penny-readings young shop-assistants, and others of their class, glad of an opportunity for exhibiting their accomplishments, declaim with great vigour; and, as a rule, select pieces which their very mixed audience might be supposed to appreciate. During my attendance at these meetings, it seemed to me that one book of selected readings was a great favourite among the reciters, and I took the trouble to buy it. Here it is."

Here Loveday took from her cloakpocket "The Reciter's Treasury," and handed it to her companion.

"Now," she said, "if you will run your eye down the index column you will find the titles of those pieces to which I wish to draw your attention. The first is 'The Suicide's Farewell;' the second, 'The Noble Convict;' the third, 'To be Let, Unfurnished.' "

"By, Jove! so it is!" ejaculated Mr. Dyer.

"In the first of these pieces, 'The Suicide's Farewell,' occur the expressions with which the black-bag letter begins—'The fatal day has arrived,' etc., the warnings against gambling, and the allusions to the 'poor lifeless body.' In the second, 'The Noble Convict,' occur the allusions to the aristocratic relations and the dying kiss to the marchioness mother. The third piece, 'To be Let, Unfurnished,' is a foolish little poem enough, although I dare say it has often raised a laugh in a not too-discriminating audience. It tells how a bachelor, calling at a house to enquire after rooms to be let unfurnished, falls in love with the daughter of the house, and offers her his heart, which, he says, is to be let unfurnished. She declines his offer, and retorts that she thinks his head must be to let unfurnished too. With these three pieces before me, it was not difficult to see a thread of connection between the writer of the black-bag letter and the thief who wrote across the empty safe at Craigen Court. Following this thread, I unearthed the story of Harry Emmett—footman, reciter, general lover and scamp. Subsequently I compared the writing on my tracing paper with that on the safe-door and, allowing for the difference between a bit of chalk and a steel nib, came to the conclusion that there could be but little doubt but what both were written by the same hand. Before that, however, I had obtained another, and what I consider the most important, link in my chain of evidence—how Emmett brought his clerical dress into use."

"Ah, how did you find out that now?" asked Mr. Dyer, leaning forward with his elbows on his knees.

"In the course of conversation with Mrs. Williams, whom I found to be a most communicative person, I elicited the names of the guests who had sat down to dinner on Christmas Eve. They were all people of undoubted respectability in the neighborhood. Just before dinner was announced, she said, a young clergyman had presented himself at the front door, asking to speak with the Rector of the parish. The Rector, it seems, always dines at Craigen Court on

Christmas Eve. The young clergyman's story was that he had been
told by a certain clergyman, whose name he mentioned, that a curate
was wanted in the parish, and he had travelled down from London
to offer his services. He had been, he said, to the Rectory and had
been told by the servants where the Rector was dining, and fearing
to lose his chance of the curacy, had followed him to the Court.
Now the Rector had been wanting a curate and had filled the va-
cancy only the previous week; he was a little inclined to be irate at
this interruption to the evening's festivities, and told the young man
that he didn't want a curate. When, however, he saw how disappointed the poor young fellow looked—I believe he shed a tear
or two—his heart softened; he told him to sit down and rest in the
hall before he attempted the walk back to the station, and said he
would ask Sir George to send him out a glass of wine. The young
man sat down in a chair immediately outside the room by which the
thieves entered. Now I need not tell you who that young man was,
nor suggest to your mind, I am sure, the idea that while the servant
went to fetch him his wine, or, indeed, so soon as he saw the coast
clear, he slipped into that little room and pulled back the catch of the
window that admitted his confederates, who, no doubt, at that very
moment were in hiding in the grounds. The house-keeper did not
know whether this meek young curate had a black bag with him.
Personally I have no doubt of the fact, nor that it contained the cap,
cuffs, collar, and outer garments of Harry Emmett, which were
most likely re-donned before he returned to his lodgings at Wreford,
where I should say he repacked the bag with its clerical contents,
and wrote his serio-comic letter. This bag, I suppose, he must have
deposited in the very early morning, before anyone was stirring, on
the door-step of the house in the Easterbrook Road."

Mr. Dyer drew a long breath. In his heart was unmitigated admiration for his colleague's skill, which seemed to him to fall little
short of inspiration. By-and-by, no doubt, he would sing her praises
to the first person who came along with a hearty good will; he had
not, however, the slightest intention of so singing them in her own
ears—excessive praise was apt to have a bad effect on the rising practitioner.

So he contented himself with saying:

"Yes, very satisfactory. Now tell me how you hunted the fellow
down to his diggings?"

"Oh, that was mere A B C work," answered Loveday. "Mrs.
Williams told me he had left his place at Colonel James's about six
months previously, and had told her he was going to look after his
dear old grandmother, who kept a sweetstuff-shop; but where she
could not remember. Having heard that Emmett's father was a cab-
driver, my thoughts at once flew to the cabman's vernacular—you

know something of it, no doubt—in which their provident association is designated by the phrase, 'the dear old grandmother,' and the office where they make and receive their payments is styled 'the sweetstuff-shop.'"

"Ha, ha, ha! And good Mrs. Williams took it all literally, no doubt?"

"She did; and thought what a dear kind-hearted fellow the young man was. Naturally I supposed there would be a branch of the association in the nearest market of town, and a local trades' directory confirmed my supposition that there was one at Wreford. Bearing in mind where the black bag was found, it was not difficult to believe that young Emmett, possibly through his father's influence and his own prepossessing manners and appearance, had attained to some position of trust in the Wreford branch. I must confess I scarcely expected to find him as I did, on reaching the place, installed as receiver of the weekly moneys. Of course, I immediately put myself in communication with the police there, and the rest I think you know."

Mr. Dyer's enthusiasm refused to be longer restrained.

"It's capital, from first to last," he cried; "you've surpassed yourself this time!"

"The only thing that saddens me," said Loveday, "is the thought of the possible fate of that poor little Stephanie."

Loveday's anxieties on Stephanie's behalf were, however, to be put to flight before another twenty-four hours had passed. The first post on the following morning brought a letter from Mrs. Williams telling how the girl had been found before the night was over, half dead with cold and fright, on the verge of the stream running through Craigen Wood—"found too"—wrote the housekeeper, "by the very person who ought to have found her, young Holt, who was, and is so desperately in love with her. Thank goodness! at the last moment her courage failed her, and instead of throwing herself into the stream, she sank down, half-fainting, beside it. Holt took her straight home to his mother, and there, at the farm, she is now, being taken care of and petted generally by everyone."

MELVILLE DAVISSON POST (1871–1930)

is usually considered one of the major writers of detective fiction between Poe and Hammett. Born in West Virginia, he practiced as a lawyer and was in politics for several years before turning to writing as a career. At the time of his death he was one of the most highly paid authors in the American magazine world.

Post first achieved fame with his stories about the strange legal figure Randolph Mason. Mason, an embittered lawyer on the edge of insanity, uses his profound knowledge of the law to enable criminals to escape punishment through quirks in the legal code. Post's stories were legally impeccable, and it is said that they were occasionally instrumental in changing the law. Post was also very highly regarded for his stories about Uncle Abner, a cattle rancher in West Virginia in the 1840s or '50s, who often acted as the embodiment of justice.

"The Sheriff of Gullmore"

[The crime of embezzlement here dealt with is statutory. The venue of this story could have been laid in many other States; the statutes are similar to a degree. See the Code of West Virginia; also the late case of The State *vs.* Bolin, 19 Southwestern Reporter, 650; also the long list of ancient cases in Russell on Crimes, 2d volume.]

I.

"It is hard luck, Colonel," said the broker, "but you are not the only one skinned in the deal; the best of them caught it to-day. By Jupiter! the pit was like Dante's Inferno!"

"Yes, it's gone, I reckon," muttered the Colonel, shutting his teeth down tight on his cigar; "I guess the devil wins every two out of three."

"Well," said the broker, turning to his desk, "it is the fortune of war."

"No, young man," growled the Colonel, "it is the blasted misfortune of peace. I have never had any trouble with the fortune of war. I could stand on an ace high and win with war. It is peace that queers me. Here in the fag-end of the nineteenth century, I, Colonel Moseby Allen, sheriff of Gullmore County, West Virginia, go up against another man's game,—yes, and go up in the daytime. Say, young man, it feels queer at the mellow age of forty-nine, after you have been in the legislature of a great commonwealth, and at the very expiration of your term as sheriff of the whitest and the freest county in West Virginia,—I say it feels queer, after all those high honors, to be suddenly reminded that you need to be accompanied by a business chaperon."

The Colonel stood perfectly erect and delivered his oration with the fluency and the abandon of a southern orator. When he had finished, he bowed low to the broker, pulled his big slouch hat down on his forehead, and stalked out of the office and down the steps to the street.

Colonel Moseby Allen was built on the decided lines of a southern mountaineer. He was big and broad-shouldered, but he was not well proportioned. His body was short and heavy, while his legs were long. His eyes were deep-set and shone like little brown beads. On the whole, his face indicated cunning, bluster, and rashness. The ward politician would have recognized him among a thousand as a kindred spirit, and the professional gambler would not have felt so sure of himself with such a face across the table from him.

When the Colonel stepped out on the pavement, he stopped, thrust his hands into his pockets, and looked up and down Wall Street; then he jerked the cigar out of his mouth, threw it into the gutter, and began to deliver himself of a philippic upon the negative merits of brokers in general, and his broker in particular. The Virginian possessed a vocabulary of smooth billingsgate that in vividness and diversity approached the sublime. When he had consigned some seven generations of his broker's ancestry to divers minutely described localities in perdition, he began to warm to his work, and his artistic profanity rolled forth in startling periods.

The passers-by stopped and looked on in surprise and wonder. For a moment they were half convinced that the man was a religious fanatic, his eloquent, almost poetic, tirade was so thoroughly filled with holy names. The effect of the growing audience inspired the speaker. He raised his voice and began to emphasize with sweeping gestures. He had now finished with the broker's ancestry and was plunging with a rush of gorgeous pyrotechnics into the certain future of the broker hmself, when a police officer pushed through the crowd and caught the irate Virginian by the shoulder.

Colonel Allen paused and looked down at the officer.

"You," he said, calmly, "I opine are a minion of the law; a hireling of the municipal authorities."

"See here," said the officer, "you are not allowed to preach on the street. You will have to come with me to the station-house."

The Colonel bowed suavely. "Sir," he said, "I, Colonel Moseby Allen, sheriff of Gullmore County in the Mountain State of West Virginia, am a respecter of the law, even in the body of its petty henchmen, and if the ordinances of this God-forsaken Gomorrah are such that a free-born American citizen, twenty-one years old and white, is not permitted the inalienable privilege of expressing his opinion without let or hindrance, then I am quite content to accompany you to the confines of your accursed jail-house."

Allen turned round and started down the street with the officer. He walked a little in advance, and continued to curse glibly in a low monotone. When they were half way to the corner below, a little man slipped out of the crowd and hurried up to the policeman. "Mike," he whispered, putting his hand under the officer's, "here is five for you. Turn him over to me."

The officer closed his hand like a trap, stepped quickly forward, and touched his prisoner on the shoulder.

As the Virginian turned, the officer said in a loud voice: "Mr. Parks, here, says that he knows you, and that you are all right, so I'll let you go this time." Then, before any reply could be made, he vanished around the corner.

Colonel Allen regarded his deliverer with the air of a world-worn cynic. "Well," he said, "one is rarely delivered from the spoiler by the hand of his friend, and I cannot now recall ever having had you for an enemy. May I inquire what motive prompts this gracious courtesy?"

"Don't speak so loud," said Parks, stepping up close to the man. "I happen to know something about your loss, Colonel Allen, and perhaps also a way to regain it. Will you come with me?"

The Virginian whistled softly. "Yes," he said.

II.

"This is a fine hotel," observed Colonel Allen, beginning to mellow under the mystic spell of a five-course dinner and a quart of Cliquot. "Devilish fine hotel, Mr. Parks. All the divers moneys which I in my official capacity have collected in taxes from the fertile county of

Gullmore, would scarcely pay for the rich embellishment of the barber shop of this magnificent edifice."

"Well, Colonel," said the bald Parks, with a sad smile, "that would depend upon the amount of the revenues of your county. I presume that they are large, and consequently the office of sheriff a good one."

"Yes, sir," answered the Virginian, "it is generally considered desirable from the standpoint of prominence. The climate of Gullmore is salubrious. Its pasture lands are fertile, and its citizens cultured and refined to a degree unusual even in the ancient and aristocratic counties of the Old Dominion. And, sir,"—here the Colonel drew himself up proudly, and thrust his hand into the breast of his coat,—"I am proud, sir,—proud to declare that from time to time the good citizens of Gullmore, by means of their suffrage, and with large and comfortable majorities, have proclaimed me their favorite son and competent official. Six years ago I was in the legislature at Charleston as the trusted representative of this grand old county of Gullmore; and four years ago, after the fiercest and most bitterly contested political conflict of all the history of the South, I was elected to that most important and honorable office of sheriff,—to the lasting glory of my public fame, and the great gratification of the commonwealth."

"That gratification is now four years old?" mused Parks.

Colonel Moseby Allen darted a swift, suspicious glance at his companion, but in a moment it was gone, and he had dropped back into his grandiloquent discourse. "Yes, sir, the banner county of West Virginia, deserting her ancient and sacred traditions, and forgetting for the time the imperishable precepts of her patriotic fathers, has gone over to affiliate with the ungodly. We were beaten, sir,—beaten in this last engagement,—horse, foot, and dragoons,—beaten by a set of carpet-baggers,—a set of unregenerate political tricksters of such diabolical cunning that nothing but the gates of hell could have prevailed against them. Now, sir, now,—and I say it mournfully, there is nothing left to us in the county of Gullmore, save only honor."

"Honor," sneered Parks, "an imaginary rope to hold fools with! It won't fill a hungry stomach, or satisfy a delinquent account." The little clerk spoke the latter part of his sentence slowly and deliberately.

Again the suspicious expression passed over the face of Colonel Allen, leaving traces of fear and anxiety in its wake. His eyes, naturally a little crossed, drew in toward his nose, and the muscles around his mouth grew hard. For a moment he was silent, looking down into his glass; then, with an effort, he went on: "Yes, the whole shooting-match is in the hands of the Philistines. From the members of the County Court up to the important and responsible position which I have filled for the last four years, and when my accounts are finally wound up, I ——"

"Your accounts," murmured Parks, "when they are finally wound up, what then?"

Every trace of color vanished from the Virginian's face, his heavy jaws trembled, and he caught hold of the arms of the chair to steady himself.

Parks did not look up. He seemed deeply absorbed in studying the bottom of his glass. For a moment Colonel Moseby Allen had been caught off his guard, but it was only for a moment. He straightened up and underwent a complete transformation. Then, bending forward, he said, speaking low and distinctly: "Look here, my friend, you are the best guesser this side of hell. Now, if you can pick a winning horse we will divide the pool."

The two men were at a table in a corner of the Hoffman café, and, as it chanced, alone in the room. Parks glanced around quickly, then he leaned over and said: "That depends on just one thing, Colonel."

"Turn up the cards," growled the Virginian, shutting his teeth down tight on his lip.

"Well," said Parks, "you must promise to stick to your rôle to the end, if you commence with the play."

The southerner leaned back in his chair and stroked his chin thoughtfully. Finally he dropped his hand and looked up. "All right," he muttered; "I'll stand by the deal; throw out the cards."

Parks moved his chair nearer to the table and leaned over on his elbow. "Colonel," he said, "there is only one living man who can set up a successful counter-plot against fate, that is dead certain to win, and that man is here in New York to-day. He is a great lawyer, and besides being that, he is the greatest plotter since the days of Napoleon. Not one of his clients ever saw the inside of a prison. He can show men how to commit crimes in such a way that the law cannot touch them. No matter how desperate the position may be, he can always show the man who is in it a way by which he can get out. There is no case so hopeless that he cannot manage it. If money is needed, he can show you how to get it—a plain, practical way, by which you can get what you need and as much as you need. He has a great mind, but he is strangely queer and erratic, and must be approached with extreme care, and only in a certain way. This man," continued the little clerk, lowering his voice, "is named Randolph Mason. You must go to him and explain the whole matter, and you must do it just in the way I tell you."

Again the Virginian whistled softly. "My friend," he said, "there is a little too much mystery about this matter. I am not afraid of you, because you are a rascal; no one ever had a face like you that was not a rascal. You will stick to me because you are out for the stuff, and there is no possible way to make a dollar by throwing the game. I am not afraid of any living man, if I have an opportunity to see his face before the bluff is made. You are all right; your game is to use me in making some haul that is a little too high for yourself. That is what you have been working up to, and you are a smooth operator, my friend. A greenhorn would have concluded long ago that you were a detective, but I knew a blamed sight better than that the moment you made your first lead. In the first place, you are too sharp to waste your time with any such bosh, and in the second place, it takes cash to buy detectives, and there is nobody following me with cash. Gullmore county has no kick coming to it until my final settlements are made, and there is no man treading shoe leather that knows anything about the condition of my official business except myself, and perhaps also that shrewd and mysterious guesser—yourself. So, you see, I am not standing on ceremonies with you. But here, young man, comes in a dark horse, and you want me to bet on him blindfolded. Those are not the methods of Moseby Allen. I must be let in a little deeper on this thing."

"All I want you to do," said Parks, putting his hand confidentially on the Virginian's arm, "is simply to go and see Randolph Mason, and approach him in the way I tell you, and when you have done that, I will wager that you stay and explain everything to him."

Colonel Allen leaned back in his chair and thrust his hands into his pockets. "Why should I do that?" he said curtly.

"Well," murmured the little man mournfully, "one's bondsmen are entitled to some consideration; and then, there is the penitentiary. Courts have a way of sending men there for embezzlement."

"You are correct," said Allen, quietly, "and I have not time to go."

"At any rate," continued Parks, "there can be no possible danger to you. You are taking no chances. Mr. Mason is a member of the New York bar, and anything you may tell him he dare not reveal. The law would not permit him to do so if he desired. The whole matter would be kept as thoroughly inviolate as though it were made in the confessional. Your objections are all idle. You are a man in a desperate position. You are up to your waist in the quicksand, now, and, at the end of the year, it is bound to close over your head. It is folly to look up at the sky and attempt to ignore this fact. I offer to help you—not from any goodness of heart, understand, but because we can both make a stake in this thing. I need money, and you must have money,—that is the whole thing in a nutshell. Now," said Parks, rising from his chair, "what are you going to do?"

"Well," said the Virginian, drawing up his long legs and spreading out his fat hands on the table, "Colonel Moseby Allen, of the county of Gullmore, will take five cards, if you please."

III.

"This must be the place," muttered the Virginian, stopping under the electric light and looking up at the big house on the avenue. "That fellow said I would know the place by the copper-studded door, and there it is, as certain as there are back taxes in Gullmore." With that, Colonel Moseby Allen walked up the granite steps and began to grope about in the dark door-way for the electric bell. He could find no trace of this indispensable convenience, and was beginning to lapse into a flow of half-suppressed curses, when he noticed for the first time an ancient silver knocker fastened to the middle of the door. He seized it and banged it vigorously.

The Virginian stood in the dark and waited. Finally he concluded that the noise had not been heard, and was about to repeat the signal when the door was flung suddenly open, and a tall man holding a candle in his hand loomed up in the door-way.

"I am looking," stammered the southerner, "for one Randolph Mason, an attorney-at-law."

"I am Randolph Mason," said the man, thrusting the silver candlestick out before him. "Who are you, sir?"

"My name is Allen," answered the southerner, "Moseby Allen, of Gullmore county, West Virginia."

"A Virginian," said Mason, "what evil circumstance brings you here?"

Then Allen remembered the instructions which Parks had given him so minutely. He took off his hat and passed his hand across his forehead. "Well," he said, "I suppose the same thing that brings the others. We get in and plunge along just as far as we can. Then Fate shuts down the lid of her trap, and we have either to drop off the bridge or come here."

"Come in," said Mason. Then he turned abruptly and walked down the hall-way. The southerner followed, impressed by this man's individuality. Allen had pushed his way through life with bluff and bluster, and like that one in the scriptural writings, "neither feared God nor regarded man." His unlimited assurance had never failed him before any of high or low degree, and to be impressed with the power of any man was to him strange and uncomfortable.

Mason turned into his library and placed the candlestick on a table in the centre of the floor. Then he drew up two chairs and sat down in one of them motioning Allen to the other on the opposite side of the table. The room was long and empty, except for the rows of heavy book-cases standing back in the darkness. The floor was bare, and there was no furniture of any kind whatever, except the great table and the ancient highback chairs. There was no light but the candle standing high in its silver candlestick.

"Sir," said Mason, when the Virginian had seated himself, "which do you seek to evade, punishment or dishonor?"

The Virginian turned round, put his elbows on the table, and looked squarely across at his questioner. "I am not fool enough to care for the bark," he answered, "provided the dog's teeth are muzzled."

"It is well," said Mason, slowly, "there is often difficulty in dealing with double problems, where both disgrace and punishment are sought to be evaded. Where there is but one difficulty to face, it can usually be handled with ease. What others are involved in your matter?"

"No others," answered the Virginian; "I am seeking only to save myself."

"From the law only," continued Mason, "or does private vengeance join with it?"

"From the law only," answered Allen.

"Let me hear it all," said Mason.

"Well," said the Virginian, shifting uneasily in his chair, "my affairs are in a very bad way, and every attempt that I have made to remedy them has resulted only in disaster. I am walking, with my hands tied, straight into the penitentiary, unless some miracle can be performed in my favor. Everything has gone dead against me from my first fool move. Four years ago I was elected sheriff of Gullmore county in the State of West Virginia. I was of course required by law to give a large bond. This I had much difficulty in doing, for the reason that I have no estate whatever. Finally I induced my brother and my father, who is a very old man, to mortgage their property and thereby secured the requisite bond. I entered upon the duties of my office, and assumed entire control of the revenues of the county. For a time I managed them carefully and kept my private business apart from that of the county. But I had never been accustomed to strict business methods, and I soon found it most difficult to confine myself to them. Little by little I began to lapse into my old habit of carelessness. I neglected to keep up the settlements, and permitted the official business to become intermixed with my private accounts. The result was that I awoke one morning to find that I owed the county of Gullmore ten thousand dollars. I began at once to calculate the possibility of my being able to meet this deficit before the expiration of my term of office, and soon found that by no possible means would I be able to raise this amount out of the remaining fees. My gambling instincts at once asserted themselves. I took five thousand dollars, went to Lexington, and began to play the races in a vain, reckless hope that I might win enough to square my accounts. I lost from the very start. I came back to my county and went on as before, hoping against hope that something would turn up and let me out. Of course this was the dream of an idiot, and when the opposition won at the last election, and a new sheriff was installed, and I was left but a few months within which to close up my accounts, the end which I had refused to think of arose and stared me in the face. I was now at the end of my tether, and there was nothing there but a tomb. And even that way was not open. If I should escape the penitentiary by flight or by suicide, I would still leave my brother and my aged father to bear the entire burden of my defalcations; and when they, as my bondsmen, had paid the sum to the county, they would all be paupers."

The man paused and mopped the perspiration from his face. He was now terribly in earnest, and seemed to be realizing the gravity and the hopelessness of his crime. All his bluster and grandiloquent airs had vanished.

"Reckless and unscrupulous as I am," he went on, "I cannot bear to think of my brother's family beggars because of my wrong, or my father in his extreme old age turned out from under his own roof and driven into the poor-house, and yet it must come as certainly as the sun will rise tomorrow."

The man's voice trembled now, and the flabby muscles of his face quivered.

"In despair, I gathered up all the funds of the county remaining in my hands and hurried to this city. Here I went to the most reliable broker I could find and through him plunged into speculation. But all the devils in hell seemed to be fighting for my ruin. I was caught in that dread and unexpected crash of yesterday and lost everything. Strange to say, when I realized that my ruin was now complete, I felt a kind of exhilaration,—such, I presume, as is said to come to men when they are about to be executed. Standing in the very gaping jaws of ruin, I have to-day been facetious, even merry. Now, in the full glare of this horrible matter, I scarcely remember what I have been doing, or how I came to be here, except that this morning in Wall Street I heard some one speak of your ability, and I hunted up your address and came without any well defined plan, and, if you will pardon me, I will add that it was also without any hope."

The man stopped and seemed to settle back in his chair in a great heap.

Randolph Mason arose and stood looking down at the Virginian.

"Sir," said Mason, "none are ever utterly lost but the weak. Answer my question."

The Virginian pulled himself together and looked up.

"Is there any large fund," continued Mason, "in the hands of the officers of your county?"

"My successor," said Allen, "has just collected the amount of a levy ordered by the county court for the purpose of paying the remainder due on the court-house. He now has that fund in his hands."

"When was the building erected?" said Mason.

"It was built during the last year of my term of office, and paid for in part out of levies ordered while I was active sheriff. When my successor came in there still remained due the contractors on the work some thirty thousand dollars. A levy was ordered by the court shortly before my term expired, but the collection of this levy fell to the coming officer, so this money is not in my hands, although all the business up to this time has been managed by me, and the other payments on the building made from time to time out of moneys in my hands, and I have been the chief manager of the entire work and know more about it than any one else. The new sheriff came into my office a few days ago to inquire how he was to dispose of this money."

Mason sat down abruptly. "Sir," he said almost bitterly, "there is not enough difficulty in your matter to bother the cheapest intriguer in Kings county. I had hoped that yours was a problem of some gravity."

"I see," said the Virginian, sarcastically, "I am to rob the sheriff of this money in such a manner that it won't be known who received it, and square my accounts. That would be very easy indeed. I would have only to kill three men and break a bank. Yes, that would be very easy. You might as well tell me to have blue eyes."

"Sir," said Randolph Mason, slowly, "you are the worst prophet unhung."

"Well," continued the man, "there can be no other way. If it were turned over to me in my official capacity what good would it do? My bondsmen would be responsible for it. I would then have it to account for, and what difference, in God's name, can it make whether I am sent to the penitentiary for stealing money which I have already used, or for stealing this money? It all belongs to the county. It is two times six one way, and six times two the other way."

"Sir," said Mason, "I retract my former statement in regard to your strong point. Let me insist that you devote your time to prophecy. Your reasoning is atrocious."

"I am wasting my time here," muttered the Virginian, "there is no way out of it."

Randolph Mason turned upon the man. "Are you afraid of courts?" he growled.

"No," said the southerner, "I am afraid of nothing but the penitentiary."

"Then," said Mason, leaning over on the table, "listen to me, and you will never see the shadow of it."

IV.

"I suppose you are right about that," said Jacob Wade, the newly elected sheriff of Gullmore county, as he and Colonel Moseby Allen sat in the office of that shrewd and courteous official. "I suppose it makes no difference which one of us takes this money and pays the contractors,—we are both under good bonds, you know."

"Certainly, Wade, certainly," put in the Colonel, "your bond is as good as they can be made in Gullmore county, and I mean no disrespect to the Omnipotent Ruler of the Universe when I assert that the whole kingdom of heaven could not give a better bond than I have. You are right, Wade; you are always right; you are away ahead of the ringleaders of your party. I don't mind if I do say so. Of course, I am on the other side, but it was miraculous, I tell you, the way you swung your forces into line in the last election. By all the limping gods of the calendar, we could not touch you!"

Colonel Moseby Allen leaned over and patted his companion on the shoulder. "You are a sly dog, Wade," he continued. "If it had not been for you we would have beaten the bluebells of Scotland out of the soft-headed farmers who were trying to run your party. I told the boys you would pull the whole ticket over with you, but they didn't believe me. Next time they will have more regard for the opinion of Moseby Allen of Gullmore." The Colonel burst out into a great roar of laughter, and brought his fat hand down heavily on his knee.

Jacob Wade, the new sheriff, was a cadaverous-looking countryman, with a face that indicated honesty and egotism. He had come up from a farm, and had but little knowledge of business methods in general, and no idea of how the duties of his office should be properly performed. He puffed up visibly under the bald flattery of Allen, and took it all in like a sponge.

"Well," said Wade, "I suppose the boys did sort of expect me to help them over, and I guess I did. I have been getting ready to run for a long time, and I ain't been doing no fool things. When the Farmers Alliance people was organizing, I just stayed close home and sawed wood, and when the county was all stirred up about that there dog tax, I kept my mouth shut, and never said nothing."

"That's what you did, Wade," continued the Colonel, rubbing his hands; "you are too smooth to get yourself mixed up with a lot of new-fangled notions that would brand you all over the whole county as a crank. What a man wants in order to run for the office of sheriff is a reputation for being a square, solid, substantial business man, and that is what you had, Wade, and besides that you were a smooth, shrewd, far-sighted, machine politician."

Jacob Wade flushed and grew pompous under this eloquent recital of his alleged virtues. Allen was handling his man with skill. He was a natural judge of men, and possessed in no little degree the rare ability of knowing how to approach the individual in order to gain his confidence and goodwill.

"No," he went on, "I am not partisan enough to prevent me from appreciating a good clear-headed politician, no matter what his party affiliations may be. I am as firm and true to my principles as any of those high up in the affairs of state. I have been honored by my party time and again in the history of this commonwealth, and have defended and supported her policies on the stump, and in the halls of legislation, and I know a smooth man when I see him, and I honor him, and stick to him out of pure love for his intelligence and genius."

The Colonel arose. He now felt that his man was in the proper humor to give ready assent to the proposition which he had made, and he turned back to it with careless indifference.

"Now, Jacob," he said lowering his voice, "this is not all talk. You are a new officer, and I am an old one. I am familiar with all the routine business of the sheriffalty, and I am ready and willing and anxious to give all the information that can be of any benefit to you, and to do any and everything in my power to make your term of office as pleasant and profitable as it can be made. I am wholly and utterly at your service, and want you to feel that you are more than welcome to command me in any manner you see fit. By the way, here is this matter that we were just discussing. I am perfectly familiar with all that business. I looked after the building for the county, collected all the previous levies, and know all about the contracts with the builders—just what is due each one and just how the settlements are to be made,—and I am willing to take charge of this fund and settle the thing up. I suppose legally it is my duty to attend to this work, as it is in the nature of unfinished business of my term, but I could have shifted the whole thing over on you and gotten out of the trouble of making the final settlements with the contractors. The levy was ordered during my term, but has been collected by you, and on that ground I could have washed my hands of the troublesome matter if I had been disposed to be ugly. But I am not that kind of a man, Wade; I am willing to shoulder my lawful duties, and wind this thing up and leave your office clear and free from any old matters."

Jacob Wade, sheriff of Gullmore county, was now thoroughly convinced of two things. First, that he himself was a shrewd politician, with an intellect of almost colossal proportions, and second, that Colonel Moseby Allen was a great and good man, who was offering to do him a service out of sheer kindness of heart.

He arose and seized Allen's hand. "I am obliged to you, Colonel, greatly obliged to you," he said; "I don't know much about these matters yet, and it will save me a deal of trouble if you will allow me to turn this thing over to you, and let you settle it up. I reckon from the standpoint of law it is a part of your old business as sheriff."

"Yes," answered Allen, smiling broadly, "I reckon it is, and I reckon I ought n't to shirk it."

"All right," said Wade, turning to leave the office, "I'll just hand the whole thing over to you in the morning." Then he went out.

The ex-sheriff closed the door, sat down in his chair, and put his feet on the table. "Well, Moseby, my boy," he said, "that was dead easy. The Honorable Jacob Wade is certainly the most irresponsible idiot west of the Alleghany mountains. He ought to have a committee,—yes, he ought to have two committees, one to run him, and one to run his business." Then he rubbed his hands gleefully. "It is working like a greased clock," he chuckled, "and by the grace of God and the Continental Congress, when this funeral procession does finally start, it won't be Colonel Moseby Allen of the county of Gullmore who will occupy the hearse."

V.

The inhabitants of the city could never imagine the vast interest aroused in the county of Gullmore by the trial of Colonel Moseby Allen for embezzlement. In all their quiet lives the good citizens had not been treated to such a sweeping tidal wave of excitement. The annual visits of the "greatest show on earth" were scarcely able to fan the interests of the countrymen into such a flame. The news of Allen's arrest had spread through the country like wildfire. Men had talked of nothing else from the moment this startling information had come to their ears. The crowds on Saturday afternoons at the country store had constituted themselves courts of first and last resort, and had passed on the matter of the ex-sheriff's guilt at great length and with great show of learning. The village blacksmith had delivered ponderous opinions while he shod the traveller's horse; and the ubiquitous justice of the peace had demonstrated time and again with huge solemnity that Moseby Allen was a great criminal, and by no possible means could be saved from conviction. It was the general belief that the ex-sheriff would not stand trial; that he would by some means escape from the jail where he was confined. So firm-rooted had this conviction become that the great crowd gathered in the little county seat on the day fixed for the trial were considerably astonished when they saw the ex-sheriff sitting in the dock. In the evening after the first day of the trial, in which certain wholly unexpected things had come to pass, the crowd gathered on the porch of the country hotel were fairly revelling in the huge sensation.

Duncan Hatfield, a long ungainly mountaineer, wearing a red hunting-shirt and a pair of blue jeans trousers, was evidently the Sir-Oracle of the occasion.

"I tell you, boys," he was saying, "old Moseby ain't got no more show than a calliker apron in a brush fire. Why he jest laid down and give up; jest naturally lopped his ears and give up like a whipped dog."

"Yes," put in an old farmer who was standing a little back in the crowd, "I reckon nobody calkerlated on jest sich a fizzle."

"When he come into court this mornin'," continued the Oracle, "with that there young lawyer man Edwards, I poked Lum Bozier in the side, and told him to keep his eye skinned, and he would see the fur fly, because I knowed that Sam Lynch, the prosecutin' attorney, allowed to go fer old Moseby, and Sam is a fire-eater, so he is, and he ain't afraid of nuthin that walks on legs. But, Jerusalem! it war the tamest show that ever come to this yer town. Edwards jest sot down and lopped over like a weed, and Sam he begun, and he showed up how old Moseby had planned this here thing, and how he had lied to Jake Wade all the way through, and jest how he got that there money, and what an everlasting old rascal he was, and there sot Edwards, and he never asked no questions, and he never paid no attention to nuthin."

"Did n't the lawyer feller do nuthin at all, Dunk?" enquired one of the audience, who had evidently suffered the great misfortune of being absent from the trial.

"No," answered the Oracle, with a bovine sneer, "he never did nothin till late this evenin. Then he untangled his legs and got up and said somethin to the jedge about havin to let old Moseby Allen go, cause what he had done was n't no crime.

"Then you ought to a heard Sam. He jest naturally took the roof off; he sailed into old Moseby. He called him nine different kinds of horse-thieves, and when he got through, I could see old

Ampe Props noddin his head back thar in the jury-box, and then I knowed that it were all up with Colonel Moseby Allen, cause that jury will go the way old Ampe goes, jest like a pack of sheep."

"I reckon Moseby's lawyer were skeered out," suggested Pooley Hornick, the blacksmith.

"I reckon he war," continued the Oracle, "cause when Sam sot down, he got up, and he said to the jedge that he didn't want to do no argufying, but he had a little paper that would show why the jedge would have to let old Moseby go free, and then he asked Sam if he wanted to see it, and Sam he said no, he cared nuthin for his little paper. Then the feller went over and give the little paper to the jedge, and the jedge he took it and he said he would decide in the mornin'."

"You don't reckon," said the farmer, "that the jedge will give the old colonel any show, do you?"

"Billdad Solsberry," said the Oracle, with a grave judicial air, as though to settle the matter beyond question, "you are a plumb fool. If the angel Gabriel war to drop down into Gullmore county, he couldn't keep old Moseby Allen from goin' to the penitentiary."

Thus the good citizens sat in judgment, and foretold the doom of their fellow.

VI.

On Monday night, the eleventh day of May, in the thirty-third year of the State of West Virginia, the judge of the criminal court of Gullmore county, and the judge of the circuit court of Gullmore county were to meet together for the purpose of deciding two matters,—one relating to the trial of Moseby Allen, the retiring sheriff, for embezzling funds of the county, amounting to thirty thousand dollars, and the other, an action pending in the circuit court, wherein the State of West Virginia, at the relation of Jacob Wade, was seeking to recover this sum from the bondsmen of Allen. In neither of the two cases was there any serious doubt as to the facts. It seemed that it was customary for the retiring sheriff to retain an office in the court building after the installation of his successor, and continue to attend to the unfinished business of the county until all his settlements had been made, and until all the matters relating to his term of office had been finally wound up and administered.

In accordance with this custom, Moseby Allen after the expiration of his term, had continued in his office in a quasi-official capacity, in order to collect back taxes and settle up all matters carried over from his regular term.

It appeared that during Allen's term of office the county had built a court-house, and had ordered certain levies for the purpose of raising the necessary funds. The first of the levies had been collected by Allen, and paid over by him to the contractors, as directed by the county court. The remaining levies had not been collected during his term, but had been collected by the new sheriff immediately after his installation. This money, amounting to some thirty thousand dollars, had been turned over to Allen upon his claim that it grew out of the unfinished affairs of his term, and that, therefore, he was entitled to its custody. He had said to the new sheriff that the levy upon which it had been raised was ordered during his term, and the work for which it was to be paid all performed, and the bonds of the county issued, while he was active sheriff, and that he believed it was a part of the matters which were involved in his final settlements. Jacob Wade, then sheriff, believing that Allen was in fact the proper person to rightly administer this fund, and knowing that his bond to the county was good and would cover all his official affairs, had turned the entire fund over to him, and paid no further attention to the matter.

It appeared that, at the end of the year, Moseby Allen had made all of his proper and legitimate settlements fully and satisfactorily, and had accounted to the proper authorities for every dollar that had been collected by him during his term of office, but had refused and neglected to account for the money which he had received from Wade. When approached upon the subject, he had said plainly that he had used this money in unfortunate speculations and could not return it. The man had made no effort to check the storm of indignation that burst upon him; he firmly refused to discuss the matter, or to give any information in regard to it. When arrested, he had expressed no surprise, and had gone to the jail with the officer. At the trial, his attorney had simply waited until the evidence had been introduced, and had then arisen and moved the court to direct a verdict of not guilty, on the ground that Allen, upon the facts shown, had committed no crime punishable under the statutes of West Virginia.

The court had been strongly disposed to overrule this motion without stopping to consider it, but the attorney had insisted that a memorandum which he handed up would sustain his position, and that without mature consideration the judge ought not to force him into the superior court, whereupon his Honor, Ephraim Haines, had taken the matter under advisement until morning.

In the circuit court the question had been raised that Allen's bond covered only those matters which arose by virtue of his office, and that this fund was not properly included. Whereupon the careful judge of that court had adjourned to consider.

It was almost nine o'clock when the Honorable Ephraim Haines walked into the library to consult with his colleague of the civil court. He found that methodical jurist seated before a pile of reports, with his spectacles far out on the end of his nose,—an indication, as the said Haines well knew, that the said jurist had arrived at a decision, and was now carefully turning it over in his mind in order to be certain that it was in spirit and truth the very law of the land.

"Well, Judge," said Haines, "have you flipped the penny on it, and if so, who wins?"

The man addressed looked up from his book and removed his spectacles. He was an angular man, with a grave analytical face.

"It is not a question of who wins, Haines," he answered; "it is a question of law. I was fairly satisfied when the objection was first made, but I wanted to be certain before I rendered my decision. I have gone over the authorities, and there is no question about the matter. The bondsmen of Allen are not liable in this action."

"They are not!" said Haines, dropping his long body down into a chair. "It is public money, and the object of the bond is certainly to cover any defalcations."

"This bond," continued the circuit judge, "provides for the faithful discharge, according to law, of the duties of the office of sheriff during his continuance in said office. Moseby Allen ceased to be sheriff of this county the day his successor was installed, and on that day this bond ceased to cover his acts. This money was handed over by the lawful sheriff to a man who was not then an officer of this county. Moseby Allen had no legal right to the custody of this money. His duties as sheriff had ceased, his official acts had all determined, and there was no possible way whereby he could then perform an official act that would render his bondsmen liable. The action pending must be dismissed. The present sheriff, Wade, is the one responsible to the county for this money. His only recourse is an action of debt, or assumpsit, against Allen individually, and as Allen is notoriously insolvent, Wade and his bondsmen will have to make up this deficit."

"Well," said Haines, "that is hard luck."

"No," answered the judge, "it is not luck at all, it is the law. Wade permitted himself to be the dupe of a shrewd knave, and he must bear the consequences."

"You can depend upon it," said the Honorable Ephraim Haines, criminal judge by a political error, "that old Allen won't get off so easy with me. The jury will convict him, and I will land him for the full term."

"I was under the impression," said the circuit judge, gravely, "that a motion had been made in your court to direct an acquittal on the ground that no crime had been committed."

"It was," said Haines, "but of course it was made as a matter of form, and there is nothing in it."

"Have you considered it?"

"What is the use? It is a fool motion."

"Well," continued the judge, "this matter comes up from your court to mine on appeal, and you should be correct in your ruling. What authorities were cited?"

"Here is the memorandum," said the criminal judge, "you can run down the cases if you want to, but I know it is no use. The money belonged to the county and old Allen embezzled it,—that is admitted."

To this the circuit judge did not reply. He took the memorandum which Randolph Mason had prepared for Allen, and which the local attorney had submitted, and turned to the cases of reports behind him. He was a hard-working, conscientious man, and not least among his vexatious cares were the reckless decisions of the Honorable Ephraim Haines.

The learned judge of the criminal court put his feet on the table and began to whistle. When at length wearied of this intellectual diversion, he concentrated all the enrgy of his mammoth faculties on the highly cultured pastime of sharpening his penknife on the back of the Code.

At length the judge of the circuit court came back to the table, sat down, and adjusted his spectacles. "Haines," he said slowly, "you will have to sustain that motion."

"What!" cried the Honorable Ephraim, bringing the legs of his chair down on the floor with a bang.

"That motion," continued the judge, "must be sustained. Moseby Allen has committed no crime under the statutes of West Virginia."

"Committed no crime!" almost shouted the criminal jurist, doubling his long legs up under his chair, "why, old Allen admits that he got this money and spent it. He says that he converted it to his own use; that it was not his money; that it belonged to the county. The evidence of the State shows that he cunningly induced Wade to turn this money over to him, saying that his bond was good, and that he was entitled to the custody of the fund. The old rascal secured the possession of this money by trickery, and kept it, and now you say he has committed no crime. How in Satan's name do you figure it out?"

"Haines," said the judge, gravely, "I don't figure it out. The law cannot be figured out. It is certain and exact. It describes perfectly what wrongs are punishable as crimes, and exactly what elements must enter into each wrong in order to make it a crime. All right of discretion is taken from the trial court; the judge must abide by the law, and the law decides matters of this nature in no uncertain terms."

"Surely," interrupted Haines, beginning to appreciate the gravity of the situation, "old Allen can be sent to the penitentiary for this crime. He is a rank, out and out embezzler. He stole this money and converted it to his own use. Are you going to say that the crime of embezzlement is a dead letter?"

"My friend," said the judge, "you forget that there is no equity in the criminal courts. The crime of embezzlement is a pure creature of the statute. Under the old common law there was no such crime. Consequently society had no protection from wrongs of this nature, until this evil grew to such proportions that the law-making power began by statute to define this crime and provide for its punishment. The ancient English statutes were many and varied, and, following in some degree thereafter, each of the United States has its own particular statute, describing this crime as being composed of certain fixed technical elements. This indictment against Moseby Allen is brought under Section 19 of Chapter 145 of the Code of West Virginia, which provides: 'If any officer, agent, clerk or servant of this State, or of any county, district school district or municipal corporation thereof, or of any incorporated bank or other corporation, or any officer of public trust in this State, or any agent, clerk or servant of such officer of public trust, or any agent, clerk or servant of any firm or person, or company or association of persons not incorporated, embezzle or fraudulently convert to his own use, bullion, money, bank notes or other security for money, or any effects or property of another person which shall have come to his possession, or been placed under his care or management, by virtue of his office, place or employment, he shall be guilty of larceny thereof.'

"This is the statute describing the offence sought to be charged. All such statutes must be strictly construed. Applying these requisites of the crime to the case before us, we find that Allen cannot be convicted, for the reason that at the time this money was placed in his hands he was not sheriff of Gullmore county, nor was he in any sense its agent, clerk, or servant. And, second, if he could be said to continue an agent, clerk, or servant of this county, after the expiration of his term, he would continue such agent, clerk, or servant for the purpose only of administering those matters which might be said to lawfully pertain to the unfinished business of his office. This fund was in no wise connected with such unfinished affairs, and by no possible construction could he be said to be an agent, clerk, or servant of this county for the purpose of its distribution or custody. Again, in order to constitute such embezzlement, the money must have come into his possession by virtue of his office. This could not be, for the reason that he held no office. His time had expired; Jacob Wade was sheriff, and the moment Jacob Wade was installed, Allen's official capacity determined, and he became a private citizen, with only the rights and liabilities of such a citizen.

"Nor is he guilty of larceny, for the very evident reason that the proper custodian, Wade, voluntarily placed this money in his hands, and he received it under a *bona fide* color of right."

The Honorable Ephraim Haines arose, and brought his ponderous fist down violently on the table. "By the Eternal!" he said, "this is the cutest trick that has been played in the two Virginias for a century. Moseby Allen has slipped out of the clutches of the law like an eel."

"Ephraim," said the circuit judge, reproachfully, "this is no frivolous matter. Moseby Allen has wrought a great wrong, by which many innocent men will suffer vast injury, perhaps ruin. Such malicious cunning is dangerous to society. Justice cannot reach all wrongs; its hands are tied by the restrictions of the law. Why, under this very statute, one who was *de facto* an officer of the county or State, by inducing some other officer to place in his hands funds to which he was not legally entitled, could appropriate the funds so received with perfect impunity, and without committing any crime or rendering his bondsmen liable. Thus a clerk of the circuit court could use without criminal liability any money, properly belonging to the clerk of the county court, or sheriff, provided he could convince the clerk or sheriff that he was entitled to its custody; and so with any officer of the State or county, and this could be done with perfect ease where the officers were well known to each other and strict business methods were not observed. Hence all the great wrong and injury of embezzlement can be committed, and all the gain and profit of it be secured, without violating the statute or rendering the officer liable to criminal prosecution. It would seem that the rogue must be stupid indeed who could not evade the crime of embezzlement."

The man stopped, removed his spectacles, and closed them up in their case. He was a painstaking, honest servant of the commonwealth, and, like many others of the uncomplaining strong, performed his own duties and those of his careless companion without murmur or comment or hope of reward.

The Honorable Ephraim Haines arose and drew himself up pompously. "I am glad," he said, "that we agree on this matter. I shall sustain this motion."

The circuit judge smiled grimly. "Yes," he said, "it is not reason or justice, but it is the law."

VII.

At twelve the following night Colonel Moseby Allen, ex-sheriff of the county of Gullmore, now acquitted of crime by the commonwealth, hurried across the border for the purpose of avoiding certain lawless demonstrations on the part of his countrymen,—and of all his acts of public service, this was the greatest.

ANNA KATHARINE GREEN

(Mrs. Charles Rohlfs) (1846–1935) was the first important female writer of detective stories and long a significant figure among American authors. Born in Brooklyn, New York, she spent most of her adult life in Buffalo, writing partly as a hobby and partly for financial reasons. Her first detective novel, The Leavenworth Case *(1878), introduced the detective Ebenezer Gryce, who appeared in many of her later works. Her stories were immensely popular, and she continued writing well up into the 1920s. Her fiction is generally considered very uneven, craftsmanlike work often being mixed with stage rhetoric and bad writing. Her plotting, however, has always been admired.*

"The Staircase at the Heart's Delight"

AS TOLD BY MR. GRYCE

"In the spring of 1840, the attention of the New York police was attracted by the many cases of well-known men found drowned in the various waters surrounding the lower portion of our great city. Among these may be mentioned the name of Elwood Henderson, the noted tea merchant, whose remains were washed ashore at Redhook Point; and of Christopher Bigelow, who was picked up off Governor's Island after having been in the water for five days, and of another well-known millionaire whose name I cannot now recall, but who, I remember, was seen to walk towards the East River one March evening, and was not met with again till the 5th of April, when his body floated into one of the docks near Peck Slip.

"As it seemed highly improbable that there should have been a concerted action among so many wealthy and distinguished men to end their lives within a few weeks of each other, and all by the same method of drowning, we soon became suspicious that a more serious verdict than that of suicide should have been rendered in the case of Henderson, Bigelow and the other gentleman I have mentioned. Yet one fact, common to all these cases, pointed so conclusively to deliberate intention on the part of the sufferers that we hesitated to take action.

"This was, that upon the body of each of the above-mentioned persons there were found, not only valuables in the shape of money and jewelry, but papers and memoranda of a nature calculated to fix the identity of the drowned man, in case the water should rob him of his personal characteristics. Consequently, we could not ascribe these deaths to a desire for plunder on the part of some unknown person.

"I was a young man in those days, and full of ambition. So, though I said nothing, I did not let this matter drop when the others did, but kept my mind persistently upon it and waited, with odd results as you will hear, for another victim to be reported at police headquarters.

"Meantime I sought to discover some bond or connection between the several men who had been found drowned, which would serve to explain their similar fate. But all my efforts in this direction were fruitless. There was no bond between them, and the matter remained for a while an unsolved mystery.

"Suddenly one morning a clew was placed, not in my hands, but in those of a superior official who at that time exerted a great influence over the whole force. He was sitting in his private room, when there was ushered into his presence a young man of a dissipated but not unprepossessing appearance, who, after a pause of marked embarrassment, entered upon the following story:

"I don't know whether or no, I should offer an excuse for the communication I am about to make; but the matter I have to relate is simply this: Being hard up last night (for though a rich man's son I often lack money), I went to a certain pawn-shop in the Bowery where I had been told I could raise money on my prospects. This place—you may see it some time, so I will not enlarge upon it—did not strike me favorably; but, being very anxious for a certain definite sum of money, I wrote my name in a book which was brought to me from some unknown quarter, and proceeded to follow the young woman who attended me into what she was pleased to call her good master's private office. He may have been a good master, but he was anything but a good man. In short, sir, when he found out who I was, and how much I needed money, he suggested that I should make an appointment with my father at a place he called Judah's in

Grand Street, where, said he, 'your little affair will be arranged, and you made a rich man within thirty days. That is,' he slyly added, 'unless your father has already made a will, disinheriting you.'

"I was shocked, sir, shocked beyond all my powers of concealment, not so much at his words, which I hardly understood, as at his looks, which had a world of evil suggestion in them; so I raised my fist and would have knocked him down, only that I found two young fellows at my elbows, who held me quiet for five minutes, while the old fellow talked to me. He asked me if I came to him on a fool's errand or really to get money; and when I admitted that I had cherished hopes of obtaining a clear two thousand dollars from him, he coolly replied that he knew of but one way in which I could hope to get such an amount, and that if I was too squeamish to adopt it, I had made a mistake in coming to his shop, which was no missionary institution, etc., etc. Not wishing to irritate him, for there was menace in his eye, I asked, with a certain weak show of being sorry for my former heat, whereabouts in Grand Street I should find this Judah. The retort was quick, 'Judah is not his name,' said he, 'and Grand Street is not where you are to go to find him. I threw out a bait to see if you would snap at it, but I find you timid, and therefore advise you to drop the matter entirely.' I was quite willing to do so, and answered him to this effect; whereupon, with a side glance I did not understand but which made me more or less uneasy in regard to his intentions towards me, he motioned to the men who held my arms to let go their hold, which they at once did.

" 'We have your signature,' growled the old man as I went out. 'If you peach on us or trouble us in any way we will show it to your father and that will put an end to all your hopes of future fortune.' Then raising his voice he shouted to the girl in the outer office, 'Let the young man see what he has signed.' She smiled and again brought forward the book in which I had so recklessly placed my name, and there at the top of the page I read these words: 'For moneys received, I agree to notify Levi Solomon, within the month, of the death of my father, that he may recover from me, without loss of time, the sum of ten thousand dollars from the amount I am bound to receive as my father's heir.' The sight of these lines knocked me hollow. But I am less a coward morally than physically, and I determined to acquaint my father at once with what I had done, and get his advice as to whether or not I should inform the police of my adventure. He heard me with more consideration than I expected, but insisted that I should immediately make known to you my experience in this Bowery pawnbroker's shop.

"The officer, highly interested, took down the young man's statement in writing, and, after getting a more accurate description of the Jew's house, allowed his visitor to go.

"Fortunately for me I was in the building at the time, and was able to respond when a man was called up to investigate this matter. Thinking that I saw a connection between it and the various mysterious deaths of which I have previously spoken, I entered into the affair with much spirit. But, wishing to be sure that my possibly unwarranted conclusions were correct, I took pains to inquire, before proceeding upon my errand, into the character of the heirs who had inherited the property of Elwood Henderson and Christopher Bigelow, and found that in each case there was one among the rest who was well known for his profligacy and reckless expenditure. It was a significant discovery, and increased, if possible, my interest in running down this nefarious trafficker in the lives of wealthy men.

"Knowing that I could hope for no success in my character of detective, I made an arrangement with the father of the young gentleman before alluded to, by which I was to enter the pawn-shop as an emissary of the latter. I accordingly appeared there, one dull November afternoon, in the garb of a certain western sporting man, who, for a consideration, allowed me the temporary use of his name and credentials.

"Entering beneath the three golden balls, with the swagger and general air of ownership I thought most likely to impose upon the self-satisfied female who presided over the desk, I asked to see her boss.

" 'On your own business?' she queried, glancing with suspicion at my short coat, which was rather more showy than elegant.

" 'No,' I returned, 'not on my own business, but on that of a young gent——'

" 'Anyone whose name is written here?' she interposed, reaching towards me the famous book, over the top of which, however, she was careful to lay her arm.

"I glanced down the page she had opened and instantly detected that of the young gentleman on whose behalf I was supposed to be there, and nodded 'Yes,' with all the assurance of which I was capable.

" 'Very well, then,' said she, 'come!' and she ushered me without much ado into a den of discomfort where sat a man, with a great beard and such heavy overhanging eyebrows that I could hardly detect the twinkle of his eyes, keen and incisive as they were.

"Smiling upon him, but not in the same way I had upon the girl, I glanced behind me at the open door, and above me at the partitions, which failed to reach the ceiling. Then I shook my head and drew a step nearer.

" 'I have come,' I insinuatingly whispered, 'on behalf of a certain party who left this place in a huff a day or so ago, but who since then has had time to think the matter over, and has sent me with an apology which he hopes'— here I put on a diabolical smile, copied, I declare to you, from the one I saw at that moment on his own lips— 'you will accept.'

"The old wretch regarded me for full two minutes in a way to unmask me had I possessed less confidence in my disguise and in my ability to support it.

" 'And what is this young gentleman's name?' he finally asked.

"For reply, I handed him a slip of paper. He took it and read the few lines written on it, after which he began to rub his palms together with a shaky unction eminently in keeping with the stray glints of light that now and then found their way through his bushy eyebrows.

" 'And so the young gentleman had not the courage to come again himself?' he softly suggested, with just the suspicion of an ironical laugh. 'Thought, perhaps, I would exact too much commission; or make him pay too roundly for his impertinent assurance.'

"I shrugged my shoulders, but vouchsafed no immediate reply, and he saw that he had to open the business himself. He did it warily and with many an incisive question which would have tripped me up if I had not been very much on my guard; but it all ended, as such matters usually do, in mutual understanding, and a promise that if the young gentleman was willing to sign a certain paper, which, by the way, was not shown me, he would in exchange give him an address which, if made proper use of, would lead to my patron finding himself an independent man within a very few days.

"As this address was the thing above all others which I most desired, I professed myself satisfied with the arrangement, and proceeded to hunt up my patron, as he was called. Informing him of the result of my visit, I asked if his interest in ferreting out these criminals was strong enough to lead him to sign the vile document which the Jew would probably have in readiness for him on the morrow; and being told it was, we separated for that day, with the understanding that we were to meet the next morning at the spot chosen by the Jew for the completion of his nefarious bargain.

"Being certain that I was being followed in all my movements by the agents of this adept in villainy, I took care, upon leaving Mr. L——, to repair to the hotel of the sporting man I was personifying. Making myself square with the proprietor, I took up my quarters in the room of my sporting friend, and, the better to deceive any spy who might be lurking about, I received his letters and sent out his telegrams, which, if they did not create confusion in the affairs of 'The Plunger,' must at least have occasioned him no little work the next day.

"Promptly at ten o'clock on the following morning I met my patron at the place of rendezvous appointed by the old Jew; and when I

tell you that this was no other than the old cemetery of which a portion is still to be seen off Chatham Square, you will understand the
uncanny nature of this whole adventure, and the lurking sense there
was in it of brooding death and horror. The scene, which in these
days is disturbed by elevated railroad trains and the flapping of long
lines of parti-colored clothes strung high up across the quiet tomb-
stones, was at that time one of peaceful rest, in the midst of a quarter
devoted to everything for which that rest is the fitting and desirable
end; and as we paused among the mossy stones, we found it hard to
realize that in a few minutes there would be standing beside us the
concentrated essence of all that was evil and despicable in human nature.

"He arrived with a smile on his countenance that completed his
ugliness, and would have frightened any honest man from his side at
once. Merely glancing my way, he shuffled up to my companion,
and leading him aside, drew out a paper which he laid on a flat
tombstone with a gesture significant of his desire that the other
should affix to it the required signature.

"Meantime I stood guard, and while attempting to whistle a
light air, was carelessly taking in the surroundings, and conjecturing,
as best I might, the reasons which had induced the old ghoul to
make use of the spot for his diabolical business, and had about decided that it was because he was a ghoul, and thus felt at home
among the symbols of mortality, when I caught sight of two or three
young fellows, who were lounging on the other side of the fence.

"These were so evidently accomplices that I wondered if the
two sly boys I had engaged to stand by me through this affair had
spotted them, and would know enough to follow them back to their
haunts.

"A few minutes later, the old rascal came sneaking towards me,
with a gleam of satisfaction in his half-closed eyes.

" 'You are not wanted any longer,' he grunted. 'The young gentleman told me to say that he could look out for himself now.'

" 'The young gentleman had better pay me the round fifty he
promised me,' I grumbled in return, with that sudden change from
indifference to menace which I thought best calculated to further my
plans; and shouldering the miserable wretch aside, I stepped up to
my companion, who was still lingering in a state of hesitation among
the gravestones.

" 'Quick! Tell me the number and street which he has given
you!' I whispered, in a tone strangely in contrast with the angry and
reproachful air I had assumed.

"He was about to answer, when the old fellow came sidling up
behind us. Instantly the young man before me rose to the occasion,
and putting on an air of conciliation said in a soothing tone:

" 'There, there, don't bluster. Do one thing more for me, and I will add another fifty to those I promised you. Conjure up an anonymous letter—you know how—and send it to my father, saying that if he wants to know where his son loses his hundreds, he must go to the place on the dock, opposite 5 South Street, some night shortly after nine. It would not work with most men, but it will with my father, and when he has been in and out of that place, and I succeed to the fortune he will leave me, then I will remember you, and——'

" 'Say, too,' a sinister voice here added in my ear, 'that if he wishes to effect an entrance into the gambling den which his son haunts, he must take the precaution of tying a bit of blue ribbon in his button-hole. It is a signal meaning business, and must not be forgotten,' chuckled the old fellow, evidently deceived at last into thinking I was really one of his own kind.

"I answered by a wink, and taking care to attempt no further communication with my patron, I left the two, as soon as possible, and went back to the hotel, where I dropped 'the sport,' and assumed a character and dress which enabled me to make my way undetected to the house of my young patron, where for two days I lay low, waiting for a suitable time in which to make my final attempt to penetrate this mystery.

"I knew that for the adventure I was now contemplating considerable courage was required. But I did not hesitate. The time had come for me to show my mettle. In the few communications I was enabled to hold with my superiors I told them of my progress and arranged with them my plan of work. As we all agreed that I was about to encounter no common villainy, these plans naturally partook of finesse, as you will see if you will follow my narrative to the end.

"Early in the evening of a cool November night I sallied forth into the streets, dressed in the habiliments and wearing the guise of the wealthy old gentleman whose secret guest I had been for the last few days. As he was old and portly, and I young and spare, this disguise had cost me no little thought and labor. But assisted as I was by the darkness, I had but little fear of betraying myself to any chance spy who might be upon the watch, especially as Mr. L—— had a peculiar walk, which, in my short stay with him, I had learned to imitate perfectly. In the lapel of my overcoat I had tied a tag of blue ribbon, and, though for all I knew this was a signal devoting me to a secret and mysterious death, I walked along in a buoyant condition of mind, attributable, no doubt, to the excitement of the venture and to my desire to test my powers, even at the risk of my life.

"It was nine o'clock when I reached South Street. It was no new region to me, nor was I ignorant of the specified drinking den on the dock to which I had been directed. I remembered it as a bright spot in a mass of ship-prows and bow-rigging, and was possessed, besides, of a vague consciousness that there was something odd in connection with it which had aroused my curiosity sufficiently in the past for me to have once formed the resolution of seeing it again under circumstances which would allow me to give it some attention. But I never thought that the circumstances would involve my own life, impossible as it is for a detective to reckon upon the future or to foresee the events into which he will be hurried by the next crime which may be reported at police headquarters.

"There were but few persons in the street when I crossed to The Heart's Delight,—so named from the heart-shaped opening in the framework of the door, through which shone a light, inviting enough to one chilled by the keen November air and oppressed by the desolate appearance of the almost deserted street. But amongst those persons I thought I recognized more than one familiar form, and felt reassured as to the watch which had been set upon the house. The night was dark and the river especially so, but in the gloomy space beyond the dock I detected a shadow blacker than the rest, which I took for the police-boat they had promised to have in readiness in case I needed rescue from the water-side. Otherwise the surroundings were as usual, and saving the gruff singing of some drunken sailor comming from a narrow side street near by, no sound disturbed the somewhat lugubrious silence of this weird and forsaken spot.

"Pausing an instant before entering, I glanced up at the building, which was about three stories high, and endeavored to see what there was about it which had once arrested my attention, and came to the conclusion that it was its exceptional situation on the dock, and the ghostly effect of the hoisting-beam projecting from the upper story like a gibbet. And yet this beam was common to many a warehouse in the vicinity, though in none of them were there any such signs of life as proceeded from the curious mixture of sail loft, boat shop and drinking saloon, now before me. Could it be that the ban of criminality was upon the house, and that I had been conscious of this without being able to realize the cause of my interest?

"Not stopping to solve my sensations further, I tried the door, and, finding it yield easily to my touch, turned the knob and entered. For a moment I was blinded by the smoky glare of the heated atmosphere into which I stepped, but presently I was able to distinguish the vague outlines of an oyster bar in the distance, and the motionless figures of some half dozen men, whose movements had been arrested by my sudden entrance. For an instant this picture remained; then the drinking and card-playing resumed, and I stood, as it were, alone on the sanded floor near the door. Improving the opportunity for a closer inspection of the place, I was struck by its picturesqueness. It had evidently been once used as a ship chandlery, and on the walls, which were but partly plastered, there still hung old bits of marlin, rusty rings and such other evidences of former traffic as did not interfere with the present more lucrative business.

"Below were the two bars, one at the right of the door, and the other at the lower end of the room near a window, through whose small, square panes I caught a glimpse of the colored lights of a couple of ferry boats, passing each other in midstream.

"At a table near me sat two men, grumbling at each other over a game of cards. They were large and powerful figures in the contracted space of this long and narrow room, and my heart gave a bound of joy as I recognized on them certain marks by which I was to know friend from foe in this possible den of thieves and murderers.

"Two sailors at the bar were *bona fide* habitués of the place, and so I judged to be the one or two other specimens of water-side character whose backs I could faintly discern in one of the dim corners. Meantime a man was approaching me.

"Let me see if I can describe him. He was about thirty, and had the complexion and figure of a consumptive, but his eye shone with the yellow glare of a beast of prey, and in the cadaverous hollows of his ashen cheeks and amid the lines about his thin drawn lips there lay for all his conciliatory smile, an expression so cold and yet so ferocious that I spotted him at once as the man to whose genius we were indebted for the new scheme of murder which I was jeopardizing my life to understand. But I allowed none of the repugnance with which he inspired me to appear in my manner, and, greeting him with half a nod, waited for him to speak. His voice had that smooth quality which betrays the hypocrite.

" 'Has the gentleman an appointment here?' he asked, letting his glance fall for the merest instant on the lapel of my coat.

"I returned a decided affirmative. 'Or rather,' I went on, with a meaning look he evidently comprehended, 'my son has, and I have made up my mind to know just what deviltry he is up to these days. You see I can make it worth your while to give me the opportunity.'

'O, I see,' he assented with a glance at the pocketbook I had just drawn out. 'You want a private room from which you can watch the young scapegrace. I understand, I understand. But the private rooms are above. Gentlemen are not comfortable here.'

" 'I should say not,' I murmured, and drew from the pocketbook a bill which I slid quietly into his hand. 'Now take me where I shall be safe,' I suggested, 'and yet in full sight of the room where the young gentlemen play. I wish to catch him at his tricks. Afterwards——'

" 'All will be well,' he finished smoothly, with another glance at my blue ribbon. 'You see I do not ask you the young gentleman's name. I take your money and leave all the rest to you. Only don't make a scandal, I pray, for my house has the name of being quiet.'

" 'Yes,' thought I, 'too quiet!' and for an instant felt my spirits fail me. But it was only for an instant. I had friends about me and a pistol at half cock in the pocket of my overcoat. Why should I fear any surprise, prepared as I was for every emergency?

" 'I will show you up in a moment,' said he; and left me to put up a heavy board-shutter over the window opening on the river. Was this a signal or a precaution? I glanced towards my two friends playing cards, took another note of their broad shoulders and brawny arms, and prepared to follow my host, who now stood bowing at the other end of the room, before a covered staircase which was manifestly the sole means of reaching the floor above.

"The staircase was quite a feature in the room. It ran from back to front, and was boarded all the way up to the ceiling. On these boards hung a few useless bits of chain, wire and knotted ends of tarred ropes, which swung to and fro as the sharp November blast struck the building, giving out a weird and strangely muffled sound. Why did this sound, so easily to be accounted for, ring in my ears like a note of warning? I understand now, but I did not then, full of expectation as I was for developments out of the ordinary.

"Crossing the room, I entered upon the staircase, in the wake of my companion. Though the two men at cards did not look up as I passed them, I noticed that they were alert and ready for any signal I might choose to give them. But I was not ready to give one yet. I must see danger before I summoned help, and there was no token of danger yet.

"When we were about half-way up the stairs the faint light which had illuminated us from below suddenly vanished, and we found ourselves in total darkness. The door at the foot had been closed by a careful hand, and I felt, rather than heard, the stealthy pushing of a bolt across it.

"My first impulse was to forsake my guide and rush back, but I subdued the unworthy impulse and stood quite still, while my companion exclaiming, 'Damn that fellow! What does he mean by shutting the door before we're half-way up!' struck a match and lit a gas jet in the room above, which poured a flood of light upon the staircase. Drawing my hand from the pocket in which I had put my revolver, I hastened after him into the small landing at the top of the stairs. An open door was before me, in which he stood bowing, with the half-burnt match in his hand. 'This is the place, sir,' he announced, motioning me in.

"I entered and he remained by the door, while I passed quickly about the room, which was bare of every article of furniture save a solitary table and chair. There was not even a window in it, with the exception of one small light situated so high up in the corner made by the jutting-up staircase that I wondered at its use, and was only relieved of extreme apprehension at the prison-like appearance of the place by the gleam of light which came through this dusty pane, showing that I was not entirely removed from the presence of my foes if I was from that of my friends.

" 'Ah, you have spied the window,' remarked my host, advancing toward me with a countenance he vainly endeavored to make reassuring and friendly. 'That is your post of observation, sir,' he whispered, with a great show of mystery. 'By mounting on the table you can peer into the room where my young friends sit securely at play.'

"As it was not part of my scheme to show any special mistrust, I merely smiled a little grimly, and cast a glance at the table on which stood a bottle of brandy and one glass.

" 'Very good brandy,' he whispered, 'Not such stuff as we give those fellows down-stairs.'

"I shrugged my shoulders and he slowly backed towards the door.

" 'The young men you bid me watch are very quiet,' I suggested, with a careless wave of my hand towards the room he had mentioned.

" 'Oh, there is no one there yet. They begin to straggle in about ten o'clock.'

" 'Ah,' was my quiet rejoinder, 'I am likely, then, to have use for your brandy.'

"He smiled again and made a swift motion towards the door.

" 'If you want anything,' said he, 'just step to the foot of the staircase and let me know. The whole establishment is at your service.' And with one final grin that remains in my mind as the most threatening and diabolical I have ever witnessed, he laid his hand on the knob of the door and slid quickly out.

It was done with such an air of final farewell, that I felt my apprehensions take a positive form. Rushing towards the door through which he had just vanished, I listened and heard, as I thought, his stealthy feet descend the stair. But when I sought to follow, I found myself for the second time overwhelmed by darkness. The gas jet, which had hitherto burned with great brightness in the small room, had been turned off from below, and beyond the faint glimmer which found its way through the small window of which I have spoken, not a ray of light now disturbed the heavy gloom of this gruesome apartment.

"I had thought of every contingency but this, and for a few minutes my spirits were dashed. But I soon recovered some remnants of self-possession, and began feeling for the knob I could no longer see. Finding it after a few futile attempts, I was relieved to discover that this door at least was not locked; and, opening it with a careful hand, I listened intently, but could hear nothing save the smothered sound of men talking in the room below.

"Should I signal for my companions? No, for the secret was not yet mine as to how men passed from this room into the watery grave which was the evident goal for all wearers of the blue ribbon.

"Stepping back into the middle of the room, I carefully pondered my situation, but could get no further than the fact that I was somehow, and in some way, in mortal peril. Would it come in the form of a bullet, or a deadly thrust from an unseen knife? I did not think so. For, to say nothing of the darkness, there was one reassuring fact which recurred constantly to my mind in connection with the murders I was endeavoring to trace to this den of iniquity.

"None of the gentlemen who had been found drowned had shown any marks of violence on their bodies, so it was not attack I was to fear, but some mysterious, underhanded treachery which would rob me of consciousness and make the precipitation of my body into the water both safe and easy. Perhaps it was in the bottle of brandy that the peril lay; perhaps—but why speculate further! I would watch till midnight and then, if nothing happened, signal my companions to raid the house.

"Meantime a peep into the next room might help me towards solving the mystery. Setting the bottle and glass aside, I dragged the table across the floor, placed it under the lighted window, mounted, and was about to peer through, when the light in that apartment was put out also. Angry and overwhelmed, I leapt down, and, stretching out my hands till they touched the wainscoting, I followed the wall around till I came to the knob of the door, which I frantically clutched. But I did not turn it immediately, I was too anxious to catch these villains at work. Would I be conscious of the harm they meditated against me, or would I imperceptibly yield to some influence of which I was not yet conscious, and drop to the floor before I could draw my revolver or put to my mouth the whistle upon which I depended for assistance and safety? It was hard to tell, but I determined to cling to my first intention a little longer, and so stood waiting and counting the minutes, while wondering if the captain of the police boat was not getting impatient, and whether I had not more to fear from the anxiety of my friends than the cupidity of my foes.

"You see I had anticipated communicating with the men in this boat by certain signals and tokens which had been arranged between us. But the lack of windows in the room had made all such arrangements futile, so I knew as little of their actions as they of my sufferings; all of which did not tend to add to the cheerfulness of my position.

"I, however, held out for a half-hour, listening, waiting and watching in a darkness which, like that of Egypt, could be felt, and when the suspense grew intolerable I struck a match and let its blue flame flicker for a moment over the face of my watch. But the matches soon gave out and with them my patience, if not my courage, and I determined to end the suspense by knocking at the door beneath.

"This resolution taken, I pulled open the door before me and stepped out. Though I could see nothing, I remembered the narrow landing at the top of the stairs, and, stretching out my arms, I felt for the boarding on either hand, guiding myself by it, and began to descend, when something rising, as it were, out of the cavernous darkness before me made me halt and draw back in mingled dread and horror.

"But the impression, strong as it was, was only momentary, and, resolved to be done with the matter, I precipitated myself downward, when suddenly, at about the middle of the staircase, my feet slipped and I slid forward, plunging and reaching out with hands whose frenzied grasp found nothing to cling to, down a steep inclined plane—or what to my bewildered senses appeared such,—till I struck a yielding surface and passed with one sickening plunge into the icy waters of the river which in another moment had closed dark and benumbing above my head.

"It was all so rapid I did not think of uttering a cry. But happily for me the splash I made told the story, and I was rescued before I could sink a second time.

"It was a full half hour before I had sufficiently recovered from the shock to relate my story. But when once I had made it known, you can imagine the gusto with which the police prepared to enter the house and confound the obliging host with a sight of my dripping garments and accusing face. And indeed in all my professional experience I have never beheld a more sudden merging of the bully into a coward than was to be seen in this slick villain's face, when I was suddenly pulled from the crowd and placed before him, with the old man's wig gone from my head, and the tag of blue ribbon still clinging to my wet coat.

"His game was up, and he saw it; and Ebenezer Gryce's career had begun.

"Like all destructive things the device by which I had been run into the river was simple enough when understood. In the first place it had been constructed to serve the purpose of a stairway and chute. The latter was in plain sight when it was used by the sailmakers to run the finished sails into the waiting yawls below. At the time of my adventure, and for some time before, the possibilities of the place had been discovered by mine host, who had ingeniously put a partition up the entire stairway, dividing the steps from the smooth runway. At the upper part of the runway he had built a few steps, wherewith to lure the unwary far enough down to insure a fatal descent. To make sure of his game he had likewise ceiled the upper room all around, including the enclosure of the stairs. The door to the chute and the door to the stairs were side by side, and being made of the same boards as the wainscoting, were scarcely visible when closed, while the single knob that was used, being transferable from one to the other, naturally gave the impression that there was but one door. When this adroit villain called my attention to the little window around the corner, he no doubt removed the knob from the stairs' door and quickly placed it in the one opening upon the chute. Another door, connecting the two similar landings without, explains how he got from the chute staircase into which he passed, on leaving me, to the one communicating with the room below.

"The mystery was solved, and my footing on the force secured; but to this day—and I am an old man now—I have not forgotten the horror of the moment when my feet slipped from under me, and I felt myself sliding downward, without hope of rescue, into a pit of heaving waters, where so many men of conspicuous virtue had already ended their valuable lives.

"Myriad thoughts flashed through my brain in that brief interval, and among them the whole method of operating this death-trap, together with every detail of evidence that would secure the conviction of the entire gang."

BRET HARTE

Francis Brett Harte (1836–1902) is remembered today as one of the bright young writers of the New (now Old) West. During his lifetime, however, he—along with Mark Twain and Ambrose Bierce—was extensively lionized, and his narrative techniques were widely imitated. Born and reared in the East, he went to California at the age of nineteen, served at the U.S. Mint for a time, and worked on various newspapers and periodicals. After the publication of "The Luck of Roaring Camp" (1868) and "The Outcasts of Poker Flat" (1869), Harte became a nationally popular author. In 1878 he accepted a post in the U.S. Diplomatic Service and left America. He served first in Germany, then in Great Britain, where he passed the remainder of his life.

Although Harte wrote no formal detective stories, he wrote very fine parodies of mystery stories by Wilkie Collins and others in Condensed Novels *(1867). "The Stolen Cigar-Case" is generally considered the best parody of Sherlock Holmes.*

"The Stolen Cigar-Case"

By A. C---n D--le

Author of "Rodney Stone, and other Light Weights"

I found Hemlock Jones in the old Brook Street lodgings, musing before the fire. With the freedom of an old friend I at once threw myself in my old familiar attitude at his feet, and gently caressed his boot. I was induced to do this for two reasons; one that it enabled me to get a good look at his bent, concentrated face, and the other that it seemed to indicate my reverence for his superhuman insight. So absorbed was he, even then, in tracking some mysterious clue, that he did not seem to notice me. But therein I was wrong—as I always was in my attempt to understand that powerful intellect.

"It is raining," he said, without lifting his head.

"You have been out then?" I said quickly.

"No. But I see that your umbrella is wet, and that your overcoat, which you threw off on entering, has drops of water on it."

I sat aghast at his penetration. After a pause he said carelessly, as if dismissing the subject: "Besides, I hear the rain on the window. Listen."

I listened. I could scarcely credit my ears, but there was the soft pattering of drops on the pane. It was evident, there was no deceiving this man!

"Have you been busy lately?" I asked, changing the subject. "What new problem—given up by Scotland Yard as inscrutable—has occupied that gigantic intellect?"

He drew back his foot slightly, and seemed to hesitate ere he returned it to its original position. Then he answered wearily: "Mere trifles—nothing to speak of. The Prince Kopoli has been here to get my advice regarding the disappearance of certain rubies from the Kremlin; the Rajah of Pootibad, after vainly beheading his entire bodyguard, has been obliged to seek my assistance to recover a jewelled sword. The Grand Duchess of Pretzel-Brauntswig is desirous of discovering where her husband was on the night of the 14th of February, and last night"—he lowered his voice slightly—"a lodger in this very house, meeting me on the stairs, wanted to know 'Why they don't answer his bell.' "

I could not help smiling—until I saw a frown gathering on his inscrutable forehead.

"Pray to remember," he said coldly, "that it was through such an apparently trivial question that I found out, 'Why Paul Ferroll killed his Wife,' and 'What happened to Jones'!"

I became dumb at once. He paused for a moment, and then suddenly changing back to his usual pitiless, analytical style, he said: "When I say these are trifles—they are so in comparison to an affair that is now before me. A crime has been committed, and, singularly enough, against myself. You start," he said; "you wonder who would have dared to attempt it! So did I; nevertheless, it has been done. *I* have been *robbed!*"

"*You* robbed—you, Hemlock Jones, the Terror of Peculators!" I gasped in amazement, rising and gripping the table as I faced him.

"Yes; listen. I would confess it to no other. But *you* who have followed my career, who know my methods; yea, for whom I have partly lifted the veil that conceals my plans from ordinary humanity; you, who have for years rapturously accepted my confidences, passionately admired my inductions and inferences, placed yourself at my beck and call, become my slave, grovelled at my feet, given up your practice except those few unremunerative and rapidly-decreasing patients to whom, in moments of abstraction over *my* problems, you have administered strychnine for quinine and arsenic for Epsom salts; you, who have sacrificed everything and everybody to me—*you* I make my confidant!"

I rose and embraced him warmly, yet he was already so engrossed in thought that at the same moment he mechanically placed his hand upon his watch chain as if to consult the time. "Sit down," he said; "have a cigar?"

"I have given up cigar smoking," I said.

"Why?" he asked.

I hesitated, and perhaps coloured. I had really given it up because, with my diminished practice, it was too expensive. I could only afford a pipe. "I prefer a pipe," I said laughingly. "But tell me of this robbery. What have you lost?"

He rose, and planting himself before the fire with his hands under his coat tails, looked down upon me reflectively for a moment. "Do you remember the cigar-case presented to me by the Turkish Ambassador for discovering the missing favourite of the Grand Vizier in the fifth chorus girl at the Hilarity Theatre? It was that one. It was incrusted with diamonds. I mean the cigar-case."

"And the largest one had been supplanted by paste," I said.

"Ah," he said with a reflective smile, "you know that?"

"You told me yourself. I remember considering it a proof of your extraordinary perception. But, by Jove, you don't mean to say you have lost it."

He was silent for a moment. "No; it has been stolen, it is true, but I shall still find it. And by myself alone! In your profession, my dear fellow, when a member is severely ill he does not prescribe for himself, but calls in a brother doctor. Therein we differ. I shall take this matter in my own hands."

"And where could you find better?" I said enthusiastically. "I should say the cigar-case is as good as recovered already."

"I shall remind you of that again," he said lightly. "And now, to show you my confidence in your judgment, in spite of my determination to pursue this alone, I am willing to listen to any suggestions from you."

He drew a memorandum book from his pocket, and, with a grave smile, took up his pencil.

I could scarcely believe my reason. He, the great Hemlock Jones! accepting suggestions from a humble individual like myself! I kissed his hand reverently, and began in a joyous tone:

"First I should advertise, offering a reward; I should give the same intimation in handbills, distributed at the 'pubs' and the pastry-cooks. I should next visit the different pawnbrokers; I should give notice at the police station. I should examine the servants. I should thoroughly search the house and my own pockets. I speak relatively," I added with a laugh, "of course, I mean *your* own."

He gravely made an entry of these details.

"Perhaps," I added, "you have already done this?"

"Perhaps," he returned enigmatically. "Now, my dear friend," he continued, putting the note-book in his pocket, and rising— "would you excuse me for a few moments? Make yourself perfectly at home until I return; there may be some things," he added with a sweep of his hand towards his heterogeneously filled shelves, "that may interest you, and while away the time. There are pipes and tobacco in that corner and whiskey on the table." And nodding to me with the same inscrutable face, he left the room. I was too well accustomed to his methods to think much of his unceremonious withdrawal, and made no doubt he was off to investigate some clue which had suddenly occurred to his active intelligence.

Left to myself, I cast a cursory glance over his shelves. There were a number of small glass jars, containing earthy substances labeled "Pavement and road sweepings," from the principal thoroughfares and suburbs of London, with the sub-directions "For identifying foot tracks." There were several other jars labeled "Fluff from omnibus and road-car seats," "Cocoanut fibre and rope strands from mattings in public places," "Cigarette stumps and match ends from floor of Palace Theatre, Row A, 1 to 50." Everywhere were evidences of this wonderful man's system and perspicacity.

I was thus engaged when I heard the slight creaking of a door, and I looked up as a stranger entered. He was a rough-looking man, with a shabby overcoat, a still more disreputable muffler round his throat, and a cap on his head. Considerably annoyed at his intrusion I turned upon him rather sharply, when, with a mumbled, growling apology for mistaking the room, he shuffled out again and closed the door. I followed him quickly to the landing and saw that he disappeared down the stairs.

With my mind full of the robbery, the incident made a singular impression on me. I knew my friend's habits of hasty absences from his room in his moments of deep inspiration; it was only too probable that with his powerful intellect and magnificent perceptive genius concentrated on one subject, he should be careless of his own belongings, and, no doubt, even forget to take the ordinary precaution of locking up his drawers. I tried one or two and found that I was right—although for some reason I was unable to open one to its fullest extent. The handles were sticky, as if someone had opened them with dirty fingers. Knowing Hemlock's fastidious cleanliness, I resolved to inform him of this circumstance, but I forgot it, alas! until—but I am anticipating my story.

His absence was strangely prolonged. I at last seated myself by the fire, and lulled by warmth and the patter of the rain on the window, I fell asleep. I may have dreamt, for during my sleep I had a vague semi-consciousness as of hands being softly pressed on my pockets—no doubt induced by the story of the robbery. When I came fully to my senses, I found Hemlock Jones sitting on the other side of the hearth, his deeply concentrated gaze fixed on the fire.

"I found you so comfortably asleep that I could not bear to waken you," he said with a smile.

I rubbed my eyes. "And what news?" I asked. "How have you succeeded?"

"Better than I expected," he said, "and I think," he added, tapping his note-book—"I owe much to *you*."

Deeply gratified, I awaited more. But in vain. I ought to have remembered that in his moods Hemlock Jones was reticence itself. I told him simply of the strange intrusion, but he only laughed.

Later, when I rose to go, he looked at me playfully. "If you were a married man," he said, "I would advise you not to go home until you had brushed your sleeve. There are a few short, brown seal-skin hairs on the inner side of the fore-arm—just where they would have adhered if your arm had encircled a seal-skin sacque with some pressure!"

"For once you are at fault," I said triumphantly, "the hair is my own as you will perceive; I have just had it cut at the hair-dressers, and no doubt this arm projected beyond the apron."

He frowned slightly, yet nevertheless, on my turning to go he embraced me warmly—a rare exhibition in that man of ice. He even helped me on with my overcoat and pulled out and smoothed down the flaps of my pockets. He was particular, too, in fitting my arm in my overcoat sleeve, shaking the sleeve down from the armhole to the cuff with his deft fingers. "Come again soon!" he said, clapping me on the back.

"At any and all times," I said enthusiastically. "I only ask ten minutes twice a day to eat a crust at my office and four hours' sleep at night, and the rest of my time is devoted to you always—as you know."

"It is, indeed," he said, with his impenetrable smile.

Nevertheless I did not find him at home when I next called. One afternoon, when nearing my own home I met him in one of his favourite disguises—a long, blue, swallow-tailed coat, striped cotton trousers, large turn-over collar, blacked face, and white hat, carrying a tambourine. Of course to others the disguise was perfect, although it was known to myself, and I passed him—according to an old understanding between us—without the slightest recognition, trusting to a later explanation. At another time, as I was making a professional visit to the wife of a publican at the East End, I saw him in the disguise of a broken-down artisan looking into the window of an adjacent pawnshop. I was delighted to see that he was evidently following my suggestions, and in my joy I ventured to tip him a wink; it was abstractedly returned.

Two days later I received a note appointing a meeting at his lodgings that night. That meeting, alas! was the one memorable occurrence of my life, and the last meeting I ever had with Hemlock Jones! I will try to set it down calmly, though my pulses still throb with the recollection of it.

I found him standing before the fire with that look upon his face which I had seen only once or twice in our acquaintance—a look which I may call an absolute concatenation of inductive and deductive ratiocination—from which all that was human, tender, or sympathetic, was absolutely discharged. He was simply an icy, algebraic symbol! Indeed his whole being was concentrated to that extent that his clothes fitted loosely, and his head was absolutely so much reduced in size by his mental compression that his hat tipped back from his forehead and literally hung on his massive ears.

After I had entered, he locked the doors, fastened the windows, and even placed a chair before the chimney. As I watched those significant precautions with absorbing interest, he suddenly drew a revolver and presenting it to my temple, said in low, icy tones:

"Hand over that cigar-case!"

Even in my bewilderment, my reply was truthful, spontaneous, and involuntary. "I haven't got it," I said.

He smiled bitterly, and threw down his revolver. "I expected that reply! Then let me now confront you with something more awful, more deadly, more relentless and convincing than that mere lethal weapon—the damning inductive and deductive proofs of your guilt!" He drew from his pocket a roll of paper and a note-book.

"But surely," I gasped, "you are joking! You could not for a moment believe——"

"Silence!" he roared. "Sit down!"

I obeyed.

"You have condemned yourself," he went on pitilessly. "Condemned yourself on my processes—processes familiar to you, applauded by you, accepted by you for years! We will go back to the time when you first saw the cigar-case. Your expressions," he said in cold, deliberate tones, consulting his paper, "were: 'How beautiful! I wish it were mine.' This was your first step in crime—and my first indication. From 'I *wish* it were mine' to 'I *will* have it mine,' and the mere detail, 'How *can* I make it mine,' the advance was obvious. Silence! But as in my methods, it was necessary that there should be an overwhelming inducement to the crime, that unholy admiration of yours for the mere trinket itself was not enough. You are a smoker of cigars."

"But," I burst out passionately, "I told you I had given up smoking cigars."

"Fool!" he said coldly, "that is the *second* time you have committed yourself. Of course, you *told* me! what more natural than for you to blazon forth that prepared and unsolicited statement to *prevent* accusation. Yet, as I said before, even that wretched attempt to cover up your tracks was not enough. I still had to find that overwhelming, impelling motive necessary to affect a man like you. That motive I found in *passion*, the strongest of all impulses—love, I suppose you would call it," he added bitterly; "that night you called! You had brought the damning proofs of it in your sleeve."

"But," I almost screamed.

"Silence," he thundered. "I know what you would say. You would say that even if you had embraced some young person in a sealskin sacque what had that to do with the robbery. Let me tell you then, that that sealskin sacque represented the quality and character of your fatal entanglement! If you are at all conversant with light sporting literature you would know that a sealskin sacque indicates a love induced by sordid mercenary interests. You bartered your honour for it—that stolen cigar-case was the purchaser of the sealskin sacque! Without money, with a decreasing practice, it was the only way you could insure your passion being returned by that young person, whom, for your sake, I have not even pursued. Silence! Having thoroughly established your motive, I now proceed to the commission of the crime itself. Ordinary people would have begun with that—with an attempt to discover the whereabouts of the missing object. These are not my methods."

So overpowering was his penetration, that although I knew myself innocent, I licked my lips with avidity to hear the further details of this lucid exposition of my crime.

"You committed that theft the night I showed you the cigar-case and after I had carelessly thrown it in that drawer. You were sitting in that chair, and I had risen to take something from that shelf. In that instant you secured your booty without rising. Silence! Do you remember when I helped you on with your overcoat the other night? I was particular about fitting your arm in. While doing so I measured your arm with a spring tape measure from the shoulder to the cuff. A later visit to your tailor confirmed that measurement. It proved to be *the exact distance between your chair and that drawer!*"

I sat stunned.

"The rest are mere corroborative details! You were again tampering with the drawer when I discovered you doing so. Do not

start! The stranger that blundered into the room with the muffler
on—was myself. More, I had placed a little soap on the drawer
handles when I purposely left you alone. The soap was on your
hand when I shook it at parting. I softly felt your pockets when you
were asleep for further developments. I embraced you when you
left—that I might feel if you had the cigar-case, or any other articles,
hidden on your body. This confirmed me in the belief that you had
already disposed of it in the manner and for the purpose I have
shown you. As I still believed you capable of remorse and confession, I allowed you to see I was on your track twice, once in the garb
of an itinerant negro minstrel, and the second time as a workman
looking in the window of the pawnshop where you pledged your
booty."

"But," I burst out, "if you had asked the pawnbroker you would
have seen how unjust——"

"Fool!" he hissed; "that was one of *your* suggestions to search
the pawnshops. Do you suppose I followed any of your suggestions—the suggestions of the thief? On the contrary, they told me
what to avoid."

"And I suppose," I said bitterly, "you have not even searched
your drawer."

"No," he said calmly.

I was for the first time really vexed. I went to the nearest
drawer and pulled it out sharply. It stuck as it had before, leaving a
part of the drawer unopened. By working it, however, I discovered
that it was impeded by some obstacle that had slipped to the upper
part of the drawer, and held it firmly fast. Inserting my hand, I
pulled out the impeding object. It was the missing cigar-case. I
turned to him with a cry of joy.

But I was appalled at his expression. A look of contempt was
now added to his acute, penetrating gaze. "I have been mistaken," he
said slowly. "I had not allowed for your weakness and cowardice. I
thought too highly of you even in your guilt; but I see now why you
tampered with that drawer the other night. By some incredible
means—possibly another theft—you took the cigar-case out of pawn,
and like a whipped hound restored it to me in this feeble, clumsy
fashion. You thought to deceive me, Hemlock Jones: more, you
thought to destroy my infallibility. Go! I give you your liberty. I
shall not summon the three policemen who wait in the adjoining
room—but out of my sight for ever."

As I stood once more dazed and petrified, he took me firmly by
the ear and led me into the hall, closing the door behind him. This
re-opened presently wide enough to permit him to thrust out my
hat, overcoat, umbrella and overshoes, and then closed against me
for ever!

I never saw him again. I am bound to say, however, that thereafter my business increased—I recovered much of my old practice—and a few of my patients recovered also. I became rich. I had a brougham and a house in the West End. But I often wondered, pondering on that wonderful man's penetration and insight, if, in some lapse of consciousness, I had not really stolen his cigar-case!

SOURCES

Grant Allen, "The Great Ruby Robbery," *The Strand Magazine*, London, 1892.

[Anonymous], "Tale of a Detective," *A Race for Life and Other Tales*, Leisure Hour Office, The Religious Tract Society, London [n.d., c. 1870].

[Anonymous], "The Woman with the Yellow Hair," *Dublin University Magazine*, Dublin, 1861.

Guy Boothby, "The Wedding Guest," *Pearson's Magazine*, London, 1897.

Mary Braddon, "Levison's Victim," *Weavers and Weft*, Simpkin, Marshall, London [n.d., c. 1895]. Originally published in *Belgravia*, London, 1870.

Wilkie Collins, "Mr. Policeman and the Cook," *Little Novels*, Chatto and Windus, London, 1887.

Charles Dickens, "Three 'Detective' Anecdotes," *Collected Works of Charles Dickens*, Carleton, New York [n.d. c. 1900]. Originally published in *Household Words*, London, 1853.

A. Conan Doyle, "The Recollections of Captain Wilkie," *Chambers's Journal*, January 19, 1895, London.

Andrew Forrester, Jr., "Arrested on Suspicion," *Revelations of a Private Detective*, Ward and Lock, London, 1863.

Tom Fox, "Revelations of a Detective," Chapter VII of *The Revelations of a Detective*, George Vickers, London, 1860.

Émile Gaboriau, "The Little Old Man of Batignolles," *Leisure Hour Library* #248, F. M. Lupton, New York, 1890. Originally published in French in 1876.

Anna Katharine Green, "The Staircase at the Heart's Delight," *A Difficult Problem*, F. M. Lupton, New York, 1900.

Bret Harte, "The Stolen Cigar-Case," *Pearson's Magazine*, London, 1900.

E. and H. Heron, "The Story of Baelbrow," *Pearson's Magazine*, London, 1898.

C. J. Cutcliffe Hyne, "The Bank Note Forger," *The Harmsworth Magazine*, London, 1899.

Charles Martel, "Hanged by the Neck," *The Detective's Note-book*, Ward and Lock, London, 1860.

L. T. Meade and Robert Eustace, "The Outside Ledge," *The Harmsworth Magazine*, London, 1900.

Arthur Morrison, "The Case of the Late Mr. Rewse," *The Windsor Magazine*, London, 1896.

C. L. Pirkis, "The Black Bag Left on a Door-Step," *The Ludgate Monthly*, London, 1893.

Melville Davisson Post, "The Sheriff of Gullmore," *The Strange Schemes of Randolph Mason*, Putnam, New York, 1896.

Mrs. J. H. Riddell, "Dr. Varvill's Prescription," *Handsome Phil and Other Stories*, F. V. White, London, 1899. Originally published in *Chemist and Druggist*, London, 1894.

"Waters," "Murder under the Microscope," *Autobiography of a London Detective*, Dick and Fitzgerald, New York, 1864. Earlier publication in *Experiences of a Real Detective*, Ward and Lock, London, 1862.

Mrs. Henry Wood, "Going through the Tunnel," *Johnny Ludlow, First Series*, Bentley, London, 1895. First published in book form 1874.